The Vampire Sextette

Edited by Marvin Kaye

BOOKSPAN

GARDEN CITY, NEW YORK

Published by GuildAmerica Books,
an imprint and registered trademark of
BOOKSPAN, Department GB,
401 Franklin Avenue,
Garden City, New York 11530

Interior Design by Paul Randall Mize
Jacket Design by Luis Royo

Compilation copyright © 2000 by Marvin Kaye

The Other Side of Midnight © 2000 by Kim Newman
Some Velvet Morning © 2000 by Nancy Collins
Sheena © 2000 by Brian Stableford
Vanilla Blood © 2000 by S. P. Somtow
In the Face of Death © 2000 by Chelsea Quinn Yarbro
The Isle is Full of Noises © 2000 by Tanith Lee

All Rights Reserved
Printed in the United States of America
ISBN 0-7394-1154-3

Contents

Introduction

The Erotic Myth of Blood

W HEN Bram Stoker's memorable *nosferatu* Dracula opens one
of his own veins and forces Mina Harker to drink, it is a moment both unholy and sexual. The count's shocking oralism is
concupiscent and, in the manner of the Black Mass, also a dark
travesty of transubstantiation.

Vampirism in its literary guise is often linked with Eros. The
two first significant vampire tales in western literature—Dr.
John Polidori's lampoon of Lord Byron, *The Vampire,* and
Sheridan LeFanu's novella, *Carmilla,* are infused with implicit
homosexuality; compared with them, *Dracula*'s sexual implica-
tions seem oblique.

One might argue that Bram Stoker was reined in by Victo-
rianism, but in fact his plot is rife with implicit carnality. The
count, in his own idiosyncratic fashion, cuckolds both Mina's
and Lucy's human lovers, and back at his old castle in Transylvania, he also maintains an undead *ménage à quatre.* (Research
reveals that one of his wives is Carmilla, which suggests she
must be bisexual.)

In his quintessential novel, Stoker introduced a third significant element to the myth: compassion. As her poor suffering
lover pounds a wooden stake through Lucy's heart, he sees upon
her countenance an expression of spiritual peace that bespeaks
her soul's delivery from the curse of the damned. This sympathy, so vital to the author's theme of holiness and the profane,
is again memorably invoked when Dracula himself is at last destroyed, and though most of the movie versions ignore this part
of the tale, it does briefly surface in the 1931 film, when Bela

Lugosi says, "To die, to be really dead, that must be glorious," and then observes, "There are far worse things awaiting man than death."

In 1976, this linkage between lust, bloodlust, and compassion reached a literary pinnacle of sorts in Anne Rice's popular *Interview With the Vampire*. In its wake came a flood of novels and short stories about vampires charismatic, eloquent, genteel, melancholy, misunderstood, noble. Some were heroic, many were equipped with paradoxically healthy libidos. Sexy vampires became such a cliché that the market for them shriveled like a cinematic vampire in the light of day* and, at several fantasy conventions, horror writer and editor of *Weird Tales* Darrell Schweitzer reminded authors that vampires, alluring though they might be, originally were supposed to be bad guys, remember?

The Vampire Sextette is my twenty-second anthology. Vampires have made relatively few appearances in my collections, partly because they don't tend to frighten me. Like demons, they are rooted in dualistic cosmology, and that has little impact on someone whose philosophy is a tad to the left of atheism. Thus, three popular horror novels, Ira Levin's *Rosemary's Baby*, William Peter Blatty's *The Exorcist*, and Stephen King's *'Salem's Lot* failed to raise a goose bump upon my jaded flesh; though, to be fair, King's novel was sufficiently well written to keep me reading to the end.

Another reason I have seldom included vampire stories is that so few have anything to offer that Stoker hasn't already done better, and some of the exceptions, notably E. F. Benson's "The Room in the Tower," Carl Jacobi's "Revelations in Black," Clark Ashton Smith's "A Rendezvous in Averoigne," and Richard Matheson's "Blood Son" have already been anthologized several times. I did reprint Matheson's gruesome "Dress of White Silk," but his most remarkable contribution to

*Only in the movies does daylight destroy vampires, but if you've read *Dracula*, you already know that.

vampire literature was too long for my gatherings: *I Am Legend,* that oft-filmed horror/science-fiction novel about a normal man trapped in a world full of vampires.

In the past twenty-plus years, however, a new spate of excellent, highly original vampire tales began to flow from the pens of such diverse stylists and storytellers as Robert Aickman, Nancy Collins, Morgan Llywelyn, George R. R. Martin, Ray Russell, Dan Simmons, S. P. Somtow, Chelsea Quinn Yarbro, and numerous others. Still, it was not until Tanith Lee and I became international pen pals that the idea for *The Vampire Sextette* was born.

I have long admired Tanith's poetically crafted fiction, and have purchased rights to several of her short stories. A few years ago, we struck up a friendly America-to-England correspondence and, at one point, exchanged works of romantic fantasy that each other had written. About this time, Tanith suggested that each I edited an anthology of a half dozen erotic vampire novellas, she would agree to write one of them. She meant to work music into her plot, and proposed the collection be called *The Vampire Sextette,* to invoke the subthemes of sensuality and music.

The idea sparked the interest of Ellen Asher, editorial director of Doubleday Direct's Science Fiction Book Club, so Ellen and I drew up a list of authors we hoped might participate with Tanith. We agreed that the eroticism might vary from X-rated down to R, that music might or might not be part of the plots, but the vampirism must not be metaphorical, like Strindberg's Vampire Cook in *The Ghost Sonata* or Harry Kressing's Conrad in *The Cook:* it must be the traditional bloodsucking variety.

The six novellas that comprise *The Vampire Sextette,* all original variations on the vampire theme, are refreshingly unlike one another. Sex and violence are equally important in "Some Velvet Morning" by Nancy Collins, "The Isle Is Full of Noises" by Tanith Lee, and S. P. Somtow's "Vanilla Blood"; gore runs stronger than carnality in Kim Newman's "The Other Side of Midnight," while the opposite is true in Brian Stableford's "Sheena" (in which music is also an important plot element).

Chelsea Quinn Yarbro's "In the Face of Death" is the least sanguine, but its poignant love affair between an elegant vampire and the redoubtable Civil War general William Tecumseh Sherman is meticulously original.

Now settle back with a Bloody Mary and meet some truly remarkable vampires . . . but before you do, don't forget to smear your windowpanes with garlic.

—Marvin Kaye
Manhattan, 2000

The Vampire Sextette

Kim Newman

The Other Side of Midnight

KIM NEWMAN *is an actor, broadcaster, film critic, and author of some of the most remarkable fantasy tales being sent our way from his hometown, London. His vampire novels include* Anno Dracula, The Bloody Red Baron, *and* Judgment of Tears, *and the theme also surfaces in his novella, "Andy Warhol's Dracula." Other fiction includes* The Night Mayor, Bad Dreams, The Quorum, *as well as nonfiction books such as* Millennium Movies: End of the World Cinema. *His affection for the great filmmaker Orson Welles surfaces in "The Other Side of Midnight," at once a startlingly different take (pun intended) on vampire films, yet deep down a delightfully old-fashioned homage to the same.*

AT MIDNIGHT, 1980 flew away across the Pacific, and 1981 crept in from the east. A muted cheer rose from the pretty folk around the barbecue pit, barely an echo of the raucous welcome to a new decade that erupted at the height of the last Paradise Cove New Year's party.

Of this company, only Geneviève clung to the old—the proper—manner of reckoning decades, centuries, and (when they came) millennia. The passing of time was important to her; born in 1416, she'd let more time pass than most. Even among vampires, she was an elder. Five minutes ago—last year, last decade—she'd started to explain her position to a greying California boy, an ex-activist they called "the Dude." His eyes glazed over with more than the weed he'd been toking throughout the party, indeed since Jefferson Airplane went Starship. She quite liked the Dude's eyes, in any condition.

"It's as simple as this," she reiterated, hearing the French in her accent ("eet's," "seemple," "ziss") that came out only when she was tipsy ("teep-see") or trying for effect. "Since there was no year nothing, the first decade ended with the end of year ten A.D.; the first century with the end of 100 A.D.; the first millennium with the end of 1000 A.D. Now, at this moment, a new decade is to begin. Nineteen-eighty-one is the first year of the 1980s, as 1990 will be the last."

Momentarily, the Dude looked as if he understood, but he was just concentrating to make out her accented words. She saw insight spark in his mind, a vertiginous leap that made him want to back away from her. He held out his twisted, tufted joint. It might have been the one he'd rolled and started in 1968, replenished on and off ever since.

"Man, if you start questioning time," he said, "what have you got left? Physical matter? Maybe you question that next, and the mojo won't work any more. You'll think holes between molecules and sink through the surface of the Earth. Drawn by gravity. Heavy things should be left alone. Fundamental things, like the ground you walk on, the air you breathe. You do breathe, don't you, man? Suddenly it hits me, I don't know if you do."

"Yes, I breathe," she said. "When I turned, I didn't die. That's not common."

She proved her ability to inhale by taking a toke from the joint. She didn't get a high like his; for that, she'd have to sample his blood as it channelled the intoxicants from his alveoli to his brain. She had the mellow buzz of him, from saliva on the roach as much as from the dope smoke. It made her thirsty.

Because it was just after midnight on New Year's Eve, she kissed him. He enjoyed it, noncommittally. Tasting straggles of tobacco in his beard and the film of a cocktail—White Russian—on his teeth and tongue, she sampled the ease of him, the defiant crusade of his back-burnered life. She understood now precisely what the expression "ex-activist" meant. If she let herself drink, his blood would be relaxing.

Breaking the kiss, she saw more sparks in his eyes, where

her face was not reflected. Her lips were sometimes like razors, even more than her fang-teeth. She'd cut him slightly, just for a taste, not even thinking, and left some of herself on his tongue. She swallowed: mostly spit, but with tiny ribbons of blood from his gums.

French-kissing was the kindest form of vampirism. From the minute exchange of fluid, she could draw a surprising sustenance. For her, just now, it was enough. It took the edge off her red thirst.

"Keep on breathing, man," said the Dude, reclaiming his joint, smiling broadly, drifting back towards the rest of the party, enjoying the unreeling connection between them. "And don't question time. Let it pass."

Licking her lips daintily, she watched him amble. He wasn't convinced 1980 had been the last year of the old decade and not the first of the new. Rather, he wasn't convinced that it mattered. Like a lot of Southern Californians, he'd settled on a time that suited him and stayed in it. Many vampires did the same thing, though Geneviève thought it a waste of longevity. In her more pompous moments, she felt the whole point was to embrace change while carrying on what was of value from the past.

When she was born and when she was turned, time was reckoned by the Julian calendar, with its annual error of eleven minutes and fourteen seconds. Thinking of it, she still regretted the ten days—the fifth to the fourteenth of October 1582—Pope Gregory XIII had stolen from her, from the world, to make his sums add up. England and Scotland, ten days behind Rome, held out against the Gregorian calendar until 1752. Other countries stubbornly stuck with Julian dating until well into the twentieth century; Russia had not chimed in until 1918, Greece not until 1923. Before the modern era, those ten-day shifts made diary-keeping a complex business for a necessarily much-travelled creature. The leap-frogged weeks were far much more jarring than the time-zone hopping she sometimes went through as an air passenger.

The Paradise Cove Trailer Park Colony had been her home for all of seven years, an eye blink which made her a senior resident among the constitutionally impermanent peoples of Malibu. Here, ancient history was Sonny and Cher and *Leave It to Beaver,* anything on the "golden oldies" station or an off-primetime rerun.

Geneviève—fully, Geneviève Sandrine de l'Isle Dieudonné, though she went by Gené Dee for convenience—remembered with a hazy vividity that she had once looked at the Atlantic and *not known* what lay between France and China. She was older than the name "America"; had she not turned, she'd probably have been dead before Columbus brought back the news. In all those years, ten days shouldn't matter, but supposedly significant dates made her aware of that fold in time, that wrench which pulled the future hungrily closer, which had swallowed one of her birthdays. By her internal calendar, the decade would not fully turn for nearly two weeks. This was a limbo between unarguable decades. She should have been used to limbos by now. For her, Paradise Cove was the latest of a long string of pockets out of time and space, cosy coffins shallowly buried away from the rush of the world.

She was the only one of her kind at the party; if she took "her kind" to mean vampires—there were others in her current profession, private investigation, even other incomers from far enough out of state to be considered foreign parts. Born in northern France under the rule of an English king, she'd seen enough history to recognise the irrelevance of nationality. To be Breton in 1416 was to be neither French nor English, or both at the same time. Much later, during the revolution, France had scrapped the calendar again, ducking out of the 1790s, even renaming the months. In the long term, the experiment was not a success. That was the last time she—Citizen Dieudonné—had really lived in her native land; the gory business soured her not only on her own nationality but humanity in general. Too many eras earned names like "the Terror." Vampires were supposed to be obscenely bloodthirsty, and she wasn't blind to the excesses of her kind, but the warm drank just as deeply from open wounds and usually made more of a mess of it.

From the sandy patio beside her chrome-finished Airstream

trailer, she looked beyond the gaggle of folks about the pit, joking over franks impaled on skewers. The Dude was mixing a pitcher of White Russians with his bowling buddies, resuming a months-long argument over the precise wording of the opening narration/song of *Branded*. An eight-track in an open-top car played "Hotel California," The Eagles's upbeat but ominous song about a vampire and her victims. Some were dancing on the sand, shoes in a pile that would be hard to sort out later. White rolls of surf crashed on the breakers, waves edged delicately up to the beach.

Out there was the Pacific Ocean and the curve of the Earth, and beyond the blue horizon, as another shivery song went, was a rising sun. Dawn didn't worry her; at her age, as long as she dressed carefully—sunglasses, a floppy hat, long sleeves—she wouldn't even catch a severe tan, let alone frazzle up into dust and essential salts like some *nosferatu* of the Dracula bloodline. She had grown out of the dark. To her owl eyes, it was no place to hide, which meant she had to be careful where she looked on party nights like this. She liked living by the sea: its depths were still impenetrable to her, still a mystery.

"Hey, Gidget," came a rough voice, "need a nip?"

It was one of the surfers, a shaggy bear of a man she had never heard called anything but Moondoggie. He wore frayed shorts, flip-flops, and an old blue shirt, and probably had done since the 1950s. He was a legendary veteran of tubes and pipes and waves long gone. He seemed young to her, though his friends called him an old man.

His offer was generous. She had fed off him before when the need was strong. With his blood came a salt rush, the sense of being enclosed by a curl of wave as his board torpedoed across the surface of the water.

Just now, she didn't need it. She still had the taste of the Dude. Smiling, she waved him away. As an elder, she didn't have the red thirst so badly. Since Charles, she had fed much less. That wasn't how it was with many vampires, especially those of the Dracula line. Some *nosferatu* got thirstier and thirstier with passing ages, and were finally consumed by their own raging red needs. Those were the ones who got to be called monsters. Beside them, she was a minnow.

Moondoggie tugged at his open collar, scratching below his salt-and-pepper beard. The LAPD had wanted to hang a murder rap on him two years ago, when a runaway turned up dead in his beach hut. She had investigated the situation, clearing his name. He would always be grateful to his "Gidget," which she learned was a contraction of "Girl Midget." Never tall, she had turned—frozen—at sixteen. Recently, after centuries of being treated almost as a child, she was most often taken for a woman in her twenties. That was: by people who didn't know she wasn't warm, wasn't entirely living. She'd have examined her face for the beginnings of lines, but looking glasses were no use to her.

Shots were fired in the distance. She looked at the rise of the cliffs and saw the big houses, decks lit by fairy-light UFO constellations, seeming to float above the beach, heavy with heavy hitters. Firing up into the sky was a Malibu New Year tradition among the rich. Reputedly started by the film director John Milius, a famous surf and gun nut, it was a stupid, dangerous thing to do. Gravity and momentum meant bullets came down somewhere, and not always into the water. In the light of New Year's Day, she found spent shells in the sand, or pocked holes in driftwood. One year someone's head would be under a slug. Milius had made her cry with *Big Wednesday*, though. Movies with coming-of-age, end-of-an-era romanticism crawled inside her heart and melted her. She would have to tell Milius it got worse and worse with centuries.

So, the 1980s?

Some thought her overly formal for always using the full form, but she'd lived through decades called "the eighties" before. For the past hundred years, "the eighties" had meant the Anni Draculae, the 1880s, when the Transylvanian Count came to London and changed the world. Among other things, the founding of his brief empire had drawn her out of the shadow of eternal evening into something approaching the light. That brought her together with Charles, the warm man with whom she had spent seventy-five years, until his death in 1959, the warm man who had shown her that she, a vampire, could still love, that she had turned without dying inside.

She wasn't unique, but she was rare. Most vampires lost more than they gained when they turned; they died and came back as different people, caricatures of their former selves, compelled by an inner drive to be extreme. Creatures like that were one of the reasons why she was here, at the far western edge of a continent where "her kind" were still comparatively rare.

Other vampires had nests in the Greater Los Angeles area: Don Drago Robles, a landowner before the incorporation of the state into the Union, had quietly waited for the city to close around his hacienda, and was rising as a political figure with a growing constituency, a Californian answer to Baron Meinster's European Transylvania Movement; and a few long-lived movie or music people, the sort with reflections in silver and voices that registered on recording equipment, had Spanish-style castles along Sunset Boulevard, like eternal child rock god Timmy Valentine or silent-movie star David Henry Reid. More, small sharks mostly, swam through Angelino sprawl, battening on marginal people to leech them dry of dreams as much as blood, or—in that ghastly new thing—selling squirts of their own blood ("drac") to sad addicts ("dhampires") who wanted to be a vampire for the night but didn't have the heart to turn all the way.

She should be grateful to the rogues; much of her business came from people who got mixed up with bad-egg vampires. Her reputation for extricating victims from predators was like gold with distressed parents or cast-aside partners. Sometimes she worked as a deprogrammer, helping kids out of all manner of cults. They grew beliefs stranger than Catholicism, or even vampirism, out here among the orange groves: the Moonies, the Esoteric Order of Dagon, Scientology, Psycho-Plasmics. Another snatch of song: "The Voice said Daddy there's a million pigeons, waiting to be hooked on new religions."

As always, she stuck it out until the party died. All the hours of the night rolled away, and the rim of the horizon turned from navy blue to lovely turquoise. January cold gathered, driving those warmer folks who were still sensible from their barbecues and beach towels to their beds.

Marty Burns, sometime sitcom star and current inhabitant of a major career slump, was passed out facedown on the chilling sands in front of her trailer space. She found a blanket to throw over him. He murmured in liquor-and-pills lassitude, and she tucked the blanket comfortably around his neck. Marty was hilarious in person, even when completely off his face, but *Salt & Pepper*, the star-making show he was squandering residuals from, was puzzlingly free of actual humour. The dead people on the laugh track audibly split sides at jokes deader than they were. The year was begun with a moderate good deed, though purging the kid's system and dragging him to AA might have been a more lasting solution to whatever was inside him chewing away.

She would sleep later, in the morning, locked in her sleek trailer, a big metal coffin equipped with everything she needed. Of all her homes over the years, this was the one she cherished the most. The trailer was chromed everywhere it could be, and customised with steel shutters that bolted over the windows and the never-used sun roof. Economy of space had forced her to limit her possessions—so few after so long—to those that really meant the most to her: ugly jewellry from her mediaeval girlhood, some of Charles's books and letters, a Dansette gramophone with an eclectic collection of sides, her beloved answering machine, a tacky Mexican crucifix with light-up eyes that she kept on show just to prove she wasn't one of *those* vampires, two decent formal dresses and four pairs of Victorian shoes (custom-cobbled for her tiny feet) which had outlasted everything made this century and would do for decades more. On the road, she could kink herself double and rest in the trunk of her automobile, a pillar-box red 1958 Plymouth Fury, but the trailer was more comfortable.

She wandered towards the sea line, across the disturbed sands of the beach. There had been dancing earlier, grown-ups who had been in Frankie and Annette movies trying to fit their old moves to current music. *Le freak, c'est chic.*

She trod on a hot pebble that turned out to be a bullet, and saluted Big John up on his A-list Hollywood deck. Milius had written *Dracula* for Francis Ford Coppola, from the Bram Stoker novel she was left out of. Not wanting to have the Count brought back to mind, she'd avoided the movie, though her vampire journalist friend Kate Reed, also not mentioned in Stoker's fiction, had worked on it as technical advisor. She hadn't heard from Kate in too long; Geneviève believed she was behind the Iron Curtain, on the trail of the Transylvania Movement, that odd faction of the Baron Meinster's which wanted Dracula's estates as a homeland for vampires. God, if that ever happened, she would get round to reapplying for American citizenship; they were accepting *nosferatu* now, which they hadn't been in 1922 when she last looked into it. Meinster was one of those Dracula wanna-bes who couldn't quite carry off the opera cloak and ruffle shirt, with his prissy little fangs and his naked need to be the new King of the Cats.

Wavelets lapped at her bare toes. Her nails sparkled under water.

Nineteen-seventies music hadn't been much, not after the 1960s. Glam rock. The Bee-Gees. The Carpenters. She had liked Robert Altman's films and *Close Encounters*, but didn't see what all the fuss was about *Star Wars*. Watergate. An oil crisis. The bicentennial summer. The Iran hostage crisis. No Woodstock. No swinging London. No one like Kennedy. Nothing like the Moon landing.

If she were to fill a diary page for every decade, the 1970s would have to be padded heavily. She'd been to some parties and helped some people, settled into the slow, pastel, dusty icecream world of Southern California, a little to one side of the swift stream of human history. She wasn't even much bothered by memories, the curse of the long-lived.

Not bad, not good, not anything.

She wasn't over Charles, never would be really. He was a constant, silent presence in her heart, an ache and a support and a joy. He was a memory she would never let slip. And Dracula, finally destroyed soon after Charles's death, still cast a long cloak-shadow over her life. Like Bram Stoker, she wondered what her life, what the world, would have been like if Vlad Tepes had never turned or been defeated before his rise to power.

Might-have-beens and the dead. Bad company.

John Lennon was truly dead, too. Less than a month ago, in New York, he had taken a silver bullet through the heart, a cruel full stop for the 1970s, for what was left of the 1960s. Annie Wilkes, Lennon's killer, said she was the musician's biggest fan, but that he had to die for breaking up the Beatles. Geneviève didn't know how long Lennon had been a vampire, but she sadly recognised in the dirge "Imagine" that copy-of-a-copy voidishness characteristic of creatives who turned to prolong their artistic lives but found the essential thing that made them who they were—that powered their talent—gone, and that the best they could hope for was a kind of rarefied self-plagiarism. Mad Annie might have done John a favour, making him immortal again. Currently the most famous vampire slayer in the world, she was a heroine to the bedrock strata of warm America that would never accept *nosferatu* as even kissing cousins to humanity.

What, she wondered as the sun touched the sky, would this new decade bring?

Count Dracula

A Screenplay
by Herman J. Mankiewicz and Orson Welles
Based on the Novel by Bram Stoker

Nov. 30, 1939

Fade In

1. Ext. Transylvania—Faint Dawn—1885

Window, very small in the distance, illuminated. All around this an almost totally black screen. Now, as the camera moves slowly towards this window, which is almost a postage stamp in the frame, other forms appear; spiked battlements, vast granite walls, and now, looming up against the still-nighted sky, enormous iron grillwork.

Camera travels up what is now shown to be a gateway of gigantic proportions and holds on the top of it—a huge initial "D" showing darker and darker against the dawn sky. Through this and beyond we see the gothic-tale mountaintop of Dracula's estate, the great castle a silhouette at its summit, the little window a distant accent in the darkness.

Dissolve

(A series of setups, each closer to the great window, all telling something of:)

2. The Literally Incredible Domain of Vlad, Count Dracula

Its right flank resting for forty miles along the Borgo Pass, the estate truly extends in all directions farther than the eye can see.

An ocean of sharp treetops, with occasionally a deep rift where there is a chasm. Here and there are silver threads where the rivers wind in deep gorges through the forests. Designed by nature to be almost completely vertical and jagged—it was, as will develop, primordial forested mountain when Dracula acquired and changed its face—it is now broken and shorn, with its fair share of carved peaks and winding paths, all man-made.

Castle Dracula itself—an enormous pile, compounded of several demolished and rebuilt structures, of varying architecture, with broken battlements and many towers—dominates the scene, from the very peak of the mountain. It sits on the edge of a very terrible precipice.

Dissolve

3. The Village

In the shadows, literally the shadows, of the mountain. As we move by, we see that the peasant doors and windows are shuttered and locked, with crucifixes and obscene clusters of garlic as further protection and sealing. Eyes peep out, timid, at us. The camera moves like a band of men, purposeful, cautious, intrepid, curious.

Dissolve

4. Forest of Stakes

Past which we move. The sward is wild with mountain weeds, the stakes tilted at a variety of Dutch angles, the execution field unused and not seriously tended for a long time.

Dissolve

5. What Was Once a Good-Sized Prison Stockade

All that now remains, with one exception, are the individual plots, surrounded by thorn fences, on which the hostages were kept, free and yet safe from each other and the landscape at large. (Bones in several of the plots indicate that here there were once human cattle, kept for blood.)

Dissolve

6. A Wolf Pit

In the f.g., a great shaggy dire wolf, bound by a silver chain, is outlined against the fawn murk. He raises himself slowly, with more thought than an animal should display, and looks out across the estates of Count Dracula, to the distant light glowing in the castle on the mountain. The wolf howls, a child of the night, making sweet music.

Dissolve

7. A Trench Below the Walls

A slow-scuttling armadillo. A crawling giant beetle. Reflected in the muddy water—the lighted window.

Dissolve

8. The Moat

Angled spears sag. An old notebook floats on the surface of the water—its pages covered in shorthand scribble. As it moves across the frame, it discloses again the reflection of the window in the castle, closer than before.

Dissolve

9. A Drawbridge

Over the wide moat, now stagnant and choked with weeds. We move across it and through a huge rounded archway into a formal courtyard, perhaps thirty feet wide and one hundred yards deep, which extends right up to the very wall of the castle. Let's see Toland keep all of it in focus. The landscaping surrounding it has been sloppy and casual for centuries, but this particular courtyard has been kept up in perfect shape. As the camera makes its way through it, towards the lighted window of the castle, there are revealed rare and exotic blooms of all kinds: *mariphasa lupino lumino,* strange orchid, *audriensis junior, triffidus celestus.* The dominating note is one of almost exaggerated wildness, sprouting sharp and desperate—rot, rot, rot. The Hall of the Mountain King, the night the last troll died. Some of the plants lash out, defensively.

Dissolve

10. The Window

Camera moves in until the frame of the window fills the frame of the screen. Suddenly the light within goes out. This stops the action of the camera and cuts the music (Bernard Herrmann) which has been accompanying the sequence. In the glass panes of the window we see reflected the stark, dreary mountainscape of the Dracula estate behind and the dawn sky.

Dissolve

11. Int. Corridor in Castle Dracula—Faint Dawn—1885

Ornate mirrors line both walls of the corridor, reflecting arches into infinity. A bulky shadow figure—Dracula—proceeds slowly, heavy with years, through the corridor. He pauses to look into the mirror, and has no reflection, no reflections, to infinity. It seems at last that he is simply not there.

Dissolve

12. Int. Dracula's Crypt—Faint Dawn—1885

A very long shot of Dracula's enormous catafalque, silhouetted against the enormous window.

Dissolve

13. Int. Dracula's Crypt—Faint Dawn—1885

An eye. An incredible one. Big impossible drops of bloody tears, the reflections of figures coming closer, cutting implements raised. The jingling of sleigh bells in the musical score now makes an ironic reference to Indian temple bells—the music freezes—

DRACULA'S OLD VOICE
Rose's blood!

The camera pulls back to show the eye in the face of the old Dracula, bloated with blood but his stolen youth lost again, grey skin parchmented like a mummy, fissures cracking open in the wrinkles around his eyes, fang-teeth too large for his mouth, pouching his cheeks and stretching his lips, the nose an improbable bulb. A flash—the descent of a guillotine-like kukri knife, which has been raised above Dracula's neck—across the screen. The head rolls off the neck and bounds down two carpeted steps leading to the catafalque, the camera following. The head falls off the last step onto the marble floor where it cracks, snaky tendrils of blood glittering in the first ray of the morning sun. This ray cuts an angular pattern across the floor, suddenly crossed with a thousand cruciform bars of light as a dusty curtain is wrested from the window.

14. The Foot of Dracula's Catafalque

The camera very close. Outlined against the uncurtained window we can see a form—the form of a man, as he raises a bowie knife over his head. The camera moves down along the catafalque as the knife descends into Dracula's heart, and rests on the severed head. Its lips are still moving. The voice, a whisper from the grave

DRACULA'S OLD VOICE
Rose's blood!

In the sunlight, a harsh shadow cross falling upon it, the head lap-dissolves into a fanged, eyeless skull.

Fade Out

Count Dracula   Cast and Credits, as of January 1940

Production Company: Mercury Productions. Distributor: RKO Radio Pictures. Executive Producer: George J. Schaefer. Producer: Orson Welles. Director: Orson Welles. Script: Herman J. Mankiewicz, Orson Welles. From the novel by Bram Stoker. Director of Photography: Gregg Toland. Editors: Mark Robson, Robert Wise. Art Director: Van Nest Polglase. Special Effects: Vernon L. Walker. Music/Musical Director: Bernard Herrmann.

Orson Welles (Dracula), Joseph Cotten (Jedediah Renfield), Everett Sloane (Van Helsing), Dorothy Comingore (Mina Murray), Robert Coote (Artie Holmwood), William Alland (Jon Harker), Agnes Moorehead (Mrs. Westenra), Lucille Ball (Lucy), George Coulouris (Dr. Walter Parkes Seward), Paul Stewart (Raymond, Asylum Attendant), Alan Ladd (Quincey P. Morris), Fortunio Bonanova (Inn-Keeper at Bistritz), Vladimir Sokoloff (Szekeley Chieftain), Dolores Del Rio, Ruth Warrick, Rita Cansino (Vampire Brides), Gus Schilling (Skipper of the *Demeter*).

"Mademoiselle Dieudonné," intoned the voice on her answering machine, halfway between a growl and a purr, "this is Orson Welles."

The voice was deeper even than in the 1930s, when he was a radio star. Geneviève had been in America over Halloween,

1938, when Welles and the *Mercury Theatre of the Air* broadcast their you-are-there dramatisation of H. G. Wells's "The Flowering of the Strange Orchid" and convinced half the Eastern seaboard that the country was disappearing under a writhing plague of vampire blossoms. She remembered also the rhetorical whisper of "who *knows* what evil *lurks* in the hearts of men?," followed by the triumphant declaration "the *Shadow* knows!" and the low chuckle which rose by terrifying lurches to a fiendish, maniacal shriek of insane laughter.

When she had first met the man himself, in Rome in 1959, the voice hadn't disappointed. Now, even on cheap tape and through the tinny, tiny amplifier, it was a call to the soul. Even hawking brandy or frozen peas, the voice was a powerful instrument. That Welles had to compete with Welles imitators for gigs as a commercial pitchman was one of the tragedies of the modern age. Then again, she suspected he drew a deal of sly enjoyment from his long-running role as a ruined titan. As an actor, his greatest role was always himself. Even leaving a message on a machine, he invested phrases with the weight—a quality he had more than a sufficiency of—of a Shakespearean deathbed speech.

"There is a small matter upon which I should like your opinion, in your capacities as a private detective and a member of the undead community. If you would call on me, I should be most grateful."

She thought about it. Welles was as famous for being broke as for living well. It was quite likely he wouldn't even come through with her modest rate of a hundred dollars a day, let alone expenses. And gifts of rare wine or Cuban cigars weren't much use to her, though she supposed she could redeem them for cash.

Still, she was mildly bored with finding lost children or bail jumpers. And no one ever accused Welles of being boring. He had left the message while she was resting through the hours of the day. This was the first of the ten or so days between the Gregorian 1980s and the Julian 1980s. She could afford to give a flawed genius—his own expression—that much time.

She would do it.

In leaving a message, Welles had given her a pause to think. She heard heavy breaths as he let the tape run on, his big man's lungs working. Then, confident that he had won her over, he cut in with address details, somewhere in Beverly Hills.

"I do so look forward to seeing you again. Until then, remember . . . *the weed of crime bears bitter fruit!*"

It was one of his old radio catchphrases.

He did the laugh, the King laugh, the Shadow laugh. It properly chilled her bones, but made her giggle, too.

She discovered Orson Welles at the centre of attention, on the cracked bottom of a drained pool behind a rented bungalow. Three nude vampire girls waved objects—a luminous skull, a Macbethian blooded dagger, a fully articulated monster-bat puppet—at him, darting swiftly about his bulky figure, nipping at his head with their Halloween props. The former boy wonder was on his knees, enormous Russian shirt open to the waist, enormous (and putty) nose glistening under the lights, enormous spade-beard flecked with red syrup. A man with a hand-held camera, the sort of thing she'd seen used to make home movies, circled the odd quartet, not minding if the vampires got between him and his director-star.

A few other people were around the pool, holding up lights. No sound equipment, though: this was being shot silent. Geneviève hung back, by the bungalow, keeping out of the way of the work. She had been on film sets before, at Cinecittà and in Hollywood, and knew this crew would be deemed skeletal for a student short. If anyone else was directing, she'd have supposed he was shooting makeup tests or a rehearsal. But with Welles, she knew that this was the real film. It might end up with the dialogue out of sync, but it would be extraordinary.

Welles was rumbling through a soliloquy.

It took her a moment to realise what the undead girls were doing, then she had to swallow astonished laughter. They were nude not for the titillation of an eventual audience, for they wouldn't be seen. Nonreflecting *nosferatu* would be completely invisible when the footage was processed. The girls were naked because clothes would show up on film, though some elders—Dracula had been one—so violated the laws of optics that they robbed any costume they wore of its reflection also, sucking even that into their black hearts. In the final film, Welles would seem to be persecuted by malignly animated objects—the skull, the dagger, and the bat. Now he tore at his garments and hair like Lear, careful to leave his nose alone, and called out to the angry heavens. The girls flitted, slender and deathly white, not feeling the cold, faces blank, hands busy.

This was the cheapest special effect imaginable.

Welles fell forward on his face, lay still for a couple of beats, and hefted himself upright, out of character, calling "cut." His nose was mashed.

A dark woman with a clipboard emerged from shadows to confer with the master. She wore a white fur coat and a matching hat. The vampire girls put the props down and stood back, nakedness unnoticed by the crew members. One took a cloak-like robe from a chair and settled it over her slim shoulders. She climbed out of the pool.

Geneviève had not announced herself. The vampire girl fixed her eye. She radiated a sense of being fed up with the supposed glamour of show business.

"Turning was supposed to help my career," she said. "I was going to stay pretty forever and be a star. Instead, I lost my image. I had good credits. I was up for the last season of *Charlie's Angels.* I'd have been the blonde."

"There's always the theatre," Geneviève suggested.

"That's not being a star," the girl said.

She was obviously a newborn, impatient with an eternity she didn't yet understand. She wanted all her presents *now,* and no nonsense about paying dues or waiting her turn. She had cropped blonde hair; very pale, almost translucent skin stretched over bird-delicate bones; and a tight, hard, cute little face, with sharp angles and glinting teeth, small reddish eyes. Her upper arm was marked by parallel claw marks, not yet healed, like sergeant's stripes. Geneviève stored away the detail.

"Who's that up there, Nico?" shouted one of the other girls.

Nico? Not the famous one, Geneviève supposed.

"Who?" the girl asked, out loud. "Famous?"

Nico—indeed, not the famous one—had picked the thought out of Geneviève's mind. That was a common elder talent, but unusual in a newborn. If she lasted, this girl might do well. She'd have to pick a new name though, to avoid confusion with the singer of "All Tomorrow's Parties."

"Another one of us," the starlet said to the girl in the pool. "An invisible."

"I'm not here for a part," Geneviève explained. "I'm here to see Mr. Welles."

Nico looked at her askew. Why would a vampire who wasn't an actress be here? Tumblers worked in the newborn's mind. It worked both ways: Nico could pick words up, but she also sent them out. The girls in the pool were named Mink and Vampi (please!), and often hung with Nico.

"You're old, aren't you?"

Geneviève nodded. Nico's transparent face showed eagerness.

"Does it come back? Your face in the mirror?"

"Mine hasn't."

Her face fell, a long way. She was a loss to the profession. Her feelings were all on the surface, projected to the back stalls.

"Different bloodlines have different qualities," Geneviève said, trying to be encouraging.

"So I heard."

Nico wasn't interested in faint hopes. She wanted instant cures.

"Is that Mademoiselle Dieudonné?" roared the familiar voice.

"Yes, Orson, it's me," she said.

Nico reacted, calculating. She was thinking that Geneviève might be an important person.

"Then that's a wrap for the evening. Thank you, people. Submit your expenses to Oja, and be back here tomorrow night, at midnight sharp. You were all stupendous."

Oja was the woman with the clipboard: Oja Kodar, Welles's

companion and collaborator. She was from Yugoslavia, another refugee washed up on this California shore.

Welles seemed to float out of the swimming pool, easily hauling his enormous girth up the ladder by the strength of his own meaty arms. She was surprised at how light he was on his feet.

He pulled off his putty nose and hugged her.

"Geneviève, Geneviève, you are welcome."

The rest of the crew came up, one by one, carrying bits of equipment.

"I thought I'd get Van Helsing's mad scene in the can," explained Welles.

"Neat trick with the girls."

The twinkle in his eye was almost Santa Clausian. He gestured hypnotically.

"Elementary movie magic," he said. "Georges Méliès could have managed it in 1897."

"Has it ever been done before? I don't recall seeing a film with the device."

"As a matter of fact, I think it's an invention of my own. There are still tricks to be teased out of the cinema. Even after so many years—a single breath for you, my dear—the talkies are not quite perfected. My little vampires may have careers as puppeteers, animators. You'd never see their hands. I should shoot a short film, for children."

"You've been working on this for a long time?"

"I had the idea at about seven o'clock this evening," he said with a modest chuckle. "This is Hollywood, my dear, and you can get anything with a phone call. I got my vampires by ordering out, like pizza."

Geneviève guessed the invisible girls were hookers, a traditional career option for those who couldn't make a showing in the movies. Some studio execs paid good money to be roughed up by girls they'd pass over with contempt at cattle calls. And vampires, properly trained, could venture into areas of pain and pleasure a warm girl would find uncomfortable, unappetising, or unhealthy.

She noticed Nico had latched on to a young, male assistant and was alternately flirting with him and wheedling at him for some favour. Welles was right: she could have a career as a puppet mistress.

"Come through into the house, Geneviève," said Welles. "We must talk."

The crew and the girls bundled together. Oja, as production manager, arranged for them to pool up in several cars and be returned to their homes or—in the case of Nico, Mink, and Vampi—to a new club where there were hours to be spent before the dawn. Gary, the cameraman, wanted to get the film to the lab and hurried off on his own to an all-night facility. Many movie people kept vampire hours without being undead.

There was an after buzz in the air. Geneviève wondered if it was genius, or had some of the crew been sniffing drac to keep going. She had heard it was better than speed. She assumed she would be immune to it; even as a blood drinker—like all of her kind, she had turned by drinking vampire blood—she found the idea of dosing her system with another vampire's powdered blood, diluted with the devil knew what, disgusting.

Welles went ahead of her, into the nondescript bungalow, turning on lights as he went. She looked back for a moment at the cast-off nose by the pool.

Van Helsing's mad scene?

She knew the subject of Welles's current project. He had mentioned to her that he had always wanted to make *Dracula*. Now, it seemed, he was acting on the impulse. It shouldn't have, but it frightened her a little. She was in two minds about how often that story should be told.

Orson Welles arrived in Hollywood in 1939, having negotiated a two-picture deal as producer-director-writer-actor with George Schaefer of RKO Pictures. Drawing on an entourage of colleagues from the New York theatre and radio, he established Mercury Productions as a filmmaking entity. Before embarking on *Citizen Kane* (1941) and *The Magnificent Ambersons* (1942), Welles developed other properties: Nicholas Blake's just-published anti-Fascist thriller *The Smiler with a Knife* (1939), Conrad's *Heart of Darkness* (1902) and Stoker's *Dracula* (1897). Like the Conrad, *Dracula* was a novel Welles had already done for the *Mercury Theatre on the Air* radio series (July 11, 1938). A script was prepared (by Welles, Herman Mankiewicz and, uncredited, John Houseman), sets were designed, the film cast, and "tests"—the extent of which have never been revealed—shot, but the project was dropped.

The reasons for the abandonment of *Count Dracula* remain obscure. It has been speculated that RKO was nervous about Welles's stated intention to film most of the story with a first-person camera, adopting the viewpoints of the various characters as Stoker does in his might-have-been fictional history. Houseman, in his memoir *Run-Through* (1972), alleges that Welles's enthusiasm for this device was at least partly due to the fact that it would keep the fearless vampire slayers—Harker, Van Helsing, Quincey, Holmwood—mostly off screen, while Dracula, object of their attention, would always be in view. Houseman, long estranged from Welles at the time of writing, needlessly adds that Welles would have played Dracula. He toyed with the idea of playing Harker as well, before deciding William Alland could do it if kept to the shadows and occasionally dubbed by Welles. The rapidly changing political situation in Europe, already forcing the Roosevelt administration to reassess its policies about vampirism and the very real Count Dracula, may have prompted certain factions to bring pressure to bear on RKO that such a film was "inadvisable" for 1940.

In an interview with Peter Bogdanovich, published in *This Is Orson Welles* (1992) but held well before Francis Ford Coppola's controversial *Dracula* (1979), Welles said: "Dracula would make a marvellous movie. In fact, nobody has ever made it; they've never paid any attention to the book, which is the most hair-raising, marvellous book in the world. It's told by four people, and must be done with four narrations, as we did on the radio. There's one scene in London where he throws a heavy bag into the corner of a cellar and it's full of screaming babies! They can go that far out now."

Jonathan Gates, "Welles's Lost Draculas,"
Video Watchdog No. 23 May–July 1994

Welles did not so much live in the bungalow as occupy it. She recognised the signs of high-end, temporary tenancy. Pieces of extremely valuable antique furniture, imported from Spain, stood among ugly, functional, modern sticks that had come with the let. The den, largest space in the building, was made aesthetically bearable by a hanging she put at sixteenth century, nailed up over the open fireplace like a curtain. The tapestry depicted a knight trotting in full armour through forest greenery, with black-faced, red-eyed-and-tongued devils peeping from behind tall, straight trees. The piece was marred by a bad burn that had caught at one corner and spread evil fingers upwards. All around were stacks of books, square-bound antique volumes and bright modern paperbacks, and rickety towers of film cans.

Geneviève wondered why Welles would have cases of good sherry and boxes of potato chips stacked together in a corner, then realised he must have been partly paid in goods for his commercial work. He offered her sherry, and she surprised him by accepting.

"I do sometimes drink wine, Orson. Dracula wasn't speaking for us all."

He arched an eyebrow and made a flourish of pouring sherry into a paper cup.

"My glassware hasn't arrived from Madrid," he apologised.

She sipped the stuff, which she couldn't really taste, and sat on a straight-backed gothic chair. It gave her a memory flash, of hours spent in churches when she was a warm girl. She wanted to fidget.

Welles plopped himself down with a Falstaffian rumble and

strain on a low couch that had a velvet curtain draped over it. He was broad enough in the beam to make it seem like a throne.

Oja joined them and silently hovered. Her hair was covered by a bright head scarf.

A pause.

Welles grinned expansively. Geneviève realised he was protracting the moment, relishing a role. She even knew who he was doing, Sydney Greenstreet in *The Maltese Falcon*. The ambiguous mastermind enjoying himself by matching wits with the perplexed private eye. If Hollywood ever remade *Falcon*, which would be a sacrilege, Welles would be in the ring for Gutman. Too many of his acting jobs were like that, replacing another big personality in an inferior retread of something already got right.

"I'll be wondering why you asked me here tonight," she prompted.

"Yes," he said, amused.

"It'll be a long story."

"I'm rather afraid so."

"There are hours before dawn."

"Indeed."

Welles was comfortable now. She understood he had been switching off from the shoot, coming down not only from his on-screen character but from his position as backyard God.

"You know I've been playing with *Dracula* for years? I wanted to make it at RKO in '40, did a script, designed sets, cast everybody. Then it was dropped."

She nodded.

"We even shot some scenes. I'd love to steal in some night and rescue the footage from the vaults. Maybe for use in the current project. But the studio has the rights. Imagine if paintings belonged to whoever mixed the paints and wove the canvas. I'll have to abase myself, as usual. The children who inherited RKO after Hughes ran it aground barely know who I am, but they'll enjoy the spectacle of my contrition, my pleading, my total dejection. I may even get my way in the end."

"Hasn't *Dracula* been made? I understand that Francis—"

"I haven't seen that. It doesn't matter to me or the world. I didn't do the first stage productions of *Macbeth* or *Caesar*, merely the best. The same goes for the Stoker. A marvellous piece, you know."

"Funnily enough, I have read it," she put in.

"Of course you have."

"And I met Dracula."

Welles raised his eyes, as if that were news to him. Was this all about picking her brain? She had spent all of fifteen minutes in the Royal Presence, nearly a hundred years ago, but was quizzed about that (admittedly dramatic) occasion more than the entire rest of her five hundred and sixty-five years. She'd seen the Count again, after his true death—as had Welles, she remembered—and been at his last funeral, seen his ashes scattered. She supposed she had wanted to be sure he was really finally dead.

"I've started *Dracula* several times. It seems like a cursed property. This time, maybe, I'll finish it. I believe it has to be done."

Oja laid hands on his shoulders and squeezed. There was an almost imperial quality to Welles, but he was an emperor in exile, booted off his throne and cast out, retaining only the most loyal and long-suffering of his attendants.

"Does the name Alucard mean anything to you?" he asked. "John Alucard?"

"This may come as a shock to you, Orson, but 'Alucard' is 'Dracula' spelled backwards."

He gave out a good-humoured version of his Shadow laugh.

"I had noticed. He is a vampire, of course."

"Central and Eastern European *nosferatu* love anagrams as much as they love changing their names," she explained. "It's a real quirk. My late friend Carmilla Karnstein ran through at least a half dozen scramblings of her name before running out. Millarca, Marcilla, Allimarc . . ."

"My name used to be Olga Palinkas," put in Oja. "Until Orson thought up 'Oja Kodar' for me, to sound Hungarian."

"The promising sculptor 'Vladimir Zagdrov' is my darling Oja, too. You are right about the undead predilection for noms de plume, alter egos, secret identities, anagrams, and palin-

dromes and acrostics. Just like actors. A holdover from the
Byzantine mind-set, I believe. It says something about the way
the creatures think. Tricky but obvious, as it were. The back
spelling might also be a compensation: a reflection on parch-
ment for those who have none in the glass."

"This Alucard? Who is he?"

"That's the exact question I'd like answered," said Welles.
"And you, my dear Mademoiselle Dieudonné, are the person I
should like to provide that answer."

"Alucard says he's an independent producer," said Oja.
"With deals all over town."

"But no credits," said Welles.

Geneviève could imagine.

"He has money, though," said Welles. "No credits, but a
line of credit. Cold cash and the Yankee dollar banish all doubt.
That seems unarguable."

"Seems?"

"Sharp little word, isn't it? Seems and is, syllables on either
side of a chasm of meaning. This Mr. Alucard, a *nosferatu,*
wishes to finance my *Dracula.* He has offered me a deal the likes
of which I haven't had since RKO and *Kane.* An unlimited
budget, major studio facilities, right of final cut, control over
everything from casting to publicity. The only condition he im-
poses is that I must make this subject. He wants not my *Don
Quixote* or my *Around the World in 80 Days,* but my *Dracula*
only."

"The Coppola—" a glare from Welles made her rephrase
"—that other film, with Brando as the Count? That broke even
in the end, didn't it? Made back its budget. *Dracula* is a box-of-
fice subject. There's probably room for another version. Not to
mention sequels, a spin-off TV series and imitations. Your Mr.
Alucard makes sense. Especially if he has deep pockets and no
credits. Being attached to a good, to a *great,* film would do him
no harm. Perhaps he wants the acclaim?"

Welles rolled the idea around his head.

"No," he concluded, almost sadly. "Gené, I have never been
accused of lack of ego. My largeness of spirit, my sense of self-

worth, is part of my act, as it were. The armour I must needs
haul on to do my daily battles. But I am not blind to my situation. No producer in his right mind would bankroll me to such
an extent, would offer me such a deal. Not even these kids, this
Spielberg and that Lucas, could get such a sweetheart deal. I am
as responsible for that as anyone. The studios of today may be
owned by oil companies and hotel magnates, but there's a trace
memory of that contract I signed when I was twenty-four and
of how it all went wrong, for me and for everyone. When I was
kicked off the lot in 1943, RKO took out ads in the trades an-
nouncing their new motto: 'Showmanship, not genius!' Hollywood doesn't want to have me around. I remind the town of its
mistakes, its crimes."

"Alucard is an independent producer, you say. Perhaps he's
a fan?"

"I don't think he's seen any of my pictures."

"Do you think this is a cruel prank?"

Welles shrugged, raising huge hands. Oja was more
guarded, more worried. Geneviève wondered whether she was
the one who had insisted on calling in an investigator.

"The first cheques have cleared," said Welles. "The rent is
paid on this place."

"You are familiar with the expression . . ."

"The one about equine dentistry? Yes."

"But it bothers you? The mystery?"

"The Mystery of Mr. Alucard. That is so. If it blows up in
my face, I can stand that. I've come to that pass before, and I
shall venture there again. But I should like some presentiment,
either way. I want you to make some discreet inquiries about
our Mr. Alucard. At the very least, I'd like to know his real
name and where he comes from. He seems very American at the
moment, but I don't think that was always the case. Most of all,
I want to know what he is up to. Can you help me, Mademoiselle Dieudonné?"

"You know, Gené," said Jack Martin wistfully, contemplating
the melting ice in his empty glass through the wisps of cigarette

smoke that always haloed his head, "none of this matters. It's not important. Writing. It's a trivial pursuit, hardly worth the effort, inconsequential on any cosmic level. It's just blood and sweat and guts and bone hauled out of our bodies and fed through a typewriter to slosh all over the platen. It's just the sick soul of America turning sour in the sunshine. Nobody really reads what I've written. In this town, they don't know Flannery O'Connor or Ray Bradbury, let alone Jack Martin. Nothing will be remembered. We'll all die and it'll be over. The sands will close over our civilisation and the sun will turn into a huge red fireball and burn even you from the face of the earth."

"That's several million years away, Jack," she reminded him.

He didn't seem convinced. Martin was a writer. In high school, he'd won a national competition for an essay entitled "It's Great to Be Alive." Now in his grumbling forties, the sensitive but creepy short stories that were his most personal work were published in small science-fiction and men's magazines, and put out in expensive limited editions by fan publishers who went out of business owing him money. He had made a living as a screenwriter for ten years without ever seeing anything written under his own name get made. He had a problem with happy endings.

However, he knew what was going on in "the Industry" and was her first port of call when a case got her mixed up with the movies. He lived in a tar-paper shack on Beverly Glen Boulevard, wedged between multimillion dollar estates, and told everybody that at least it was earthquake-proof.

Martin rattled the ice. She ordered him another Coca-Cola. He stubbed out one cigarette and lit another.

The girl behind the hotel bar, dressed as a magician, sloshed ice into another glass and reached for a small chromed hose. She squirted Coke into the glass, covering the ice.

Martin held up his original glass.

"Wouldn't it be wonderful if you could slip the girl a buck and have her fill up *this* glass, not go through all the fuss of getting a fresh one and charging you all over again. There should be infinite refills. Imagine that, a utopian dream, Gené. It's what America needs. A *bottomless* Coke!"

"It's not policy, sir," said the girl. With the Coke came a quilted paper napkin, an unhappy edge of lemon, and a plastic stirrer.

Martin looked at the bar girl's legs. She was wearing black fishnets, high-heeled pumps, a tight white waistcoat, a tail coat, and tophat.

The writer sampled his new, bottomed, Coke. The girl went to cope with other morning customers.

"I'll bet she's an actress," he said. "I think she does porno."

Geneviève raised an eyebrow.

"Most X-rated films are better directed than the slop that comes out of the majors," Martin insisted. "I could show you a reel of something by Gerard Damiano or Jack Horner that you'd swear was Bergman or Don Siegel. Except for the screwing."

Martin wrote "scripts" for adult movies, under well-guarded pseudonyms to protect his Writers' Guild membership. The guild didn't have any moral position on porno, but members weren't supposed to take jobs which involved turning out a full-length feature script in two afternoons for three hundred dollars. Martin claimed to have invented Jamie Gillis's catchphrase, "Suck it, bitch!"

"What can you tell me about John Alucard?"

"The name is—"

"Besides that his name is 'Dracula' written backwards."

"He's from New York. Well, that's where he was last. I heard he ran with that art crowd. You know, Warhol and Jack Smith. He's got a first-look deal at United Artists, and something cooking with Fox. There's going to be a story in the trades that he's set up an independent production company with Griffin Mill, Julia Phillips, and Don Simpson."

"But he's never made a movie?"

"The word is that he's never *seen* a movie. That doesn't stop him calling himself a producer. Say, are you working for him? If you could mention that I was available. Mention my rewrite on

Can't Stop the Music. No, don't. Say about that TV thing that didn't happen. I can get you sample scripts by sundown."

Martin was gripping her upper arm.

"I've never met Alucard, Jack. I'm checking into him for a client."

"Still, if you get the chance, Gené. You know what it would mean to me. I'm fending off bill collectors, and Sharkko Press still hasn't come through for the *Tenebrous Twilight* limiteds. A development deal, even a rewrite or a polish, could get me through winter and spring. Buy me time to get down to Ensenada and finish some stories."

She would have to promise. She had learned more than the bare facts. The light in Jack Martin's eyes told her something about John Alucard. He had some sort of magic effect, but she didn't know whether he was a conjurer or a wizard.

Now she would have to build on that.

Short of forcing her way into Alucard's office and asking outright whether he was planning on leaving Orson Welles in the lurch, there wasn't much more she could do. After Martin, she made a few phone calls to industry contacts, looked over recent back numbers of *Variety* and the *Hollywood Reporter* and hit a couple of showbiz watering holes, hoping to soak up gossip.

Now, Geneviève was driving back along the Pacific Coast Highway to Paradise Cove. The sun was down, and a heavy, unstarred darkness hung over the sea. The Plymouth, which she sometimes suspected of having a mind of its own, handled gently, taking the blind curves at speed. She twiddled the radio past a lot of disco and found a station pumping out two-tone. That was good, that was new, that was a culture still alive.

". . . mirror in the bathroom, recompense all my crimes of self-defence . . ."

She wondered about what she had learned.

It wasn't like the old days, when the studios were tight little fiefdoms and a stringer for Louella Parsons would know everything going on in town and every current scandal. Most movies weren't even made in Hollywood any more, and the studios were way down on the lists of interests owned by multinational corporations with other primary concerns. The buzz was that United Artists might well be changing its name to TransAmerica Pictures.

General word confirmed most of what Martin had told her, and turned up surprisingly few extra details. Besides the Welles deal, financed off his own line of credit with no studio production coin as yet involved, John Alucard had projects in development all over town, with high-end talent attached. He was supposed to be in bed with Michael Cimino, still hot off *The Deer Hunter*, on *The Lincoln County Wars*, a Western about the vampire outlaw Billy the Kid and a massacre of settlers in Roswell, New Mexico, in the 1870s. With the Mill-Simpson-Phillips setup, he was helping the long-in-development Anne Rice project, *Interview With the Mummy*, which Elaine May was supposed to be making with Cher and Ryan O'Neal, unless it was Nancy Walker, with Diana Ross and Mark Spitz.

In an interview in the *Reporter*, Alucard said, "The pursuit of making money is the only reason to make movies. We have no obligation to make history. We have no obligation to make art. We have no obligation to make a statement. Our obligation is to make money." A lot of execs, and not a few directors and writers, found his a refreshing and invigorating stance, though Geneviève had the impression Alucard was parroting someone else's grand theory. If he truly believed what he said, and was not just laying down something the studios' corporate owners wanted to hear, then John Alucard did not sound like someone who would happily want to be in business with Orson Welles. Apart from anything else, his manifesto was a 1980s rewrite, at five times the length with in-built repetition to get through to the admass morons at the back of the hall, of "showmanship, not genius."

The only thing she couldn't find out was what his projects really were. Besides Welles's *Dracula,* which wasn't mentioned by anyone she had talked with, and the long-gestating shows he was working with senior production partners, he had a half dozen other irons in the fire. Directors and stars were attached, budgets set, start dates announced, but no titles ever got mentioned, and the descriptions in the trades—"intense drama," "romantic comedy"—were hardly helpful. That was interesting and unusual. John Alucard was making a splash, waves radiating outwards, but surely he eventually would have to say what the pictures were. Or had that become the least important part of the package? An agent at CAA told her that for men like Alucard, the art was in the deal not on the screen.

That did worry her.

Could it be that there wasn't actually a pot of gold at the end of this rainbow? The man was a vampire, but was he also a phantom? No photographs existed, of course. Everyone had a secondhand description, always couched as a casting suggestion: a young Louis Jourdan, a smart Jack Palance, a rough-trade David Niven. It was agreed that the man was European, a long time ago. No one had any idea how long he had been a vampire, even. He could be a newborn, fresh-killed and risen last year, or a centuried elder who had changed his face a dozen times. His name always drew the same reaction: excitement, enthusiasm, fear. There was a sense that John Alucard was getting things on the road, and that it'd be a smart career move to get close to him, to be ready to haul out of the station with him.

She cruised across sandy tarmac into the trailer park. The seafood restaurant was doing a little New Year's Day business. She would be thirsty soon.

Someone sat on the stairs of her trailer, leaning back against her door, hands loose in his lap, legs in chinos, cowboy boots. Someone dead.

Throughout Welles's career, *Dracula* remained an *idée fixe*. The Welles-Mankiewicz script was RKO property, and the studio resisted Welles's offer to buy it back. They set their asking price at the notional but substantial sum accountants reckoned had been lost on the double debacle of *Ambersons* and the unfinished South American project, *It's All True*.

When Schaefer, Welles's patron, was removed from his position as Vice-President in Charge of Production and replaced by Charles Koerner, there was serious talk of putting the script into production through producer Val Lewton's unit, which had established a reputation for low-budget supernatural dramas with *Cat People* (1942). Lewton got as far as having DeWitt Bodeen and then Curt Siodmak take runs at further drafts, scaling the script down to fit a straitjacket budget. Jacques Tourneur was attached to direct, though editor Mark Robson was considered when Tourneur was promoted to A pictures. Stock players were assigned supporting roles: Tom Conway (Dr. Seward), Kent Smith (Jonathan Harker), Henry Daniell (Van Helsing), Jean Brooks (Lucy), Alan Napier (Arthur Holmwood), Skelton Knaggs (Renfield), Elizabeth Russell (Countess Marya Dolingen), Sir Lancelot (a calypso-singing coachman). Simone Simon, star of *Cat People,* was set for Mina, very much the focus of Lewton's take on the story, but the project fell through because RKO were unable to secure their first and only choice of star, Boris Karloff, who was committed to *Arsenic and Old Lace* on Broadway.

In 1944, RKO sold the Welles-Mankiewicz script, along with a parcel of set designs, to 20th Century-Fox. Studio head Darryl F. Zanuck offered Welles the role of Dracula, promising Joan Fontaine and Olivia de Havilland for Mina and Lucy, suggesting Tyrone Power (Jonathan), George Sanders (Arthur), John Carradine (Quincey) and Laird Cregar (Van Helsing). This *Dracula* would have been a follow-up to Fox's successful Welles-Fontaine *Jane Eyre* (1943), and Welles might have committed if Zanuck had again assigned weak-willed Robert Stevenson, allowing Welles to direct in everything but credit. However, on a project this "important," Zanuck would consider only two directors; John Ford had no interest—sparing us John Wayne, Victor McLaglen, Ward Bond, and John Agar as brawling, boozing, fearless vampire slayers—so it inevitably fell to Henry King, a specialist in molasses-slow historical subjects like *Lloyd's of London* (1936) and *Brigham Young* (1940). King, a plodder who had a brief flash of genius in a few later films with Gregory Peck, had his own, highly developed, chocolate box style and gravitas, and was not a congenial director for Welles, whose mercurial temperament was unsuited to methods he considered conservative and dreary. The film still might have been made, since Welles was as ever in need of money, but Zanuck went cold on Dracula at the end of the war when the Count was moving into his Italian exile.

Fox wound up backing *Prince of Foxes* (1949), directed by King, with Power and Welles topping the cast, shot on location in Europe. A lavish bore, enlivened briefly by Welles's committed Cesare Borgia, this suggests what the Zanuck *Dracula* might have been like. Welles used much of his earnings from the long shoot to pour into film projects made in bits and pieces over several years: the completed *Othello* (1952), the unfinished *Don Quixote* (begun 1955) and, rarely mentioned until now, yet another *Dracula*. *El conde Dràcula*, a French-Italian-Mexican-American-Irish-Liechtensteinian-British-Yugoslav-Moroccan-Iranian coproduction, was shot in snippets, the earliest dating from 1949, the latest from 1972.

Each major part was taken by several actors, or single actors over a span of years. In the controversial edit supervised by the Spaniard Jesus Franco—a second-unit director on Welles's *Chimes at Midnight* (1966)—and premiered at Cannes in 1997, the cast is as follows: Akim Tamiroff (Van Helsing), Micheál MacLiammóir (Jonathan), Paola Mori (Mina), Michael Redgrave (Arthur), Patty McCormick (Lucy), Hilton Edwards (Dr. Seward), Mischa Auer (Renfield). The vampire brides are played by Jeanne Moreau, Suzanne Cloutier, and Katina Paxinou, shot in different years on different continents. There is no sight of Francisco Reiguera, Welles's Quixote, cast as a skeletal Dracula, and the Count is present only as a substantial shadow voiced (as are several other characters) by Welles himself. Much of the film runs silent, and a crucial framing story, explaining the multinarrator device, was either never filmed or shot and lost. Jonathan's panicky exploration of his castle prison, filled with steam like the Turkish bath in *Othello*, is the most remarkable, purely Expressionist scene Welles ever shot. But the final ascent to Castle Dracula, with Tamiroff dodging patently *papier-mâché* falling boulders and wobbly zooms into and out of stray details hardly seems the work of anyone other than a fumbling amateur.

In no sense "a real film," *El conde Dràcula* is a scrapbook of images from the novel and Welles's imagination. He told Henry Jaglom that he considered the project a private exercise, to keep the subject in his mind, a series of sketches for a painting he would execute later. As Francis Coppola would in 1977, while his multimillion-dollar *Dracula* was bogged down in production problems in Romania, Welles often made comparisons with the Sistine Chapel. While Coppola invoked Michelangelo with some desperation as the vast machine of his movie seemed to be collapsing around him, Welles always resorted playfully to the metaphor, daring the interviewer with a wave and a wink and a deep chuckle to suggest the Pope probably did turn up every day wanting to know when the great artist would be finished and how much it was going to cost.

In 1973, Welles assembled some *El conde Dràcula* footage, along with documentary material about the real Count Dracula and the scandals that followed his true death in 1959: the alleged, much-disputed will that deeded much of his vast fortune to English housewife Vivian Nicholson, who claimed she had encountered Dracula while on a school holiday in the early fifties;

the autobiography Clifford Irving sold for a record-breaking advance in 1971, only to have the book exposed as an arrant fake written by Irving in collaboration with Fred Saberhagen; the squabbles among sundry vampire elders, notably Baron Meinster and Princess Asa Vajda, as to who should claim the Count's unofficial title as ruler of their kind. Welles called this playful, essaylike film—constructed around the skeleton of footage shot by Calvin Floyd for his own documentary, *In Search of Dracula* (1971)—*When Are You Going to Finish el conde Dràcula?*, though it was exhibited in most territories as *D Is for Dracula*. On the evening Premier Ceausescu withdrew the Romanian Cavalry needed for Coppola's assault on Castle Dracula in order to pursue the vampire banditti of the Transylvania Movement in the next valley, Francis Ford Coppola held a private screening of *D Is for Dracula* and cabled Welles that there was a curse on anyone who dared invoke the dread name.

Gates, ibid.

The someone on her steps was *truly* dead. In his left chest, over his punctured heart, a star-shaped blotch was black in the moonlight.

Geneviève felt no residue. The intangible thing—immortal soul, psychic energy, battery power—which kept mind and body together, in *nosferatu* or the warm, was gone.

Broken is the golden bowl, the spirit flown forever.

She found she was crying. She touched her cheek and looked at the thick, salt, red tears, then smeared them away on her handkerchief.

It was Moondoggie. In repose, his face looked old, the lines his smile had made appealing turned to slack wrinkles.

She took a moment with him, remembering the taste of the living man, that he was the only one who called her "Gidget," his inability to put in words what it was about surfing that made him devote his life to it (he'd been in pre-med once, long,

long ago—when there was a crack-up or a near-drowning, the doctor he might have been would surface and take over), and the rush of the seas that came with his blood.

That man was gone. Besides sorrow at the waste, she was angry. And afraid.

It was easy to see how it had happened. The killer had come close, face-to-face, and stuck Moondoggie through the heart. The wound was round, not a slit. The weapon was probably a wooden stake or a sharpened metal pole. The angle of the wound was upwards, so the killer was shorter than the rangy surfer. Stuck through, Moondoggie had been carefully propped up on her doorstep. She was being sent a message.

Moondoggie was a warm man, but he'd been killed as if he were like her, a vampire.

He was not cold yet. The killing was recent.

Geneviève turned in a half circle, looking out across the beach. Like most vampires, she had above average night vision for a human being—without sun glare bleaching everything bone white, she saw better than by day—but no hawklike power of distinguishing far-off tiny objects or magical X-ray eyesight.

It was likely that the assassin was nearby, watching to see that the message was received. Counting on the popular belief that vampires did have unnatural eyesight, she moved slowly enough that anyone in concealment might think she was looking directly at them, that they had been seen.

A movement.

The trick worked. A couple of hundred yards off, beyond the trailer park, out on the beach, something—someone—moved, clambering upright from a hollow depression in the dry sand.

As the probable murderer stood, Geneviève saw a blonde ponytail whipping. It was a girl, mid-to-late teens, in halter top and denim shorts, with a wispy gauze neck scarf, and—suggestive detail—running shoes and knee pads. She was undersized but athletic. Another girl midget: no wonder she'd been able to get close enough to Moondoggie, genial connoisseur of young bodies, to stab him in the heart.

She assumed the girl would bolt. Geneviève was fast enough to run her down, but the killer ought to panic. In California, what people knew about vampires was scrambled with fantasy and science fiction.

For once, Geneviève was tempted to live up to her image. She wanted to rip out the silly girl's throat.

(and drink)

She took a few long steps, flashing forwards across the beach.

The girl stood her ground, waiting.

Geneviève had pause. The stake wasn't in the dead man's chest. The girl still had it. Her right hand was out of sight, behind her back.

Closer, she saw the killer's face in the moonlight. Doll-pretty, with an upturned nose and the faintest fading traces of freckles. She was frowning with concentration now but probably had a winning smile, perfect teeth. She should be a cheerleader, not an assassin.

This wasn't a vampire, but Geneviève knew she was no warm cream puff, either. She had killed a strong man twice her weight with a single thrust, and was prepared for a charging *nosferatu*.

Geneviève stood still, twenty yards from the girl.

The killer produced her stake. It was stained.

"Meet Simon Sharp," she said. She had a clear, casual voice. Geneviève found her flippancy terrifying.

"You killed a man," Geneviève said, trying to get through to her, past the madness.

"Not a man. One of you, undead vermin."

"He was alive."

"You'd snacked on him, Frenchie. He would have turned."

"It doesn't work like that."

"That's not what I hear, not what I *know*."

From her icy eyes, this teenager was a fanatic. There could be no reasoning with her.

Geneviève would have to take her down, hold her until the police got here.

Whose side would the cops take? A vampire or a prom queen? Geneviève had fairly good relations with the local law, who were more uneasy about her as a private detective than as a vampire, but this might stretch things.

The girl smiled. She did look awfully cute.

Geneviève knew the mad bitch could probably get away with it. At least once. She had the whole Tuesday Weld thing going for her, pretty poison.

"You've been warned, not spared," said the girl. "My plan A was to skewer you on sight, but the Overlooker thinks this is better strategy. It's some English thing, like cricket. Go figure."

The Overlooker?

"It'd be peachiest all around if you left the state, Frenchie. The country, even. Preferably, the planet. Next time we meet, it won't be a warning. You'll get a formal introduction to the delightful Simon. *Capisce?*"

"Who are you?"

"The Slayer," said the girl, gesturing with her stake. "Barbie, the Vampire Slayer."

Despite herself, despite everything, Geneviève had to laugh. That annoyed Barbie.

Geneviève reminded herself that this silly girl, playing dress-up-and-be-a-heroine, was a real live murderess.

She laughed more calculatedly.

Barbie wanted to kill her but made no move. Whoever this Overlooker—bloody silly title—was, his or her creature didn't want to exceed the brief given her.

(Some English thing, like cricket.)

Geneviève darted at the girl, nails out. Barbie had good reactions. She pivoted to one side and launched a kick. A cleated shoe just missed Geneviève's midriff but raked her side painfully. She jammed her palm heel at Barbie's chin, and caught her solidly, shutting her mouth with a click.

Simon Sharp went flying. That made Geneviève less inhibited about close fighting.

Barbie was strong, trained, and smart. She might have the brain of a flea, but her instincts were pantherlike, and she went all out for a kill. But Geneviève was still alive after five hundred and fifty years as a vampire.

Barbie tried the oldest move in girly martial arts and yanked her opponent's hair, cutting her hand open. Geneviève's hair was fine but stronger and sharper than it looked, like pampas grass. The burst of hot blood was a distraction, sparking lizardy synapses in Geneviève's brain, momentarily blurring her thoughts. She threw Barbie away, skittering her across the sand on her can in an undignified tangle.

Mistake.

Barbie pulled out something that looked like a mace spray and squirted at Geneviève's face.

Geneviève backed away from the cloud, but got a whiff of the mist. Garlic, holy water, and silver salts. Garlic and holy water didn't bother her—more mumbo-jumbo, ineffective against someone not of Dracula's bloodline—but silver was deadly to all *nosferatu*. This spray might not kill her, but it could scar her for a couple of centuries, or even life. It was vanity, she supposed, but she had got used to people telling her she was pretty.

She scuttled away, backwards, across the sand. The cloud dissipated in the air. She saw the droplets, shining under the moon, falling with exaggerated slowness, pattering onto the beach.

When the spray was gone, so was Barbie the Slayer.

". . . and, uh, this is exactly where you found Mr. Griffin, miss?" asked the LAPD homicide detective.

Geneviève was distracted. Even just after dawn, the sun was fatiguing her. In early daylight, on a gurney, Moondoggie— whose name turned out to have been Jeff Griffin—looked colder and emptier, another of the numberless dead stranded in her past while she went on and on and on.

"Miss Dew-dun-ee?"

"Dieudonné," she corrected, absentmindedly.

"Ah yes, Dieudonné. Accent *grave* over the *e*. That's French, isn't it? I have a French car. My wife says—"

"Yes, this is where I found the body," she answered, catching up.

"Ah. There's just one thing I don't understand."

She paid attention to the crumpled little man. He had curly hair, a gravel voice, and a raincoat. He was working on the first cigar of the day. One of his eyes was glass, and aimed off to the side.

"And what might that be, Lieutenant?"

"This girl you mentioned, this—" he consulted his notebook, or pretended to, "—this 'Barbie.' Why would she hang around after the murder? Why did she have to make sure you found the body?"

"She implied that she was under orders, working for this Overlooker."

The detective touched his eyebrow as if to tuck his smelly cigar behind his ear like a pen, and made great play of thinking hard, trying to work through the story he had been told. He was obviously used to people lying to him, and equally obviously unused to dealing with vampires. He stood between her and the sun, as she inched into the shrinking shadow of her trailer.

She wanted to get a hat and dark glasses, but police tape still barred her door.

" 'Overlooker,' yes. I've got a note of that, miss. Funny expression, isn't it? Gives the impression the 'Overlooker' is supposed *not* to see something, that the whole job is about, ah, overlooking. Not like my profession, miss. Or yours either, I figure. You're a PI, like on TV?"

"With fewer car chases and shoot-outs."

The detective laughed. He was a funny little duck. She realised he used his likability as a psychological weapon, to get close to people he wanted to nail. She couldn't mistake the situation: she was in the ring for the killing, and her story about Barbie the Slayer didn't sound straight in daylight. What sane professional assassin gives a name, even a partial name, to a witness?

"A vampire private eye?" The detective scratched his head.

"It makes sense. I don't mind staying up all night. And I've got a wealth of varied experience."

"Have you solved any big cases? Really big ones?"

Without thinking, she told a truth. "In 1888, I halfway found out who Jack the Ripper was."

The detective was impressed.

"I thought no one knew how that panned out. Scotland Yard still have it open. What with you folk living longer and longer, it's not safe to close unsolved files. The guy who took the rap died, didn't he? These days, the theorists say it couldn't have been him."

"I said I halfway found out."

She had a discomfiting memory flash, of her and Charles in an office in Whitechapel in 1888, stumbling over the last clue, all the pieces falling into place. The problem was that solving the mystery hadn't meant sorting everything out, and the case had continued to spiral out of control. There was a message there.

"That wouldn't be good enough for my captain, I'm afraid, miss. He has to answer to Police Chief Exley, and Chief Exley insists on a clearance and conviction rate. I can't just catch them, I have to prove they did it. I have to go to the courts. You'd be surprised how many guilty parties walk free. Especially the rich ones, with fancy lawyers. In this town, it's hard to get a conviction against a rich man."

"This girl looked like a high-school kid."

"Even worse, miss. Probably has rich folks."

"I've no idea about that."

"And pretty is as good as being rich. Better. Juries like pretty girls as much as lawyers like rich men."

There was a shout from the beach. One of the uniformed cops who had been combing the sand held up a plastic evidence bag. Inside was Barbie's bloody stake.

"Simon Sharp," Geneviève said. The detective's eyebrows rose. "That's what she called it. What kind of person gives a pet name to a murder weapon?"

"You think you've heard everything in this business and then something else comes along and knocks you flat. Miss, if you don't mind me asking, I know it's awkward for some women, but, um, well, how old are you?"

"I was born in 1416," she said.

"That's five hundred and, um, sixty-five."

"Thereabouts."

The detective shook his head again and whistled.

"Tell me, does it get easier? Everything?"

"Sadly, no."

"You said you had—uh, how did you put it?—'a wealth of varied experience.' Is that like getting cleverer every year? Knowing more and more of the answers?"

"Would that it did, Lieutenant. Sometimes I think it just means having more and more questions."

He chuckled. "Ain't that the truth."

"Can I get into my trailer now?" she asked, indicating the climbing sun.

"We were keeping you out?" he asked, knowing perfectly well he was. "That's dreadful, with your condition and everything. Of course you can go inside, miss. We'll be able to find you here, if there are any more questions that come up? It's a trailer, isn't it? You're not planning on hitching it up to your car and driving off, say, out of state?"

"No, Lieutenant."

"That's good to know."

He gallantly tore the police tape from her door. She had her keys out. Her skin tingled, and the glare off the sea turned everything into blobby, indistinct shapes.

"Just one more thing," said the detective, hand on her door.

The keys were hot in her fingers.

"Yes," she said, a little sharply.

"You're on a case, aren't you? Like on TV?"

"I'm working on several investigations. May I make a bet with you, Lieutenant? For a dime?"

The detective was surprised by that. But he fished around in his raincoat pocket and, after examining several tissues and a book of matches, came up with a coin and a smile.

"I bet I know what you're going to ask me next," she said. "You're going to ask me who I'm working for."

He was theatrically astonished.

"That's just incredible, miss. Is it some kind of vampire mind-reading power? Or are you like Sherlock Holmes, picking up tiny hints from little clues, like the stains on the cigar band or the dog not howling in the night?"

"Just a lucky guess," she said. Her cheeks were really burning, now.

"Well, see if I can luckily guess your answer. Client confidentiality privilege, like a lawyer or a doctor, eh?"

"See. You have hidden powers, too, Lieutenant."

"Well, Miss Dieudonné, I do what I can, I do what I can. Any idea what I'm going to say next?"

"No."

His smile froze slightly, and she saw ice in his real eye.

"Don't leave town, miss."

On rising, she found Jack Martin had left a message on her machine. He had something for her on "Mr. A." Geneviève listened to the brief message twice, thinking it over.

She had spent only a few hours asking about John Alucard, and someone had gotten killed. A connection? It would be weird if there wasn't. Then again, as the detective reminded her, she'd been around for a long time. In her years, she'd ticked off a great many people, not a few as long-lived as she was herself. Also, this was Southern California, La-La Land, where the nuts came from: folk didn't necessarily need a reason to take against you, or to have you killed.

Could this Overlooker be another Manson? Crazy Charlie was a vampire hater, too, and used teenage girls as assassins. Everyone remembered the death of Sharon Tate, but the Manson Family had also destroyed a vampire elder, Count von Krolock, up on La Cienaga Drive, and painted bat symbols on the walls with his old blood. Barbie the Slayer was cutie-pie where the Family had been skaggy, but that could be a 1980s thing as opposed to a 1960s one.

Geneviève knew she could take care of herself, but the people who talked to her might be in danger. She must mention it to Martin, who wasn't long on survival skills. He could at least

scurry down to Mexico for a couple of months. In the meantime, she was still trying to earn her fifty dollars a day, so she
returned Martin's call. The number he had left was (typically) a
bar, and the growling man who picked up had a message for
her, giving an address in the valley where she could find Martin.

This late in the afternoon, the sun was low in the sky. She
loved the long winter nights.

In a twist-tied plastic bag buried among the cleaning products and rags under her sink unit was a gun, a ladylike palm-size
automatic. She considered fishing it out and transferring it to
the Plymouth Fury but resisted the impulse. No sense in esca-
lating. As yet, even the Overlooker didn't want her dead.

That was not quite a comfort.

The address was an anonymous house in an anonymous neigh-
bourhood out in the diaspora-like sprawl of ranchos and villas
and vistas, but there were more cars and vans outside than a single family would need. Either there was a party on, or this was
a suburban commune. She parked on the street and watched for
a moment. The lights from the windows and the patio were a
few candles brighter than they needed to be. Cables snaked out
of a side door and round to the backyard.

She got out of the Plymouth and followed the hose-thick
Cables, passing through a cultivated arbour into a typical yard
space, with an oval pool, currently covered by a heavy canvas
sheet that was damp where it rested on water, and a white
wooden gazebo, made up with strands of dead ivy and at the
centre of several beams of light. There were a lot of people
around, but this was no party. She should have guessed: it was
another film set. She saw lights on stands and a camera crew,
plus the usual assortment of hangers-on, gophers, rubberneck-
ers, fluffers, runners, and extras.

This was more like a "proper" movie set than the scene she
had found at Welles's bungalow, but she knew from the naked
people in the gazebo that this was a far less proper movie.
Again, she should have guessed. This was a Jack Martin lead,
after all.

"Are you here for 'Vampire Bitch Number Three'?"

The long-haired, chubby kid addressing her wore a tie-dyed T-shirt and a fisherman's waistcoat, pockets stuffed with goodies. He carried a clipboard.

Geneviève shook her head. She didn't know whether to be flattered or offended. Then again, in this town, everyone thought everyone else was an actor or actress. They were usually more or less right.

She didn't like the sound of the part. If she had a reflection that caught on film and were going to prostitute herself for a skin flick, she would at least hold out for "Vampire Bitch Number One."

"The part's taken, I'm afraid," said the kid, not exactly dashing her dreams of stardom. "We got Seka at the last minute."

He nodded towards the gazebo, where three warm girls in pancake makeup hissed at a hairy young man, undoing his Victorian cravat and waistcoat.

"I'm here to see Jack Martin?" she said.

"Who?"

"The writer?"

She remembered Martin used pseudonyms for this kind of work, and spun off a description: "Salt-and-pepper beard, *Midnight Cowboy* jacket with the fringes cut off, smokes a lot, doesn't believe in positive thinking."

The kid knew who she meant. "That's 'Mr. Stroker.' Come this way. He's in the kitchen, doing rewrites. Are you sure you're not here for a part? You'd make a groovy vampire chick."

She thanked him for the compliment, and followed his lead through a mess of equipment to the kitchen, torn between staring at what was going on between the three girls and one guy in the gazebo and keeping her eyes clear. About half the crew were of the madly ogling variety, while the others were jaded enough to stick to their jobs and look at their watches as the shoot edged towards golden time.

"Vampire Bitch Number Two, put more tongue in it," shouted an intense bearded man whose megaphone and beret marked him as the director. "I want to see fangs, Samantha. You've got a jones for that throbbing vein, you've got a real lust for blood. Don't slobber. That's in bad taste. Just nip nicely. That's it. That's colossal. That's the cream."

"What is the name of this picture?" Geneviève asked.

"*Debbie Does Dracula*," said the kid. "It's going to be a four-boner classic. Best thing Boris Adrian has ever shot. He goes for production values, not just screwing. It's got real crossover potential, as a 'couples' movie. Uh-oh, there's a gusher."

"Spurt higher, Mr. Jeremy," shouted the director, Boris Adrian. "I need the arc to be highlit. Thank you, that's perfect. Seka, Samantha, Desiree, you can writhe in it if you like. That's outstanding. Now, collapse in exhaustion, Mr. Jeremy. That's perfect. Cut, and print."

The guy in the gazebo collapsed in real exhaustion, and the girls called for assistants to wipe them off. Some of the crew applauded and congratulated the actors on their performances, which she supposed was fair enough. One of the "Vampire Bitches" had trouble with her false fang-teeth.

The director got off his shooting stick and sat with his actors, talking motivation.

The kid held a screen door open and showed her into the kitchen. Martin sat at a tiny table, cigarette in his mouth, hammering away at a manual typewriter. Another clipboard kid, a wide girl with a frizz of hair and Smiley badges fastening her overall straps, stood over him.

"Gené, excuse me," said Martin. "I'll be through in a moment."

Martin tore through three pages, working the carriage return like a gunslinger fanning a Colt, and passed them up to the girl, who couldn't read as fast as he wrote.

"There's your Carfax Abbey scene," Martin said, delivering the last page.

The girl kissed his forehead and left the kitchen.

"She's in love with me."

"The assistant?"

"She's the producer, actually. Debbie W. Griffith. Had a

monster hit distributing *Throat Sprockets* in Europe. You should see that. It's the first real adult film for the vampire market. Plays at midnight matinees."

"She's 'D. W. Griffith,' and you're . . . ?"

Martin grinned, "Meet 'Bram Stroker.' "

"And why am I here?"

Martin looked around to make sure he wasn't overheard, and whispered, "This is it, this is his. Debbie's a front. This is *un film de* John Alucard."

"It's not Orson Welles."

"But it's a start."

A dark girl, kimono loose, walked through the kitchen, carrying a couple of live white rats in one hand, muttering to herself about "the Master." Martin tried to say hello, but she breezed past, deeply into her role, eyes drifting. She lingered a moment on Geneviève, but wafted out onto the patio and was given a mildly sarcastic round of applause.

"That's Kelly Nicholls," said Martin. "She plays Renfield. In this version, it's not *flies* she eats, not in the usual sense. This picture has a great cast: Dirk Diggler as Dracula, Jennifer Welles as Mina, Holly Body as Lucy, Big John Holmes as Van Helsing."

"Why didn't you tell me about this yesterday?"

"I didn't know then."

"But you're the screenwriter. You can't have been hired and written the whole thing to be shot this afternoon."

"I'm the rewriter. Even for the adult industry, their first pass at the script blew dead cats. It was called *Dracula Sucks*, and boy did it ever. They couldn't lick it, as it were. It's the subject, *Dracula*. You know what they say about the curse, the way it struck down Coppola in Romania. I've spent the day doing a page one rewrite."

Someone shouted, "Quiet on set," and Martin motioned Geneviève to come outside with him to watch the shooting.

"The next scene is Dracula's entrance. He hauls the three vampire bitches—pardon the expression—off Jonathan and, ah, well, you can imagine, *satiates* them, before tossing them the baby in a bag."

"I was just offered a role in the scene. I passed."

Martin harrumphed. Unsure about this whole thing, she began to follow.

A movement in an alcove distracted her. A pleasant-faced warm young man sat in there, hunched over a sideboard. He wore evening dress trousers and a bat-winged black cloak but nothing else. His hair was black and smoothed back, with a prominent widow's peak painted on his forehead. For a supposed vampire, he had a decent tan.

He had a rolled-up ten-dollar bill stuck in his nose.

A line of red dust was on the sideboard. He bent over and snuffed it up. She had heard of drac but never seen it.

The effect on the young man was instant. His eyes shone like bloodied marbles. Fang-teeth shot out like switchblades.

"Yeah, that's it," he said. "Instant vamp!"

He flowed upright, unbending from the alcove, and slid across the floor on bare feet. He wasn't warm, wasn't a vampire, but something in between—a dhampire—that wouldn't last more than an hour.

"Where's Dracula?" shouted Boris Adrian. "Has he got the fangs-on yet?"

"I am Dracula," intoned the youth, as much to himself, convincing himself. "I *am* Dracula!"

As he pushed past her, Geneviève noticed the actor's trousers were held together at the fly and down the sides by strips of Velcro. She could imagine why.

She felt obscurely threatened. Drac—manufactured from vampire blood—was extremely expensive and highly addictive. In her own veins flowed the raw material of many a valuable fangs-on instant vamp fugue. In New York, where the craze came from, vampires had been kidnapped and slowly bled empty to make the foul stuff.

Geneviève followed the dhampire star. He reached out his arms like a wingspread, cloak billowing, and walked across the covered swimming pool, almost flying, as if weightless, skipping over sagging puddles and, without toppling or using his hands, made it over the far edge. He stood at poolside and let the cloak settle on his shoulders.

"I'm ready," he hissed through fangs.

The three fake vampire girls in the gazebo huddled together, a little afraid. They weren't looking at Dracula's face, his hypnotic eyes and fierce fangs, but at his trousers. Geneviève realised there were other properties of drac that she hadn't read about in the newspapers.

The long-haired kid who had spoken to her was working a pulley. A shiny cardboard full moon rose above the gazebo. Other assistants held bats on fishing lines. Boris Adrian nodded approval at the atmosphere.

"Well, Count, go to it," the director ordered. "Action."

The camera began to roll as Dracula strode up to the gazebo, cloak rippling. The girls writhed over the prone guy, Jonathan Harker, and awaited the coming of their dark prince.

"This man is mine," said Dracula, in a Californian drawl that owed nothing to Transylvania. "As you all are mine, you vampire bitches, you horny vampire bitches."

Martin silently recited the lines along with the actor, eyes alight with innocent glee.

"You never love," said the least-fanged of the girls, who had short blonde hair, "you yourself have never loved."

"That is not true, as you know well and as I shall prove to all three of you. In succession, and together. Now."

The rip of Velcro preceded a gasp from the whole crew. Dirk Diggler's famous organ was bloodred and angry. She wondered if he could stab a person with it and suck their blood, or was that just a rumour like the Tijuana werewolf show Martin spent his vacations trying to track down.

The "vampire bitches" huddled in apparently real terror.

"Whatever he's taking, I want some of it," breathed Martin.

Later, in an empty all-night diner, Martin was still excited about *Debbie Does Dracula*. Not really sexually, though she didn't underestimate his prurience, but mostly high on having his words read out, caught on film. Even as "Bram Stroker," he had pride in his work.

"It's a stopgap till the real projects come through," he said, waving a deadly cigarette. "But it's cash in hand, Gené. Cash in hand. I don't have to hock the typewriter. Debbie wants me for the sequel they're making next week, *Taste the Cum of Dracula*, but I may pass. I've got something set up at Universal, near as damn it. A remake of *Buck Privates*, with Belushi and Dan Aykroyd. It's between me and this one other guy, *Lionel Fenn*, and Fenn's a drac-head from the East with a burn-out date stamped on his forehead. I tell you, Gené, it's adios to "Bram Stroker" and "William Forkner" and "Charles Dickings." You'll be my date for the premiere, won't you? You pretty up good, don't you? When the name Jack Martin means something in this town, I want to direct."

He was tripping on dreams. She brought him down again.

"Why would John Alucard be in bed with Boris Adrian?" she asked.

"And Debbie Griffith," he said. "I don't know. There's an invisible barrier between adult and legit. It's like a parallel world. The adult industry has its own stars and genres and awards shows. No one ever crosses. Oh, some of the girls do bit parts. Kelly was in *The Toolbox Murders*, with Cameron Mitchell."

"I missed that one."

"I didn't. She was the chickie in the bath, who gets it with a nail gun. Anyway, that was a fluke. You hear stories that Stallone made a skin flick once, and that some on-the-skids directors take paying gigs under pseudonyms."

"Like 'Bram Stroker'?"

Martin nodded, in his flow. "But it's not an apprenticeship, not really. Coppola shot nudies, but that was different. Just skin, no sex. Tame now. Nostalgia bait. You've got to trust me, Gené, don't tell anyone, and I mean not anyone, that I'm 'Bram Stroker.' It's a crucial time for me, a knife edge between the big ring and the wash-out ward. I really need this *Buck Privates* deal. If it comes to it, I want to hire you to scare off Fenn. You do hauntings, don't you?"

She waved away his panic, her fingers drifting through his nicotine cloud.

"Maybe Alucard wants to raise cash quickly?" she suggested.

"Could be. Though the way Debbie tells it, he isn't just a sleeping partner. He originated the whole idea, got her and Boris together, borrowed Dirk from Jack Horner, even—and I didn't tell you this—supplied the bloody nose candy that gave Dracula's performance the added *frisson*."

It was sounding familiar.

"Did he write the script?" she asked. "The first script?"

"Certainly no writer did. It might be Mr. A. There was no name on the title page."

"It's not a porno movie he wants, not primarily," she said. "It's a Dracula movie. Another one. Yet another one."

Martin called for a coffee refill. The ancient, slightly mouldy character who was the sole staff of the Nighthawks Diner shambled over, coffee sloshing in the glass jug.

"Look at this guy," Martin said. "You'd swear he was a goddamned reanimated corpse. No offence, Gené, but you know what I mean. Maybe he's a dhamp. I hear they zombie out after a while, after they've burned their bat cells."

Deaf to the discussion, the shambler sloshed coffee in Martin's mug. Here, in Jack Martin heaven, there were infinite refills. He exhaled contented plumes of smoke.

"Jack, I have to warn you. This case might be getting dangerous. A friend of mine was killed last night, as a warning. And the police like me for it. I can't prove anything, but it might be that asking about Alucard isn't good for your health. Still, keep your ears open. I know about two John Alucard productions now, and I'd like to collect the set. I have a feeling he's a one-note musician, but I want that confirmed."

"You think he only makes Dracula movies?"

"I think he only makes Dracula."

She didn't know what she meant by that, but it sounded horribly right.

There was night enough left after Martin had peeled off home to check in with the client. Geneviève knew Welles would still be holding court at four in the morning.

He was running footage.

"Come in, come in," he boomed.

Most of the crew she had met the night before were strewn on cushions or rugs in the den, along with a few newcomers, movie brats and law professors and a very old, very grave black man in a bright orange dashiki. Gary, the cameraman, was working the projector.

They were screening the scene she had seen shot, projecting the picture onto the tapestry over the fireplace. Van Helsing tormented by vampire symbols. It was strange to see Welles's huge, bearded face, the luminous skull, the flapping bat and the dripping dagger slide across the stiff, formal image of the mediaeval forest scene.

Clearly, Welles was in midperformance, almost holding a dialogue with his screen self, and wouldn't detach himself from the show so she could report her preliminary findings to him.

She found herself drifting into the yard. There were people there, too. Nico, the vampire starlet, had just finished feeding, and lay on her back, looking up at the stars, licking blood from her lips and chin. She was a messy eater. A too-pretty young man staggered upright, shaking his head to dispel dizziness. His clothes were Rodeo Drive, but last year's in a town where last week was another era. She didn't have to sample Nico's broadcast thoughts to put him down as a rich kid who had found a new craze to blow his trust-fund money on, and her crawling skin told her it wasn't a sports car.

"Your turn," he said to Nico, nagging.

She kept to the shadows. Nico had seen her, but her partner was too preoccupied to notice anyone. The smear on his neck gave Geneviève a little prick of thirst.

Nico sat up with great weariness, the moment of repletion

spoiled. She took a tiny paring knife from her clutch purse. It glinted, silvered. The boy sat eagerly beside her and rolled up the left sleeve of her loose muslin blouse, exposing her upper arm. Geneviève saw the row of striped scars she had noticed last night. Carefully, the vampire girl opened a scar and let her blood trickle. The boy fixed his mouth over the wound. She held his hair in her fist.

"Remember, lick," she said. "Don't suck. You won't be able to take a full fangs-on."

His throat pulsed, as he swallowed.

With a roar, the boy let the girl go. He had the eyes and the fangs, even more than Dirk Diggler's Dracula. He moved fast, a temporary newborn high on all the extra senses and the sheer sense of power.

The dhampire put on wraparound mirror shades, ran razor-nailed hands through his gelled hair and stalked off to haunt the La-La night. Within a couple of hours, he would be a real live boy again. By that time, he could have got himself into all manner of scrapes.

Nico squeezed shut her wound. Geneviève caught her pain. The silver knife would be dangerous if it flaked in the cut. For a vampire, silver rot was like bad gangrene.

"It's not my place to say anything," began Geneviève.

"Then don't," said Nico, though she clearly received what Geneviève was thinking. "You're an elder. You can't know what it's like."

She had a flash that this newborn would never be old. What a pity.

"It's a simple exchange," said the girl. "Blood for blood. A gallon for a scratch. The economy is in our favour. Just like the President says."

Geneviève joined Nico at the edge of the property.

"This vampire trip really isn't working for me," said Nico. "That boy, Julian, will be warm again in the morning, mortal and with a reflection. And when he wants to, he'll be a vampire. If I'm not here, there are others. You can score drac on Hollywood Boulevard for twenty-five dollars a suck. Vile stuff, powdered, not from the tap, but it works."

Geneviève tidied Nico's hair. The girl lay on her lap, sobbing silently. She hadn't just lost blood.

This happened when you became an elder. You were mother and sister to the whole world of the undead.

The girl's despair passed. Her eyes were bright, with Julian's blood.

"Let's hunt, Elder, like you did in Transylvania."

"I'm from France. I've never even been to Romania."

Now she mentioned it, that was odd. She'd been almost everywhere else. Without consciously thinking of it, she must have been avoiding the supposed homeland of the *nosferatu*.

"There are human cattle out there," said Nico. "I know all the clubs. X is playing at the Roxy, if you like West Coast punk. And the doorman at After Hours always lets us in, vampire girls. There are so few of us. We go to the head of the line. Powers of fascination."

"Human cattle" was a real newborn expression. This close to dawn, Geneviève was thinking of her cosy trailer and shutting out the sun, but Nico was a race-the-dawn girl, staying out until it was practically light, bleeding her last as the red circle rose in the sky.

She wondered if she should stick close to the girl, keep her out of trouble. Why? She couldn't protect everyone. She barely knew Nico, probably had nothing in common with her.

She remembered Moondoggie. And all the other dead, the ones she hadn't been able to help, hadn't tried to help, hadn't known about in time.

This girl really was none of her business.

"What's that?" said Nico, head darting. There was a noise from beyond the fence at the end of the garden.

Dominating the next property was a three-storey wooden mansion, California cheesecake. Nico might have called it old. Now Geneviève's attention was drawn to it, her night eyes saw how strange the place was. A rusted-out pickup truck was on cinderblocks in the yard, with a pile of ragged auto tires next to it. The windshield was smashed out, and dried streaks—which any vampire would have scented as human blood, even after ten years—marked the hood.

"Who lives there?" Geneviève asked.

"In-bred backwoods brood," said Nico. "Orson says they struck it rich down in Texas, and moved to Beverly Hills. You know: swimming pools, movie stars . . ."

"Oil?"

"Chili sauce recipe. Have you heard of Sawyer's Sauce?" Geneviève hadn't. "I guess not. I've not taken solid foods since I turned, though if I don't feed for a night or two I get this terrible phantom craving for those really shitty White Castle burgers. I suppose that if you don't get to the market, you don't know the brand names."

"The Sawyers brought Texas style with them," Geneviève observed. "That truck's a period piece."

The back porch was hung with mobiles of bones and nail-impaled alarm clocks. She saw a napping chicken, stuffed inside a canary cage.

"What's that noise?" Nico asked.

There was a wasplike buzzing, muted. Geneviève scented burning gas. Her teeth were on edge.

"Power tool," she said. "Funny time of the night for warm folks to be doing carpentry."

"I don't think they're all entirely warm. I saw some gross Grandpaw peeping out the other night, face like dried leather, licking livery lips. If he isn't undead, he's certainly nothing like alive."

There was a stench in the air. Spoiled meat.

"Come on, let's snoop around," said Nico, springing up. She vaulted over the low fence dividing the properties and crept across the yard like a four-legged crab.

Geneviève thought that was unwise, but followed, standing upright and keeping to shadows.

This really was none of her business.

Nico was on the porch now, looking at the mobiles.

Geneviève wasn't sure whether it was primitive art or voodoo. Some of the stick-and-bone dangles were roughly man-shaped.

"Come away," she said.

"Not just yet."

Nico examined the back door. It hung open, an impenetrable dark beyond. The buzzing was still coming from inside the ramshackle house.

Geneviève *knew* sudden death was near, walking like a man. She called to Nico, more urgently.

Something small and fast came, not from inside the house but from the flatbed of the abandoned truck. The shape cartwheeled across the yard to the porch and collided purposefully with Nico. A length of wood pierced the vampire girl's thin chest. A look, more of surprise than pain or horror, froze on her face.

Geneviève felt the thrust in her own heart, then the silence in her mind. Nico was gone, in an instant.

"How do you like your stake, ma'am?"

It was Barbie. Only someone truly witless would think stake puns the height of repartee.

This time, Geneviève wouldn't let her get away.

"Just the time of night for a little leech-on-a-spit," said the Slayer, lifting Nico's deadweight so that her legs dangled. "This really should be you, Frenchie. By the way, I don't think you've met Simon's brother, Sidney. Frenchie, Sidney. Sidney, hellbitch creature of the night fit only to be impaled and left to rot in the light of the sun. That's the formalities out of the way."

She threw Nico away, sliding the dead girl off Sidney the Stake. The newborn, mould already on her still-startled face, flopped off the porch and fell to the yard.

Geneviève was still shocked by the passing, almost turned to ice. Nico had been in her mind, just barely and with tiny fingers, and her death was a wrench. She thought her skull might be leaking.

"They don't cotton much to trespassers down Texas way," said Barbie, in a bad cowboy accent. "Nor in Beverly Hills, neither."

Geneviève doubted the Sawyers knew Barbie was here.

"Next time, the Overlooker says I can do you, too. I'm wishing and hoping and praying you ignore the warning. You'd look so fine on the end of a pole, Frenchie."

An engine revved, like a signal. Barbie was bounding away, with deerlike elegance.

Geneviève followed.

She rounded the corner of the Sawyer house and saw Barbie climbing into a sleek black Jaguar. In the driver's seat was a man wearing a tweed hunting jacket with matching bondage hood. He glanced backwards as he drove off.

The sports car had vanity plates: OVRLKER1.

Gravel flew as the car sped off down the drive.

"What's all this consarned ruckus?" shouted someone from the house.

Geneviève turned and saw an American gothic family group on the porch. Blotch-faced teenage boy, bosomy but slack-eyed girl in a polka-dot dress, stern patriarch in a dusty black suit, and hulking elder son in a stained apron and crude leather mask. Only the elder generation was missing, and Geneviève was sure they were up in rocking chairs on the third storey, peeking through the slatted blinds.

"That a dead'n'?" asked the patriarch, nodding at Nico.

She conceded that it was.

"*True* dead'n'?"

"Yes," she said, throat catching.

"What a shame and a waste," said Mr. Sawyer, in a tone that made Geneviève think he wasn't referring to a life but to flesh and blood that was highly salable.

"Shall I call the sheriff, Paw?" asked the girl.

Mr. Sawyer nodded gravely.

Geneviève knew what was coming next.

". . . there's just one thing I don't understand, miss."

"Lieutenant, if there were 'just one thing' I didn't understand, I'd be a very happy old lady. At the moment, I can't think of 'just one thing' I do understand."

The detective smiled craggily.

"You're a vampire, miss. Like this dead girl, this, ah, Nico. That's right, isn't it?"

She admitted it. Orson Welles had lent her a crow-black umbrella which she was using as a parasol.

"And this Barbie, who again nobody else saw, was, ah, a living person?"

"Warm."

"Warm, yes. That's the expression. That's what you call us."

"It's not offensive."

"That's not how I take it, miss. No, it's that aren't vampires supposed to be faster than a warm person, harder to catch hold of in a tussle?"

"Nico was a newborn, and weakened. She'd lost some blood."

"That's one for the books."

"Not any more."

The detective scratched his head, lit cigar end dangerously near his hair. "So I hear. It's called 'drac' on the streets. I have friends on the Narco Squad. They say it's a worse blight than heroin, and it's not illegal yet."

"Where is this going, Lieutenant?"

He shut his notebook and pinned her with his eye.

"You could have, ah, *taken* Miss Nico? If you got into a fight with her?"

"I didn't."

"But you could have."

"I could have killed the Kennedys and Sanford White, but I didn't."

"Those are closed cases, as far as I'm concerned. This is open."

"I gave you the plate number."

"Yes, miss. OVRLKER1. A Jaguar."

"Even if it's a fake plate, there can't be that many English sports cars in Los Angeles."

"There are, ah, one thousand, seven hundred and twenty-two registered Jaguars. Luxury vehicles are popular in this city, in some parts of it. Not all the same model."

"I don't know the model. I don't follow cars. I just know it was a Jaguar. It had the cat on the bonnet, the hood."

"Bonnet? That's the English expression, isn't it?"

"I lived in England for a long time."

With an Englishman. The detective's sharpness reminded her of Charles, with a witness or a suspect.

Suspect.

He had rattled the number of Jaguars in Greater Los Angeles off the top of his head, with no glance at the prop notebook. Gears were turning in his head.

"It was a black car," she said. "That should make it easier to find."

"Most automobiles look black at night. Even red ones."

"Not to me, Lieutenant."

Uniforms were off, grilling the Sawyers. Someone was even talking with Welles, who had let slip that Geneviève was working for him. Since the client had himself blown confidentiality, she was in an awkward position; Welles still didn't want it known what exactly she was doing for him.

"I think we can let you go now, miss," said the detective.

She had been on the point of presenting him her wrists for the cuffs.

"There isn't 'just one more thing' you want to ask?"

"No. I'm done. Unless there's anything you want to say."

She didn't think so.

"Then you can go. Thank you, miss."

She turned away, knowing it would come, like a hand on her shoulder or around her heart.

"There is one thing, though. Not a question. More like a circumstance, something that has to be raised. I'm afraid I owe you an apology."

She turned back.

"It's just that I had to check you out, you know. Run you through the books. As a witness, yesterday. Purely routine."

Her umbrella seemed heavier.

"I may have got you in trouble with the state licensing board. They had all your details correctly, but it seems that every time anyone looked at your license renewal application, they misread the date. As a European, you don't write an open four. It's easy to mistake a four for a nine. They thought you were born in 1916. Wondered when you'd be retiring, in fact. Had you down as a game old girl."

"Lieutenant, I am a game old girl."

"They didn't pull your license, exactly. This is really embarrassing, and I'm truly sorry to have been the cause of it, but they want to, ah, review your circumstances. There aren't any other vampires licensed as private investigators in the state of California, and there's no decision on whether a legally dead person can hold a license."

"I never died. I'm not legally dead."

"They're trying to get your paperwork from, ah, France."

She looked up at the sky, momentarily hoping to burn out her eyes. Even if her original records existed, they'd be so old as to be protected historical documents. Photostats would not be coming over the wire from her homeland.

"Again, miss, I'm truly sorry."

She just wanted to get inside her trailer and sleep the day away.

"Do you have your license with you?"

"In the car," she said, dully.

"I'm afraid I'm going to have to ask you to surrender it," said the detective. "And that until the legalities are settled, you cease to operate as a private investigator in the state of California."

At sunset, she woke to another limbo, with one of her rare headaches. She was used to knowing what she was doing tonight, and the next night, if not specifically then at least generally. Now, she wasn't sure what she *could* do.

Geneviève wasn't a detective any more, not legally. Welles had not paid her off, but if she continued working on John Alucard for him she'd be breaking the law. Not a particularly important one, in her opinion . . . but vampires lived in such a twilight world that it was best to pay taxes on time and not park in towaway zones. After all, this was what happened when she drew attention to herself.

She had two other ongoing investigations, neither promising. She should make contact with her clients, a law firm and an Orange County mother, and explain the situation. In both cases, she hadn't turned up any results and so would not in all conscience be able to charge a fee. She didn't even have that much Welles could use.

Money would start to be a problem around Valentine's Day. The licensing board might have sorted it out by then.

(in some alternate universe)

She should call Beth Davenport, her lawyer, to start filing appeals and lodging complaints. That would cost, but anything else was just giving up.

Two people were truly dead. That bothered her, too.

She sat at her tiny desk, by a slatted window, considering her telephone. She had forgotten to switch her answering machine on before turning in, and any calls that might have come today were lost. She had never done that before.

Should she rerecord her outgoing message, stating that she was (temporarily?) out of business? The longer she was off the bus, the harder it would be to get back.

On TV, suspended cops, disbarred private eyes, and innocent men on the run never dropped the case. And this was Southern California, where the TV came from.

She decided to compromise. She wouldn't work Alucard, which was what Welles had been paying her for. But, as a concerned—indeed, involved—citizen, no law said she couldn't use her talents unpaid to go after the Slayer.

Since this was a police case, word of her status should have filtered down to her LAPD contacts but might not yet have reached outlying agencies. She called Officer Baker, a contact in the Highway Patrol, and wheedled a little to get him to run a license plate for her.

OVRLKER1.

The callback came within minutes, excellent service she admitted was well worth a supper and cocktails one of these nights. Baker teased her a while about that, then came over.

Amazingly, the plate *was* for a Jaguar. The car was registered in the name of Ernest Ralph Gorse, to an address in a town up the coast, Shadow Bay. The only other forthcoming details were that Gorse was a British subject—not citizen, of course—and held down a job as a high-school librarian.

The Overlooker? A school librarian and a cheerleader might seem different species, but they swam in the same tank.

She thanked Baker and rang off.

If it was that easy, she could let the cops handle it. The Lieutenant was certainly sharp enough to run a Gorse down and scout around to see if a Barbie popped up. Even if the detective hadn't believed her, he would have been obliged to run the plate, to puncture her story. Now he was obliged to check it out.

But wasn't it all too easy?

Since when did librarians drive Jaguars?

It had the air of a trap.

She was where the Lieutenant must have been seven hours ago. She wouldn't put the crumpled detective on her list of favourite people, but didn't want to hear he'd run into another of the Sharp brothers. Apart from the loss of a fine public servant who was doubtless also an exemplary husband, it was quite likely that if the cop sizing her up for two murders showed up dead, she would be even more suitable for framing.

Shadow Bay wasn't more than an hour away.

Welles's final Dracula project came together in 1981, just as the movies were gripped by a big vampire craze. Controversial and slow-building, and shut out of all but technical Oscars, Coppola's *Dracula* proved there was a substantial audience for vampire subjects. This was the film era of Werner Herzog's *Renfield, Jeder fur Sich und die Vampir Gegen Alle,* a retelling of the story from the point of the fly-eating lunatic (Klaus Kinski); of Tony Scott's *The Hunger,* with Catherine Deneuve and David

Bowie as New York art patrons Miriam and John Blay-
lock, at the centre of a famous murder case defended by
Alan Dershowitz (Ron Silver); of John Landis's *Scream,
Blacula, Scream,* with Eddie Murphy as Dracula's
African-get Prince Mamuwalde, searching for his lost
bride (Vanity) in New York—best remembered for a
plagiarism lawsuit by screenwriter Pat Hobby that
forced Paramount to open its books to the auditors; of
Richard Attenborough's bloated, mammoth, Oscar-
scooping *Varney,* with Anthony Hopkins as Sir Francis
Varney, the vampire Viceroy overthrown by the Second
Indian Mutiny; of Brian DePalma's remake of *Scarface,*
an explicit attack on the Transylvania Movement, with
Al Pacino as Tony Sylvana, a Ceausescu cast-out rising
in the booming drac trade and finally taken down by a
Vatican army led by James Woods.

Slightly ahead of all this activity, Welles began
shooting quietly, without publicity, working at his own
pace, underwritten by the last of his many mysterious
benefactors. His final script combined elements from
Stoker's fiction with historical fact made public by the
researches of Raymond McNally and Radu Florescu—
associates as far back as *D Is for Dracula*—and concentrated on the last days of the Count, abandoned in
his castle, awaiting his executioners, remembering the
betrayals and crimes of his lengthy, weighty life. This
was the project Welles called *The Other Side of Midnight.* From sequences filmed as early as 1972, the director culled footage of Peter Bogdanovich as Renfield,
while he opted to play not the stick insect vampire but
the corpulent slayer, finally gifting the world with his
definitive Professor Van Helsing. If asked by the trade
press, he made great play of having offered the role of
Dracula to Warren Beatty, Steve McQueen, or Robert
DeNiro, but this was a conjurer's distraction, for he had
fixed on his Count for some years and was now finally

able to fit him for his cape and fangs. Welles's final
Dracula was to be John Huston.

                                        Gates, ibid.

She parked on the street but took the trouble to check out the
Shadow Bay High teachers' parking lot. Two cars: a black
Jaguar (OVRLKER1), a beat-up silver Peugeot ("I have a French
car"). Geneviève checked the Peugeot and found LAPD ID on display. The interior was a mess. She caught the after-whiff of cigars.

The school was as unexceptional as the town, with that
faintly unreal movie-set feel that came from newness. The oldest building in sight was put up in 1965. To her, places like this
felt temporary.

A helpful map by the front steps of the main building told
her where the library was, across a grassy quadrangle. The
school grounds were dark. The kids wouldn't be back from
their Christmas vacation. And no evening classes. She had
checked Gorse's address first and found no one home.

A single light was on in the library, like the cover of a gothic
romance paperback.

Cautious, she crossed the quad. Slumped in the doorway of
the library was a raincoated bundle. Her heart plunging, she
knelt and found the Lieutenant insensible but still alive. He had
been bitten badly and bled. The ragged tear in his throat
showed he'd been taken the old-fashioned way—a strong grip
from behind, a rending fang bite, then sucking and swallowing.
Nonconsensual vampirism, a felony in anyone's books, without
the exercise of powers of fascination to cloud the issue. It was
hard to mesmerise someone with one eye, though some vampires worked with whispers and could even put the fluence on a
blind person.

There was another vampire in Shadow Bay. By the look of
the leavings, one of the bad uns. Perhaps that explained Barbie's
prejudice. It was always a mistake to extrapolate a general rule
from a test sample of one.

She clamped a hand over the wound, feeling the weak pulse,

pressing the edges together. Whoever had bitten the detective hadn't even had the consideration to shut off the faucet after glutting themselves. The smears of blood on his coat and shirt collar overrode her civilised impulses: her mouth became sharp-fanged and full of saliva. That was a good thing. A physical adaption of her turning was that her spittle had antiseptic properties. Vampires of her bloodline were evolved for gentle, repeated feedings. After biting and drinking, a full-tongued lick sealed the wound.

Angling her mouth awkwardly and holding up the Lieutenant's lolling head to expose his neck, she stuck out her tongue and slathered saliva over the long tear. She tried to ignore the euphoric if cigar-flavoured buzz of his blood. She had a connection to his clear, canny mind.

He had never thought her guilty. Until now.

"Makes a pretty picture, Frenchie," said a familiar girlish voice. "Classic Bloodsucker 101, vamp and victim. Didn't your father-in-darkness warn you about snacking between meals? You won't be able to get into your party dresses if you bloat up. Where's the fun in that?"

Geneviève knew Barbie wasn't going to accept her explanation. For once, she understood why.

The wound had been left open for her.

"I've been framed," she said around bloody fangs.

Barbie giggled, a teen vision in a red ra-ra skirt, white ankle socks, mutton-chop short-sleeved top, and faux metallic choker. She had sparkle glitter on her cheeks and an Alice band with artificial antennae that ended in bobbling stars.

She held up her stake and said, "Scissors cut paper."

Geneviève took out her gun and pointed it. "Stone blunts scissors."

"Hey, no fair," whined Barbie.

Geneviève set the wounded man aside as carefully as possible and stood up. She kept the gun trained on the Slayer's heart.

"Where does it say vampires have to do kung fu fighting? Everyone else in this country carries a gun, why not me?"

For a moment, she almost felt sorry for Barbie the Slayer.

Her forehead crinkled into a frown, her lower lip jutted like a sulky five-year-old's, and tears of frustration started in her eyes. She had a lot to learn about life. If Geneviève got her wish, the girl would complete her education in Tehachapi Womens' Prison.

A silver knife slipped close to her neck.

"Paper wraps stone," suaved a British voice.

"Barbie doesn't know, does she? That you're *nosferatu*?"

Ernest Ralph Gorse, high-school librarian, was an epitome of tweedy middle-aged stuffiness, so stage English that he made Alistair Cooke sound like a Dead End Kid. He arched an elegant eyebrow, made an elaborate business of cleaning his granny glasses with his top-pocket hankie, and gave out a little I'm-so-wicked moue that let his curly fangs peep out from beneath his stiff upper lip.

"No, 'fraid not. Lovely to look at, delightful to know, but frightfully thick, that's our little Barbara."

The Overlooker—"Yes," he had admitted, "bloody silly name, means nothing, just sounds 'cool' if you're a twit"—had sent Barbie the Slayer off with the drained detective to call at the hospital ER and the Sheriff's office. Geneviève was left in the library in the custody of Gorse. He had made her sit in a chair, and kept well beyond arm's length.

"You bit the Lieutenant?" she stated.

Gorse raised a finger to his lips and tutted.

"Shush now, old thing, mustn't tell, don't speak it aloud. Jolly bad show to give away the game and all that rot. Would you care for some instant coffee? Ghastly muck, but I'm mildly addicted to it. It's what comes of being cast up on these heathen shores."

The Overlooker pottered around his desk, which was piled high with unread and probably unreadable books. He poured water from an electric kettle into an oversize green ceramic apple. She declined his offer with a headshake. He quaffed from his apple-for-the-teacher mug, and let out an exaggerated ahh of satisfaction.

"That takes the edge off. Washes down *cop au nicotin* very nicely."

"Why hasn't she noticed?"

Gorse chuckled. "Everything poor Barbara knows about the tribes of *nosferatu* comes from me. Of course, a lot of it I made up. I'm very creative, you know. It's always been one of my skills. Charm and persuasion, that's the ticket. The lovely featherhead hangs on my every word. She thinks all vampires are gruesome creatures of the night, demons beyond hope of redemption, frothing beasts fit only to be put down like mad dogs. I'm well aware of the irony, old thing. Some cold evenings, the hilarity becomes almost too much to handle. Oh, the stories I've spun for her, the wild things she'll believe. I've told her she's the Chosen One, the only girl in the world who can shoulder the burden of the crusade against the forces of evil. Teenage girls adore that I'm-a-secret-Princess twaddle, you know. Especially the Yanks. I copped a lot of it from *Star Wars*. Bloody awful film, but very revealing about the state of the national mind."

Gorse was enjoying the chance to explain things. Bottling up his cleverness had been a trial for him. She thought it was the only reason she was still alive for this performance.

"But what's the point?"

"Originally, expedience. I've been 'passing' since I came to America. I'm not like you, sadly. I can't flutter my lashes and have pretty girls offer their necks for the taking. I really am one of those hunt-and-kill, rend-and-drain sort of *nosferatu*. I tried the other way, but courtship dances just bored me rigid, and I thought, well, why not? Why not just rip open the odd throat? So, after a few months here in picturesque Shadow Bay, empties were piling up like junk mail. Then the stroke of genius came to me. I could hide behind a Vampire Slayer, and since there were none in sight I made one up. I checked the academic records to find the dimmest dolly bird in school and recruited her for the cause. I killed her lunk of a boyfriend—captain of football team, would you believe it?—and a selection of snack-type teenagers. Then, I revealed to Barbara that her destiny was to be the Slayer. Together, we tracked and destroyed that first dread fiend—the school secretary who was nagging me about getting my employment records from Jolly Old England, as it happens—and staked the bloodlusting bitch. However, it seems she spawned before we got to her, and ever since we've been doing away with her murderous brood. You'll be glad to know I've managed to rid this town almost completely of real estate agents. When the roll is called up yonder, that must count in the plus column, though it's my long-term plan not to be there."

Actually, Gorse was worse than the vampires he had made up. He'd had a choice, and *decided* to be evil. He worked hard on fussy geniality, modelling his accent and speech patterns on *Masterpiece Theatre,* but there was ice inside him, a complete vacuum.

"So, you have things working your way in Shadow Bay?" she said. "You have your little puppet theatre to play with. Why come after me?"

Gorse was wondering whether to tell her more. He pulled a half-hunter watch from his waistcoat pocket and pondered. She wondered if she could work her trick of fascination on him. Clearly, he loved to talk, was bored with dissimulation, had a real need to be appreciated. The sensible thing would have been to get this over with, but Gorse had to tell her how brilliant he was. Everything up to now had been his own story; now there was more important stuff, and he was wary of going on.

"Still time for one more story," he said. "One more *ghost* story."

Click. She had him.

He was an instinctive killer, probably a sociopath from birth, but she was his elder. The silver-bladed letter opener was never far from his fingers. She would have to judge when to jump.

"It's a lonely life, isn't it? Ours, I mean. Wandering through the years, wearing out your clothes, lost in a world you never made? There was a golden age for us once, in London when Dracula was on the throne. Eighteen eighty-eight and all that. You, famous girl, did your best to put a stop to that, turned us all back into nomads and parasites when we might have been masters of the universe. Some of us want it that way again, my darling. We've been getting together lately, sort of like a pressure group. Not like those Transylvania fools who want to go back to the castles and the mountains, but like Him, battening onto a new, vital world, making a place for ourselves. An exalted place. He's still our inspiration, old thing. Let's say I did it for Dracula."

That wasn't enough, but it was all she was going to get now.

People were outside, coming in.

"Time flies, old thing. I'll have to make this quick."

Gorse took his silver pig sticker and stood over her. He thrust.

Faster than any eye could catch, her hands locked around his wrist.

"Swift filly, eh?"

She concentrated. He was strong, but she was old. The knife point dimpled her blouse. He tipped back her chair and put a knee on her stomach, pinning her down.

The silver touch was white hot.

She turned his arm and forced it upwards. The knife slid under his spectacles and the point stuck in his left eye.

Gorse screamed, and she was free of him. He raged and roared, fangs erupting from his mouth, two-inch barbs bursting from his fingertips. Bony spars, the beginnings of wings, sprouted through his jacket around the collar and pierced his leather elbow patches.

The doors opened, and people came in. Barbie and two crucifix-waving sheriff's deputies.

The Slayer saw

(and recognised?)

the vampire and rushed across the room, stake out. Gorse caught the girl and snapped her neck, then dropped her in a dead tangle.

"Look what you made me do!" he said to Geneviève, voice distorted by the teeth but echoing from the cavern that was his reshaped mouth. "She's *broken* now. It'll take ages to make another. I hadn't even got to the full initiation rites. There would have been bleeding, and I was making up something about tantric sex. It would have been a real giggle, and you've spoiled it."

His eye congealed, frothing grey deadness in his face.

She motioned for the deputies to stay back. They wisely kept their distance.

"Just remember," said Gorse, directly to her, "You can't stop Him. He's coming back. And then, oh my best beloved, you will be as sorry a girl as ever drew a sorry breath. He is not big on forgiveness, if you get my drift."

Gorse's jacket shredded, and wings unfurled. He flapped into the air, rising above the first tier of bookshelves, hovering at the mezzanine level. His old-school tie dangled like a dead snake.

The deputies tried shooting at him. She supposed she would have, too.

He crashed through a tall set of windows and flew off, vast shadow blotting out the moon and falling on the bay.

The deputies holstered their guns and looked at her. She wondered for about two minutes whether she should stick with her honesty policy.

Letting a bird flutter in her voice, she said, "That man . . . he was a v-v-vampire."

Then she did a pretty fair imitation of a silly girl fainting. One deputy checked her heartbeat while she was "out," and was satisfied that she was warm. The other went to call for backup.

Through a crack in her eyelids, she studied "her" deputy. His hands might have lingered a little too long on her chest for strict medical purposes. The thought that he was the type to cop a feel from a helpless girl just about made it all right to get him into trouble by slipping silently out of the library while he was checking out the dead Slayer.

She made it undetected back to her car.

In her trailer, after another day of lassitude, she watched the early evening bulletin on Channel 6. Anchorpersons Karen White and Lew Landers had details of the vampire killing in

Shadow Bay. Because the primary victim was a cute teenage girl, it was top story. The wounding of a decorated LAPD veteran—the Lieutenant was still alive, but off the case—also rated a flagged mention. The newscast split-screened a toothpaste commercial photograph of "Barbara Dahl Winters," smiling under a prom queen tiara, and an "artist's impression" of Gorse in giant bat form, with blood tastefully dripping from his fangs. Ernest "Gory" Gorse turned out to be a fugitive from Scotland Yard, with a record of petty convictions before he turned and a couple of likely murders since. Considering a mug shot from his warm days, Karen said the killer looked like such a nice fellow, even scowling over numbers, and Lew commented that you couldn't judge a book by its cover.

Geneviève continued paying attention, well into the next item—about a scary candlelight vigil by hooded supporters of Annie Wilkes—and turned the sound on her portable TV set down only when she was sure her name was not going to come up in connection with the Shadow Bay story.

Gorse implied she was targeted because of her well-known involvement in the overthrow of Count Dracula nearly a century ago. But that didn't explain why he had waited until now to give her a hard time. She also gathered from what he had let slip in flirtatious hints that he wasn't the top of the totem pole, that he was working with or perhaps for someone else.

Gorse had said: "You can't stop Him. He's coming back."

Him? He?

Only one vampire inspired that sort of *quondam rex que futurus* talk. Before he finally died, put out of his misery, Count Dracula had used himself up completely. Geneviève was sure of that. He had outlived his era, several times over, and been confronted with his own irrelevance. His true death was just a formality.

And He was not coming back.

A woodcut image of Dracula appeared on television. She turned the sound up.

The newscast had reached the entertainment roundup, which in this town came before major wars on other continents.

A fluffy-haired woman in front of the Hollywood sign was talking about the latest studio craze, Dracula pictures. A race was on between Universal and Paramount to get their biopics of the Count to the screens. At Universal, director Joel Schumacher and writer-producer Jane Wagner had cast John Travolta and Lily Tomlin in St. *George's Fire;* at MGM, producer Steven Spielberg and director Tobe Hooper had Peter Coyote and Karen Allen in *Vampirgeist.* There was no mention of Orson Welles—or, unsurprisingly, Boris Adrian—but another familiar name came up.

John Alucard.

"Hollywood dealmakers have often been characterised as bloodsuckers," said the reporter, "but John Alucard is the first actually to be one. Uniquely, this vampire executive is involved in *both* these competing projects, as a packager of the Universal production and as associate producer of the MGM film. Clearly, in a field where there are too few experts to go around, John Alucard is in demand. Unfortunately, Mr. A—as Steven Spielberg calls him—is unable because of his image impairment to grant interviews for broadcast media, but he has issued a statement to the effect that he feels there is room for far more than two versions of the story he characterises as 'the most important of the last two centuries.' He goes on to say, 'There can be no definitive Dracula, but we hope we shall be able to conjure a different Dracula for every person.' For decades, Hollywood stayed away from this hot subject but, with the Francis Coppola epic of a few years ago cropping up on Best of All Time lists, it seems we are due, like the Londoners of 1885, for a veritable *invasion* of Draculas. This is Kimberley Wells, for Channel 6 KDHB *Update News,* at the Hollywood sign."

She switched the television off. The whole world, and Orson Welles, knew now what John Alucard was doing, but the other part of her original commission—who he was and where he came from—was still a mystery. He had come from the East, with a long line of credit. A source had told her he had skipped New York ahead of an investigation into insider-trading or junk bonds, but she might choose to put that down to typical Los

Angeles cattiness. Another whisper had him living another life up in Silicon Valley as a consultant on something hush-hush President Reagan's people were calling the Strategic Defense Initiative, supposedly Buck Rogers stuff. Alucard could also be a Romanian shoe salesman with a line of great patter who had quit his dull job and changed his name the night he learned his turning vampire wasn't going to take in the long run and set out to become the new Irving Thalberg before he rotted away to dirt.

There must be a connection between the moviemaking mystery man and the high-school librarian. Alucard and Gorse. Two vampires in California. She had started asking around about one of them, and the other had sent a puppet to warn her off.

John Alucard could not *be* Count Dracula.

Not yet, at least.

On her way up into the Hollywood Hills, to consult the only real magician she knew, she decided to call on Jack Martin, to see if he wanted to come along on the trip. The movie mage would interest him.

The door of Martin's shack hung open.

Her heart skipped. Loose manuscript pages were drifting out of Martin's home, catching on the breeze, and scuttling along Beverly Glen Boulevard, sticking on the manicured hedges of the million-dollar estates, brushing across the white-painted faces of lawn jockeys who had been coal black until Sidney Poitier made a fuss.

She knocked on the door, which popped a hinge and hung free.

"Jack?"

Had Gorse gotten to him?

She ventured inside, prepared to find walls dripping red and a ruined corpse lying in a nest of torn-up screenplays.

Martin lay on a beat-up sofa, mouth open, snoring slightly. He was no more battered than usual. A Mexican wrestling magazine was open on his round tummy.

"Jack?"

He came awake, blearily.

"It's you," he said, cold.

His tone was like a silver knife.

"What's the matter?"

"As if you didn't know. You're not good to be around, Gené. Not good at all. You don't see it, but you're a wrecker." She backed away.

"Someone tipped off the Writers' Guild about the porno. My ticket got yanked; my dues were not accepted. I'm off the list. I'm off all the lists. All possible lists. I didn't get *Buck Privates*. They went with Lionel Fenn."

"There'll be other projects," she said.

"I'll be lucky to get *Buck's Privates*."

Martin had been drinking, but didn't need to get drunk to be in this despair hole. It was where he went sometimes, a mental space like Ensenada, where he slunk to wallow, to soak up the misery he turned into prose. This time, she had an idea he wasn't coming back; he was going lower than ever and would end up a beachcomber on a nighted seashore, picking broken skulls out of bloody seaweed, trailing bare feet through ink black surf, becoming the exile king of his own dark country.

"It just took a phone call, Gené. To smash everything. To smash me. I wasn't even worth killing. That hurts. You, they'll kill. I don't want you to be near me when it happens."

"Does this mean our premiere date is off?"

She shouldn't have said that. Martin began crying, softly. It was a shocking scene, upsetting to her on a level she had thought she had escaped from. He wasn't just depressed, he was scared.

"Go away, Gené," he said.

This was not a jaunt any more. Jack Martin was as lost to her as Moondoggie, as her license.

How could things change so fast? It wasn't the second week of January, wasn't the Julian 1980s, but everything that had seemed certain last year, last decade, was up for debate or thrown away.

There was a cruelty at work. Beyond Gorse.

She parked the Plymouth and walked across a lawn to a ranch-style bungalow. A cabalist firmament of star signs decorated the mailbox.

The mage was a trim, fiftyish man, handsome but small, less a fallen angel than a fallen cherub. He wore ceremonial robes to receive her into his *sanctum sanctorum*, an arrangement of literal shrines to movie stars of the 1920s and '30s: Theda Bara, Norma Desmond, Clara Bow, Lina Lamont, Jean Harlow, Blanche Hudson, Myrna Loy. His all-seeing amulet contained a long-lashed black-and-white eye, taken from a still of Rudolph Valentino. His boots were black leather motorcycle gear, with polished chrome buckles and studs.

As a boy, the mage—Kenneth Anger to mortals of this plane—had appeared as the Prince in the 1935 Max Reinhardt film of *A Midsummer Night's Dream*. In later life, he had become a filmmaker, but for himself not the studios (his "underground" trilogy consisted of *Scorpio Rising, Lucifer Rising* and *Dracula Rising*), and achieved a certain notoriety for compiling *Hollywood Babylon*, a collection of scurrilous but not necessarily true stories about the seamy private lives of the glamour gods and goddesses of the screen. A disciple of Aleister Crowley and Adrian Marcato, he was a genuine movie magician.

He was working on a sequel to *Hollywood Babylon*, which had been forthcoming for some years. It was called *Transylvania Babylon*, and contained all the gossip, scandal, and lurid factoid speculation that had ever circulated about the elder members of the vampire community. Nine months ago, the manuscript and all his research material had been stolen by a couple of acid-heads in the employ of a pair of New Orleans–based vampire elders who were the focus of several fascinating, enlightening, and perversely amusing chapters. Geneviève had recovered the materials, though the book was still not published, as Anger had to negotiate his way through a maze of injunctions and magical threats before he could get the thing in print.

She hesitated on the steps that led down to his slightly

sunken *sanctum*. Incense burned before the framed pictures, swirling up to the low stucco ceiling.

"Do you have to be invited?" he asked. "Enter freely, spirit of dark."

"I was just being polite," she admitted.

The mage was a little disappointed. He arranged himself on a pile of harem cushions and indicated a patch of Turkish carpet where she might sit.

There was a very old bloodstain on the weave.

"Don't mind that," he said. "It's from a thirteen-year-old movie extra deflowered by Charlie Chaplin at the very height of the Roaring Twenties."

She decided not to tell him it wasn't hymenal blood (though it was human).

"I have cast spells of protection, as a precaution. It was respectful of you to warn me this interview might have consequences."

Over the centuries, Geneviève had grown out of thinking of herself as a supernatural creature, and was always a little surprised to run into people who still saw her that way. It wasn't that they might not be right, it was just unusual and unfashionable. The world had monsters, but she still didn't know if there was magic.

"One man who helped me says his career has been ruined because of it," she said, the wound still fresh. "Another, who was just my friend, died."

"My career is beyond ruination," said the mage. "And death means nothing. As you know, it's a passing thing. The lead-up, however, can be highly unpleasant, I understand. I think I'd opt to skip that experience, if at all possible."

She didn't blame him.

"I've seen some of your films and looked at your writings," she said. "It seems to me that you believe motion pictures are rituals."

"Well put. Yes, all real films are invocations, summonings. Most are made by people who don't realise that. But I do. When I call a film *Invocation of My Demon Brother*, I mean it exactly as it sounds. It's not enough to plop a camera in front of a ceremony. Then you only get religious television, God help you. It's in the lighting, the cutting, the music. Reality must be banished, channels opened to the beyond. At screenings, there are always manifestations. Audiences might not realise on a conscious level what is happening, but they always know. Always. The amount of ectoplasm poured into the auditorium by drag queens alone at a West Hollywood revival of a Joan Crawford picture would be enough to embody a minor djinni in the shape of the Bitch Queen, with a turban and razor cheekbones and shoulder pads out to here."

She found the image appealing, but also frightening.

"If you were to make a dozen films about, say, the devil, would the Prince of Darkness appear?"

The mage was amused. "What an improbable notion! But it has some substance. If you made twelve ordinary films about the devil, he might seem more real to people, become more of a figure in the culture, get talked about and put on magazine covers. But let's face it, the same thing happens if you make one ordinary film about a shark. It's the thirteenth film that makes the difference, that might work the trick."

"That would be your film? The one made by a director who understands the ritual?"

"Sadly, no. A great tragedy of magic is that the most effective must be worked without conscious thought, without intent. To become a master mage, you must pass beyond the mathematics and become a dreamer. My film, of the devil you say, would be but a tentative summoning, attracting the notice of a spirit of the beyond. Fully to call His Satanic Majesty to Earth would require a work of surpassing genius, mounted by a director with no other intention but to make a wonderful illusion, a von Sternberg or a Frank Borzage. That thirteenth film, a *Shanghai Gesture* or a *History Is Made at Night,* would be the perfect ritual. And its goaty hero could leave his cloven hoofprint in the cement outside Grauman's Chinese."

In January 1981, Welles began filming *The Other Side of Midnight* on the old Miracle Pictures lot, his first studio-shot—though independently-financed—picture since *Touch of Evil* in 1958, and his first "right of final cut" contract since *Citizen Kane*. The ins and outs of the deal have been assessed in entire books by Peter Bart and David J. Skal, but it seems that Welles, after a career of searching, had found a genuine "angel," a backer with the financial muscle to give him the budget and crew he needed to make a film that was truly his vision but also the self-effacing trust to let him have total artistic control of the result.

There were nay-saying voices and the industry was already beginning to wonder whether still in-progress auteur movies like Michael Cimino's *The Lincoln County Wars* or Coppola's *Dracula* follow-up *One from the Heart* were such a great idea, but Welles himself denounced those runaways as examples of fuzzy thinking. As with his very first *Dracula* movie script and *Kane*, *The Other Side of Midnight* was meticulously preplanned and precosted. Forty years on from *Kane*, Welles must have known this would be his last serious chance. A boy wonder no longer, the pressure was on him to produce a "mature masterpiece," a career bookend to the work that had topped so many Best of All Time lists and eclipsed all his other achievements. He must certainly have been aware of the legion of cineastes whose expectations of a film that would eclipse the flashy brilliance of the Coppola version were sky-rocketing. It may be that so many of Welles's other projects were left unfinished deliberately, because their creator knew they could never compete with the imagined masterpieces that were expected of him. With *Midnight,* he had to show all his cards and take the consequences.

The Other Side of Midnight occupied an unprecedented three adjacent soundstages, where Ken Adam's sets for Bistritz and Borgo Pass and the exteriors and interiors of Castle Dracula were constructed. John Huston shaved his beard and let his moustache sprout, preparing for the acting role of his career, cast apparently because Welles admired his predator-patriarch Noah Cross (*Chinatown*, 1974). It has been rumoured that the seventy-four-year-old Huston went so far as to have transfusions of vampire blood and took to hunting the Hollywood night with packs of newborn vampire brats, piqued because he couldn't display trophies of his "kills." Other casting was announced, a canny mix of A-list stars who would have worked for scale just to be in a Welles film, long-time associates who couldn't bear to be left out of the adventure and fresh talent. Besides Welles (Van Helsing), the film would star Jack Nicholson (Jonathan Harker), Richard Gere (Arthur Holmwood), Shelley Duvall (Mina), Susan Sarandon (Lucy), Cameron Mitchell (Renfield), Dennis Hopper (Quincey), Jason Robards (Dr. Seward), Joseph Cotten (Mr. Hawkins), George Couloris (Mr. Swales) and Jeanne Moreau (Peasant Woman). The three vampire brides were Anjelica Huston, Marie-France Pisier and then-unknown Kathleen Turner. John Williams was writing the score, Gary Graver remained Welles's preferred cinematographer, Rick Baker promised astounding and innovative special make-up effects and George Lucas's ILM contracted for the optical effects.

There were other vampire movies in pre-production, other *Dracula* movies, but Hollywood was really only interested in the Welles version.

Finally, it would happen.

Gates, ibid.

Geneviève parked the Plymouth near Bronson Caverns, in sight of the Hollywood sign, and looked out over Los Angeles, transformed by distance into a carpet of Christmas lights. MGM used to boast "more stars than there were in the heavens," and there they were, twinkling individually, a fallen constellation. Car lights on the freeways were like glowing platelets flowing through neon veins. From up here, you couldn't see the hookers on Hollywood Boulevard, the endless limbo motels and real estate developments, the lost, lonely, and desperate. You couldn't hear the laugh track, or the screams.

It came down to magic. And whether she believed in it.

Clearly, Kenneth Anger did. He had devoted his life to rituals. A great many of them, she had to admit, had worked. And so did John Alucard and Ernest Gorse, vampires who thought themselves magical beings. Dracula had been another of the breed, thanking Satan for eternal nightlife.

She just didn't know.

Maybe she was still undecided because she had never slipped into the blackness of death. Kate Reed, her Victorian friend, had done the proper thing. Kate's father-in-darkness, Harris, had drunk her blood and given of his own, then let her die and come back, turned. Chandagnac, Geneviève's mediaeval father-in-darkness, had worked on her for months. She had transformed slowly, coming alive by night, shaking off the warm girl she had been.

In the last century, since Dracula came out of his castle, there had been a lot of work done on the subject. It was no longer possible to disbelieve in vampires, even in a country like the United States which was still comparatively free of them. With the *nosferatu* in the open, vampirism had to be incorporated into the prevalent belief systems, and this was a scientific age. These days, everyone generally accepted the "explanation" that the condition was a blood-borne mutation, an evolutionary quirk adapting a strain of humankind for survival. But, as geneticists probed ever further, mysteries deepened: vampires retained the DNA pattern they were born with as warm humans, and yet they were *different* creatures. And, despite a lot of cracked theorising, no one had ever convincingly adjusted the laws of optics to account for the business with mirrors.

If there were vampires, there could be magic.

And Alucard's ritual—the mage's thirteen movies—might work. He could come back, worse than ever.

Dracula.

She looked up from the city lights to the stars.

Was the Count out there, on some intangible plane, waiting to be summoned? Reinvigorated by a spell in the beyond, thirsting for blood, vengeance, power? What might he have learned in hell, that he could bring to the Earth?

She hated to think.

She drove through the studio gates shortly before dawn, waved on by the uniformed guard. She was accepted as a part of Orson's army, somehow granted an invisible armband by her association with the genius.

The Miracle Pictures lot was alive again. "If it's a good picture, it's a Miracle!" had run the self-mocking, double-edged slogan, all the more apt as the so-called fifth-wheel major declined from mounting Technicolor spectacles like the 1939 version of *The Duelling Cavalier*, with Errol Flynn and Fedora, to financing drive-in dodos like *Machete Maidens of Mora Tau*, with nobody and her uncle. In recent years, the fifty-year-old soundstages had mostly gone unused as Miracle shot their product in the Philippines or Canada. The standing sets—seen in so many vintage movies—had been torn down to make way for bland office buildings where scripts were "developed" rather than shot. There wasn't even a studio tour.

Now it was different.

Orson Welles was in power, and legions swarmed at his command, occupying every department, beavering away in the service of his vision. They were everywhere: gaffers, extras, carpenters, managers, accountants, makeup men, effects technicians, grips, key grips, boys, best boys, designers, draughtsmen, teamsters, caterers, guards, advisors, actors, writers, planners, plotters, doers, movers, shakers.

Once Welles had said this was the best train set a boy could have. It was very different from three naked girls in an empty swimming pool.

She found herself on Stage 1, the Transylvanian village set. Faces she recognised were on the crew: Jack Nicholson, tearing through his lines with exaggerated expressions; Oja Kodar, handing down decisions from above; Debbie W. Griffith (in another life, she presumed), behind the craft services table; Dennis Hopper, in a cowboy hat and sunglasses.

The stage was crowded with onlookers. Among the movie critics and TV reporters were other directors—she spotted Spielberg, DePalma, and a shifty Coppola—intent on kibbitzing on the master, demonstrating support for the abused genius or suppressing poisonous envy. Burt Reynolds, Gene Hackman, and Jane Fonda were dressed up as villagers, rendered unrecognisable by makeup, so desperate to be in this movie that they were willing to be unbilled extras.

Somewhere up there, in a platform under the roof, sat the big baby. The visionary who would give birth to his Dracula. The unwitting magician who might, this time, conjure more than even he had bargained for.

She scanned the rafters, a hundred feet or more above the studio floor. Riggers crawled like pirates among the lights. Someone abseiled down into the village square.

She was sorry Martin wasn't here. This was his dream.

A dangerous dream.

The Other Side of Midnight

A Script by Orson Welles
Based on *DRACULA,* by Bram Stoker

Revised final, January 6, 1981

1: An ominous chord introduces an extreme CU of a crucifix, held in a knotted fist. It is sunset, we hear sounds of village life. We see only the midsection of the VILLAGE WOMAN holding the crucifix. She pulls tight the rosary-like string from which the cross hangs, like a strangling chord. A scream is heard off camera, coming from some distance. The WOMAN whirls around abruptly to the left, in the direction of the sound. Almost at once the camera pans in this direction, too, and we follow a line of PEASANT CHILDREN, strung out hand in hand and dancing, towards the INN, of the Transylvanian Village of Bistritz. We close on a leaded window and pass through—the set opening up to let in the camera—to find JONATHAN HARKER, a young Englishman with a tigerish smile, in the centre of a tableau Breughel interior, surrounded by peasant activity, children, animals, etc. He is framed by dangling bulbs of garlic, and the VILLAGE WOMAN's crucifix is echoed by one that hangs on the wall. Everyone, including the animals, is frozen, shocked. The scream is still echoing from the low wooden beams.

HARKER: What did I say?

The INNKEEPER crosses himself. The peasants mutter.

HARKER: Was it the place? Was it [relishing each syllable] Castle Dra-cu-la?

More muttering and crossing. HARKER shrugs and continues with his meal. Without a cut, the camera pans around the

cramped interior, to find MINA, HARKER's new wife, in the doorway. She is huge-eyed and tremulous, more impressed by "native superstitions" than her husband, but with an inner steel
core which will become apparent as JONATHAN's outward bluff
crumbles under assaults. Zither and fiddle music conveys the
bustle of this border community.

MINA: Jonathan dear, come on. The coach.

JONATHAN flashes a smile, showing teeth that wouldn't shame a
vampire. MINA doesn't see the beginnings of his viperish second
face, but smiles indulgently, hesitant. JONATHAN pushes away his
plate and stands, displacing children and animals. He joins MINA
and they leave, followed by our snakelike camera, which almost
jostles them as they emerge into the twilight. Some of the crowd
hold aloft flaming torches, which make shadow-featured flickering
masks of the worn peasant faces. JONATHAN, hefting a heavy bag,
and MINA, fluttering at every distraction, walk across the village
square to a waiting COACH. Standing in their path, a crow-black
figure centre-frame, is the VILLAGE WOMAN, eyes wet with fear, crucifix shining. She bars the HARKER' way, like the Ancient Mariner,
and extends the crucifix.

VILLAGE WOMAN: If you must go, wear this. Wear it for your
mother's sake. It will protect you.

JONATHAN bristles, but MINA defuses the situation by taking the
cross.

MINA: Thank you. Thank you very much.

The WOMAN crosses herself, kisses MINA's cheek, and departs.
JONATHAN gives an eyebrows-raised grimace, and MINA shrugs,
placatory.

COACHMAN: All aboard for Borgo Pass, Visaria, and Klausen-
burg.

We get into the coach with the HARKERS, who displace a fat MER-CHANT and his "secretary" ZITA, and the camera gets comfortable opposite them. They exchange looks, and MINA holds JONATHAN's hand. The coach lurches and moves off—it is vital that the camera remain fixed on the HARKERS to cover the progress from one soundstage to the next, with the illusion of travel maintained by the projection of reflected Transylvanian mountain road scenery onto the window. We have time to notice that the MERCHANT and ZITA are wary of the HARKERS; he is middle-aged and balding, and she is a flashy blonde. The coach stops.

COACHMAN (v.o.): Borgo Pass.
JONATHAN: Mina, here's our stop.
MERCHANT: Here?
MINA (proud): A carriage is meeting us here, at midnight. A nobleman's.
MERCHANTS: Whose carriage?
JONATHAN: Count Dracula's.

JONATHAN, who knows the effect it will have, says the name with defiance and mad eyes. The MERCHANT is terror-struck, and ZITA hisses like a cat, shrinking against him. The HARKERS, and the camera, get out of the coach, which hurries off, the COACH-MAN whipping the horses to make a quick getaway. We are alone in a mountain pass, high above the Carpathians. Night sounds: wolves, the wind, bats. The full moon seems for a moment to have eyes, DRACULA's hooded eyes.

JONATHAN (pointing): You can see the castle.
MINA: It looks so . . . desolate, lonely.

JONATHAN: No wonder the Count wants to move to London. He must be raging with cabin fever, probably ready to tear his family apart and chew their bones. Like Sawney Beane.

MINA: The Count has a family?

JONATHAN (delighted): Three wives. Like a Sultan. Imagine how that'll go down in Piccadilly.

Silently, with no hoof or wheel sounds, a carriage appears, the DRIVER a black, faceless shape. The HARKERS climb in, but this time the camera rises to the top of the coach, where the DRIVER has vanished. We hover as the carriage moves off, a LARGE BAT flapping purposefully over the lead horses, and trundles along a narrow, vertiginous mountain road towards the castle. We swoop ahead of the carriage, becoming the eyes of the BAT, and take a flying detour from the road, allowing us a false perspective view of the miniature landscape to either side of the full-side road and carriage, passing beyond the thick rows of pines to a whited scrape in the hillside that the HARKERS do not see, an apparent chalk quarry which we realise consists of a strew of complete human skeletons, in agonized postures, skulls and rib cages broken, the remains of thousands and thousands of murdered men, women, children, and babies. Here and there, skeletons of armoured horses and creatures between wolf or lion and man. This gruesome landscape passes under us, and we close on CASTLE DRACULA, a miniature constructed to allow our nimble camera to close on the highest tower and pass down a stone spiral stairway that affords COVERT access to the next stage . . .

. . . and the resting chamber of DRACULA and his BRIDES. We stalk through a curtain of cobweb, which parts unharmed, and observe as the three shroud-clad BRIDES rise from their boxes, flitting about before us. Two are dark and feral, one is blonde and waiflike. We have become DRACULA and stalk through the corridors of his castle, brass-bound oaken doors opening before us. Footsteps do not echo, and we pass mirrors that reveal nothing—reversed sets under glass, so as not to catch our crew—but a spindle-fingered, almost animate shadow is cast, impossibly long arms reaching out, pointed head with bat-flared ears momentarily sharp against a tapestry. We move faster and faster through the CASTLE, coming out into the great HALLWAY at the very top of a wide staircase. Very small, at the bottom of the steps, stand JONATHAN and MINA, beside their luggage. Sedately, we fix on them and move downwards, our cloaked shadow contracting. As we near the couple, we see their faces: JONATHAN awestruck, almost in love at first sight, ready to become our slave; MINA horrified, afraid for her husband, but almost on the point of pity. The music, which has passed from lusty human strings to ethereal theremin themes, swells, conveying the ancient, corrupt, magical soul of DRACULA. We pause on the steps, six feet above the HARKERS, then leap forwards as MINA holds up the crucifix, whose blinding light fills the frame. The music climaxes, a sacred choral theme battling the eerie theremin.

2: CU on the ancient face, points of red in the eyes, hair, and moustaches shocks of pure white, pulling back to show the whole stick-thin frame wrapped in unrelieved black.

THE COUNT: I . . . am . . . Dracula.

Welles had rewritten the first scenes—the first shot—of the film to make full use of a new gadget called a Louma crane, which gave the camera enormous mobility and suppleness. Combined with breakaway sets and dark passages between stages, the device meant that he could open *The Other Side of Midnight* with a single tracking shot longer and more elaborate than the one he had pulled off in *Touch of Evil.*

Geneviève found Welles and his cinematographer on the road to Borgo Pass, a full-size mock-up dirt track complete with wheel ruts and milestones. The night-black carriage, as yet not equipped with a team of horses, stood on its marks, the crest of Dracula on its polished doors. To either side were forests, the nearest trees half life-size, and those beyond getting smaller and smaller as they stretched out to the studio backdrop of a Carpathian night. Up ahead was Dracula's castle, a nine-foot-tall edifice, currently being sprayed by a technician who looked like a colossal man, griming and fogging the battlements.

The two men were debating a potentially thorny moment in the shot, when the camera would be detached from the coach and picked up by an aerial rig. Hanging from the ceiling was a contraption that looked like a Wright brothers–Georges Méliès collaboration, a man-shaped flying frame with a camera hooked onto it, and a dauntless operator inside.

She hated to think what all this was costing.

Welles saw her, and grinned broadly.

"Gené, Gené," he welcomed. "You must look at this cunning bit of business. Even if I do say so myself, it's an absolute stroke of genius. A simple solution to a complex problem. When *Midnight* comes out, they'll all wonder how I did it."

He chuckled.

"Orson," she said, "we have to talk. I've found some things out. As you asked. About Mr. Alucard."

He took that aboard. He must have a thousand and one mammoth and tiny matters to see to, but one more could be accommodated. That was part of his skill as a director, being a master strategist as well as a visionary artist.

She almost hated to tell him.

"Where can we talk in private?" she asked.

"In the coach," he said, standing aside to let her step up.

The prop coach, as detailed inside as out, creaked a lot as Welles shifted his weight. She wondered if the springs could take it.

She laid out the whole thing.

She still didn't know who John Alucard was, though she supposed him some self-styled last disciple of the King Vampire, but she told Welles what she thought he was up to.

"He doesn't want a conjurer," Welles concluded, "but a sorcerer, a magician."

Geneviève remembered Welles had played Faustus on stage.

"Alucard needs a genius, Orson," she said, trying to be a comfort.

Welles's great brows were knit in a frown that made his nose seem like a baby's button. This was too great a thing to get even his mind around.

He asked the forty-thousand-dollar question: "And do you believe it will work? This conjuring of Dracula?"

She dodged it. "John Alucard does."

"Of that I have no doubt, no doubt at all," rumbled Welles. "The colossal conceit of it, the enormity of the conception, boggles belief. All this, after so long, all this can be mine, a real chance to, as the young people so aptly say, do my thing. And it's part of a Black Mass. A film to raise the devil himself. No mere charlatan could devise such a warped, intricate scheme."

With that, she had to agree.

"If Alucard is wrong, if magic doesn't work, then there's no harm in taking his money and making my movie. That would truly be beating the devil."

"But if he's right . . ."

"Then I, Orson Welles, would not merely be Faustus, nor even Prometheus, I would be Pandora, unloosing all the ills of the world to reign anew. I would be the father-in-darkness of a veritable Bright Lucifer."

"It could be worse. You could be cloning Hitler."

Welles shook his head.

"And it's my decision," he said wearily. Then he laughed, so loud that the interior of the prop carriage shook as with a thunderbolt from Zeus.

She didn't envy the genius his choice. After such great beginnings, no artist of the twentieth century had been thwarted so consistently and so often. Everything he had made, even *Kane*, was compromised as soon as it left his mind and ventured into the marketplace. Dozens of unfinished or unmade films, unstaged theatrical productions, projects stolen away and botched by lesser talents, often with Welles still around as a cameo player to see the potential squandered. And here, at the end of his career, was the chance to claw everything back, to make good on his promise, to be a boy wonder again, to prove at last that he was the king of his world.

And against that, a touch of brimstone. Something she didn't even necessarily believe.

Great tears emerged from Welles's clear eyes and trickled into his beard. Tears of laughter.

There was a tap at the coach door.

"All ready on the set now, Mr. Welles," said an assistant.

"This shot, Gené," said Welles, ruminating, "will be a marvel, one for the books. And it'll come in under budget. A whole reel, a quarter of an hour, will be in the can by the end of the day. Months of planning, construction, drafting, and setting up. Everything I've learned about the movies since 1939. It'll all be there."

Had she the heart to plead with him to stop?

"Mr. Welles," prompted the assistant.

Suddenly firm, decided, Welles said, "We take the shot."

On the first take, the sliding walls of the Bistritz Inn jammed, after only twenty seconds of exposure. The next take went perfectly, snaking through three stages, with more than a hundred performers in addition to the principles and twice that many technicians focusing on fulfilling the vision of one great man. After lunch, at the pleading of Jack Nicholson—who thought he could do better—Welles put the whole show on again. This time, there were wobbles as the flying camera went momentarily out of control, plunging towards the toy forest, before the operator (pilot?) regained balance and completed the stunt with a remarkable save.

Two good takes. The spontaneous chaos might even work for the shot.

Geneviéve had spent the day just watching, in awe.

If it came to a choice between a world without this film and a world with Dracula, she didn't know which way she would vote. Welles, in action, was a much younger man, a charmer and a tyrant, a cheerleader and a patriarch. He was everywhere, flirting in French with Jeanne Moreau, the peasant woman, and hauling ropes with the effects men. Dracula wasn't in the shot, except as a subjective camera and a shadow puppet, but John Huston was on stage for every moment, when he could have been resting in his trailer, just amazed by what Welles was doing, a veteran as impressed as parvenus like Spielberg and DePalma, who were taking notes like trainspotters in locomotive heaven.

Still unsure about the outcome of it all, she left without talking to Welles.

Driving up to Malibu, she came down from the excitement. In a few days, it would be the Julian 1980s. And she should start working to get her license back. Considering everything, she should angle to get paid by Welles, who must have enough of John Alucard's money to settle her bill.

When she pulled into Paradise Cove, it was full dark. She took a moment after parking the car to listen to the surf, an eternal sound, pre- and posthuman.

She got out of the car and walked towards her trailer. As she fished around in her bag for her keys, she sensed something that made quills of her hair.

As if in slow motion, her trailer exploded.

A burst of flame in the sleeping section spurted through the shutters, tearing them off their frames, and then a second, larger fireball expanded from the inside as the gas cylinders in the kitchen caught, rending the chromed walls apart, wrecking the integrity of the vessel.

The light hit her a split-second before the noise.

Then the blast lifted her off her feet and threw her back, across the sandy lot.

Everything she owned rained around her in flames.

After a single day's shooting, Orson Welles abandoned *The Other Side of Midnight*. Between 1981 and his death in 1985, he made no further films and did no more work on such protracted projects as *Don Quixote*. He made no public statement about the reasons for his walking away from the film, which was abandoned after John Huston, Steven Spielberg and Brian DePalma in succession refused to take over the direction.

Most biographers have interpreted this willful scuppering of what seemed to be an ideal, indeed impossibly perfect, setup as a final symptom of the insecure, self-destructive streak that had always co-existed with

genius in the heart of Orson Welles. Those closest to
him, notably Oja Kodar, have argued vehemently
against this interpretation and maintained that there
were pressing reasons for Welles's actions, albeit reasons which have yet to come to light or even be tenta-
tively suggested.

As for the exposed film, two full reels of one extended shot, it has never been developed and, due to a
financing quirk, remains sealed up, inaccessible, in the
vaults of a bank in Timisoara, Romania. More than one
cineaste has expressed a willingness to part happily with
his immortal soul for a single screening of those reels.
Until those reels, like Rosebud itself, can be discovered
and understood, the mystery of Orson Welles's last, lost
Dracula will remain.

Gates, ibid.

"Do you know what's the funny side of the whole kit and ka-
boodle," said Ernest Gorse. "I didn't even think it would work.
Johnny Alucard has big ideas, and he is certainly making something of himself on the coast, but this 'Elvis lives' nonsense is
potty. Then again, you never know with the dear old Count.
He's been dead before."

She was too wrung out to try to get up yet.

Gorse, in a tweed ulster and fisherman's hat, leaned on her
car, scratching the finish with the claws of his left hand. His face
was demonised by the firelight.

Everything she owned.

That's what it had cost her.

"And, who knows, maybe Orson wasn't the genius?" suggested Gorse. "Maybe it was Boris Adrian. Alucard backed all
those Dracula pictures equally. Perhaps you haven't thwarted
him after all. Perhaps He really is coming back."

All the fight was out of her. Gorse must be enjoying this.

"You should leave the city, maybe the state," he said.
"There is nothing here for you, old thing. Be thankful we've left
you the motor. Nice roadboat, by the way, but it's not a Jag, is

it? Consider the long lines, all the chrome, the ostentatious muscle. D'you think the Yanks are trying to prove something? Don't trouble yourself to answer. It was a rhetorical question."

She pushed herself up on her knees.

Gorse had a gun. "Paper wraps stone," he said. "With silver foil."

She got to her feet, not brushing the sand from her clothes. There was ash in her hair. People had come out of the other trailers, fascinated and horrified. Her trailer was a burning shell.

That annoyed her, gave her a spark.

With a swiftness Gorse couldn't match, she took his gun away from him. She broke his wrist and tore off his hat, too. He was surprised in a heart-dead British sort of way, raising his eyebrows as far as they would go. His quizzical, ironic expression begged to be scraped off his face, but it would just grow back crooked.

"Jolly well done," he said, going limp. "Really super little move. Didn't see it coming at all."

She could have thrown him into the fire, but just gave his gun to one of the onlookers, the Dude, with instructions that he was to be turned over to the police when they showed up.

"Watch him, he's a murderer," she said. Gorse looked hurt. "A common murderer," she elaborated.

The Dude understood and held the gun properly. People gathered round the shrinking vampire, holding him fast. He was no threat any more: he was cut, wrapped, and blunted.

There were sirens. In situations like this, there were always sirens.

She kissed the Dude good-bye, got into the Plymouth, and drove north, away from Hollywood, along the winding coast road, without a look back. She wasn't sure whether she was lost or free.

Nancy A. Collins

Some Velvet Morning

NANCY A. COLLINS, *a resident of Atlanta, is the award-winning author of ten novels, including* Lynch: A Gothik Western *and* Angels on Fire, *and more than fifty short stories.* "Some Velvet Morning" *is a new installment in a cycle of stories about Sonja Blue, a punk vampire/vampire slayer first introduced in* Sunglasses After Dark *(1989), and whose adventures continue in* In the Blood *(1992),* Paint It Black *(1995), and* A Dozen Black Roses *(1996), as well as in her own comic-book series. A collected series of Sonja Blue stories has recently been reissued by White Wolf Publishing in a special illustrated tenth-anniversary edition.*

SHE WAS the most attractive woman he'd ever seen outside a movie theatre. She was not just pretty, she was beautiful, and the way models and starlets are beautiful. Her skin was creamy, as translucent as pearl; her long, wavy hair was the color of raw honey. Her fire-engine-red lips matched her low-cut one-piece with spaghetti straps and revealing side slit. She was wearing black-patent-leather open-toed shoes with four-inch heels, which revealed that her toenails, as well as fingernails, were painted the exact same shade as her lips. And she was smiling at him from across the hotel bar.

First he had to double-check to make sure there wasn't another, younger man possibly sitting directly behind him before he dared respond. No. There wasn't anyone else she could possibly be paying attention to. It had to be him.

"Hey, buddy," he said, pushing a ten across the damp bar top. "I'd like to buy that lady a drink."

The bartender nodded and palmed the bill without saying a word. A couple of minutes later a fresh Bloody Mary was placed in front of the woman in red.

She lifted the drink in a half toast and smiled at him. And this time there was no mistaking it: she was smiling one hundred percent at him.

He nervously slicked back his thinning hair and coughed lightly into his fist, surreptitiously sniffing it to make sure his breath was passable. Satisfied, he slid off the barstool and tried to look nonchalant as he strolled to the end of the bar.

"I couldn't help noticing you were alone," he said, trying not to sound nervous. "Would you mind terribly much if I joined you for a drink?"

"Why should I mind?" she said, flashing yet another one of those smiles. "After all, you were the one kind enough to buy it for me."

He moved to sit next to her, then stopped and looked around the bar. He was a thousand miles away from home, his wife, and their friends and associates, but old habits were hard to break.

"Would you mind if we sat somewhere a little more . . . private?" he said, gesturing to a booth in one of the shadowy corners.

"Whatever you like—?" She paused, waiting for him to supply his name.

"John," he said, his cheeks coloring slightly. "My name is John."

"Of course it is," she replied, no hint of irony in her honeyed voice. "My name is Phaedra."

"That's an unusual name," he said as he slid into the booth beside her.

"It's from the classics. Phaedra was a queen who was possessed by unnatural desires."

"How fascinating," he said, feigning interest. He suspected Phaedra was as much her name as John was his. It sounded too deliberate to be real.

Once they were safely in the booth, he went into the same

little song and dance he always did on business trips: he inflated his importance at the firm, while avoiding telling her the exact company he worked for and what it was he really did for a living; and when she asked him where he was from, he gave her the correct state but lied about the city. And some time during the small talk he let his hand fall on Phaedra's leg just above the knee. To his relief, she did not shift about uncomfortably or demand that he remove his hand. Her dress was silky smooth under his palm, and beneath its flimsiness he could feel warm flesh and taut muscle. It had been years since his wife's thigh had felt like anything besides a bag of suet.

He had to fight to keep from choking on his drink when she shifted her leg so that his hand slid further up her thigh, towards the heat between her legs. His suspicions were confirmed: she wasn't wearing panties. He began to sweat, his scalp itching under his thinning hair. His crotch throbbed like a high-school freshman with a case of blue balls.

"I, uh, have a room here at the hotel . . ." he stammered clumsily.

She shook her head and wrinkled her nose in disgust. "I *detest* hotel rooms. They're so impersonal. Why don't we go to my place, instead?"

"Sure. Whatever you want, baby."

As he heard himself saying those words, he wondered what the hell he thought he was doing. He had to catch a flight first thing in the morning, not to mention turn the rental car back in at the airport. He didn't have the time to waste going to some hottie's apartment out in the 'burbs. But when he looked into Phaedra's eyes, he knew he would do whatever it took to get her into bed, even if it meant flying standby.

As he signed for the drinks, she slid out of the booth and motioned for him to follow.

"Let's go in my car," she said, holding up a key ring attached to a pair of red plastic dice.

He knew he should protest. The last thing he needed was to get stranded out in the middle of nowhere, unable to get back to the hotel in time to pick up his bags and make his flight home. There was something about the arrangement that set off an alarm in the back of his head, but it was quickly muffled by the lust rising from belowdecks.

Phaedra led him out the side door of the hotel bar to the parking lot outside. She walked ahead of him with quick, purposeful strides, which made her jiggle in all the right places.

"Here's my car," she said, gesturing to a little convertible, painted the same color red as her lips and nails. "Hop in, John."

He opened the passenger door halfway, then paused, indecision flickering across his brow.

"I don't know . . . maybe I should follow you. . . ."

"You can do that, if you like," she said with a shrug. "I live out on the lake; it's not that far, but it's easy to get lost if you don't know where you're going."

He suddenly had a vivid mental picture of himself driving around unfamiliar suburbs in the dark, a raging hard-on in his pants, and with no clear idea of how to get back to the hotel.

"Okay," he said with a resigned sigh. "I'll ride with you."

He wasn't sure if Phaedra was driving particularly fast, or if merely riding in an open convertible in the dead of night made it seem that way. The wind tore at him, turning his tie into a wind sock and exposing his comb-over for the lie it was.

As they sped through the night, she rubbed his thigh gently, moving her hand closer and closer to his groin. He licked his lips and coughed nervously into his fist. The lights of the strip malls and main boulevard had long since disappeared, plunging them into an inky darkness that was relieved only by the glow from the dashboard and the beams of the headlights on the road ahead.

"Where is it you said you live?" he shouted over the roar of the wind and the engine.

"Red Velvet manor!" she shouted back.

"Is that some kind of subdivision?"

"Lord, no!" She laughed. "That's what it was called a hundred years ago! It's something of an unofficial landmark around here. It used to be a brothel for the superrich. All the rooms had red velvet wallpaper—that's where it got its name. Now it's a private residence. I live there."

"All by yourself?"

"No."

Before he could ask another question, the car rounded a turn in the road, and he saw their final destination. It was an impressive late Victorian pile, with turrets and huge picture windows that glowed like the eyes of a jack-o'-lantern, situated on a clifflike outcropping that overlooked the lake. Judging from the utter darkness surrounding the estate, the nearest neighbors had to be over a mile away in every direction.

Phaedra steered the car up the lengthy drive that led to the old-fashioned covered carriage port at the side of the house, the gravel crunching loudly under the wheels.

"Wow, this place really is something," he said, leaning back in his seat to ogle the building. "How much does a house like this go for, nowadays?"

Phaedra shrugged indifferently. It was clear that the subject did not interest her in the slightest. "A million, maybe two, if you count the lakefront that's attached to it. The Contessa says it's been in the family for generations, and that's probably where it's going to stay."

She switched the car off and turned to face him. She moved quickly, leaning in to plant a deep, passionate kiss on his mouth. His thoughts of money and real estate disappeared entirely, turned to steam by the heat growing within his belly. He took her in his arms, holding her body tight against his own. In twelve years of marriage, he had never experienced anything as sensuous as Phaedra's lips moving against his own.

Phaedra broke away from the kiss, studying him with hooded eyes, a sly smile on her lips. "You're shivering," she said. "How sweet."

"I don't know what to say. This is all so new to me," he lied.

"I think we better go inside before you cum outside," she said with a wink.

"Uh, yeah," he grunted.

The interior of the house was as impressive as its exterior.

The first thing he saw was a grand foyer with an elaborate parquet floor and a grand staircase that split on the second floor into two separate wings. An antique chandelier swayed in the air above their heads like a giant gold and crystal wind chime. The walls of the reception hall were paneled in the finest cherry wood, burnished to a healthy glow. Marble hamadryads sported with marble fauns while a massive grandfather's clock with a zodiac face counted out the time nearby. Twin mirrors in gilt rococo frames, each the size of a door, made the foyer seem even larger than it already was.

"Man, this must have really been something, back in the day," John marveled aloud, his voice echoing in the hall.

"You have no idea how grand it was, young man. No idea at all."

There was a buzzing sound, and an electric wheelchair emerged from the parlor off the foyer. The rider was an old woman dressed in a velvet housecoat the color of oxblood, a woolen throw draped across her lap for extra warmth. Her face was as wrinkled as that of an apple-doll, her swan white hair bound in a long braid and coiled about her fragile shoulders like an albino python. The old woman's hands were as gnarled and twisted as the claws of a vulture, the nails long and yellowish.

None of this was unusual, given her obvious great age. However, what he was unprepared for was the sight of metal legs that resembled a cross between stilts and pogo sticks emerging from underneath the fringe of the blanket covering the old lady's lap. Upon noticing his stare, the Contessa hastily rearranged the throw, screening the prostheses from view.

"Contessa! What are you doing up at this hour?" Phaedra said mock-reproachfully, bending to kiss her benefactor's withered cheek.

"It's these bones of mine. The older they get, the harder it is to sleep the night through. I did not mean to startle your gentleman friend, my dear."

"Allow me to introduce you: Contessa, this is . . . John."

The Contessa offered her gnarled hand to him. There was a

ring with a diamond the size of a man's thumb glinting on one arthritic finger.

"*Enchanted,* my dear," she said, smiling crookedly.

"My pleasure, ma'am."

"I have no doubt it will be," the old woman said, a sly grin on her face.

"Uh, right." He smiled awkwardly and pulled away, unsure of how to react.

"Can I get you anything, Contessa?" Phaedra asked, apparently unfazed by the old woman's behavior towards her guest.

"No, my dear. Do not mind me," she said, toggling the joystick so that the chair went back the way it came. "You two have fun," she said over her shoulder. "That is what youth is for, after all!" Something about what she had just said must have struck the old woman as funny, because she began to laugh. It was a wild sound, like the call of a screech owl.

Phaedra took his hand and led him towards the stairs. He paused to look back towards the parlor, where the Contessa sat chuckling to herself.

"She doesn't mind you bringing men home?"

"Mind? Why should she mind?" Phaedra snorted. "Remember what I told you about Red Velvet Manor? She used to run the joint."

A leer spread across his face. "You mean she was a—?"

"Yes. But not since they closed the place back in '44. She married an expatriate Romanian nobleman who didn't have anything but a title. But that's okay, because that's all she wanted from him."

"What happened to her, uh, you know . . . ?"

"Her legs were amputated a few years ago, due to complications from diabetes. That's when I began working for her."

"You're her nurse?"

"She prefers the title 'companion.' So do I. I've accompanied her on numerous trips around the world. It's only recently that her condition forced her to return here."

"Real jet-setter, eh?"

"She knew them all: Rita and Ali, Liz and Dick, Rainier and

Grace, Coward, Capote, Warhol . . ." She turned suddenly to fix him with her gaze. "But that's enough about the Contessa. We've got *better* things to do. Don't you agree?"

He tried to answer, but something in the way she looked at him made it hard for him to formulate a coherent sentence, so he contented himself with nodding his head. As she resumed her climb, he lagged behind a few steps, watching her perfectly formed ass. This was all too good to be true. She had to be a pro. He'd been around enough to know the difference between a call girl and a bored housewife on the prowl. Her mentioning the old lady's former profession had to be a tip-off. No doubt once the credit card clicker finally made its appearance, she'd be charging for her services, but something told him it would be well worth the expense. He'd had his share of paid women before, but none of them had this amount of style or heat.

She paused in front of an elaborately carved wooden door at the end of the second-floor hallway. "This is my room," she said with a smile. "Come on in." She opened the door and stepped inside, motioning for him to follow.

He followed, moving cautiously into the darkened room.

"Hey . . . where did you go?" he said with a nervous laugh. All of a sudden he was aware of the fact that nobody knew he was miles from the city, in an isolated house occupied by strangers whose last names he didn't know.

"Wait a second—I'll get the lights." Phaedra's voice came out of the darkness, behind and to one side of where he stood.

The lights came on with a sudden flash of brilliance, enough to make him wince. The first thing he noticed was that the walls were the color of spilled blood. The second thing he noticed was the huge mirror mounted on the ceiling, which reflected plush carpeting a shade lighter than the walls. The overhead light fixtures and wall sconces were shaped like gilded cherubs armed with cornucopias. In the middle of the room was a king-size circular bed outfitted with red satin sheets. Heavy crimson velvet curtains covered the windows.

"We can do whatever we like without disturbing anyone,"

Phaedra said. She was still behind him, near the light switch. "All the bedrooms are soundproofed."

He turned to face her, but whatever he was planning to say never found its way past his lips. Phaedra was leaning against the bloodred wall, stark nude except for her shoes. Her dress lay in a pool at her feet, as if it had melted off her body.

"You like?" She smiled.

Unable to find his voice, he nodded vigorously.

She gave a little chuckle and did something with the light switch, and the room abruptly dimmed. "That's better," she said, stepping towards him.

He began to remove his own clothes, but his fingers kept fumbling because he couldn't take his eyes off her. Her skin was as white and flawless as an alabaster statue, her hips shapely and inviting, without a hint of cellulite. Her belly was flat, and her pubic hair carefully trimmed. She smelled of sex and expensive perfume and did not want to discuss children, in-laws, bank balances, mortgage payments, or any of the things that defined the confines of his life. She was young and desirable and available. And the knowledge that he was none of these things made his penis so painfully rigid it vibrated like a tuning fork.

He was breathing fast and his mouth was open as Phaedra approached him. She stood facing him, close enough that he could feel the heat from her body. She looked into his eyes, then down at his penis, jutting forward from underneath the swell of his middle-management paunch.

As Phaedra's hand wrapped around his erection, his wife's face shimmered across the back of his eyes like a summer haze, then was gone. Phaedra began to rub his cock up and down with sure, practiced strokes. He gave a choked little cry and placed his hand atop her own, staying the movements.

"That feels too good," he whispered hoarsely.

"But I *want* you to feel good," she purred. "I want you to feel better than you *ever* have . . . or ever will again." She pressed herself tightly against his body, rubbing her breasts against the naked expanse of his chest. "That's why you're here, isn't it? To make yourself feel good?"

With a sly smile, she gracefully dropped to her knees before him. He gave a groan of approval and tilted his head back, staring up at his reflection in the mirrored ceiling.

As his cock slid into her ready mouth, his vision grew blurry around the edges and a groan of intense pleasure escaped him. Phaedra's lips glided over the shaft, her tongue exploring every inch of him. He'd never felt anything so incredible in his life, not with his wife or any of the coworkers or call girls he had used over the years. At first her movements were slow, but quickly picked up speed and intensity. He could feel her fingernails dig into his ass cheeks, urging him onward.

That was all the encouragement he needed to surrender to the urge that had been gnawing at his loins all night long. He dug his fingers tight into the hair at the back of Phaedra's head and began fiercely pumping in and out of her mouth. Even if she had wanted to stop, there was no way he was going to let her. He wanted—no, *needed*—to cum in her mouth more than anything in his life. He needed it more than a promotion, more than food and shelter. Somehow, everything that was wrong and dull and empty in his life would be set right, if only he could reach orgasm with this woman. And at that moment he was willing to sacrifice everything he had ever held dear—his wife, his children, his career—if it meant he could empty himself between her bloodred lips.

A sweat broke out all over his body as his balls jerked up to the sides of his cock, flooding her mouth with their warm, bitter cream. His head dropped back, his mouth open, as his hips continued to thrust blindly forward. A deep groan escaped him, and then his hands let go of her head as he stepped back on numbed legs, his wilted penis sliding free of her lips. He was light-headed and rubber-kneed, as weak and vulnerable as a freshly foaled colt.

Phaedra was still kneeling before him, wiping spittle and semen from her lower lip with the back of her hand. There was a distance in her eyes he had not seen before, or at least had not allowed himself to notice. Although less than five seconds before they had been as intimate as two humans could possibly be, it was as if she were miles away.

"I-I need to pee," he stammered.

Phaedra pointed silently in the direction of the bathroom door. He staggered away from her, glad to be free of her thousand-yard stare. She was probably thinking he was a jerk for coming so soon. He meant to apologize, say something about her being so sexy he couldn't hold back, but he couldn't work up the energy to bother with it. Besides, she didn't seem so much disappointed as kind of dazed. Maybe those Bloody Marys were finally catching up with her, after all.

The bathroom, in keeping with the rest of the house, was much larger and far grander than anything he'd ever seen in a private residence. The walls were mirrored, casting myriad images of his nakedness into infinity. The floor was ceramic tile, embossed with starfish and crustaceans painted in Mediterranean blue. The oceanic theme was continued by a wash basin fashioned from a gigantic conch shell and solid gold fixtures shaped like medieval dolphins. As impressive as those features were, the pièce de résistance was the huge, oval-shaped marble tub that sat atop its own dais in the middle of the room. The bathroom looked like something you might expect to see in an old-fashioned movie star's home . . . or a high-class knocking shop.

He climbed up the steps that led to the tub and gazed down at it. It was easily the width of a child's swimming pool, and twice as deep. The sides were worn smooth from use and sloped steeply towards the drain, which looked somewhat rusty, set squarely in the bottom of the tub. Still, he couldn't help but feel that there was something not quite right. Then he realized there was no faucet anywhere in sight. Perplexed, he looked upward, thinking there might be a showerhead in the ceiling.

There was something affixed to the ceiling, but it wasn't plumbing. As he stood gaping up at the ceiling, he was dimly aware of Phaedra having joined him in the bathroom.

"What the fuck is that doing up there?" he asked, pointing at the old-fashioned block and tackle suspended over the tub.

Phaedra's answer came in the form of a baseball bat connecting with the side of his head.

The first thing he felt upon regaining consciousness was the congestive pressure of his own blood in his ears. The second thing he felt was pain from his broken jaw. He tried to open his eyes, but his right one was swollen shut. Still, he didn't need both eyes to know that he was hanging upside down by his heels over the marble tub.

"That didn't take long."

He recognized the voice as the Contessa's. He caught a glimpse of her in one of the mirrors, her wheelchair parked in the open door of the bathroom.

"Thank God for small favors. And I *do* mean small," Phaedra sneered. She was seated on the toilet, smoking a cigarette. "I prefer it when they cum in my mouth. I hate it when they stick it in me." She shivered with revulsion at the very thought.

"Yes, my dear. I understand all too well," the Contessa said sympathetically. "The penis is such a *transgressive* organ."

He tried to open his mouth to demand that they let him go, but the pain from his shattered jaw turned his shout into an agonized moan. The two women glanced up at him as if he were nothing more than a chiming clock.

"He's awake," Phaedra said, flicking the cigarette into the conch-shaped wash basin.

"Good," the Contessa said, tossing aside her lap blanket and levering herself out of the wheelchair. "Let's get this over with."

Compared to the rest of her body, the tubular metal and carbon filaments of her prosthetic limbs were frighteningly sturdy. She wavered like a young tree in a stiff wind, then took a step forward, the hydraulic knees and tendons hissing and popping like steam-driven pogo sticks.

Phaedra moved to meet the Contessa, helping the older woman to remove her garment. Her body was so wrinkled it was almost impossible to tell what sex she was, her dried-up dugs hanging flat against her chest like deflated wine-skins. With trembling, gnarled fingers, the Contessa loosened her hair, allowing it to spill down upon her shoulders like a fall of snow.

The old woman nodded to the younger one, and Phaedra began methodically to unfasten the elaborate suspension gear—half corset, half truss—that held the Contessa's artificial legs in place. When the last strap was finished with, the Contessa linked her arms around Phaedra's neck as her companion lifted her free of the legs. The prostheses, empty of their operator, dropped to the tiled floor with a loud clatter.

Phaedra carried her mistress easily up the steps of the dais and carefully balanced her on its worn lip. Using her arms to propel her, the Contessa scuttled down the side of the tub like a pallid crab.

The man who said his name was John was finally beginning to figure out that whatever plans Phaedra and the Contessa had for him, they were not sexual. At least not as he understood the term. His initial indignation and anger turned to fear, then panic. He tried to call out Phaedra's name, but the best he could manage was a cry of animal-like pain. Phaedra was standing at the edge of the tub. Even though he was disoriented from the blow and able to see out of only one eye, he was still able to glimpse the knife she held in her hand. His mind was racing so fast it was standing still, unable to gain the traction necessary to escape as Phaedra grabbed his hair and yanked back-wards, exposing his Adam's apple. He didn't have enough spirituality to find comfort in faith; but he *had* watched enough TV to delude himself into thinking that someone—Kojak, maybe, or Rockford—would kick open the door, right in the nick of time.

He was still waiting on the cops when Phaedra slit his throat from ear to ear.

The last thing he saw before escaping, mercifully, into

unconsciousness, then death, was the sight of his life's blood jetting forth shot from his severed jugular vein and carotid arteries, like wine from a newly tapped keg. His body involuntarily jerked with the release, much as it had during his orgasm.

The rich red splashed against the smooth marble surface with a thick, wet sound, like rain gushing from a choked gutter. The Contessa thrust herself under the grisly downpour, eagerly massaging it into her thirsty flesh with obscene abandon. The stolen blood did not smear or clot upon her skin, but was absorbed, like rain falling on a sun-baked riverbed. The Contessa's withered flesh grew firm and taut, smoothing out the creases and wrinkles that crosshatched her face from within. Like ink dropped into a glass of milk, darkness reclaimed her hair. Her eyes shed their clouds to burn as brightly as twin goblets of fine claret held before a fire. She smiled up at her companion, who knelt on the lip of the tub, watching her with the keen attention of a surgeon overseeing an operation.

"You shouldn't frown so, my dear," the Contessa said, clucking her tongue. "It leaves wrinkles. Don't just stand there—help me out."

Phaedra leaned forward and gathered her mistress into her arms, lifting her free of the gore-streaked tub. The Contessa's head lolled against her shoulder like that of a newborn child. Rejuvenation always left her torpid. The languor would pass after a few minutes, but until then she needed to be guarded and protected.

Phaedra carried the Contessa out of the bathroom and placed her on the circular bed, carefully arranging the red velvet bolster and satin pillows against the headboard.

"The night," the Contessa said with a breathy sigh. "I want to see the night."

Phaedra nodded and picked up a remote-control device from atop the bedside table and pointed it at the heavy velvet drapes. She pressed a button and the curtains parted, revealing a picture window that filled the wall. Phaedra assumed that during the day the view was spectacular, but now it was dark as only night on the water can be. The sky was clear, undimmed by the glare from city lights and suburban development, and the millions of stars that filled the night sky were twinned in the inky surface of the lake. The Contessa loved to stare out at the lake for hours on end, although nothing moved except the twinkling of the stars and the gentle motion of the lake's surface. At least nothing Phaedra's mortal eyes could see.

"So beautiful," the Contessa said, slurring the words slightly. She patted the coverlet beside her with her hand. "Come. Sit by me, child."

Phaedra sat beside her, her naked body pressed close to the Contessa's own. The older woman looked at her for a long moment, then motioned to Phaedra's hair.

"Take that dreadful thing off."

Phaedra nodded and tossed the blonde wig to the foot of the bed.

The Contessa stroked Phaedra's close-cropped, mousy hair as she would the fur of a cat. "That's better," she said. "You must be tired after all that. Come, child, rest your head."

With a grateful sigh, Phaedra pillowed her cheek against the smooth curve of her mistress's right stump. The Contessa's hands, no longer twisted by arthritis, continued to play with her hair.

"Contessa—?" Phaedra's voice was high and sweet, like that of a little girl.

"Yes, my precious?"

"Tell me a story."

"Very well, my dear. Which story would you like to hear? How about the one about the Secret Princess?"

"No. The other one."

The Contessa smiled and nodded her understanding. "Ah, yes. *That* one. Very well. As you wish, my pet. Now, how does that one begin . . . ?"

"'Once upon a time, long, long ago, there was a beautiful young girl named Elizabeth' . . ." Phaedra prompted.

"Of course!" The Contessa chuckled. "Now I remember!

Once upon a time, long, long ago, there was a beautiful young girl named Elizabeth, who lived in a land far, far away. This far-away land was very beautiful, and because it was so beautiful, everyone wanted to own it. So there was constant war for control of the land. Life was very hard for the peasants and commoners who lived in the battle-torn land, as there was little money and rarely enough food.

"But since Elizabeth's family was very rich and very powerful, none of this concerned her. As she grew to womanhood, she quickly learned that because one cousin was the Prime Minister, another the ruler of an allied kingdom, and her great-uncle a cardinal in the Church, there was nothing she could do that would not be overlooked or forgiven.

"When Elizabeth was but fifteen, her family married her to the Black Count, eleven years her senior. He was not as politically important, but he had a great deal of money and possessed considerable property, and the marriage was deemed a good one in the eyes of her family. So Elizabeth was sent away against her wishes to live in her new husband's castle in the farthest reaches of the land.

"Things did not go well from the very start. Although the Black Count was not unhandsome, he was always going off to some battle or another, leaving his young bride alone with only his mother and castle retainers for company. The wicked mother-in-law was a horrible woman with a shrewish tongue and a narrow mind. All she did day in and day out was pray to God and berate poor Elizabeth for not being perfect. There was nothing Elizabeth could do that the wicked mother-in-law approved of. If Elizabeth had the servants put more logs on the fire, the wicked mother-in-law accused her of being a spendthrift; if Elizabeth did not order the servants to light a fire, the wicked mother-in-law accused her of stinginess. But what the wicked mother-in-law complained the most about was how Elizabeth had failed to provide an heir. She was most eager to have the marriage annulled, so that the Black Count might take a more 'suitable' wife, one who could give him children—and plenty of them. It did not matter that her son was rarely home long enough to change his clothes, much less impregnate his wife. The fault, it was clear, lay with Elizabeth.

"As much as she resented being married, Elizabeth knew that to be sent back to her family as a failed wife would be her undoing. Determined to secure her place as lady of the castle, she began to scheme how to bear a child. When folk remedies and old wives' tales proved useless, she took as lovers men similar in build and appearance to the Black Count, but nothing came of those liaisons.

"Despairing, she begged her old nurse to help her. The loyal servant introduced her mistress to a witch, who claimed she could use her dark arts to place a child within Elizabeth's womb. So, during the dark of the moon, the witch smuggled Elizabeth out of the castle and into the surrounding forest, to a magic grove used by her kind since the days of Rome. The witch had Elizabeth strip naked and anoint her body with an unguent made from the fat of unbaptized babies. Then she poured the blood of a black goat upon the ground and called upon her master—

" 'With this blood I summon thee, He Who Makes Shadows. With my will I bring thee forth, He Who Makes War. With these words I beseech thee, He Who Makes Dreams. Come forth from your world into this!' "

"A cold wind blew down from the mountaintops, and the shadows in the darkness shaped themselves into the semblance of a tall, dark man with the legs of a goat, eyes of flame, and six fingers on each hand.

" 'Who calls me forth upon this plane?' asked the dark man, his voice echoing like thunder through the mountains. 'Who would summon He Who Makes?' "

"The very sound of the demon lord's voice was enough to make Elizabeth's breath freeze in her mouth. But although she was frightened, she was even more fearful of being sent back to her people in disgrace.

" 'I would make a child, lord.' "

"He Who Makes looked at Elizabeth's naked belly as if it

was glass and shook his head. 'Daughter of Eve, no seed sown by a human husband can ever take root in such rocky soil as yours.'

" 'Then I have no choice but to take an inhuman husband, lord,' she replied.

"The flames within the demon lord's eyes leapt like burning bonfires as Elizabeth knelt before him. With a fearsome roar, he took her under the moonless sky like a beast of the field, hard as horn and cold as ice. Elizabeth cried out as her demon lover loosed his seed, which burned like that of oil of peppermint poured upon an open wound. Once he was finished with her, the dark man returned to the shadows, leaving Elizabeth collapsed on the ground, clutching her belly as if she had been stabbed in the vitals. The witch quickly dressed her mistress and hurried her back to the castle before any of the courtiers noticed she was gone. For several days Elizabeth lay abed, wracked by fever; when she awoke from her delirium, she could feel the seed He Who Makes had planted within her womb.

"That night she crept into her husband's bedchamber and made herself available to him, but as the Black Count placed his member inside her, he cried out in alarm, for she was cold as ice. He Who Makes had placed his mark upon her. In her own way, Elizabeth realized she was bound to her demon lover in unholy chastity as surely as the Brides of Christ are wed to their resurrected lord.

"If the Black Count suspected the child she claimed he had placed within her belonged to any but himself, he showed no sign. The impending arrival of an heir appeased, somewhat, the wicked mother-in-law, and her scoldings grew less frequent.

"Elizabeth's belly grew, and she took to lying in, attended by her loyal nurse, the witch, and her majordomo. Then, seven months into her maternity, she fell into heavy labor, her body struggling to bring forth the thing within her. What emerged from Elizabeth's womb resembled something dragged from the bowels of the sea, for it was without bones or limbs, its skin the color and consistency of fresh pitch broken only by patches of hair, a lipless mouth ringed with tiny, razorlike teeth, and a single red eye. The witch screeched and wailed and called it a name unspoken in a thousand years. Then as the nurse and the majordomo whispered whether or not to slay the wretched thing as it lay shivering on the counterpane, it gave a solitary cry and surrendered its breath.

"Elizabeth gnashed her teeth and cursed herself for not having been more specific when she bargained with the demon. She had asked for a child, but had not said she wanted a human one or that it should be born alive and healthy. She was ruined for childbirth, her womb rendered as icy as a tombstone in the dead of winter.

"The thing that she delivered forth was not given a name, nor was it buried in holy ground. The witch placed it in a bag and left with it hidden under her cloak, no doubt with intentions of rendering it for its unbaptized fat. To allay suspicions, Elizabeth's loyal nurse bought the corpse of a newborn from a midwife, who specialized in the disposal of unwanted children, and presented it to the Black Count as his stillborn son and heir. The Black Count, more interested in warfare than posterity, seemed slightly grieved by the loss, while the wicked mother-in-law was visibly relieved she no longer had to be civil to Elizabeth. With the entombment of the infant imposter in the family vault, the subject of annulment was no longer whispered in the castle.

"As the wicked mother-in-law grew older and more and more feeble, Elizabeth's power within the castle strengthened. The years became decades, and the wicked mother-in-law's sharp tongue became blunted for fear of Elizabeth and her allies within the court. She kept more and more to her chambers, until she was little more than a memory. Then, one day, a courtier came bearing news of the Black Count's death on the field of battle.

"Upon her husband's passing, Elizabeth assumed the title and power of Countess and lost no time in banishing the wicked mother-in-law to a small hunting lodge atop a distant mountain; there the elderly woman was forced to chop her own firewood, draw her own water, and subsist on nothing but black bread and stone soup. She quickly joined her son in the grave. For the first time in her life, Elizabeth was free from her husband and the control his family had exerted over her.

"None could compare to her when it came to her riches, station, and comeliness. But of these three attributes, it was her beauty that Elizabeth treasured most. It pleased her that men would be moved by the sight of her to unthinking lust. For, as she had long ago learned, men possessed by lust have their uses in the political arena.

"Since she no longer enjoyed the embrace of men, she developed a taste for the pleasure of others, and orchestrated orgies for her amusement. As the years passed, they became more and more extreme in nature, involving erotic circuses complete with acrobats, trained animal acts, and freak shows. Black Sabbaths were held within the castle's chapel, where highborn guests ritually desecrated the altar and baptismal font in honor of He Who Makes. There were whispers of the goings-on amongst the villagers, but the rumors rarely made it to the royal court. And even if they did, the Countess was a blood cousin of the vice chamberlain. Who would dare to lift a hand against her?

"And so it went for several years. But as roses fade and silver tarnishes, as the sun will one day lose its fire, Elizabeth's great beauty finally began to dim. Her breasts were no longer firm like apples, but more like ripened plums. Her buttocks and belly were starting to sag; silver threads were woven throughout her dark hair, and her hands resembled more the claws of a crow than the wings of doves. For a woman such as Elizabeth, the effects of aging were no more to be suffered than the stare of an insolent peasant. She instructed the witch to find a rejuvenation spell or she would put her to death.

"The witch pored through her collection of spells and incantations until she came upon a ritual described within the pages of an ancient tome known as *The Aegrisomnia*. It promised the restoration of youth and vigor and, eventually, the gift of immortality, but only by bathing in the freshly shed blood of young virgins.

"Elizabeth decided that if Cleopatra became one of the great beauties of the civilized world with the help of asses' milk, then she would have her bath of blood. The majordomo, in collaboration with the witch, butchered one of the servant girls and bled her into a large cauldron, in which Elizabeth steeped herself. From that day on, the ravages of age held no sway over her.

"For ten years, Elizabeth's loyal inner circle scoured the countryside in search of suitable young girls, free of sin and untainted by illness, which, in those days, was not as easy as it sounds. Numerous peasant girls, born into ignorance and poverty, were offered positions as chambermaids and scullery servants in the comparative grandeur of the castle. But the moment the new 'serving girls' arrived, they were drugged, bound, and butchered like sheep.

"Over the next ten years, more than forty young girls were fed to Elizabeth's beauty, and it would have continued for another decade, possibly a third, if a fatal case of mistaken identity had not been made. When the young daughter of the archduke arrived at the castle for an unannounced visit after a particularly long and arduous journey, she was mistaken for the most recent recruit and summarily drugged and bled out before anyone realized who she was.

"The archduke became concerned when his favorite daughter did not return. He wrote several letters to Elizabeth, asking what had become of his child. At first Elizabeth assured the archduke that the girl was fine and had merely decided to extend her stay. But when he still did not hear from his daughter, the archduke became more insistent. Elizabeth then claimed that the young girl had contracted a fever and could not be moved. This news upset the archduke greatly, and he promptly sent a messenger to the castle to inform Elizabeth that he would be leaving his palace to personally attend his ailing daughter.

"Halfway to the castle, the archduke was met by one of Elizabeth's retainers, who said his daughter had died of the plague and the castle was under quarantine. The Countess had been forced to burn the body of the archduke's daughter, for fear of contamination.

"This last piece of news was more than the archduke could bear. He had heard rumors of the goings-on at the castle but had not given them much credence. He knew his child was dead, but he suspected her end had come by mortal hands. He petitioned the king for an investigation. Elizabeth's cousin, the vice chamberlain, tried to block the request, but since the king was the cousin of the archduke, he was unable to stop it.

"A division of the king's army, led by the archduke and accompanied by church inquisitors, stormed the castle. They found the archduke's dear, departed daughter moldering in the dungeon, her highborn corpse alongside the daughters of swineherds and hod carriers.

"The lowborn accomplices who had served Elizabeth so loyally were put to the question, and quickly turned evidence against their mistress. For collaborating with the State, the witnesses privy to the secret behind Elizabeth's unique beauty treatments were rewarded by having their fingernails pulled out with pliers, their kneecaps broken, and then were hanged and dismembered in the public square. The witch, for the additional crime of blasphemy, was broken on the wheel and then burned at the stake.

"Because of her high station, Elizabeth was not put to death. Indeed, she was not even placed on trial. Instead, it was decreed that she would spend the rest of her natural life under house arrest, and to make sure that her sentence would be as short as possible, her jailer was the archduke.

"The day after sentence was passed, the archduke arrived at her castle and ordered all the fixtures removed. The beds, chairs, tables, tapestries, even the chamber pots, were taken from the castle and distributed amongst the families of those who had lost their daughters to the bloodbath. Once the interior of the castle was bleak and bare, the archduke ordered what few servants remained to leave. By the end of the second day, all that was left inside was a pallet of dirty straw, a crooked footstool, a rough-hewn table . . . and Elizabeth.

"The archduke then summoned his master mason and ordered him to brick up every door and window . . . save for one. The sole egress was a small window in Elizabeth's bedchamber, accessible only via a long ladder. Through this narrow portal Elizabeth's jailers pushed her daily meal of black bread and stone soup.

"Elizabeth's isolation from the world was total, as she was forbidden pen and paper to pass her days, candles or fire to illuminate the darkness or warm herself, and her keepers were forbidden to speak even one word to her, under pain of death.

"She spent four years sealed away from the light of day. Four years spent shitting in the ballroom fireplace. Four years spent prowling the dark for rats and mice to supplement her diet. Four years spent licking condensation off the walls to quench her thirst. Four years freezing in winter and sweltering in summer. Her only clothes were those upon her back the day the master mason sealed her away. Her only blanket was a tattered piece of tapestry overlooked by the archduke's men. Finally, after years of such treatment, she collapsed in her bedchamber, too weak to rise. As she lay dying on the hard, chill floor, the shadows in the corner of the room took a form familiar to her and knelt beside her, its eyes flickering in the eternal gloom.

" 'Thou breathest thy last, fair Elizabeth, but despair not. In life thou embraced monstrosity and, in doing so, secured for thyself Unlife never-ending. In three days' time, thou shalt walk the earth once more, as one Made in mine own image.'

"They found the body of Elizabeth, reduced to little more than a skeleton, covered in filth and open sores. Although the archduke would have gladly thrown her corpse on the dung heap for dogs to tear apart, he had no desire to offend her powerful relatives, so he had her body placed in the family tomb without the benefit of clergy, alongside her long-dead husband.

"And so ended the story, as far as most people were concerned. But the night following her entombment, Elizabeth rose from her resting place and walked out into the darkness, never to return to her native land. For He Who Makes was as good as his word; although dead, she was now one of the Unliving, who walk by night and feed upon the blood of mortals. But Elizabeth was different in many ways from common *enkidu,* those creatures whom humans know as vampires. She did not have fangs to bite her victims, but instead absorbed their blood directly through her skin. And now that she was Undead, she no longer had to worry about the blood being that of a male or a female, virgin or sinner.

"So Elizabeth wandered the world, eager to quench her thirst and continue the existence she had once known. She soon learned that the best cover for her operations was that of the brothel. Men, as a rule, were far easier to entice to their deaths . . . and much less likely to be missed than virginal young maidens.

"Over the centuries she went from country to country, city to city, establishing a series of bordellos notorious for their willingness to cater to the more perverse—and wealthy—patrons. Rome, Vienna, Paris, Stockholm, Copenhagen, Venice, Moscow, and London: she knew them all, and they knew her, under a dozen different names. But always the same title: Countess.

"Empires rose and fell. Religions were founded and destroyed. The ancestral line of which she was once so proud grew anemic and fell into decline. To her eyes, human society was like a castle made of sand, constantly being washed away and rebuilt. The one thing that remained unchanged was her beauty . . . and the blood that fed it.

"And so things would have remained until the world's end, except for the Blue Monster.

"The Blue Monster was a fearsome creature that hated all things inhuman. It had mirrors for eyes, a leathery black skin, and a single, deadly silver tooth, which it plunged into the hearts of its hapless victims. It scoured the world in search of vampires and other nonhumans, stalking its prey without mercy.

"One day, not too long ago, while returning from an exclusive sex club in Monte Carlo, Elizabeth was accosted by the

Blue Monster, who attacked without warning or provocation, slicing her with its horrible silver tooth. It took all of Elizabeth's strength to escape the dreadful beast.

"Although she had avoided true death at the hands of her enemy, the Blue Monster's silver tooth had done its damage, turning her legs gangrenous. To keep the rot from spreading, Elizabeth had no other choice but to have her legs removed. Although the surgery was successful, her existence was forever changed. As all vampires know, wounds dealt by silver weapons never truly heal, and limbs lost to silver never regenerate.

"For the first time in centuries, Elizabeth was unable to feed her beauty, and without the blood of her admirers, the full weight of her years began to bear down on her brittle bones. Elizabeth needed a companion to help restore her youth and beauty; a companion who would do her bidding without question or qualm; a companion who would deceive, seduce and kill for her. Most of all, she needed a companion who would protect her from the Blue Monster.

"Elizabeth looked in penthouses and boxcars, prep schools and prisons for such a companion. Then, one night, while at an interstate travel plaza, she noticed a young girl dressed in a tank top and cut-off jeans going from rig to rig, soliciting the truckers for sex. She watched as the girl climbed into one of the cabs, then exited ten minutes later, her hands stained with blood and clutching a large roll of paper currency. It was then that Elizabeth knew she had found her companion.

"Elizabeth took the girl away from the truck stops and rest areas that had been her world and gave her nice clothes, money, expensive cars, and took her traveling around the globe. And in exchange, all the companion—who was, in reality, a Secret Princess—had to do was keep Elizabeth's beauty fed with fresh blood. Which proved very, very easy. The End."

"But you didn't say if Elizabeth and the Secret Princess lived happily ever after," Phaedra said.

"How remiss of me! And Elizabeth and the Secret Princess lived happily ever after forever and ever. The End."

"I like it when you do the voices," Phaedra said, her voice drowsy.

The next john whose name wasn't John was a Japanese business executive with an Osaka electronics concern. She picked him up at a gentleman's club while wearing the red wig and driving the Lamborghini. He had insisted on vaginal intercourse but hadn't lasted three minutes. Not that it mattered. In the end he met the same fate as all the other nameless Johns she had slaughtered in the service of the Contessa's beauty.

Still, she was beginning to worry. They had been in one place far too long. And the cycles between baths were becoming disturbingly short. When Phaedra first began working for her, the Contessa had required only one bath a week. Now it was two, sometimes three. The local police would eventually tie the various disappearances together, despite Phaedra's care in changing her appearance and making sure she didn't trawl in a discernible pattern.

Even if the cops were slow on the uptake, there was no guarantee the papers wouldn't smell a story and start writing about the sudden spate of missing midlevel executives. Neither the cops nor reporters really concerned Phaedra overmuch. She was used to dodging both. But what she was afraid of was the story getting picked up by the wire services. That meant the Blue Monster would be headed their way.

Phaedra felt much safer in Europe than the States. Part of that was personal. After all, nothing bad had ever happened to her on the Continent. She had repeatedly begged her mistress to leave the country, but the Contessa remained adamant about staying put. Phaedra feared that the Contessa's frequent aging cycles had somehow affected her mind. Sometimes she seemed distant and disjointed, as if centuries of memory were playing inside her head at the same time. On occasion she called Phaedra by different names and spoke in languages she didn't recognize.

There were other changes, too. The torpor that followed her rejuvenation now lasted hours. Now all the Contessa seemed interested in doing was sitting on her bed and staring out at the night, watching the moon's reflection on the lake's liquid surface. The only thing that seemed to interest the Contessa, besides watching the night, were the fairy tales.

Phaedra liked lying with her head in her mistress's truncated lap while the Contessa absently stroked her hair and told her bedtime stories. It was something her mother had never done for her as a child. Her stepfather used to come into her room and put her head in his lap, but that was different.

If there was one thing Phaedra had learned in her short life, it was that love was not to be trusted. Need was better than love, safer than want, more reliable than lust. The Contessa needed her more than anyone else ever had. She needed her like Phaedra needed to eat and breathe. That, more than the money, was what kept her bound to the old woman.

The Contessa had done more for her than any other person on the face of the Earth, including her mother. All that bitch ever did was give birth to her. The Contessa, on the other hand, had lifted her up from the gutter, taught her how to act and dress and talk in such a way as to attract a more affluent john. It was the Contessa who exposed her to the world beyond the grim, gray confines of truck-stop plazas, trailer parks, and cheap motels.

It was the Contessa who had taught her how best to butcher a human being and disassemble him with a hacksaw and a cleaver; it was she who had showed Phaedra how to dispose of a body without attracting attention. When they first met, Phaedra was a callow young girl with a lot of anger and a straight razor; the Contessa had turned her into a sophisticated femme fatale and a world-class serial killer.

The Contessa had given her a life where before there had been nothing but day-to-day existence. Phaedra owed it to her mistress to protect her and make her safe from her enemies. But there was only so much she could do for her lady. Why the Contessa chose to come back to this place, she was not certain.

Phaedra knew the Contessa had lived in Red Velvet Manor

far longer than any other place in the nearly four hundred years of her existence. Then again, perhaps the old woman's reasons for returning were more practical than sentimental. After all, Red Velvet Manor was already outfitted for her special needs.

It was Phaedra's job to protect her mistress, and that meant making sure their camouflage within the community remained intact. The best way to do that was to maintain a low profile, make sure the curious stayed at arm's length, and keep moving. The longer they stayed at Red Velvet Manor, the more likely it was that the Blue Monster would sniff them out. Phaedra had never seen the Blue Monster, but she did not doubt it existed. The Contessa's legs were proof enough of that.

In the years spent making sure the Contessa was one step ahead of the Blue Monster, Phaedra had come to realize it was as smart as it was tenacious. While Red Velvet Manor was isolated, it did have a historical connection to the Contessa; one that was easily accessible to anyone with access to the Internet and knowledge of the Contessa's various pseudonyms.

If her lady wished to remain at Red Velvet Manor, then they would stay put. But Phaedra could not shake the sensation that things were about to go bad. It was the same feeling she used to get when she stood on the concrete block that served as the trailer's front stoop, sniffing the summer wind while cicadas sang in the trees. On the surface everything seemed safe, but there was always an edge of potential disaster in the rising wind.

There was a storm coming. But would it be just another summer squall . . . or a twister? Do you run for cover or stand your ground? Do you batten down the hatches or flee for your life? There was no way of knowing, really, until the storm was upon you. And by then it was too late to do anything but ride it out.

"Have you seen this woman?"

"Nope," the bartender grunted, barely glancing in the direction of the photo on the top of the bar.

A fresh twenty suddenly appeared atop the photograph.

"You *sure* about that?"

The bartender stopped cleaning the highball glass and glanced up, for the first time, at the woman standing opposite him. His eyebrow went up even higher. Hotel Orso was a four-star establishment, catering to wealthy business executives. It rarely saw young women tricked out in leather motorcycle jackets, mirrored sunglasses, and tattered Black Flag T-shirts, even when rock stars were staying in the hotel.

The bartender palmed the twenty and picked up the photo, knitting his brows as he frowned. It was a candid surveillance shot, taken with a telephoto lens.

"Which one you mean? The old lady?"

"No. The blonde pushing the wheelchair," the woman in the leather jacket said, tapping the picture.

The bartender shook his head and tossed the photograph back onto the counter. "Naw. Can't say I recognize her. Sorry."

"How about this one?" She flipped a second photo out of a small deck held in a fan like playing cards.

The other photograph was in better focus, although taken under the same conditions. It was of a sexy brunette in a red cocktail dress being helped into a sports car by a slightly balding middle-aged man in evening clothes. The bartender's eyes narrowed.

"Now *this* one looks familiar. She wears her hair different, but I'm pretty sure it's her. She comes in from time to time. Checks out the bar. Working girl, from what I've seen of her."

"She ever talk to you?"

The bartender shook his head. "Just to order drinks. Virgin Marys. Keeps to herself, unless she hooks a john."

"When's the last time you saw her?"

"Couple of weeks ago, I guess. She left with some suit." He tilted his head to one side. "Are you a cop, lady?"

"Do I look like a cop?"

"Hell, no!" the bartender snorted. "The reason I asked, see . . . that suit she walked out of here with turned up missing a couple of days later."

"You don't say?"

"Cops were all over this place, asking questions. I guess he was some kind of business bigwig," he said, turning to slide one of the long stems into its overhead rack. "The cops seemed to think the bastard high-tailed it to Rio with company funds. The way I see it—" The bartender turned back to face his questioner, only to find himself addressing empty space. He shrugged and resumed polishing his highball glass. Fucking tourists.

Sonja strode purposefully across the Hotel Orso's lobby, oblivious to the stares from the staff and guests. She had more important things on her mind. The blood witch was in the area. There was no doubt the Contessa's renfield was out and about, doing her mistress's work.

She had spent the better part of two years tracking down the old bitch. She had come close to killing her back in Vienna, only to have her escape. Now it was up to her to track down the Contessa and finish her off, much like a master hunter would a wounded deer.

Vampires as ancient as the Contessa were never easy prey. You didn't get to be hundreds of years old without honing to a fine art the ability to go to ground. If one identity got too hot for them, they would switch to another as easily as they would change their socks. This made her quarry especially difficult to keep track of. However, since ancients rarely had to worry about being recognized from one generation to another, they tended to use the same identities over and over again. Another thing in her favor was the inherent difficulty ancients seemed to have in understanding the importance of technology, which to her meant commissioning a computer database, based on her own design, that could access and cross-reference real estate records, land titles, newspaper reports, census information, birth and death certificates, and maps, scanning them for known identities and pseudonyms of the so-called Ruling Class. As an afterthought, she had an anagram generator incorporated into the system, just in case someone decided to get cute.

A search on the Contessa pulled up newspaper reports dating from the Depression of a notorious "high-class house of ill repute" called Red Velvet Manor. Its madam was one Eliza Bayroth, who was rumored to have catered to the more outré tastes of captains of industry, Supreme Court justices, and the occasional President. After the start of World War II, rumors began to circulate of occult rituals, which may or may not have been a cover for Fifth Columnist activities.

The brothel shut down shortly after a newspaperman famous for underworld reportage announced his intention of publishing an exposé of Red Velvet Manor. The reporter disappeared off the face of the Earth not long after that. A year later, a badly decomposed body, believed to be that of the missing journalist, was found in a nearby landfill. It was assumed to be a gangland killing. By the time the body was uncovered, Madame Bayroth had married a dissolute Romanian nobleman and set sail for the Continent, where, from there on in, she was known simply as the Contessa.

This information dovetailed into what she herself had uncovered from her European sources and from microfiched issues of *Le Figaro*, *Paris-Match*, and *Der Spiegel*. Studied in its totality, the data answered several nagging questions Sonja had concerning her quarry.

She had been hunting vampires for almost thirty years. Her knowledge of their strengths and weaknesses, their abilities and limits, did not come from reading books or watching movies, but from hands-on experience. But, for all her familiarity with the world and ways of the Undead, she had been baffled by the Contessa. For one, she did not seem to possess the telltale fangs, nor did she surround herself with lesser vampires of her own Making. And, most important, she had survived an attack with a silver weapon, albeit as a double amputee.

Sonja realized now that she had made a grave mistake in classifying the Contessa as a garden-variety vampire. From what she had since learned from various sources and her own research, the Contessa was not a true vampire, but a *strega*— those who transform themselves into Undead through the use of black magic. Such creatures were rare, but those that existed were crafty and possessed different strengths and weaknesses than "typical" vampires. While the Contessa's means of feeding on her victims did not spread the taint, that didn't make her any less dangerous. Like all vampires, she was a corrupting force on any human who fell into her sphere of influence. To allow such a monster to continue to exist was anathema to Sonja.

After all, it was one such monster that had attacked Sonja, over thirty years ago . . . and made her one of them.

Phaedra was wearing the short red wig and the black silk sheath that night. It hadn't taken her very long to reel in the next john whose name wasn't John. As they headed for the Boxter, he began to drag his heels. She turned to look at him.

"Is there something wrong, sugar?"

"Look, lady . . ." he said, his face coloring. "I thought I could go through with this."

"What do you mean?" she asked, genuinely baffled.

"It's not you!" he said with a nervous laugh. "God knows, you're one of the most beautiful women I've ever met! It's just that—well, I keep thinking of my wife and the kids. And, well, I'm sure you're a *great* person and all that . . . but I just *can't* go through with this. I'm sorry if I led you on back at the bar."

Phaedra blinked and shifted around uncomfortably, uncertain of what she should do. She had never had a john throw the hook before. The one or two who had gotten away in the past had done so simply because someone who would have been able to give a description to the local authorities or remember a license plate number had walked up at an inopportune moment. But nothing like actual rejection had ever happened to her before. It had never once crossed her mind that a man might be capable of passing up sex. In her experience, given the chance, men fucked anything that was willing, and much that was not.

"I feel like I haven't been honest with you or myself. My name isn't John, it's Frank. Frank Hensley," he said, an abashed look on his face. "Believe me, I would love to spend the night with you—"

"Get in the car," she said.

"Beg pardon?" Frank blinked, uncertain he'd heard her correctly.

"Get in the car, damn you!"

Frank's eyes widened at the sight of the gun aimed at his midsection. "Whoa, lady!" he said, automatically raising his hands. "Don't you think you're overreacting?"

Bartenders, like cops, develop a sixth sense for trouble. And the chick in the leather jacket was definitely that. Over the years he learned never to trust anyone who wore sunglasses after the sun went down, since it usually meant they were strung out on something. Still, potential trouble or not, it was his job to serve her, just as he would any other customer who happened to stroll into the Embers Lounge.

"What'll it be, ma'am?"

"I don't want a drink, just information. Have you seen this woman?" she asked, pushing a snapshot wrapped in a twenty towards him.

"What's the deal?" he said, eyeing her suspiciously. "She owe you money or something?"

The woman in the sunglasses smiled crookedly without showing her teeth. "Far from it. In fact, *I'm* the one who owes *her.* I'm just trying to track her down so I can pay her back."

The bartender hesitated for a moment, but the twenty was too tempting to ignore. He picked up the photo and frowned at it for a moment.

"Yeah, I recognize her."

The stranger in the leather jacket and mirrored shades grew attentive. "When was the last time you saw her?"

"Just a few minutes ago." He nodded in the direction of the side door. "She just left with some suit."

To his surprise, the stranger bared her teeth in a snarl and headed in the direction he'd indicated as if the joint had suddenly caught fire. The bartender wasn't certain, but he could have sworn he'd glimpsed fangs. He shook his head, doing his best to forget what he had just seen as he pocketed the twenty. Yeah, she was trouble all right. But not his, thank God.

"Shut up and get in the car!" Phaedra said, jerking open the passenger door.

Frank stared at the gun, then at Phaedra. What he saw in her eyes was enough to turn him on his heel and send him sprinting back in the direction of the motel. He managed to get halfway across the parking lot before she dropped him with a single shot to the right leg. Frank lay on the asphalt, writhing in pain as he clutched what remained of his kneecap.

Phaedra hurried to claim her prize, removing the handcuffs she kept hidden in her purse as she crossed the lot with brisk, purposeful strides. Frank cringed in fear, lifting his bloodied hands to shield his face, as she loomed over him.

"Take my wallet, if that's what you want! I don't care! Just don't kill me! *Please!* I've got a wife and kids!"

Phaedra cursed under her breath and quickly scanned the parking lot for witnesses. The bastard was making too much noise. She would be better off popping him here and now and fleeing the scene, then starting from scratch in one of the gentlemen's clubs across town. Phaedra returned the handcuffs to her purse and raised the gun. Frank began to alternately pray and sob out loud.

Before Phaedra could squeeze the trigger, the side door of the bar banged open, causing her to swing the gun in the direction of the noise. She saw a strange woman standing framed in the doorway, dressed in a black leather motorcycle jacket and wearing a pair of mirrored sunglasses, even though it was the dead of night.

The stranger did not seem surprised by the sight of a man wallowing on the asphalt, nor was she frightened by the gun pointed in her direction. Instead of turning and running back into the building, the stranger let the door close behind her and gave her right wrist a small, sharp snap and a silver blade in the shape of a frozen flame sprouted from her hand as if by magic.

Phaedra gasped in recognition, even though she had never seen the woman before.

The Blue Monster fixed Phaedra with its horrible mirrored eyes and moved towards her with determined, measured steps, its hideous silver fang reflecting the glow from the streetlights.

Phaedra squeezed the trigger of the gun, firing on her approaching enemy. The Blue Monster moved with the fluid grace of underwater ballet, twisting its upper torso one-quarter turn to allow the bullet to pass by. The second bullet, however, caught it in the upper shoulder, knocking it to the ground.

Phaedra looked down at Frank, still cowering at her feet, then at the Blue Monster, which was already painfully picking itself up off the ground, and, with a scream of angry frustration, fled to the waiting Boxter, leaving six feet of smoking rubber in her wake.

Sonja sat up and grimaced at the pain radiating from her shoulder. She bit her lower lip, her fangs inadvertently drawing more blood. It felt like the renfield had broken her damn collarbone. Then again, she'd taken slugs to the heart and lungs without much to show for it except some scars. She grunted as she got to her feet, pushing the throbbing in her shoulder to the back of her mind.

She walked over to where the renfield's intended victim lay huddled on the asphalt. He was alive, although his face was starting to go gray from shock. He flinched as she leaned over him.

"Don't shoot me," he whispered.

"I'm not her."

The side door opened, and the bartender stuck his head outside. "What the fuck's going on out here?"

"This man's been shot! Call 911!" she shouted in reply.

The bartender nodded and disappeared back inside the Embers.

Frank shook his head, a look of baffled pain on his face. "Why'd she shoot me?"

"You must have broken the script. You did something she was unprepared for."

Frank laughed without humor. "All I said was that I didn't want to go home with her." His laughter turned into a moan, causing him to close his eyes. When he opened them again, the woman with the mirrored sunglasses was gone. Which suited him just fine. There was something about the way she stared at the blood from his wound that scared him even more than being shot again.

The sound of the front door slamming shut reverberated throughout the house. Startled, the Contessa looked around at the red velvet wallpaper and the gilded rococo statuary that surrounded her on all sides, a look of bafflement on her face. This wasn't Vienna. And she was reasonably sure it wasn't Budapest. But if she was in neither of these places, then where was she? And, more important, *when* was she?

Her confused gaze fell to her lap, and she caught sight of the grotesque contraptions that served as her legs. Ah, yes. The New World. The city that sprawled along the shores of the great inland freshwater sea. She stared at a heavily brocaded mahogany love seat and saw a long-dead Chief Justice being fellated by a twelve-year-old boy. She shook her head, dislodging the ghost memory. It was so easy to forget where and when she was these days.

If it wasn't for Magda . . . no, her name was Gretchen. Wait, that wasn't right, either. Phaedra? Yes. That was it. If it weren't for her faithful companion, Phaedra, she would become lost within the world inside herself, wandering the shadow-haunted palaces and ballrooms of centuries past.

"*Contessa!*"

Phaedra burst into the parlor, her mascara smeared and hair in disarray. That more than the look of fear on her companion's face shocked the Contessa back into her senses.

"What is it, child? You look a fright."

Phaedra grabbed the handles of the old woman's wheelchair

and began quickly pushing her towards the converted dumb-waiter. "We have to leave! We have to leave *right now!*"

"Phaedra, what's going on?" The Contessa twisted around in her seat so she could face her companion. "Answer me, young lady!"

Phaedra fumbled with the door to the elevator, her eyes blinded by tears. "I'm so sorry, mistress. I'm so, *so* sorry."

"Sorry? For *what?*"

Phaedra's shoulders shook as she began to sob. "I've *failed* you, mistress. Please forgive me."

"Speak plainly, Phaedra! You're starting to annoy me!"

"The Blue Monster is here."

The Contessa gasped involuntarily as phantom pain shot through the stumps of her legs. She put a trembling hand to her mouth, her eyes wide with fear.

"Are you *certain* it's her?"

"As sure as sunlight burns," Phaedra replied. "Please, Con-tessa, we've got to leave right now! Take the elevator to the ground floor and wait for me by the boathouse. I'll go upstairs and get the strongbox and passports, then I'll bring the car around. I'll have to put you in the trunk—just in case sunrise catches us before I can reach a safe haven."

"But I don't *want* to ride in the trunk," the Contessa said petulantly.

"Please, mistress, not *now!* Just do as I ask!" Phaedra pushed the wheelchair into the elevator and pulled the doors shut behind it. "I'll be down to get you in a couple of minutes. I promise."

The Contessa sat in the darkened elevator, staring at the control panel for a long moment, before punching the button.

Phaedra grabbed the top drawer of the bedroom dresser and yanked it out, sending crotchless panties and Wonder Bras fly-ing in every direction. She flipped the drawer over, revealing the manila envelope taped to its bottom. Inside the envelope were numerous identity papers, passports, and documents made out in the various names the Contessa had used over the years. Exactly which pseudonym they would be using to flee the country would be decided later.

Phaedra stuffed the envelope inside a leather satchel, then hurried over to the red leather ottoman and removed its padded lid. Inside the hollowed out footrest was a metal strongbox containing two hundred thousand dollars in bundled currency, a number of credit cards, seven gold Rolex watches, and various pieces of male jewelry they had yet to convert into ready cash. Still, it was enough to take them somewhere far away. The French Riviera, perhaps, maybe the Golden Triangle. Anywhere but here.

As she lifted the strongbox from its hiding place, she was surprised to hear the sound of the Contessa's private elevator coming to a stop. She turned and saw the Contessa wheeling herself out of the converted dumbwaiter.

Cursing under her breath, she put aside what she was doing and strode forward, trying her best to keep the panic from showing in her face. "Why aren't you downstairs?"

"I *can't* leave," the Contessa replied, shaking her head.

Phaedra knelt so she could look her mistress in the face, placing a soft, young hand on the Contessa's withered shoulder. "*Why* can't you leave?"

"Because it's time for my bath," the Contessa said matter-of-factly, her gnarled hand closing on Phaedra's throat, its grip as tight and inescapable as death's.

There was no mistaking Red Velvet Manor for anything else, even from a distance. The red curtains, lit from behind, caused the windows to glow like the eyes of an animal.

Sonja cut the headlights as she came up the long, winding drive approaching the house. She could see the Boxter in which the renfield had made her escape earlier by the side of the house, the driver's-side door still hanging open. She pulled up behind the sports car, blocking its path. She twitched her right arm, cupping her hand so it caught the switchblade as it dropped from its hidden sheath within the sleeve.

The front door was standing slightly ajar, the light from the foyer spilling across the front veranda. Sonja frowned and glanced up at the second-floor windows. Her prey was still here. She could feel it. The question was *why?*

It had taken Sonja twenty minutes to find this place. The renfield, the one called Phaedra, had that advantage, on top of a good five-minute lead. She cautiously pushed the front door, but it swung open without incident. She stepped inside the grand foyer, eyeing the decor for hidden trip wires or skulking bodyguards. There were none.

She tilted her head, allowing her mirrored sunglasses to slide to the end of her nose, and dropped her vision into the occult spectrum. What had been empty air a moment before was filled with dark energies that seethed like heat shadows cast against a summer sidewalk.

Out of the corner of her eye, she glimpsed men dressed in old-fashioned evening clothes, brandy snifters in their hands, watching a large dog mount a naked woman. But it couldn't be a dog, because it had hands. As Sonja turned to get a better look, the shades flickered and disappeared.

Sonja shook her head. She had to keep her guard up and not allow herself to be distracted by shadows. Even though the Contessa might be crippled, she hadn't gotten to be four centuries old on just luck and blood.

Sonja started up the grand staircase, scanning the doors that lined the second floor. They all seemed to be locked save for the one at the end, which stood slightly ajar. She nudged that door all the way open with the toe of her boot. The interior of the room was dark, save for a sliver of light from the half-open bathroom door that fell across the floor, illuminating the blood-red carpet.

"Do not be so hesitant, my dear," said the Contessa from somewhere inside the darkened room. "You have nothing to fear from me."

"Forgive me if I do not believe you," Sonja replied as she crossed the threshold.

The Contessa sat propped up against the padded headboard

of a large oval-shaped bed, dressed in a red velvet robe trimmed with monkey fur. Her hair spilled over her shoulders and across the red satin pillows like ink from an overturned bottle. Her skin was milky white and as smooth as alabaster, unmarred by age or imperfection. Her delicate, long-fingered hands were folded in her lap, cradling what looked like the remote control for a TV set.

Sonja glanced about, probing the shadows for signs of an ambush, but all she saw were a pair of prosthetic legs draped over a nearby chair like a pair of empty pants.

"Where is she, witch?"

"*She?*" the Contessa asked, arching an eyebrow.

"The renfield."

The Contessa pointed with the remote control in the direction of the bathroom door, which stood slightly ajar. Sonja gave it a wary push, and it swung all the way open on its hinges, revealing Phaedra—born into the world as Faye Alice Baker—hung by her heels over the marble tub, her throat slit from ear to ear like a summer hog. The sight didn't surprise Sonja; after all, she had caught the scent of blood the moment she entered the house.

"I *hated* having to do that," the Contessa said, turning the remote control she held over and over again in her hands. "Really I did. But I had no choice. There was no point in running away again. I knew it, and so did Phaedra, although she could not bring herself to admit it. It wouldn't be fair to her, leaving her on her own. . . . What would she do without me? I did her a kindness, really."

"So you put her down, rather than leave her to face life without you. How altruistic of you. I notice you didn't let her blood go to waste."

"I will meet eternity in no skin but this one."

"Once a vain, psychotic bitch, always a vain, psychotic bitch, eh? Put down the remote, old woman. I'll be as quick about this as I can."

The Contessa shook her head in defiance. "No! I refuse to die at the hands of a monster such as you! My family once strode the world as kings! What right does a lowborn freak of nature such as yourself have to destroy me? I was Made by my own hand, and by my own hand shall I be Unmade!"

The Contessa pointed the remote at the heavy velvet drapes and pushed the button a final time. The curtains parted like those of a stage, and the first rays of the rising sun spilled across the room. Both women instinctively lifted their arms to shield their faces from the sunlight, but only one burst into flames.

The Contessa screamed as her skin and hair caught fire, the flames quickly spreading to her gown and bedclothes. Sonja backed away, both repulsed and fascinated as the ancient vampire's flesh bubbled and melted, dripping from her bones like wax from a candle. Within seconds the Contessa had been reduced to a thrashing skeleton, and yet she continued to scream.

The fire, having consumed the bed, quickly spread to the red velvet wallpaper. The walls ignited like dry kindling, and suddenly the entire room was ablaze. Sonja leapt through the curtain of fire and smoke that swallowed the door, rolling as she hit the hallway floor in order to extinguish the flames clinging to her jacket. The hair on the right side of her head was burned to the scalp and heat blisters were rising across her back, but she barely noticed.

The interior of the mansion was already filling with heavy, acrid smoke. As she hurried down the stairs towards the front door, Sonja felt a chill on her spine. Someone, or something, was watching her. She turned and saw what looked like a tall man the color of shadow standing on the landing above her, watching her with eyes made of fire.

Sonja ran out the front door and all the way to her car, throwing it into gear the second the engine turned over. She was halfway down the drive before she bothered to close the door. She didn't know why the old blood-witch's patron had chosen to lay low, and she didn't care. Vampire slaying was one thing, but demon hunting was a whole other ball game.

. . .

Inside the funeral pyre that once was known as Red Velvet Manor, a shadow shaped like a man stood in the grand foyer and laughed as the grandfather clock with the zodiac face struck thirteen. Upon the final strike, a pillar of fire punched through the roof, and the final visitor to its gilded halls closed its burning front door behind him.

Brian Stableford

Sheena

BRIAN STABLEFORD *is a prolific writer living in Reading, England. His fiftieth novel (and seventy-fifth book),* Year Zero, *appeared in June 2000, close on the heels of* The Fountains of Youth, *which is the third volume in a future-history science-fiction series that began in 1998 with* Inherit the Earth. *Earlier novels include* The Empire of Fear, Young Blood, *and* The Hunger *and* Ecstasy of Vampires. *In 1999, he was the recipient of the Science Fiction Research Association's Pilgrim Award for his contributions to SF scholarship. His other awards include the SFRA's Pioneer Award (1996), the Distinguished Scholarship Award of the International Association for the Fantastic in the Arts (1987), and the J. Lloyd Eaton Award (1987). His recent nonfiction includes* Yesteryear's Bestsellers *and* Glorious Perversity: The Decline and Fall of Literary Decadence. *"Sheena" is a story that I privately consider third-stage romanticism; when you've lost faith in love and still have to live and live and live, you might as well believe in the nonbelievable . . .*

N.B. A glossary of British "localisms" provided by the author begins on page 203.

IF I'D HAD a quid for every time I heard the old joke beginning, "What do you say to a sociology graduate?," I wouldn't have had to get a stopgap job at all, but nobody pays you a wage to listen to put-downs. Anyway, it's not true—not any more. Ever since the minimum wage came in, fast-food outlets are deeply reluctant to hire anyone who qualifies for it. The sacred right to be on the wrong end of orders for a Big Mac and fries is now reserved to seventeen- and eighteen-year-olds. Because I was twenty-one when I left university, I had no alternative but to raise my sights.

Fortunately, the introduction of the minimum wage coincided with the wildfire spread of call centres, which allowed me to cash in on the only asset I had—apart, of course, from my sociology degree. Although I was born and bred just off Easterly Road and never had an elocution lesson in my life, my accent isn't nearly as thick as it might have been. I'd learned to suppress it even further while I was doing my three years at the uni; paradoxical as it may seem, the only way for a Leeds lad to fit in at the local wastepaper factory is to ape the manners and mores of the southern majority. When I left home I got a flat in Harehills Lane, not to be just a bus ride away from Mum and the sibs—although that's what I told *them*—but because it allowed me to tell my new friends that I lived in Dorset. It was a waste of irony, of course. None of them ever thought for an instant that I might mean the posh southern county, and some of them even knew where its humbler namesake was. "Oh, yeah," they'd say smugly. "Out past St James's and the Corporation Cemetery." I might have done better simply to tell the smartarses that I'd been to school in Dorset, saving the revelation that I meant Thorn Walk Secondary for a punch line.

The people at the call centre weren't, of course, allowed to say that one of the qualifications for the job was a posher voice than most people who'd go for that kind of a job possessed. Their ads only specified a "good telephone manner"—but I could do politeness and patience, too, even though I wasn't female. Ninety percent of the front liners were lasses, perhaps because a "good telephone manner" is one of those things that most females develop naturally in their teenage years, like bulimia, PMT, and deodorant addiction. Lads don't usually develop a "good telephone manner" because boys take an essentially utilitarian view of the phone, making short and functional calls, whereas lasses find a perverse kind of intimacy in the form and touch of a plastic receiver which delivers gossip as if by magic. Not that I was a common or garden male chauvinist, of course, even before I changed—we northern scum don't always conform to stereotype.

All call centres are pretty much alike, although the one on Scott Hall Road where I went to work seemed distinctly incestuous, by virtue of the fact that we were fielding queries on behalf of a firm that made, installed, and customized all kinds of telephone equipment, up to and including call centres. Although there was only one other graduate in my intake and two already on the strength it was stopgap work for practically everyone who manned the phones, because people can take only so much of a job which involves dealing sensitively with boorish clients who are confused or angry before they're put on HOLD and twice as bad afterwards. We got calls from customers who were resentful because they were too stupid to follow the instructions telling them how to work their kit, customers who were livid because the kit couldn't do what they wanted it to, and customers who were incandescent because they thought they'd been overcharged—that was about it. Although I did two weeks' basic training in the kinds of products the company sold, the only advice I was allowed to give was script-based stuff that didn't get much more sophisticated than "have you checked that the unit's plugged in?" My job was to take down details of problems so that I could refer them to the appropriate technical staff or accounts department, with profuse assurances that somebody would phone back shortly with real help.

I didn't expect the work to be difficult, and it wasn't, but it was peculiarly taxing to have to maintain a polite front in the face of such relentless incompetence and hostility. Apart from the fact that the money was enough to feed me, pay the rent, and nibble away at my overdraft, the job's main advantage was the flexible shift system. This allowed me to vary my hours—taking time out to attend interviews for real jobs whenever they came up—and made overtime easily available if I wanted it. There was a period when I thought there was an even greater advantage—the fact that females were in such a large majority that no shift ever had more than three blokes working alongside twenty nubile females—but I soon learned better. In a competitive environment like that, I thought at first, even a sweeper with lead boots could score at regular intervals, but it didn't take long to encounter the downside of the situation.

It wasn't that the lasses weren't up for it. Quite the reverse, in fact. I doubt that there was one among them who hadn't lost her virginity at thirteen and taken to the sport like a duck to water, but they certainly didn't play by the rules I'd got used to at the uni. Maybe it was a side effect of the working environment and maybe it was just a sign of the times, but the great majority didn't bother with "dating" or "relationships" at all. What they did were "girls' nights out," on which they'd go out in gaggles of eight or ten, drinking like fish and laughing like lunatics with one another, until the time came to go home—at which time, if they happened to fancy a shag, they'd just pick some bloke at random and drag him off. It was easy to arrange to be one of the blokes—the slags weren't at all shy about inviting their male colleagues to join them on their riotous nights off, and if you stuck with them all night you were absolutely guaranteed to cop off with someone—but there was a price to be paid. I tagged along only once before I realised exactly why the other lads at work were so reluctant to accept any invitations from their female workmates.

The problem with being a male hanger-on on a girls' night out in Leeds is that it's rather like being a male stripper at a hen party—in fact, you have to be bloody careful that it doesn't turn out *exactly* like that. You're the butt of all the banter, and the talk gets filthier with every unit of alcohol that's sunk—and we're talking double figures by eight o'clock—so the suggestive remarks, the lewd questions, and the probing fingers become increasingly intrusive and increasingly aggressive. It's not just that they're mimicking what they see as the essential features of lad culture—which would be more than bad enough, believe me—but that while they're doing it they feel that they're *getting their own back* for thousands of years of indignity heaped upon their mothers, grandmothers, and so on, all the way back to Eve. Because of that aspect, lasses don't go over the top in the kind of relaxed, natural way that their male counterparts do; in over-the-top terms, every girls' night out is the second day of the

Somme, and the troops sure as hell aren't in any mood for taking prisoners. I suppose it isn't so bad if you can just grit your
teeth and wait for the payoff at the end, even though *you* don't
get to choose which of the witches will eventually take you
home, but for anyone with an ounce of sensibility the path to
that consummation is way too thorny. Even for blokes, pull-a-
pig contests are pretty tacky, but when lasses start, it gets posi-
tively disgusting. After two hours of listening to those kinds of
reminiscences and hypotheticals, no man alive can get any kind
of kick out of scoring, even if it happens to be the one he actually fancies who eventually drags him off. No matter what she
whispers in his ear when they're finally alone, he always feels
like a prize porker ripe for the Polaroid laugh track.

All of which is beside the point, really—except that it's the
context that explains exactly how and why I became fascinated
by Sheena Howell. She seemed to be the only lass on the various shifts who never went on girls' nights out and never in-
dulged in any of the ritual humiliations that gave the others such
insane delight.

You might think that as an obvious singleton Sheena would be
the prime target of all the lads who'd ever been battered and
bruised by a night out with one or other of the gaggles, but she
wasn't. The others thought she was "too weird."

When I asked one of the old hands, Jez, how Sheena had
come to have this reputation, when she seemed so inoffensive,
he filled me in readily enough.

"She's dressed for work right now," he said, "but those are
her civvies. She's a Goth—nights out she wears nothing but
black, hair in spikes, eyes made up like fireworks. Wouldn't be
so bad if it were only the outfit, but she's a vampire Goth—not
just an Anne Rice fan, though that'd be bad enough, but a full-
blown pretender. Says she learned to hypnotise herself so she
could access her past lives, and maybe she did, because she
surely doesn't seem to be living in the present. A mate of mine
who knew her years ago told me her name's really Susan—they
all make up names, although they usually pick something

classier than *Sheena*. She's seriously crazy, and a bit feeble to boot—takes more time off than the others. Bad legs, apparently."

You couldn't tell any of that by watching Sheena at work. She was small and thin, and couldn't possibly have weighed more than seven stone, but she seemed more ethereal than feeble to me. The fact that her hair was black with mousy roots was only exceptional because the regular harpies mostly had hair that was blonde with mousy roots. She was usually clad in worn black jeans and grey T-shirts implausibly declaring that she was a member of the Royal Redondan Naval Reserve or the Israeli Defence Forces, which qualified as dressing down even by the relaxed standards of Phoneland. She did seem as if she wasn't quite there, but not because she looked as if she were mad, in spite of Jez's slanders. To me, it seemed that she was slightly *faded*, like a photocopy of a photocopy. Her telephone manner was exquisite, though. She spoke softly, with perfect, almost musical clarity. Unlike the members of the slag legion, she didn't give the impression of having momentarily switched off a natural and otherwise-everpresent coarseness. She seemed—to me, at least—to be naturally gentle of tone and manner. She never got pissed off by the callers, which spoke of incredible fortitude, and had a happy knack of calming them down, no matter how irate they were when they finally got past the Chopin prelude that we tortured them with while they were on HOLD.

"I don't think she's crazy at all," I told Jez forthrightly, after making my own preliminary observations. "All that Goth stuff is just posing, anyway. It's an affectation—a lifestyle fantasy way past its sell-by date. She must be about ready to get over it."

"Fucking sociology graduate," was Jez's immediate response, although he had two A levels himself.

"Has she got a boyfriend?" I wanted to know.

"Used to live with some guy almost as weird as she is. They were in a shitty band, but they broke up—the band as well as the living-together bit. She moved back with her mum. She'll probably go out with you if you ask, but she won't let you fuck her, and you'll have to wear black—to go out, that is. Don't know what you'd have to do in bed—never got that far. Watch your jugular."

The next time Sheena and I were on the same two-to-ten shift, I came to work in black Levis and a black T-shirt, whose Gothic qualifications were only slightly compromised by the luminous green *X-Files* logo on the back. When the shift was about to finish, I logged off five minutes early, having already taken my quota of calls, and went over to her cubbyhole.

"Hi," I said. "I'm Tony Weever, with a double *e*. Started a couple of weeks back. Wondered if you'd like to go for a drink with me before we go home. We've got an hour before closing time."

I was steeled for some kind of scornful put-off, but all she said was, "Okay."

"You're Sheena, right?" I prompted.

"That's right," she said, turning away so that she could take one more call, although I was certain that she'd already made her score. I waited patiently for her to finish, then guided her to the recently redecorated Cock and Crown in Sholebrooke Avenue, which was safely distant from any watering hole that the harpy patrol might be nipping into for a quick one. She asked for a half of Dry Blackthorn, showing commendable restraint.

"Never been in here," she observed. "The maroon plastic upholstery's seriously revolting."

"You should have seen it before," I told her. "Bad case of Oscar Wilde wallpaper—three pints and you wanted to fight it to the death."

She didn't laugh, but she contrived to give the impression that it wasn't because she didn't understand the joke.

"Jez told me you used to be in a band," I said when we sat down.

"Yes," she said. "It split. Davy and I are hoping to do something else."

"Davy?"

"We used to live together, but we don't now. It's just a music thing now."

"You sing?"

"And write lyrics. He does the music. We'll record a CD when we're ready."

"A DIY job?"

"That's right. It's normal, with our kind of thing."

"I was at the university for three years—did your band ever play there?"

"No. What did you do?"

"Sociology."

"So why aren't you a social worker?"

"That's social admin. If I wanted to do something like that, I'd have to do a vocational qualification. I considered the probation service, but only for a minute. Much safer to deal with the criminal classes over the phone, and I'm too deeply in debt to do another year's training right away. I'm hoping to get a job in the media, but so's everybody else in the world. Where do you live?"

"With my mum, in Cross Gates. You?"

"Out past St James's and the Corporation Cemetery. No dad?"

"No. Mum was married, but I was too young to notice when it broke up. He died soon afterwards. Mum took Libby— that's my older sister—to the funeral, because she remembered him, but I didn't go."

"I don't know my dad either," I admitted, "although he's still alive. Mum and he were never married. My two brothers and I all have different fathers, so it all got a bit complicated."

"Lib's my full sister," she said, "but my little brother's only a half."

The conversation was flowing more easily now that we'd established things in common, but it was way too downbeat. "So why'd you change your name to Sheena?" I asked, in a blatant attempt to lighten it up.

"Libby went to see the Cramps on their last British tour, shortly after I joined the scene. They had a song called 'Sheena's in a Goth Gang.' Lib started calling me Sheena because she thought it was funny, in a contemptuous sort of way. The best way to deal with put-downs is to accept them and take them one step further, don't you think? Now I'm Sheena to every-body."

"While the real you remains secret. Why not? Does the fact that you sometimes wear an Israeli Defence Forces T-shirt mean that you're Jewish?"

"No. Davy brought it back for me from Jerusalem. He bought it in an Arab shop on the Via Dolorosa. He thought it was funny that the Arab shops were making money out of them. Maybe the Arabs did, too. The Redondan Naval Reserve one was from him, too. He gets the Redondan Cultural Foundation Newsletter. You'd probably like him."

I had my own ideas about the likelihood of that, but I wasn't about to spoil things by saying so. Nor was I about to ask her opinion of past-life regression or vampires unless and until she introduced the topic first. A changed name is one thing; esoteric interests that she might be taking a shade too se-riously were another.

"I don't know much about Goths," I confessed, thinking that it was probably safe to go that far. "I've seen them around, of course, ever since the good old days when the Sisters of Mercy were *the* local heroes."

"That's retro-Goth now," she said. "Things have moved on."

"To Marilyn Manson?"

"That's flash metal—bastard son of Alice Cooper."

"Nick Cave?" I queried, getting slightly desperate.

"He's still okay, but basically mainstream. The whole point is not to like the things that other people like, not to think the things that other people think, not to want the things that other people want, and not to do the things that other people do. Every time an idol becomes generally popular, the insiders lose interest. If you'd ever heard of any of the bands that I'd pick as favourites, I'd probably be disappointed."

"Try me," I said bravely.

"I like to dance to Inkubus Sukkubus and the Horatii. I also listen to Ataraxia, Mantra, and Sopor Aeternus, and dark am-bient stuff like Endura."

The bright side was that I didn't have to disappoint her.

"Even an oppositional subculture has to have norms of its own," I pointed out, letting my sociology degree show. "You still have to think the things that *certain* other people think, etcetera, etcetera. Want another?"

"I can afford to buy a round."

"Yes, but I'm drinking pints and you're on halves, so it's only fair if I buy two before you buy one."

"Okay. But it's not true about the conformist nonconformity thing. There's a dress code of sorts, and shared tastes in music, but that doesn't mean that we all think the same things or want the same things, etcetera. We can be as weird as we like, but we don't have to be *similarly* weird. No such thing as *too weird*, of course." She was obviously familiar with Jez's opinion of her fuckability.

I fetched the drinks before I said: "And exactly how weird are you?"

"Didn't the little bird tell you?"

"Only bullshit. I didn't take him seriously."

"That's because you didn't want to. You were going to ask me out, so you didn't want to believe anything too silly."

"No, honestly," I said valiantly. "It was bullshit, but I wouldn't have minded. Be a pity if we were all the same, as Gran used to say."

" 'There's nowt so queer as folk,' " she quoted. "But Jez doesn't know the half of it. Do you believe in reincarnation?"

"No. Do you?"

"Yes. And how. How about vampires?" She was being deliberately provocative.

"Well," I said carefully, "that would depend what you meant by vampire."

"Oh, right," she said. "The 'anyone can drink blood if they want to' routine. That's not what I mean."

"If you mean the undead rising from their graves by night, perennially in danger of crumbling to dust in sunlight, invisible in mirrors, then no," I said. "It doesn't make any sense. Anyway, blood is just blood, not some magical elixir."

"We die every night," she said, in her scrupulous telephone

voice. "We surrender our hold on consciousness, and we rise from the grave every time we dream, hungry as well as invulnerable. We all wake up different—even those of us who never meet an incubus or succubus. Our true selves are invisible to us, especially when we look in mirrors. Blood is just blood if you cut yourself, or while it's sloshing around your veins, but to a vampire, blood is life—and when your blood's been drunk by a vampire, you wake up *very* different. If it happens often enough, you can never go back to what you were before. All that stuff about shrivelling up in the sunlight is complete crap, though— the movies invented that."

I burst out laughing, because I thought it was a punch line— and when she kept a studiously straight face I *still* thought it was a punch line.

"You're cheating," I pointed out. "You're changing the supernatural into the merely metaphorical."

"No I'm not," she said. "That's your interpretation, not mine. Most people don't realise how supernatural even the everyday things are. Not just all dreaming but all feeling. Life itself, even reason. It's all supernatural. Vampires are ordinary *because* they're supernatural, not in spite of it."

"Ah, I get it," I said, figuring that I'd cottoned on to what she was doing and why. "It's more Sheena, isn't it? You take the put-downs and you run with them, taking them so much further that all the mockery's discharged. If people accuse you of being crazy, you take the bullshit on and double it, until it becomes surreal. Cool. I like it. I really do."

"That's your interpretation," she repeated, "not mine"— but I thought I had the measure of her, and I thought I understood the way she played the game. I wasn't lying to her. I really did like it.

"It's getting late," I said. "Maybe I should take you home."

"I knew you wouldn't let me get a round," she said. "Too macho. Not exactly convincing, is it, from a sociology graduate? You should go out with the girls a few more times. That'd toughen you up."

"I'm not in the least macho," I assured her, figuring that I might as well get in on the game. "I always wanted to be—even took masculinity A level. I was okay on the theory, but I failed the practical. I only became a sociologist so I could learn to understand my own dismal failings as a mere male. I would have done psychology, but in psychology you have to blame everything on your parents, and it didn't seem fair to Mum. In sociology, it's the entire society's fault. Share the wealth and share the blame, I say. So much more PC than blaming bad karma left over from Atlantis. Not that I don't believe in Atlantis, of course. I believe United are going to win the league and that New Labour still intend to cut hospital waiting lists and help the pensioners, so why would I have any difficulty believing in Atlantis?"

"Which United?" she asked.

"Darling," I said, "there is, by definition, only one United, whatever fools may think in Manchester, Sheffield, or bloody Dundee. Did you know that Elland Road has the only five-stall dog track in the country?"

"No."

"Well then, it's obviously true what they say. You *do* learn something new every day. Tell you what—I'll get them in and you can slip me the money under the table when nobody's looking."

"Somebody would see us out of the corner of his eye and get the wrong idea," she said. "Anyway, it's nearly last orders. I think I'll owe you one and get the last bus. You don't have to see me home. We creatures of the night can look after ourselves."

All in all, it was a perfectly satisfactory predate. Even after the intensity of the vampire discussion, I didn't think Jez could be taken seriously. I didn't think Sheena was crazy—and even if she was, I figured, I should still be able to worm my way into her knickers, given time and a little native wit.

"You want to take me ten-pin bowling at the Merrion Centre?" she asked when I laid out my proposition for a first real date.

"Why not?" I said. "Bright lights and polished lanes—the

pastel pullovers are optional. Wouldn't want to go somewhere dark and gloomy where we'd fade into the background, would we?" I figured that the blind-side approach was best, although I'd already done what any university man would do when faced with a tactical problem—I'd visited the Central Library and Miles's secondhand bookshop in search of research materials.

"Oh, all right," she said. "Anything's better than television—and if it's good enough for Homer Simpson, it's good enough for me."

We were on eight-to-four, so we had time to go home and make ourselves beautiful before meeting up at the Merrion. I'd decided that too safe a compromise would look wimpy, so I'd borrowed a black leather jacket from half-brother Jack. I already had a black silk shirt, which I'd bought under the mistaken impression that the creases wouldn't be so obvious if it didn't get ironed in an emergency, and a decent pair of black trousers. My gingery hair did let the ensemble down somewhat, but I wasn't ready to start dyeing it yet.

I half expected Sheena to have gone the whole hog, but she hadn't. Her boots had only two-inch heels and her leggings only had a slight sheen. Her velvety jacket was cut like a Tudor doublet with a drawstring at the waist, but she hadn't done anything extravagant with her hair except for renewing the dye. Her mascara was almost conservative.

"You're not quite ready for the *real* me," she told me when I told her she looked beautiful.

"I'm working on it," I assured her.

I figured that I'd have no difficulty at all beating her on the lane. Even if she'd played before, I reasoned, she couldn't have had much practice recently, and she was bound to feel bad about having to check her boots in favour of style-disaster flatties. It turned out, however, that she was every bit as neat and meticulous with a bowling ball as she was with a phone and keyboard, and I made the mistake of starting with a heavy ball. It wasn't until I put the black one aside and accepted that I was one of nature's reds that I got into a groove. Sheena won the first game by 120–113, and I had to sweat to get the best out of three; I needed 160 to outscore her on the third and I only just managed it.

"I knew you could do it," she said when I collected the necessary eight on a final-frame spare. "You're the sort who raises his game under pressure. Not many of those about in this town. Wasted in Phoneland."

"It's just a stopgap." I said, revelling in the compliment as we reclaimed our footwear and gravitated towards the bar.

"Course it is," she said. "According to the techies, it'll only be a couple of years before the whole place disappears up its own arse. The next-generation software will let them farm the work out to people's homes. I'll have to jack it in then, mind—no way I'm spending all day with Mum and Marty the brat. Lib says she can get me a job at Gap, but I wouldn't want to work in a mall, and I certainly wouldn't want a job where I was somebody's crazy little sister."

"Maybe your singing career will take off," I suggested as I ordered a pint and a half of Dry Blackthorn.

"I'll get these," she said. I let her; in a bowling alley, anything goes. "Davy's not ready yet," she added, as we made our way to a cubicle. "He gave me a tape last week, but he says it's only half cooked. I'll find the words, but I'll probably have to change them later. He says he's a perfectionist, but he's really just a ditherer."

I wondered whether it had been a mistake to turn the conversation in that direction, but it seemed better to follow it through and kill it off rather than backtrack. "That's how you work, is it?" I said. "He does the tunes, then you fit words to them?"

"I find the words," she repeated. "Davy finds the music; I find the words."

"Why put it like that?" I asked. "Why pretend that it's not your own effort?" It had always seemed to me to be a peculiar form of false modesty when writers talked about their work having a life and logic of its own which they had no alternative but to follow—as if they were merely passive agents of fate, puppets in the hands of their own creations.

"Because it's what happens," she said. "Don't you believe in muses?"

I was more than ready for any sentence beginning "Don't you believe in . . . ?"

"Of course I do," I said. "I'm intimately acquainted with the muse of sociology. She wasn't one of the original nine, of course, but they had to make concessions after the publication of the Communist Manifesto or there'd have been a revolution on Olympus. Which one's yours?" I hadn't been expecting muses, so I didn't have any names to drop; I was sufficiently grateful to have remembered that there were nine.

"In seventeenth-century France," she said with a half smile that seemed to be a polite acknowledgement of my ready grasp of the game, "poets thought that their muses were vampiric—that they had to pay in blood for artistic inspiration. Geniuses paid so high a price that they wasted away."

I figured that it was a test—maybe the crucial test that would decide whether she was willing to let me get closer. "In nineteenth-century France," I countered, "they thought the same about the clap—that because genius was close to madness, tertiary syphilis was the M1 to enlightenment." I said it lightly, so that she would know that it was the kind of put-down that was laid on to be picked up and run to healthy absurdity.

"By that time," she said, "the art of dreaming had gone to pot, ruined by laudanum. If you know how to let yourself go when you fall asleep, you don't need dope. You only have to attract the right kinds of night visitors to make the connections you need."

"Must be why I got only a two-two," I said. "The muse of sociology didn't come through when I needed her most. My mistake—I should have fed her better."

"It's not just blood, of course," she said. "There are other bodily fluids that will do as well—and some which definitely won't."

I got the joke immediately. "Muses never take the piss," I said.

"Neither should you," she riposted immediately, in her very best telephone manner.

I could take a hint. Sheena was telling me that if we were to devote ourselves to the game in earnest, I had to be careful to stay within the field of play—even if, like Elland Road dog track, it was too narrow to accommodate the sixth stall that the normal rules demanded.

"So how do you find the words," I asked earnestly, "if you can't just make them up the way other lyricists do?"

"You lose yourself in the music," she said, with equal seriousness. "You shut your eyes and you let it take over. It's like self-hypnosis—it's not really a trance, but it *is* an altered state of consciousness. Music's a natural language, with its own meanings built in. It speaks to the emotions. It's the purest magic of all, and the greatest mystery. And if you listen—really *listen*—you know what it's about. A piece of music doesn't mean the same thing to everybody, of course, because our emotional profiles are so different. Music resonates in different ways in different souls. If you want to understand your own meanings—the nature of your true self—you have to find your own music, and then you have to find the words that fit it. Otherwise, you might as well be taking calls at work, reciting crap from somebody else's script."

It *was* a test, and I knew that it was a crucial one. If I couldn't take what she was saying seriously, it would all be off—but she didn't want it to be off. She liked me, at least enough not to prefer loneliness, so she'd warned me as gently as she could about the dangers of taking the piss. All I had to do was play ball.

I nodded sagely and resisted the pseudo-intellectual temptation to quote Walter Pater about all art aspiring to the condition of music. "I see what you mean," I said. "Our moods have musical reflections, and it goes much deeper than the ratio of backbeat to heartbeat. To produce the right lyrics, you have to find words that have the same emotional quality as the music. It makes sense."

"No, it doesn't," she said quietly. "It goes way beyond *sense*, in either meaning of the term. It's supernatural."

"And it costs," I added, trying not to sound too tentative. "In blood, sweat, and tears. It takes something out of you."

"It takes everything out of you," she said. "Everything that isn't just waste."

Jez's comments about the band she and her boyfriend had been in—and their living-together thing having broken up at the same time—took on new significance then. The one topic you should normally steer clear of when you're trying to charm a lass into bed is her ex-boyfriend, but I already knew that Sheena wasn't subject to the normal rules of engagement.

"It must be difficult," I observed delicately, "to find the right words to fit the music of a guy you used to live with."

"The sex was always a mistake," she said. "That wasn't the way we gelled."

Under normal circumstances I'd have deduced from that remark that wee Davy must be queer, but in this particular instance I was prepared to believe that he might really be wedded to his vampire muse. In any case, that wasn't the important issue. "We all make mistakes," I said. "I never thought it was possible for sex to be among them, but that was before I met the Phoneland harpies. One night with them was enough to teach me that it really does matter whether or not you gel."

"You could probably get used to it," Sheena informed me coolly. "After the third or fourth time they'd go easier on you. One or other of them would probably develop a soft spot for you and let you separate her from the pack. They don't really go in for pull-a-pig contests—what's the point of playing a game it's impossible to lose? They just resent the fact that lads do, and they know it puts the fear of God into lads to think that they might be victims of that kind of contempt."

"Actually," I said, "I think the whole pull-a-pig thing's an urban legend."

"No it's not," she said quietly.

She was right; I'd never done it myself, but I'd seen the Polaroids. I'd even laughed at them, because that was what was expected, even though they weren't at all funny.

"I wouldn't want to get used to it," I said. "And it's definitely my round. The next one, too."

"In that case," she said, "let's go somewhere a little less naff. We've both made our points, haven't we?"

We had. The only places within easy walking distance where the oak beams weren't plastic and there wasn't a trace of maroon were the downmarket Upin Arms and the upmarket Countess of Cromartie. I took her to the Countess, even though the harpies sometimes used it for girls' nights out. I figured that the risk was worth it.

Afterwards, I saw her home. Sheena lived on what passes for the wrong side of the tracks in Cross Gates, north of the railway and east of the ring road, but the terraced street she lived in was neatly kept—what gran would have called respectable poor. It was obvious that Sheena wasn't about to introduce me to her mum or her big sister right away, so I left her on the doorstep—but that was okay, because we'd already fixed up another date. She had agreed to bring some of her tapes over to my place and let me cook her a meal. Nobody said anything about bringing an overnight bag, but it was tacitly understood that we liked one another well enough to find out whether or not we gelled.

I don't claim to be much of a cook, but I'd felt the pinch of student poverty sharply enough in the previous three years to appreciate how much money you can save by peeling your own potatoes and sticking your own toppings on a pizza base. For Sheena I splashed out on steaks—from the butcher's, not Tesco—and a bottle of French red. I draw the line at attempted baking, though, so I bought a couple of slices of cheesecake from the Harehills Delicatessen to serve as dessert. I'd managed to acquire three more black shirts by scouring the local charity shops, and I took the best one up to Roundhay so Mum could pass the iron over it.

"Not going into the church, I hope," Mum said wearily.

" 'Fraid so," I told her. "I get my dog collar next week, but I'm not allowed to hear confessions until I've done the moral obstacle course."

Mum only humphed, but I was proud enough of the quip to save it up to tell Sheena later.

Sheena turned up fashionably late, but only by fifteen minutes. She was wearing the same mock-doublet-and-hose she'd worn at the Merrion Centre, but her boots were longer and shinier and she'd gone all out with the makeup and silver-plate jewellery. Her earrings were bats, and her necklace looked like something out of an ancient Saxon tomb. Her eyes looked fabulous, like pale blue suns with black holes at the core, pouring all manner of strange radiance over her lids and lashes.

She'd brought four tapes, but she told me to put them on one side until later. While I made busy in the kitchenette she inspected my bookshelves with minute care.

"Research?" she said, when I popped my head around the door to check that she was okay. She was pointing a long black fingernail at the Freda Warrington paperbacks I'd picked up at Miles's—but I'd taken care to hide the books on Atlantis and past-life regression I'd borrowed from the Central Library. A conscientious bullshitter has a duty not to reveal his sources.

"Sure," I said. "Have you read them?"

"Oh yes. I could have lent them to you if you'd asked."

"That's okay," I told her. "How rare do you want your steak?"

"Somewhere between well done and ruined."

That was a relief. If she'd felt forced to conform to stereotype and eat it bloody, I'd have felt obliged to do likewise, but she was obviously a Yorkshire lass first and a vampire second.

"So what's your favourite past life?" I asked her, once we were tucking in. "Priestess, princess, or courtesan?"

"Those sorts of existences aren't what they're cracked up to be," she retorted. "History being what it was, the most comfortable incarnations have usually been male—except for the really remote ones, back in the days when the Mother Goddess was all-powerful. Being a dryad in Arcadia was okay—satyrs put merely human males in the shade, equipment-wise—but being an Amazon was even better. The two lives I led in Atlantis were good, too."

"I meant to ask you about that," I said. "Where exactly was Atlantis—Thera or north of the Azores?"

"Malta," she said unhesitatingly.

"Malta isn't underwater," I pointed out.

"No," she admitted, "but it did get comprehensively drowned and scrubbed clean of all habitation during the disaster. It was an asteroid, I think, like the Tunguska object. The tidal wave wiped out the whole of civilization in the Middle East and Africa, thousands of years before the eruption that destroyed Thera."

"It must have been painful amputating your left breast so that you could use a bow when you were an Amazon," I observed. "I hope it didn't get infected."

"Oh, we had anaesthetics and antibiotics in Arcadia," she said. "It wasn't until the Dark Ages that the last remnants of traditional female learning were wiped out by male doctors. Don't knock it—*you*'d love getting in touch with an Amazon self. Think of all that lesbian sex!"

"You'll have to teach me to do the self-hypnosis thing," I said. "Not that I expect too much, of course. I realise that finding out I'd been Napoleon—or even Max Weber—would be the equivalent of winning the lottery on a rollover week. With my luck, I'd probably turn out to have been a eunuch in a Caliph's harem."

"I was one of those once," she told me serenely. "Great singing voice. Every incarnation leaves its mark, but some are more welcome than others."

"On the other hand," I said speculatively, "maybe it would spoil my enjoyment of the present to be always comparing it with the edited highlights of a thousand lifetimes. Don't you find that?"

"Other way about," she came back, presumably having met the argument before. "The only way to get a true appreciation of what it means to be alive—or undead—is to have died a thousand times. Until you've lived and lost a million joyful moments, you don't realise how precious they are. Anyway, once you've had a glimpse of other worlds, this one can never be enough. If you don't learn to dream, you're letting most of life's potential go to waste."

"Does the soul have any choice about its incarnations?" I asked, aware as I did so that my pretended curiosity was becoming real. "Does it simply get assigned to the baby whose birth coincides most closely with the extinction of the previous incumbent, or can it hang about and wait for a better opportunity?"

"The more closely you're in touch with the sequence of your past lives, the more control you obtain," she assured me. "Some ghosts are just souls that get stuck, but others are exercising a precious skill. Vampires tend to be experts at hanging around— it makes it much easier to visit sleepers and take their blood. If necessary, you can get right inside the beating heart, bathing in the oxygen-rich flood from the pulmonary vein. In some ways, though, shed blood is better, especially if it's *offered*, as a kind of libation."

I thought she might mean the pulmonary *artery*, but I'd dropped biology at thirteen so I wasn't sure, and it wasn't the kind of conversation into which one could insert an abrupt dose of pedantry.

"Forgive me if I'm being stupid," I said instead, "but how is it possible to remember having been a vampire in a past existence? Do the memories of the undead impress themselves on the eternal unconscious of the wandering soul in the same fashion as memories of life?"

"Yes, they do," she said. "And how. Once you've been a vampire, you never forget it. Of all the things that make their mark, that's the most powerful. It's not quite 'once a vampire, always a vampire,' but there's a definite predilection."

"Like a curse, handed down from generation to generation?"

"Some might think so."

"Not you?"

"Not me. All vampires aren't alike, Tony. Didn't the muse of sociology explain that to you?"

"I forgot about the muse thing," I admitted. "It's all very well for poets to pay in blood for inspiration, but if it were just the blood, I wonder whether the vampire muse would bother with the trade-off. Why give anything in return, unless she gets more than she could have for free? On the other hand, maybe if I'd given more freely of my blood, sweat, and tears, the muse of sociology would have let me in on a few more secrets—like how to get a better degree and immediate employment. But I've got you now, haven't I?"

"Have you?" she countered. She was making a tokenistic show of being hard to get. I reminded myself that it was *all* just a show, just an exotic lifestyle fantasy, but it no longer mattered. All lifestyle is fantasy, and there's no virtue in buying a mass-produced one off the peg in Gap if you have the wherewithal to design and make your own.

We saved a little of the wine until we'd finished the cheesecake, so that we could carry our half-full glasses to the couch. It was difficult to tell how mellow Sheena was, because her veiled eyes and meticulous pronunciation didn't give much away, but I saw the tension in her limbs as she went to put one of the tapes on. This, I knew, was the final test—and I had a shrewd suspicion that I wasn't going to be able to fake it. If I couldn't relate to the music, no amount of bluster and empty flattery would cover up. She'd know. Although she still didn't know a damn thing about the real me, she would know enough, somehow, to see right through me in that one vital respect.

I didn't really know what to expect, but if I'd had to guess I'd probably have opined that heartbreaker Davy's music would tend to the gloomy, the ethereal, and the tuneless. Sheena's remark about seventeenth-century French poets had given me an impression, although I'd never read a word of seventeenth-century French poetry in my life. I just assumed that it was dark, nebulous, and leaden.

I was dead wrong, about twentieth-century Leeds if not about seventeenth-century Paris. These days, with fancy keyboards, synthesizers and samplers, drum machines and computer software, one guy can pretend to be a whole ensemble, or even an orchestra. Davy didn't seem to want to be an orchestra, but he didn't want to be some morose bastard sitting in the dark with an acoustic guitar, either. The backing track on the tape was multilayered, replete with insistent percussion, but by no means unmelodious. It was dark and strange, but there was nothing in the least effete about it. If anything, it was a trifle too full-blooded for my pop-educated taste.

Sheena was so softly spoken, and so seemingly fragile, that I'd expected her voice to be thin, maybe tending towards falsetto or whispery, but it wasn't. The register was lower than I'd anticipated, but the notes were well rounded, not in the least hoarse. If her lyrics had been written out as if they were prose or blank verse, they would probably have looked clumsy, maybe even meaningless, but I could see right away what she meant about finding meaning implicit in the music and choosing words to echo and amplify it.

I knew that I wouldn't be able to follow or remember the convolutions of the lyrics until I'd heard them at least a half dozen times, but certain phrases and repetitive refrains immediately stuck in my head. The dark romanticism of the music was reflected in images of night and death, but there was a lot more that obviously derived from Sheena's fascination with remote and probably imaginary pasts. There were no explicit references to Atlantis or Amazons, although vampires featured in such tracks as "Graveyard Love," but the half-whimsical conversation in which we'd touched on those subjects allowed me to catch references I might otherwise have missed—to the extent that I began to wonder whether I'd really been as much in charge of its subject matter as I'd thought.

When Sheena sang about falling stars or the wings of time or the loneliness of castaways, she wasn't simply redistributing the standard pick-and-mix materials of teenage angst. I knew that I'd have to go a lot deeper into her fantasies if I were to get to the bottom of her lyrics, and that I'd have to put some work into solving the mysteries with which they'd been liberally salted. Because I had other things on my mind—well, *one* other thing on my mind—I didn't really make much effort to listen with more than half an ear, but that half ear was sincerely appreciative, and some of the couplets penetrated deeply enough to recur long after the tapes had run through.

"I like that," I said, of one refrain which ran: "To kiss and sting through some emergent world / Reeking and dank from out of the slime."

For the first time, she blushed.

"It's Byron," she admitted. "I borrow, sometimes."

If there were more misappropriations, I didn't recognise them—but I probably wouldn't have. One that seemed to me to be more than likely to be hers, though, was: "I need to be free, of myself, of myself / I need to be free, of myself."

I hadn't a clue what it was supposed to mean, but it seemed to me to be heartfelt.

First impressions don't always cut deepest, but if they stick, they stick hard, and Sheena must have known that before she selected the order in which she played the tapes. The couplets that wormed its way into my consciousness most avidly, and stuck most securely, were on the earliest tracks she played. There were other neat refrains, but the one I seized upon as if it were a key was "I want to be free, of myself." It didn't sound, in Sheena's voice, like a mere artifact or affectation. It sounded intensely personal, and somehow found a resonance in me that the more fanciful imagery didn't.

Davy's compositions weren't the kind of music you'd ever hear on *Top of the Pops*, and I wasn't sure that they were the kind of alternative that John Peel would ever have championed before he turned into a comedy teddy bear, but they certainly weren't amateurish or inept. When the first tape clicked off I relaxed, no longer afraid that I was going to blow my chances with Sheena by being unable to take this aspect of her seriously—and when she saw me relax, she relaxed, too. She'd remained standing after putting the tape on, but after three or four minutes of the second side she sat down.

"I brought some earlier stuff as well," she said. "But that's more or less where we're up to. Davy says it's not right yet. It's partly the mix, he says, but bits of it need rethinking. When he's got the fundamentals right, he says, I'll be able to find the right words." Her telephone manner had cracked at last, and she was rambling slightly.

"It's good," I said. "It works. It's weird, but it works."

"Would you like to meet him? Davy, I mean."

I hadn't been in any doubt as to her meaning, but I wasn't sure what the right answer was.

"Not tonight, of course," she added swiftly. "Sunday, maybe, if you're not doing a shift."

"Would he want to meet me?" I asked. I didn't want to be paraded before an ex-boyfriend as some kind of trophy, displayed in order to make him think again about the wisdom of casting her aside like a worn-out sock.

"He wouldn't be jealous," she assured me, having recovered enough of her composure to read my hesitation. "He really wouldn't mind—and it would help you to understand." She didn't specify whether she meant the music, or her, or both.

"Sure," I said. "Sunday. Why not? Not as if I'm due in church. Still have to pass the moral obstacle course."

After I'd explained the reference, she said: "You've been hearing my confessions."

"Yes," I said, "but you don't need absolution—and if you did, eating my cooking is penance enough for anyone."

"It was good," she said. "I'm impressed."

"Can't go wrong with meat," I said. "Stick it under the grill till it turns brown."

"It only seems easy," she assured me. "The accumulated unconscious wisdom of a thousand unremembered lifetimes. Who knows? Back in the Stone Age, you might have been the caveman who first came up with the idea of cooking."

"I think it was earlier than that," I said. "I seem to remember being an *Australopithecus* at the time. Weren't you the woman who came up with the idea of cutting up gazelle skins to make clothes? I thought we'd met before."

I wondered briefly what the United strikers could have been

doing since the days of Mitochondrial Eve to have so completely mastered the art of kicking a ball the size of a dead man's head into a rectangular goal. I drank the last of my wine and reminded myself that there was no hurry at all, and that the more tapes we played through, the later it would get. Within her lifestyle fantasy, Sheena and I had already had all the time in the world, and we could take that legacy to bed with us when the time came, even though I couldn't remember a single damn thing that had happened before 1984—by which time I'd already been five years undead for what still seemed to me to be the one and only time.

"It *is* good," I said again, cocking an ear towards the music centre. "It's too weird to sell, but it's okay."

"Weird *is* okay," she informed me, although there was no longer any need. "And there's no such thing as *too weird*, in this world."

The sex wasn't terrible, which was good, for a first time. It wasn't weird either, which was also good, for a first time. Not that it was ordinary, of course, and not just because looking down at those fantasised eyes was almost as strange as looking up at them. No first time is ever ordinary, because it's all exploration. Maybe there'll come a day when I've experienced all the different shapes, sizes, and textures that lasses come in, but I can't believe that any more than I can believe that in the course of a thousand lifetimes I've already done it.

There's no point trying to describe how Sheena felt, because even if I had anything to liken it to, I'd have no way of knowing whether anyone else could understand the likenesses—and in a way, I'd prefer to believe that nobody could. She was slim and silky, firm and flowing, but none of those words really signifies anything, because they're all mere measuring devices, which only operate in a world of common sense and common sensibility. Even the kind of perfunctory and dismissive sex that the harpies went in for can't entirely be reduced to that. Sheena would have said that even that was supernatural, and that sex with her was much further out, but she would have been speaking metaphorically, at least about the harpies.

We were both nervous, of course. We both knew that it could be a lot better, and maybe would be, but we both took comfort from the awareness that it was okay. In fact, if I were honest enough to put the discretion of hindsight aside and try to recall how I felt at the time, it was much better than okay. We'd had only the one bottle of wine between us, so there was plenty of margin left for further intoxication. We went at it hard enough to exhaust ourselves, and if we hadn't been on such tenterhooks we'd probably have fallen straight into Dreamland. In fact, we were too uneasy to release each other from our mutual embrace in order to relax into sleep, and just uneasy enough to play one more round of the collusion game.

"You didn't bite," I said, neither wonderingly nor accusatively.

"Didn't have to," she said. She didn't mean that she'd had her fill of other bodily fluids; the vital ones were safely contained in a twentieth-century French letter. She meant something subtler.

"If I don't feed you properly, how can you become my muse?"

"I can't," she murmured, very softly. "But that's not what you want me for. Even if it was more than just one more notch on the bedhead, that's not what you need from me. Don't think you got off lightly, though. You can't escape unscathed—and if this goes on, you'll be changed forever. I don't need to bite to draw blood, and if you give me enough chances, I'll get right into the chambers of your heart and change you forever. You might be the kind of vampire who sinks blood like a pint of bitter, but I'm not. I belong to a rarer and more discerning kind."

As the monologue went on the musical quality of her voice was enhanced, as if she were fitting her words to secret music— or finding her sentiments in some melody that only she could hear. The way we were entangled allowed me to feel the heartbeat behind her ribs—and I knew, even though I couldn't hear the secret music, that it had a greater surge and power than any-one would have realised who was only conscious of her slen-derness and physical frailty.

"A lamia," I suggested.

"A lamia's a snake," she whispered. "I'm not a snake. Human through and through. A thousand times over, but al-ways a human vampire. No curse at all, just lust for blood and every clever way to take it in. It won't kill you, but it will change you forever. Better make up your mind whether you want in or out."

I wanted in. I wanted in again and again and again. I was in love, and not just with her fragile flesh. She was too weird for Jez and everyone like him, but she wasn't too weird for me. The best way to defuse a put-down is to pick it up and run with it, until you've transformed it into a way to fly, and I decided that I was with her a hundred percent when she said that there was no such thing as too weird in our world.

I wanted in. Again and again and again. It only takes one psychotherapist to change a lightbulb, but the lightbulb has to want to be changed. I wanted to be changed. I wanted to shine, as brightly and as darkly as her paradoxical eyes. I had glimpsed new possibilities, and I wanted them actualised.

If you fall asleep in that kind of mood, you can hardly be surprised if you dream. So I did, and I wasn't.

In my dream, I looked at myself in a mirror and couldn't see myself. I asked Mum if she could see me in the mirror, and she couldn't, but she merely told me, in that no-nonsense Yorkshire way of hers, that it didn't matter, because she could see me in the flesh, and why would she ever feel the need to look at me in a mirror? I knew she was right, in the dream, but I wasn't sure that it was as simple as that, even though I used an electric razor and didn't need to see myself in order to shave. Perhaps Mum would need to see me in a mirror, I thought, if I became a gor-gon when I changed, with snakes for hair and a gaze that could petrify people.

Afterwards, in the dream, I did become a gorgon, and it was wicked. I went around petrifying people deliberately, and it gave me a real thrill to do it. Mercifully, Sheena—who was, of course, undead—wasn't affected by my baleful gaze, so we could still get together and wander through the frozen world like two playful demons, mocking the comical Polaroids that everyone else had become, lads and lasses alike. It was as if all the people in the world had become victims of our lust. Their clothes weren't petrified, though, and the mobile phones in their pockets kept going off, like the phones that escaped the Paddington train wreck unscathed, as the distant loved ones of the dead tried to find out what had happened to them. All the stupid customized ringing tones formed a crazy symphony that had far too much percussion in it to be plausible, and the beat went on and on and on until the only way to stop it was to wake up, and ease myself slowly away from Sheena's sleeping body.

I woke up, but she didn't. She was sleeping very deeply indeed, as if her spirit really had fled her undead body to go wandering, as a blood-sucking succubus. She couldn't bite anyone if she were insubstantial, but I knew now that she didn't have to. She didn't even have to suck semen into her cunt, or lick the tears from grief-stricken eyes. For her, vampirism wasn't a matter of sinking pints the way lads sup ale. It was authentically supernatural. She could leech the blood out of a man's veins, the marrow out of his bones, the elixir of life out of his very soul, with the most delicate touch of her purple-stained lips, or maybe even the hypnotic gaze of her neutron-star eyes.

"I can do this," I said to myself, not quite aloud. It was the most joyful discovery I had made in twenty-one years ten months and twenty-two days, or maybe in a thousand lifetimes. I felt like the missing link who'd invented cooking, or a new-born sceptic unexpectedly risen as a vampire from the coffin where he'd fully expected to rot. I didn't just think I could do it—I *knew*. It's like that, being in love; your powers of apprehension become supernatural.

I believed in the supernatural, at that moment. At least, I half believed—which is fair enough, given that when I'd told myself "I can do this" without the slightest shadow of doubt, I was really only half right.

It wasn't until we got out of bed the next morning that I saw the bruises on her thighs.

"Christ!" I said. "Did I do that?"

"Not all of it," she said. "Maybe some. Don't worry about it. It comes, and it goes. Sometimes I bruise really easily, other times hardly at all. No sense to it. It's the same with my periods—one month it's red Niagara, the next it's almost a no-show. The pregnancy scares I had with Davy . . . well, I soon learned not to worry too much. My legs get bad sometimes, and I have to live on aspirin for days. Had to go to casualty a couple of times—but it's okay. I'm not as fragile as I look. Honestly."

I knew that she hadn't put in the comment about the pregnancy scares to remind me that she had a real history as well as a thousand imaginary ones. She was preparing the ground for a lasting relationship. If I'd been a United player, I'd have been over the moon or extremely chuffed, but as a conscientious avoider of cheap footballing clichés, I was content to be very, very pleased indeed.

The rumour that I'd "slipped the ferret to the Queen of the Jungle" (as Jez so ineloquently put it) went round the call centre like a dose of the flu. I hadn't said anything to anyone and neither had Sheena—and neither of us wasted a moment suspecting the other of so doing—but they knew anyway. It wasn't quite supernatural, but it was a divinatory talent the harpies had by virtue of being harpies, so it was the next best thing. If I'd been able to collect a quid every time some red-lipped monster invited me to "show us yer love bites, then" I could have quit the job, but I couldn't. We simply had to weather the jokes and shrug off the cackling laughter.

"Of course I'm as weird as she is," I told Jez, playing the game with the zest of a recent convert. "In fact, I'm weirder. Supporting United and voting Labour is just camouflage. I have the heart of a psychopathic serial killer. I keep it in the second drawer of my desk."

"Fucking sociology graduate," he observed glumly. "I never thought you'd pull it off. Anyway, I'm going out with the girls tonight."

"Well, bully for you," I said. "If I run across you in the Headrow stark naked and handcuffed to a lamppost, I'll call you a locksmith but I won't lend you my coat."

Even Mum figured out that I'd got a girlfriend, although the fact that I took round all my shirts and underpants to be ironed probably gave her enough of a clue to save her from needing any uncanny powers of divination.

"Make sure you clean the lavvy," she advised. "Strong bleach, mind—*and buy a brush*. Peeling your own potatoes won't impress her for long—lasses expect more than that nowadays. And whatever else you do, don't get her pregnant."

"That's okay," I said. "She's a vampire. Vampires don't get pregnant."

"They do if you don't use protection, love," she said. "Believe me—I know."

Facing up to the petrifying leers of the Phoneland gorgons and the anxious solicitations of my own dear mother wasn't the worst aspect of the rite of passage, though. The worst of it, I knew, wouldn't be encountered until bloody Sunday, when I had agreed to meet Davy, Sheena's partner in musical endeavour.

I'd expected another terraced house in lesser suburbia, but it turned out that Davy lived south of the railway and west of the ring road, off Whitkirk High Street. He lived in what had once been a single-storey detached cottage in the long-gone days when Whitkirk was a village. It must have been worth nearly a hundred thou. When I raised my eyebrows, Sheena explained, slightly shamefacedly, that Davy rented it from his uncle.

"He's kind of the black sheep of the family," she said, "but they haven't completely cut him off."

The incompleteness of that severance was equally obvious in the interior, not so much in the cheesy 1940s furniture that wasn't quite old enough to qualify as antique as in the equipment that Davy had installed to assist him in pursuit of the vocation that his parents probably thought of as "Bohemian." He had a computer with twice the clout of mine, three heavy-duty keyboards, amps the size of sideboards, and various accessories I couldn't even put a name to.

The shock of Davy's surroundings was almost matched by the man himself. I had somehow begun thinking of Davy as "wee Davy," perhaps as a subconscious strategy to minimise the vague threat he posed to my future happiness, but he turned out to be anything but wee. I don't think of myself as short, by Yorkshire standards, but he towered over me by a good four inches, and his exceedingly long black hair seemed to exaggerate the advantage. He wasn't exactly handsome, especially with the bags under his eyes that made him look as if he hadn't slept for a week, but he was *imposing*. He looked more like a young Howard Stern than your average primped-up Goth-boy, and he moved with a stately unhurriedness that suggested that he was seriously laid-back. I tried telling myself that he'd probably smoked far too much dope since deciding to cultivate his black-sheep status in earnest, but I knew that it was a hopeful invention. Somehow, he reminded me of one of those spindly nocturnal proto-primates that you sometimes see in zoos: a slow loris, writ large. He was probably a year or two younger than me, although he certainly didn't look it.

"Tony," he echoed, when Sheena introduced us. His voice was a profound baritone, which added a little more dignity to the name than it had ever possessed in anyone else's mouth, but also a little more absurdity. Sheena immediately retreated to the kitchen—a *real* kitchen, not a glorified cupboard like the one bundled into a spare corner of my flat—to make coffee.

"Sheena's told me a lot about you," I said foolishly. "I liked the tapes."

"It's half cooked," he said apologetically, "but it's coming along. I think I'm almost there. I hope you won't be too bored while Sheen and I get on with things."

Sheen! I thought. *She told me that she was Sheena to everybody.*

"No, that's okay," I said. "She warned me that you'd be working. I won't get in the way."

He leaned closer, exaggerating the looming effect. He seemed to be looking down at me from a mountainous height. Knowing that it was just an optical illusion didn't make it any more comfortable.

"There's no polite way to say this," he whispered, "so I'll just come right out with it. If you're pissing Sheen about, and you don't stop right away, I'll come after you and rip your fucking head off."

I'd heard of people's jaws dropping in amazement, but I'd never experienced it until then. The only reply I could contrive was a strangled: "I'm not."

"Because," he added, without any evident change of mental gear, "you could be really good for her, you know, if you're serious."

"Right," I said. It never even occurred to me to try to play the game. Extrapolating to the surreal was definitely not called for in this instance. I knew it was a man-to-man thing, although it wasn't like any man-to-man thing I had ever encountered before. "I'm serious."

He nodded his huge-seeming head and politely retreated to the margins of what we in Yorkshire consider to be a man's personal space. Then he retreated an extra step, as if to emphasize that he needed more personal space than most.

"Everything okay?" said Sheena, as she brought in three coffee mugs, two in her right hand and one in her left.

"Peachy," I said. "He says he'll rip my head off if I do you wrong, but apart from that we're practically blood brothers already."

"He'll have to join the queue," Sheena said with perfect equanimity. "If it came to that, I think I could persuade him to back off until I'd had my own pound of flesh. Blood included, of course. After that, you probably wouldn't feel your head coming off. A mere coup de grâce."

It was no good complaining that this was a side of her I hadn't seen before. She had as many sides as I had new ideas to feed her extrapolative compulsion, and I wouldn't have wanted it any other way. "Well," I said, "at least we all know where we stand, future-mutilation-wise."

"You mustn't think it's jealousy," Sheena observed punctiliously. "Davy doesn't do jealousy. He doesn't care who I fuck. He just needs my input into the music."

"I care," said Davy. "I could do jealousy, too, if need be. Not the point. You're happy, I'm happy, too."

The conversation was becoming tedious, and I was glad when it lapsed. I remembered Sheena saying that I would probably like Davy, and that I'd decided to reserve my judgement. It had been a wise decision; I didn't like Davy *at all*. But when he started his back-up tapes running and began fingering his keyboards, I had to admit that he had a certain style. He had the amps turned up so that the music sounded far louder than it did on tape, and there was something about the acoustics of the cottage's main room that made the produce of his drum machine seem even more insistent than it ever had before. I felt it vibrating in my rib cage, not unpleasantly by any means, but more intrusively than I could have wished.

I sat in a corner, already feeling like a spectre at a feast. I knew that the feeling was going to get worse and worse. I was certain that Sheena had only the best of motives for letting me into this part of her life, and I certainly wouldn't have felt good about being left out of it, but it wasn't comforting to be made to see that Sheena already had an intimate relationship that ours—however close it might become—couldn't weaken or reduce. I was prepared to be convinced that Davy genuinely didn't envy me any part of Sheena that was actually accessible to me, but that didn't mean that I had to refrain from envying him the part of Sheena that was accessible only to him. I could do jealousy, and then some. I couldn't help myself.

I'd never seen musicians at work before, so I didn't know what to expect, but I certainly hadn't imagined that it would be so fragmentary or so repetitive. Davy would play a bit, then Sheena would supply a few words, and then they'd break off—for no particular reason that I could discern—and start again. It wouldn't have been so bad if they'd seemed to be building something that got longer and longer each time they tried it, converging on completion, but every time they seemed satisfied with the way one fragment was going they'd switch to something else. They seemed to make such switches without any significant discussion, as if by instantaneous common consent. The intensity of their communion increased by slow degrees, until they both seemed utterly lost. I wondered whether they would even notice if I got up and left, or if I started yelling at them, but I didn't want to try it in case I was right.

It would have been horribly tedious and mildly annoying if the fragments hadn't been so loud, but I found that the assault on my ears had a peculiar progressive effect on my imagination. Even though I wasn't involved in the making of the shattered soundscape, I was sucked into it regardless. The insistent beat didn't lose its authority in being so frequently interrupted; in a curious fashion, the incompleteness of the many repetitions began to create a kind of physical need in the parts of my body that were reverberating, which gradually confused and disoriented me—but as if in answer to that penetrating loss of focus, I thought that I began to see the relationship between Sheena and Davy much more clearly.

They worked on the Byronic kiss-and-sting motif for a while, but not as long as they worked on the ramifications of "I want to be free, of myself." Davy seemed to know what it meant, or was at least prepared to pretend.

As I watched the two of them together, exploring esoteric fractions of some vaster and inchoate scheme, I began to fancy that they were both serving as muses for the other, each drawing the other out and each changing the other's perceptions of their collaborative endeavour. I might once have thought of it as a kind of symbiosis, but I'd heard and read too much of vampires in the last couple of weeks. I couldn't help seeing it as a mutual parasitism that was taking a toll of both of them rather than working to their mutual advantage.

I tried to put such ominous thoughts aside by letting my mind wander. As the train of thought ran off, seemingly under its own steam, it got a little lighter—but it never left the realm of the macabre.

How long could a vampire survive on a desert island, I wondered, if she had only her own blood to drink?

At first, it seemed to me that her predicament wouldn't be much different from that of other hypothetical castaways, who had nothing to eat but slices carved from their own flesh and nothing to drink but their own piss, but then I remembered the difference that Sheena had taught me. To a vampire, blood isn't mere food. To a vampire, blood is life itself, and anyone who feeds a vampire is profoundly changed in the process. So the vampire castaway drinking from her own veins wouldn't simply be wasting away; she'd be embarked upon some mysterious process of self-induced metamorphosis. But suppose that on this desert island there was not one vampire but two, who thus had the alternative of sustaining themselves on each other's blood rather than their own. They, too, would be in a situation very different from two castaways who attempted to dine on each other's meat, or two snakes who tried to swallow each other's tails. They, too, would be remaking the other as they fed, inducing mysterious metamorphoses of flesh and spirit alike.

If a vampire muse needed nothing but blood, I remembered saying to Sheena, she surely wouldn't bother trading inspiration for what she could have for free—but if she, too, obtained her share of inspiration, of creativity, the trade-off would be more understandable. Not necessarily fair and equal, of course, but *understandable*. Even if it were a crooked game, you might have to play, if it were the only game in town.

It was all a flight of fancy, of course. Davy and Sheena were just making music, after their own conscientiously esoteric fashion. They weren't drinking each other's blood. And yet, those bags under Davy's eyes made it look as if he hadn't slept for a week, and Sheena was so slim that anyone who hadn't seen her eat a well-done steak could easily have wondered whether she was anorexic. Now I'd seen the bruises, I knew what a delicate flower she could be—but only *could be*, because I had her assurance that there were also times when she hardly bruised at all.

I could do jealousy, and then some. If anyone were feeding on the substance of Sheena's soul, metaphorically or supernaturally, I wanted it to be me. Obviously, I thought, Davy felt exactly the same way. He didn't mind my fucking her, but if I upset the equilibrium on which her singing depended, he'd rip my head off—always provided that he could get to the head of the queue in time.

Eventually, they finished. They seemed happy with what they'd done, although it didn't seem to me as if they'd completed anything. Unfortunately, I wasn't like Big Bad Davy. It wasn't enough for me to be happy that she should be happy. For me to be happy, I had to be the cause of her happiness—and if that made me a kind of vampire that neither of us could admire, I had to live with it.

I knew that I couldn't woo her away from the music, and I knew that I shouldn't even try, but that didn't mean that I couldn't try to compete, to make my own demands on the blood that coursed through her body. I didn't have to settle for being the only one who was changed. I could change her, too, if only I put my mind and heart into the attempt. As she'd said herself, anyone can be a vampire, and everything that we take too readily for granted is really supernatural.

Sheena went to the loo before we left, and I took the opportunity to have another wee word with Big Davy.

"So who were you in a previous life?" I asked. "Beethoven or Jack the Ripper—or both?"

He grinned. "What you see is what you get," he said. "I don't do past lives. Do you?"

That was what I wanted to hear. I'd suspected as much. Sheena had told me that Goths had a licence to be weird in any way they wanted—nothing ruled out, and nothing compulsory.

"Yes I do," I said. "And how."

In the next few weeks Sheena and I went dog racing at Elland Road and horse racing at Wetherby. We went dancing wherever there were dark-clad bands playing to legions of dark-clad acolytes—even if we had to go as far as Nottingham or Derby—and we went drinking in the Cock and Crown, the Upin Arms, and the Countess of Cromartie. Mostly, however, we went to Atlantis and Arcadia.

While I was still figuring out the best way to work it I let Sheena do most of the talking. The kind of self-hypnosis she practised wasn't much more complicated than relaxing into a mental gear somewhere west of neutral, and once I'd learned how not to be an inhibitory presence, she didn't have any obvious difficulty in getting there, or in free-associating fantasies of quite extraordinary elaboration. I had a lot of catching up to do, so I was content at first to offer prompts and nonleading questions. As time went by, however, I began to feed more and more information into the fantasies.

I discovered that Sheena was right about the nature of the creative process—that it really did seem that I was *finding* the material I fed in, not in the books that I read but within the fantasy itself, as if they had always been there waiting to be noticed or uncovered. It was perhaps as well, because the Atlantis we wove out of words wasn't much like any of the Atlantises in the books I dug up—which ranged from Plato to Madame Blavatsky—and the Arcadia would have been hardly recognisable to the scrupulous author of *Dr Smith's Classical Dictionary*. If I'd had to plagiarise the material I used in the continuing reconstruction of Sheena's favourite past lives, the wheels would probably have come off the entire enterprise. I'd never have become an authentic collaborator. Fortunately, my own imagination proved equal to the continual challenge. Necessity is the mother of improvisation, and I needed to cement that link with Sheena because it was the only way I could see to go one better than Davy, to be the perfect partner he had failed to be in spite of the hold his music exercised upon her.

It was inevitable, of course, that the fantasies would come to occupy much of my thought even when I was not with Sheena. At work, once I was able to cruise through calls on autopilot, I often found myself slipping away into daydreams of discovery, in which I would conjure up new titbits of information and imagery that fit one or other of the jigsaws we were patiently bringing towards completion. Whenever I was walking from home to work, or filling in time at home while Sheena was working with Davy, Atlantis and Arcadia were always there to provide temporary avenues of escape. Bit by bit, slyly and shyly, they even managed to work their way into my dreams.

Sheena introduced me to her mother within a week of introducing me to Davy, but I didn't see her big sister then or on any of the next few times when I had occasion to cross her home threshold, because she was always at work or out. Mrs. Howell was no taller than her daughter, but she was much stouter. She had probably been pretty thirty years before, but she hadn't aged well, perhaps because she was so nervous, indecisive, and fluttery that she must have been hyped up with adrenaline practically all her life. I never mentioned Atlantis, Arcadia, vampires, or Goths in front of Mrs. Howell, who seemed to take some comfort from the fact that I did not have dyed-black hair. Sheena was careful not to leave me alone with her mother, but on the one occasion when Mrs. Howell did manage to snatch a private word, she said: "I hope you'll be patient with Suzy. She's often unwell, you know, and her imagination sometimes runs away with her."

"She's been fine lately," I assured her, tacitly taking credit for the fact that Sheena's bad legs had almost ceased to bother her. "I love her imagination." It was the truth, if not the whole truth. I adored her pliant, fleshy reality *and* her runaway imagination, and saw no need to separate the two in my own mind, even if diplomacy circumscribed what I could say to her mother.

The sex was even better once we began to take it for granted, although I did try to be as gentle as possible, even when she told me that she was in one of her unbruising phases. For me—but not, I suspect, for her—the sex functioned in the beginning as a kind of anchor in reality, tethering the flights of fancy that became, in essence, a leisurely kind of foreplay. I thought of the sex, to begin with, as "coming down to Earth" after an excursion into Neverland, and it wasn't difficult to draw that distinction while our mutual hypnosis sessions weren't really mutual at all. While we were exploring past lives sitting at a table, or in two chairs placed so that we could stare into each other's eyes, the act of *going to bed* was always an obvious transition from one state of mind to another. As time went by, however, we began to indulge our flights of fancy while lying together on the couch. Sometimes we went to bed *before* we began to explore the still-hidden treasures of Sheena's supposed memories, and added the physical into the imaginary as if one could be subtly dissolved into the other without crossing of any obvious boundary. I had no alternative, then, but to enter more fully into the fantasies myself.

It was natural enough, during my early attempts to help Sheena recall her supposed past lives in Atlantis and Arcadia, for me to ask her whether there was anyone among her past selves' acquaintances who might be one of my own former incarnations. She denied it with such apparent assurance that I never thought the point worth pressing—and it seemed, at first, to make my own part as a prompter easier to play. As time went by, however, I began to wonder if her confident denials were a way of keeping me safely distant from the deep core of her dream. The only thing which stopped me making more strenuous efforts to intrude myself into the scenarios we spun out was the fact that she was just as emphatic that none of Davy's previous incarnations was present, even though Atlantis and Arcadia were both places where music flourished. In Sheena's Atlantis, in fact, choral singing was the highest art, much more vital to the coherence and solidarity of society than religion.

"I wish I could sing the songs of Atlantis for you," she said, "but I can't. I've tried before—" I presumed she meant that she had tried to sing them for Davy "—and it can't be done. The language of Atlantis is dead, and I can't pronounce the words, but even if I could, they're not the kind of songs that can be sung solo."

That was, of course, one of the many aspects of her fantasies that were intrinsically mysterious. For instance, all her memories of Atlantis were nighttime memories, although her memories of being a dryad or an Amazon in Arcadia were usually sunlit, pleasantly if not gloriously. This was not because Sharayah or Morgina—the two Atlanteans she remembered most frequently and more clearly—had not been active by day, although they had both been vampires after their fashion, but because they were deliberately shielding their memories of day from her miraculous hindsight.

"Our past selves can do that," she explained. "Access to such memories is a privilege, not a right. In fact, access to our own memories is a privilege, too. Sometimes, when we repress aspects of our present histories, it's not because they're traumatic in themselves but because they're linked to recurrent patterns extending across the centuries, like wormholes."

"There must be something terrible in Atlantis that can be seen only by day," I suggested. "Some monster that retires to its lair at sunset and returns at dawn, like a movie vampire in reverse."

"It's not as simple as that," she assured me. "I think it might be something to do with colour. At night, no matter how bright the stars are, it's very difficult to perceive colour. Candlelight helps, but it's not like real daylight. I think the Atlanteans may have had more colours than we have, and that Sharayah and Morgina don't want me to realise what we've lost."

"Perhaps that's why the magical creatures of Arcadia were destined to die out," I said. "We may flatter ourselves that satyrs and centaurs, dryads and the gods themselves became intangible when humans ceased to believe in them, but it's hard to see why they'd be impressed by our scepticism. Perhaps their hearts were broken, although they didn't know why, by the loss of the secret colours of Atlantis. Perhaps that's why they lost the ability to sing in proper harmony, or even to speak in the language of the authentic Golden Age. Did the Arcadians invent art and drama in the hope of being able to rebuild what they dimly remembered? And is that why the arts have been going downhill ever since, as the memory is slowly obscured from all but a frustrated few? Except, of course, that you're not frustrated, are you?"

"No," she said, ignoring the double entendre. "What I do remember only makes me more complete."

There's nothing in the least surprising in the fact that I began to hypnotise myself with these same fancies, occasionally slipping into a mental gear where disbelief was totally suspended. The only real cause for surprise is that I couldn't make any progress inventing or summoning up the memories of any past lives of my own. I *wanted* to find my Atlantean and Arcadian selves, even if it turned out that they didn't overlap in time with any of Sheena's selves and couldn't actually meet, but it seemed that I was to be limited to the role of disembodied voice, accompanying Sheena when she flew upon the wings of time, a mere parasite of her remembrance.

"I wish I could be more," I said once.

"Don't fret about it," she advised. "What was, was—the past is unchangeable. It's not the worst of fates, to be a passenger in my memories. It's a far easier way to my heart. I just wish you could hear, if only for a moment, the song of Atlantis, the song of the world as it was. I can describe the people to you, the buildings, the flowers, and the animals. I can even describe the chimeras and the spirits, at least as they seem by moonlight, but I can't describe the music, because that can't be put into any words *we* know."

"I have more than enough," I assured her, repenting of the suggestion that I could be in any way dissatisfied with our relationship. "I have everything I need."

I had, too. I had everything. It took me a little longer to show Sheena off to my mother and my half-brothers than it might have done, because I was paranoid that one or other of them was going to say something horribly wrong, but when the time came to bite the bullet, the occasion passed harmlessly.

"She's that thin," was Mum's verdict afterwards. "But it seems to be the fashion nowadays. Look at that Ally McBeal." The last remark was not a veiled reference to Sheena's talent for invention, but merely evidence of the censorious frame of mind in which Mum invariably watched TV.

The last remaining piece of our personal jigsaw fell into place a couple of days later, when we were in overlapping shifts. I got home about five, while Sheena was on two-to-ten, and I'd been in for an hour or so when the doorbell rang. It was a woman, who looked to be about four years older than me. She had bleached blonde hair, but she was too well dressed and neatly polished to be placed in the same category as the slags at work.

"I'm Elizabeth Howell," she said.

It took a full ten seconds for the penny to drop; I had never taken the trouble to work out what "Libby" must be short for. When it did, reflex made me say: "Sheena's not here. She's at work."

"I know," she said. "Can I come in for a minute?"

I opened the door wide and stood aside to let her go past. By the time I'd closed it and turned around again, she was already well into her tour of inspection. She made not the slightest attempt to cover up the fact that that was what she was doing. She carefully examined my furniture, my bookshelves, my CD collection, and my PC before turning her critical eyes on me. I tried to meet them squarely, taking note of the fact that although they were blue, they were much darker than Sheena's. Physically, Libby favoured her mother. She was handsome, even voluptuous, but anyone who had seen Mrs. Howell would have been able to imagine her slowly morphing into something wide and soft.

"Crockett says you're all right," she observed.

"Crockett?" I queried. Again the penny was ridiculously slow to drop. She meant Davy, obviously.

"Wasn't as obliging as our Suzy," she admitted. "Wouldn't take the nickname on—but I keep trying. Don't like to fail."

"Davy told you I was all right?" I said, slightly surprised.

"Said you'd probably be good for her. Don't know about that, myself. She's head over heels. Never good to be that dependent. If you muck her about, you know—"

"You'll do terrible things to me," I finished for her. "Fine. By the time Sheena's had her pound of flesh, blood included, and Davy's ripped my head off, I'll be past caring."

"Fucking sociology graduate," she said. "Think you know it all. Well, you don't."

"So tell me the rest," I said, trying to suppress my annoyance and keep my tone light. She was Sheena's sister, after all.

"I will," she said, "when the time's right. Until then—"

"Don't muck her about. Believe me, Elizabeth—can I call you Libby?—I'm not about to do that."

"Call me what you like," she said. "Just tell me that you're as mad on her as she is on you, and that you're man enough to handle it." She was staring at me, trying to give the impression that she had a built-in lie detector.

"I'm as mad on her as she is on me," I told her. "I hope I can handle it, because it's going to fuck me up worse than anything it can do to her if I can't. Satisfied?"

She didn't go so far as to nod. "Mum says come to dinner on Saturday," she said instead, finally condescending to complete the errand on which she'd presumably been sent, probably because her mother didn't trust Sheena to deliver it or bring back an accurate answer. "It's her wedding anniversary."

"*Wedding anniversary?*" I echoed.

"Is there any law that says a widow can't celebrate her wedding anniversary with her daughters?" Elizabeth Howell demanded. It would have been anything but safe to enquire, even in jest, whether Mrs. Howell also celebrated the anniversary of her divorce, or the anniversary of her son's conception. I guessed that the anniversary was just an excuse, although I couldn't quite figure out what it was that Libby and her mother were excusing.

"We'll be there," I assured her.

"Seven-thirty," Libby said in a much friendlier tone. "Maybe you *are* all right. Our Suzy certainly thinks so."

"Our Suzy?" I challenged, having realised that I had failed in my duty when I'd let it go before.

"Oh, all right," she said. "Sheena. Don't see why I should

keep it up, now that she's as good as out of the Goth gang, but if it's what she wants . . . do me a favour, will you, and tell her no if she asks you to dye your hair."

"She seems to like it the way it is," I said, "but if she were to ask, it'd be black before you could count to five. Sorry."

Libby shrugged. "Probably the right answer," she conceded grudgingly. "See you Saturday."

I relayed the entire conversation to Sheena, virtually word for word, when I met her from work.

"They're just trying to be friendly," she assured me. "It's just an excuse to make a big show. It'll be hell, but it's best to go through it."

"Well," I said, "if ever Mum approaches you about springing a surprise birthday party for me, you have my permission to tell her to go jump off Wigan Pier."

It wasn't hell, although it was a bit of an ordeal—more like purgatory, really. No mention was made of the supposed anniversary, which had served its purpose in getting us to turn up. The food was average and the canned lager Mrs. Howell had thoughtfully but mistakenly laid in for me was drinkable in spite of the gas. I probably put one too many away while Libby and Sheena shared a six-pack of Strongbow. Little brother Martin had obviously been instructed to talk to me about football, but he felt that his duty had been done once we had exchanged a few ritualistic utterances about the leakiness of the United defence away from home and the falsity of the assumption that a four-all draw at Everton counted as "value-for-money entertainment," when all that really mattered was bagging the three points. Libby was friendly enough, although her relentless campaign to win Sheena away from Phoneland by extolling the virtues of Gap became rather tedious once the cider had loosened her up.

We managed to escape at half-past ten. Sheena made a show of having to see me home and muttered vaguely about getting a taxi back, although no one was really under the illusion that she had any intention of coming back. We could have stayed on the bus all the way into town and then got another outward-bounder practically to the door, but it was easier and a little quicker to get off opposite Rookwood Recreation Ground and walk up Harehills Lane, so that's what we did.

By the time we got to my place it was ten past eleven, and I thought there wasn't enough time for adventures in imaginary history, but Sheena had other ideas. She was happy enough to go directly to bed, but once there she didn't want to pass Go without going all around the board, so we took refuge under the duvet and turned out the light. Knowing that she'd have to do a little work to get me into the mood, Sheena started talking while I lay back and listened. It was standard stuff, at first.

Morgina was in the principal harbour of Atlantis—what would now, I guess, be Valletta—about to board a ship. The sailing ships of Atlantis were akin to dhows, but tended to be much larger than the Arab vessels that inherited their design. They often carried passengers to Atlantean colonies in Clarica— the modern Sicily—and the north African coast, and they often set sail by night if the tides and winds were favourable. Morgina was bound for the Clarican city of Avra.

Morgina was excited, because she had never left the Atlantean mainland before, and slightly frightened by the awful silence of the sea. The night was bright enough when the boat set sail, but the sky soon darkened as clouds gathered, overtaking the craft because the wind blew faster at altitude. It began to rain, but it wasn't a storm, and Morgina didn't take shelter down below. The raindrops weren't cold, and they fell with an eerie gentleness, like sentimental tears—not tears of grief but the kind you shed at the end of a film when lovers are reunited after an interval of heart-rending separation and danger.

Belowdecks, some of Morgina's fellow passengers began to sing, as if to shut out the rain and the loneliness, but Morgina resisted the inevitable temptation to join in, because she wanted to savour the rain. When she opened her mouth to take in the falling drops, she found it sweet, almost as if there were a trace of blood in every slowly descending drop . . .

We were touching all the while, caressing each other, slowly and unhurriedly. We were perfectly relaxed, all the more so for having escaped the tension and embarrassment of the family dinner. If I'd had to set my mind to the serious business of invention I would have had to concentrate, but even that obligation had released its hold. I wasn't entranced, and I wasn't drifting off to sleep . . .

But for the first time, I *remembered*. I really and truly remembered, with a certainty that would have instantly dismissed all doubts and confusions arising from the knowledge that there had, after all, never been any such place as Atlantis, had some such dismissal been necessary. As it happened, though, I didn't remember being in Atlantis or any of its satellite states.

What I remembered was being on a tiny island, not much larger than a sandbar. The interior was covered with thorn-laden scrub, interrupted by a few scrawny date palms, but I'd already stripped the trees of their unripe fruit—at considerable cost to the integrity of my skin, which was scored all over with streaky scabs. I'd managed to squeeze a little moisture from leaves and a few inedible fruits, but there was no gentle rain to supply me with fresh water, and I was fearfully thirsty. I was lying on the thin strip of sand that separated the scrub from the breaking waves, and would certainly have been unconscious had it not been for the torment of my thirst, because I was very weak. My eyes were open, and I was staring up at the sky, desperately wishing that the clouds obscuring the stars would break, although I rolled my head from side to side occasionally, hoping that I might glimpse the lanterns of a passing ship.

I never said a word to Sheena. I was too startled, too amazed. I felt that if I spoke, I would break the spell, and I didn't want the experience to evaporate like a dream. I wanted to examine every detail of the apparent memory, and the fact that it was painful only made it more fascinating, more intriguing. If I gave any indication at all to Sheena that I had been transported, it could only have been my body language that conveyed the hint. I said *nothing*—but she knew. Or maybe it was Morgina who knew. One way or another, the tale that

Sheena was spinning changed, seamlessly, into an account of an errand of mercy.

"The ship is too slow," Sheena/Morgina reported. "It'll never get there in time, and I know it. I can't go below to join in with the singing. I have to use magic. It's dangerous, but it's the only way. I have to fly, no matter what the risk or the cost. It's very difficult, to sing my own song when I can still hear the other, but it has to be done, and the sound of the rain on the sea helps me. I sing my spell, and I know it's going to work, even though I've never sung such a spell before, because the need is so great. I sing the spell, and I take wing from the deck of the ship. I fly so fast that I'm out of the shadow of the rainclouds within minutes, although I can see darkness on the horizon again almost as soon as the moonlight touches me. The clouds on the horizon are different, high and cold, remote and uncaring, but they don't matter."

I couldn't remember my name, but I didn't think of that as strange, I was in dire straits, and names didn't matter. Only thirst mattered, and the possibility of relief. I had known, once, exactly who I was and where I was bound and how I'd come to be marooned on that tiny strip of land somewhere between Europe and Africa, but all of that had been driven deep into my mind, to leave the surface of my thoughts free for desperation and hope. In another world, the hope would have died, and in due course the desperation would have died, too, as I shrivelled into a desiccated corpse, silver-grey upon the amber sand, fading by slow degrees to whiteness. But this was an age of miracles, and there was no need to die.

A winged shadow fell out of the soulless night, and metamorphosed into a human female. I had no idea who she was, and could not have recognised her had I known her name. There were no mirrors in Atlantis; for all Morgina's skill in description, she could not describe her own face.

She was small and slender, and the pale features of her black-framed face were so perfect that I wished I could see their true colours. But I was also seized by a premonition that something was wrong, that my need had demanded something from her that was more than she had to give, no matter how clever or willing she might be.

She had no water, but she cut her forearm above the wrist and gave me blood to drink. The blood was sweeter and more intoxicating than wine, and it quenched my dreadful thirst, if only for a little while.

Having done that, my saviour sank down beside me on the sand utterly exhausted, and began to caress me with her fingers, and what had been memory faded by slow degrees into a dream, which extended in the way dreams sometimes do, rendering time elastic, so that the night went on forever . . . or would have done, had forever been a possibility.

But forever was not a possibility, and the dream was already faded, like a photocopy of a photocopy. It evaporated, as did the darkness of the night.

Morgina tried to pull away then, but I caught and held her.

Stay, I said, insistently but not aloud—and she consented to be held while the sun rose and the dark world filled with colour.

Newton only pretended that there are seven colours in our rainbow because he thought that seven was the appropriate number. In fact, there are five: red, yellow, green, blue, and violet—but Newton must have remembered fragments of past lives spent in imaginary histories, and must have known that there really were seven colours in the rainbows that shone in Atlantean skies. Two of them have been lost, and no longer have names, but I know now that they lay beyond red and violet, not within like Newton's invented colours.

The colour of the sun was yellow, and the sea was blue. The date palms and the thorn bushes were green—but Morgina's face and costume were tinted with colours I had never seen before. I know now that we only think that blood is red because we have lost the ability to see the other colour with which the red is mingled, just as we have lost the ability to taste blood as vampires taste it, and draw that special nourishment from it for which vampires ceaselessly thirst.

Had I drunk more frequently or more abundantly of

Morgina's blood, I would have been more vampire than I was when the sun rose on that tiny island, forgotten even though it lay within the boundaries of the empire of Lost Atlantis. Alas, I remained far too human.

As soon as the light hit her, she began to dissolve. I felt a terrible sense of betrayal, because I had always believed—always *known*—that vampires did not dissolve in sunlight, because that was the one aspect of the myth that really was a myth—but I stifled a scream when she tried to speak. I needed to hear what she was saying, even though her voice had already decayed to the merest whisper.

"The spell was too costly," she told me. "But nothing really dies, and nothing changes its inmost nature. Don't be afraid. I shall return with the night, and you will not go thirsty, no matter how long you remain here."

I was already awake, as far as far could be from any mere dream, but it wasn't until I opened my eyes that I found Sheena dead.

I was hysterical, of course, but I think I managed to do all the right things in the right order. I phoned an ambulance, and then I set about trying to resuscitate her. I breathed air into her lungs and I pummelled her chest until the paramedics from St James's arrived and took over. It was only after their arrival that I actually lost control. I remember shouting "She's only nineteen fucking years old, for fuck's sake—how the fuck can she have a fucking heart attack?," but I don't think the paramedics held it against me. That wasn't why they wouldn't let me accompany the corpse to the hospital. I was sufficiently coherent, in any case, to give them the address and phone number of her official next of kin, so that they could send someone else to deliver the terrible news.

I couldn't stay in the flat, and I certainly couldn't face Mrs. Howell and Libby, so I started walking eastwards, towards the rising sun, and I continued until I reached the urban wilderness of Whitkirk.

Davy was already up and about, busy with noise. I leaned

on the doorbell until it penetrated the wall of sound. When he opened the door, he seemed angry, but as soon as he saw me the anger metamorphosed into something else—something essentially unfathomable.

"Is she . . . ?" he asked, but couldn't force the final word past his lips.

"This might be a good time to rip my head off," I told him angrily. "You seem to have got to the head of the queue—but then, you always knew that you would, didn't you?"

"It wasn't your fault," he said, standing aside to let me in, then closing the door to exclude the world from our private business. "However it happened, it wasn't your fault."

"If you weren't so much bigger than me," I told him, "I'd be seriously considering the possibility of ripping *your* head off. I must have been blind and stupid not to see it. First you, then her sister. I thought it was just run-of-the-mill protectiveness. Even when she spelled it out in letters of fire, telling me in so many words that there was something I didn't know, it didn't click. But *you* knew, didn't you? Whatever the big secret was, *you* were in on it and I wasn't."

"We would have told you," he said. "When the time . . . we didn't expect . . . I'm sorry. We didn't know . . . so soon."

The message was clear even though the sentences weren't complete. They hadn't expected it to happen so soon—but they *had* expected it. They would have told me eventually, but they wanted to be sure that it was serious first. They wanted to convince themselves, as far as it was possible, that I was, in Libby's phrase, "man enough to handle it." I understood all that. The one thing I didn't understand, and desperately needed to know, was why Sheena had been part of the conspiracy of silence. She had known me through and through, even if her sister and her ex-boyfriend hadn't.

"So tell me," I said to Big Bad Davy, "exactly how it comes about that a nineteen-year-old girl can have a heart attack."

Davy sighed. "Do you know what protein C is?" he asked.

"No," I answered sourly. "I'm only a fucking sociology graduate."

"It's one of the clotting factors in the blood. Do you know what homeostasis is?"

"Feedback," I said. "Like a thermostat. If you're talking about people, it's the control mechanism that regulates body temperature. You get too cold, you shiver to generate heat. You get too hot, you sweat to lose it."

"It's not just temperature," he told me. "All kinds of bodily processes have to be regulated by chemical feedback systems. Blood clotting is one of them. If blood doesn't clot readily enough, you can bleed to death from a trivial cut. If it clots too readily, clots form even when there isn't any damage, and they get stuck—usually in the capillaries in the legs, but sometimes in more dangerous places. A clot in the brain can cause a stroke, a clot in a heart valve can cause heart failure. Nowadays, doctors can treat conditions like haemophilia with clotting factors like thrombin and protein C, and conditions of the opposite kind with warfarin and hirudin, but Sheena's condition wasn't amenable to any kind of continuous therapy. They didn't even know it existed until ten years ago. Her father was one of the first people to be properly diagnosed—posthumously, unfortunately."

"How can you have *both* problems?" I demanded. "It doesn't make sense."

"The level of protein C in the blood is controlled by a feedback mechanism," he said. "Unfortunately, Sheena's father had a bad gene which made a faulty version of the enzyme which is supposed to switch off protein C production when it reaches the right level. It wasn't that the mechanism didn't work at all—just that it was dodgy. Sometimes, his levels went way up, and sometimes they went way down. His children had a fifty-fifty chance of inheriting the dodgy gene, and that's the way it worked out. Libby was clear, Sheena wasn't. They didn't actually have a test for the gene until a couple of years ago, when they finally managed to locate it, but the symptoms were pretty obvious. Given two or three more years of the Human Genome Project, they'll probably be able to sequence the protein and identify the fault in the dodgy version, and that might open up the possibility of finding an effective treatment, but at the time Mrs. Howell and Libby got the diagnosis there was nothing that could be done except treat Sheena's symptoms as and when they appeared, according to type, so . . . "

"So they decided not to tell her," I finished for him, as enlightenment dawned. "Because they didn't want her to know that she was living under a death sentence." And then, as further enlightenment dawned, I said: "Is that why you broke up with her, you bastard? Is that why Libby hesitated over telling *me*?"

"*No!*" he said. "At least, not in the way you think. Okay, I admit, it made a difference when Libby told me. I got scared. Look at me! I'm twice her size. I'd always felt like I was handling precious porcelain—how do you think it made me feel when I was told that a bad bruise could kill her? Maybe I did overdo the carefulness, and maybe she did begin to wonder whether I might be going off her, but that wasn't it. It *wasn't*. We just weren't *right*, except for the music . . . and I knew that if she didn't have time to spare, she shouldn't have to spend it making do. *I didn't dump her.* We just . . . fell apart."

Maybe it was self-justificatory bullshit and maybe it wasn't, but that didn't matter. It had been the right result, after all. Sheena and I had been *right*. If anything was ever meant to be, we'd have been one of the things that was meant to be—but whether we live a million lifetimes or one, nothing is ever really *meant to be*. What isn't pure chance is what you make of the cards you're dealt, and Sheena and I had made the most of each other once chance had thrown us together. No one could have made any more of either of us than we'd made of each other, and there was no use complaining about the unfairness of the ill-luck that had torn us apart. It hadn't been cruel fate, or any god that any human had ever believed in. Life never had been fair, even in Atlantis or Arcadia.

I couldn't blame Davy. I certainly couldn't hold it against him that he hadn't told me what Libby and Mrs. Howell wouldn't, and I couldn't even rail at him for not having told Sheena—because I knew that even if she hadn't heard the ugly clinical details, Sheena *had* known everything she actually needed to know. She'd always known, even if she'd never raised it to consciousness or connected it to her absent father's premature demise, that she was living in mortal danger. Why else would she have been so implacably determined to get in touch with her past selves, to cram a thousand lifetimes into one horribly narrow span?

I had helped. I had to cling to that. I had helped.

The funeral was absolute hell. The crematorium was sterile, the reality of the process carefully hidden by velvet curtains and passionless smiles, but it was even worse at the house, afterwards. Libby and her mother kept giving me books, pictures, CDs, and tapes, saying: "I think she'd have wanted *you* to have these." She probably would have, but that didn't make it any easier standing beside a chair piled high with the obscene loot of her brief life. Davy had already given me a dozen spare tapes and had promised me faithfully that when the CD came off the presses I'd get the very first copy.

On the other hand, I certainly wasn't going to turn anything down that had anything of Sheena in it, even if it were just a secondhand paperback whose pages had been turned by her black-painted fingernails.

I couldn't eat anything, and the tea was vile as well as weak. It wouldn't have tasted any better even if I hadn't still been nursing the remains of the previous night's hangover.

After hell, it was back to purgatory again when I turned up for work. A dreadful hush seemed to have descended on the call centre, and the muted ringing tones of the multitudinous phones were transmuted by the lack of competition into a sinister symphony.

I got seven invitations to go out with the girls, and seven assurances that they'd behave themselves if I did. I believed them. They'd have sat quietly in a corner, with me in the middle, sipping their drinks. Although they'd all have made themselves available, just in case I needed further comfort, they would have done so with unprecedented discretion and sensitivity.

I said no seven times, very politely. Only five of them went on to say: "Well, if you need to talk . . ."

I didn't. I needed to listen.

I played the tapes over and over, and when Davy arrived to make me a present of the newly cut CD—from which "Graveyard Love" had been sensitively omitted, although Byron's kiss-and-sting was still there—I played it over and over and over. I wanted to be free, of myself, but hearing Sheena sing those words, far less plaintively than seemed warranted, didn't do the trick. I wasn't free, especially of myself, even though my true self was invisible. Every time I looked into a mirror, I saw nothing but emptiness.

Davy told me that the songs on the CD were the best of her work as well as the best of his, but they weren't. They weren't even the *rest* of her work, left over when body and soul had fled, because I knew full well—although I could hardly confide the truth to anyone else—that her soul hadn't fled at all.

Sheena was a vampire, and she knew how to remain disembodied. She was in no hurry to be reborn, because she understood well enough how much future remained for serial embodiment. The Earth had existed for four billion years, while humankind had been around for a mere million; it would exist for four billion more, and humankind stood a better than even chance of seeing far more than a million of that, provided that the next falling asteroid was no bigger than the one that had drowned Atlantis and scoured its relics from the soil of Malta. She didn't need to rush for her own sake, and she knew that I needed her to linger. If she had wanted to be free of herself when she wrote that song, she didn't want it now. She had met me in the interim. Now she wanted to kiss and sting in an emergent world, reeking and damp from out of the slime. Now she had a reason to remain, suspended between death and life.

I played the songs over and over regardless of the fact that their message was out of date, because I knew that music as the purest magic of all as well as the greatest mystery, and I needed magic. I needed to go way beyond *sense*, into the supernatural.

I needed the music to take everything out of me that wasn't just waste, because there was so much in me that *was* just waste, and I couldn't bear it.

Sheena had been right when she told me that the only way to get a true appreciation of what it means to be alive is to have died a thousand times, and I knew that I didn't have that true appreciation. She had been right to tell me that until I'd lived and lost a million joyful moments, I wouldn't realise how precious they were. And above all, she was right to tell me that once I'd had the even briefest glimpse of other worlds, this one would never be enough.

I knew that I had only to attract the right kind of night visitor, and feed her, to make the connection I needed, to find the muse who would teach me the art of living in a shattered and shambolic world.

Every night, I opened a vein in my forearm in order that Sheena could feed. It wasn't strictly necessary, given that she could install herself readily enough within the chambers of my heart, but I wanted her beside me as well as inside me. I wanted to make an offering, an honest libation. I always had to lick the remaining blood away, as if I were a vampire castaway on some desert island, driven to desperate measures in the hope of sustaining myself till rescue came, but the nourishment it provided me was meagre by comparison with the need it filled in her. For her, vampirism wasn't a matter of sinking pints the way lads sup ale. She could leech the blood out of my veins, the marrow out of my bones, the elixir of life out of my very soul, without requiring the delicate touch of her purple-stained lips or the hypnotic gaze of her neutron-star eyes—but she needed the gift, the demonstration of my love.

I tried my utmost to remember Atlantis and Arcadia, or even to dream of them, but I couldn't. I could have made things up, of course, but I didn't. Fiction is all about contriving happy endings in a world where the only real endings are fire and the grave, but real comfort has to be found and not contrived, and if the supernatural is the only place where real comfort can be

found, that's where you have to look for it. If you also find
nightmares there, that's the price you have to pay.

I paid.

You can't just *make things up*. You have to *find* what you
need, even if that makes you a puppet in the hands of your own
creation. I knew where to look. I knew how. I paid the price. But
I couldn't remember. I couldn't even dream. I had to be content
with cutting myself, and watching the blood flow down my
arm, clotting with minutely judged alacrity, neither too quickly
nor too slowly.

There was always time for Sheena to drink her fill, and she
never took too much. She knew the value of extravagance, but
she knew the value of economy, too. Her spirit had none of the
inbuilt irresponsibility of her body and her blood. She was a
vampire—and how!

I talked to her, of course. Oh, how I talked! But I didn't talk
about Atlantis or Arcadia, because she no longer needed my
help to recall her past lives. The wandering soul remembers
everything. Even Plato, who really didn't know the first thing
about Atlantis, knew that. I talked to her about the future, because the future was unmade, and the future was where we'd
meet again, if we ever did.

"In the future," I told her, "all things are possible. In the future, our descendants will learn to see those two lost colours all
over again, and they'll find out how to sing again, in all the languages that ever were or ever will be, in true harmony. It won't
always be like that, of course, because the course of progress
never runs smoothly, and there'll be dark days when civilization
all but vanishes and even vampires starve, but as long as the sun
shines there'll be new dawns, and because light sustains life, it
also, in the ultimate analysis, sustains all the forms of undeath,
even the photophobic ones. In time, of course, the sun will begin
to fade, reddening as it ages, always reaching for that *other*
colour which is the better part of the colour of blood. In the
end, that colour will be all that's left, and even that will fade as
the sun shrinks and dies, until there's nothing left of it but the
black hole at its core and a surrounding chaos of strange ener-

gies. With luck, my love, you'll survive even that; in four billion years even humans ought to be able to reach the stars, and the undead will surely lead the way."

She didn't answer, but I didn't really expect her to. After all, her voice was the one part of her that I still had in superabundance, and it was always there, filling the space between me and the walls.

I want to be free, of myself, of myself,
I want to be free, of myself.

I didn't really need her voice, although I was very glad to have it, and in such abundance. In the final analysis, I needed only her thirst. It would have been better if I'd been able to remember, or even to dream, but life isn't fair, and you have to play the cards you're dealt to the best of your ability. All I could give her was blood, and for that, she wasn't obliged to be a generous muse.

But still, *I had her thirst.*

I knew she was there every time I cut myself. She was there the rest of the time, too, day and night. She was with me when I slept, no matter how dark and bleak my dreaming was, and she was with me when I went to work, to play the puppet in my best telephone manner, always speaking softly and always following the script with minute precision. She was with me in the Headrow and Harehills Lane, at the Merrion Centre and Elland Road . . . but when I cut myself, I *knew* she was there, because I knew exactly how thirsty she was, and exactly what she needed to satisfy her thirst.

She'd have done as much for me.

In another life, she already had, even though it set her free upon the tides of time, incapable for a little while of anything but drifting. I'd lost her then, but I didn't have to lose her this time around, and I didn't.

I clung on, and I clung hard.

The more blood I shed, and the more I consumed, the greater the change in me became, but I didn't become the kind of vampire she had been. She'd never promised me that. All she'd promised me was that I would be changed, and changed forever, and I was.

In a way, it might have been easier to become a shadow of my former self, to pine away and die of a broken heart, but I didn't have a broken heart. My heart was healthy—a fit abode for the sickliest of disembodied vampire spirits—and I didn't want to be a shadow while I still had blood to feed a shadow's thirst.

Sheena had needed me while she was alive, because nobody else could give her what she needed then, and she needed me just as much now that she was dead, because mine was the blood that she wanted more than any other. When her body had been more than ash and dust, it had been my body that she had needed to give her comfort, and now that there was nothing left of her flesh but ash and dust, it was my blood that she needed *for comfort*. Any body might have done for warmth, and any blood might have slaked her thirst, but *for comfort*, it had to be my blood, exactly as it had to be my body. I offered it, as a testament of love.

It was for comfort, too, that I needed her. For me, nobody else would have sufficed, even for warmth—but what I needed her for most urgently and most ardently was comfort. That was why I cut myself, night after night after night, to feed her and to try—crudely and hopelessly—to feed myself. She was always satisfied, but I never was. I continued to thirst, because no matter how much I had changed, I wasn't the kind of vampire who could sustain myself on a desert island, with none but a ghostly spirit for company.

"Life goes on, love," Mum said—and she was absolutely right. She had no idea how right she was. Life does go on, but that doesn't mean that it doesn't hurt.

"It could have been either of us," Libby told me, once when she came to the flat to see how I was doing. "It could have been both, or neither. It could have been me and not her. Maybe it should have been. I was the older one, after all. If I said I wished I could trade places with her, I'd be a liar, but maybe that's the way it should have been."

"No," I said, in my best telephone manner. "It shouldn't. You couldn't have handled it the way Sheena handled it."

"We never even talked about it," she went on. "That was absolutely the worst thing about not telling her. We never talked about it. It's almost as if we weren't sisters at all."

"It doesn't matter," I assured her. "She knew what she needed to know. She said what she needed to say. She heard what she needed to hear."

"From you," she said. "What did I ever give her, apart from that stupid name?"

"It was what she needed," I pointed out. "If it hadn't been, she wouldn't have taken it."

Libby went away happy that we'd shared a few confidences, genuinely pleased that I was bearing up and doing well. She didn't offer me any more than her good wishes because she was being loyal to her little sister. She knew, even though she'd never be able to say so, that Sheena wasn't entirely gone. She might even have known what Sheena was, even though she couldn't actually *believe* in ghosts, let alone in vampires. Working in Gap and living at home had fixated her mind on superficial things. Her mother was like my mother, full of common sense and well-tried saws. I never heard Mrs. Howell say, "Life goes on, love," but I expect she did, even when there was no one in the room to hear her.

The first person to see my scars—inevitably, I suppose—was Mum, but she didn't see them for what they were. "What *have* you been doing, love?" she asked. I could have told her that I'd been out collecting blackberries and she'd have believed it, but what I actually said was a far more blatant lie, even though it was nearer to the truth.

"I've had them for ages," I said. "They'll be fine, as long as I never get scurvy. Collagen dissolves when you get scurvy, apparently, and the wounds open up."

"You and your books," she said—which was a tamer version of *fucking sociology graduate*. I kept drinking the orange juice, though. I didn't want to start coming apart at the seams.

They say that time heals, but it doesn't. At best, time scars, and there's no orange juice for the soul that will keep you safe from those occasional moments of spiritual scurvy when the scars break down and everything pours out. Even though I couldn't remember, or even dream, I still had those nightmare moments when everything seemed to fall apart and it felt as if all the blood was flooding out of me at once, inviting every supernatural carrion drinker for miles to fall upon me like a flock of crows. The flock was sometimes so dense that my own guardian vampire had no chance to defend her territory—but such moments did pass as my spiritual clotting factors cut in, never more than a little too late.

I always got through the night, ready to return to puppet life in Phoneland, where even the harpies still touched me tenderly and the gorgons looked at me with naked pity.

"Actually," I confided to Jez one night in the Countess of Cromartie, when I finally allowed him to bully me into letting him buy me a pint of bitter, "life doesn't go on. We begin to die as soon as we begin to live. It's death that whittles the embryo into human shape, death that clears out all the cellular compost day by day, as life takes its toll. Life doesn't go on at all—it just flows away, bit by bit, emptying us out even though we were never really full."

"Yeah," he said wisely. "Too bloody right. That's why you have to make the most of what you've got. Fight it, mate. You might lose, but you've got to fight." He couldn't quite see that that was exactly what I was doing, far more cleverly than he could know. At least he had the grace to refrain from making observations about the number of pebbles on the beach or fish in the sea. He'd been out with the girls too many times to be under any delusions about any fuck being a good fuck. He didn't know enough to envy me what I now had, but he knew enough to envy me what I'd had before.

"She was a grand lass," he said. "A bit strange, but who can blame her? We take our health too much for granted."

"Yes, she was," I said. "And yes we do. Do you mind if I don't get another round in—no offence, but I think I'd rather be at home."

"No, mate," he said. "Another time, eh?"

"Another time," I echoed. That was where I was headed. I didn't necessarily expect to get there that night, but I intended to travel hopefully. Contrary to proverbial wisdom, it's far better actually to arrive, but the momentum of hopeful travelling does have its own compensations.

When I got back to the flat, I made myself eat. I had to "keep my strength up," as Mum would have put it. I peeled and chipped my own potatoes, although the processed peas came out of a tin. It had been a while since I'd been to the supermarket and the skinless sausages were a couple of days past their sell-by date, but I knew it didn't matter. English sausages have so much preservative in them that they keep for at least a week after they've supposedly given up the ghost—it's one of the nation's finest traditions.

While I ate I put on the CD Davy had given me, and filled the flat with Sheena's voice. Afterwards, I put it on again, and then again. I wasn't always that obsessive; some nights I didn't play it at all, preferring other items from what had been Sheena's Gothic rock collection and was now—thanks to the generosity of Libby and Mrs. Howell—mine. Listening to the Fields of the Nephilim's *Elizium* or Dreadful Shadows performing "Sea of Tears" or anything at all by Sopor Aeternus brought back tender memories of listening with Sheena as well as creating an appropriately heartaching mood. Most nights, though, I arrived home without having been sidetracked, and there was something about drinking in a pub with Jez that smacked ever so slightly of betrayal, so I felt that I needed to mainline the real thing, to go directly to the source. I had mixed feelings now about Davy's decision to omit "Graveyard Love" from the album, because I had begun to think of that as the most prophetic and deeply felt of all Sheena's non-Byronic lyrics.

Eventually, I put the kettle on to boil. Then I got the kitchen devil from the drawer and used the jet of vapour gushing from the kettle's spout to sterilise the blade. It wasn't for my own sake that I was frightened of infection, but I needed to preserve the purity of my blood.

The inner surface of my left forearm already had too many scars crisscrossing it, and the outer part was far too hairy, and I wasn't sure I could make a neat enough cut with the blade in my left hand, so I took off my shirt before sitting down on the bed. There were hairs on my chest too, but they were mostly above nipple-level and I was pretty sure that I could draw a good line across my heart if only I could figure out exactly where it was hiding behind my rib cage.

By this time I'd read enough about the circulation of the blood to know that Sheena had been right and I had been wrong about the pulmonary vein, but I didn't intend to cut that deep. Freshly oxygenated blood is undoubtedly the best kind—the vampire's champagne—but as soon as you open up the meanest, bluest vein the outflow sucks life from the air and becomes pure scarlet, pure intoxication.

When I'd made the cut I lay back, closed my eyes, and listened. One day, I knew, I'd be able to lie back like that and keep on going: falling through the space-time continuum, across the fragile borderlands that separate our own universe from all the parallel alternatives, not merely to Arcadia and Atlantis but to venues even more exotic.

But not yet.

For the time being, I was still an amateur, still a hopeful fellow traveller, not yet an initiate into the brotherhood and sisterhood of blood. For the time being, I stood in need of guidance, of education, of moulding—but that, at least, I already had. I had the best teacher in the world, perhaps the best in all the worlds.

Although I could always hear and feel her, I didn't often see her—but that night I did. That night, she came to me *vividly*, in all her posthumous glory. Her face was pale but her lips were purple and her black hair shone as it tumbled vibrantly about her shoulders. She was dressed for the grave, in a shroud that had once been white, but the night had infected the filmy fabric, filling it with darkness and the stars.

The lust in her eyes was limitless, but when she settled upon me and lowered her head to feed she was as light as a cloud and as dainty as a moth.

When I first threw my arms around her, I hardly dared to hug her, for fear that she would break or dissolve into mist, but I felt the thrill in her flesh as she lapped the blood from the horizontal well, and I felt the force of her caresses, as she ran her delicate fingers over my face and my neck, my hips and my thighs.

When we kissed, she nipped my lip between her teeth to prove that I wasn't dreaming. I needed the reassurance, because I needed to know that the ecstasy was real and not just a product of my wishful mind. Sheena had assured me that even the everyday was supernatural, and we'd had our moments of ecstasy while she was still imperfectly incarnate, but the supernatural is at its best when it's bold and blatant, and ecstasy achieves its greatest heights when it's properly unfettered. To get the best from a vampire lover, you have to do more than dream. You have to overcome your fear of true commitment.

When I came, Sheena absorbed the milky fluid as easily as she'd absorbed the rich claret that flowed from the gash beneath my nipple.

It's traditional for supernatural visitors to prove their reality by leaving behind some physical token of their presence, and Sheena did that, too, but it was the substance that she took to nourish her own fugitive solidity that provided the firmer proof to me. It didn't make sense, but I knew that she was way beyond sense now, as truly supernatural as any creature that had ever defied the crippling demands of mortality.

She had always been a vampire, but I never had before. The final proof of the preciousness of our love would be the future we would share, once we were united in nature and in purpose.

When she had had her fill of me, she lingered, as only the most loving vampire can or will. She let me run my hands over her body and look into her fabulous eyes. As I looked, it seemed to me that I could see *through* her eyes, into the dark essence of her emotion and intelligence, where her lust for blood, life, and eternity was manifest in the tortured energies swirling around the event horizon of her appetites. The display was alight not merely with all the colours of the Atlantean rainbow but with others not yet manifest in any of the lives that she and I had lived.

One day, I know, we'll find the identities that would allow us to perceive those colours, and more besides.

That night, with all my heart, I wanted to be free, especially of myself—but I knew that the kind of freedom I wanted was the kind that had to be won, and that the winning of it wouldn't be easy.

Silence fell while we held each other, but it didn't break the spell. Sheena still lay upon me, her head cradled on my shoulder, the weight of her slender torso pressed against my heart, and her legs parted to either side of my lumpen thighs. She was so very peaceful, now that she had fed, that I could have rolled us over and pinned her down, and threatened to detain her until morning, but she would have laughed at me, because vampires can't be caught like that.

"There's no hurry," she whispered when she caught the stray thought. "We have all the time in the world."

I know that—but sometimes it's hard to be patient. Sometimes, when you hold a vampire lover in your arms, you want it to go on—if not forever, at least until the sun comes up. But vampires are definitely creatures of the night, even though the notion that they crumble to dust in sunlight is something the movies made up to provide their tall tales with some sort of closure.

"When will I see you again?" I asked, although I knew she wouldn't give me a specific answer.

"Another time," she said.

That's where I'm headed, for now and always.

I truly believe that I'll get there. I'm changed and I'm changing, and it's only a matter of feeding the muse until she forgives me for the time it took to see her for what she really is, and to understand what I really am, even if I'll never be able to see it in a mirror.

The inhabitants of other times saw more in light than we can see, and they heard more in music than we can hear. There's not much we can do to compensate for that, but we should all do what we can. We can all try our utmost not to think the way other people think, not to do the things other people do, not to like the things that other people like, and not to want the things that other people want. We can all feed the creatures of the night, and hope that whichever of them deigns to accept our loving offerings will eventually set us free, in one or another of the nine secret ways that only muses know.

Sheena told me her secret even before she died: that the only way to get a true appreciation of what it means to be alive is to die a thousand times. Until I've lived and lost a million joyful moments, I can't begin to know what such moments are really worth—and that's not the kind of task you can rush.

I'm working on it, but I know that even with her to help me, it'll take a lot longer than a single lifetime.

Another time?

If only.

GLOSSARY OF LOCAL AND
OTHER ESOTERIC TERMS

arse: the English word mistranscribed by Americans as "ass" (in the non-Biblical sense).

civvies: military slang for civilian dress.

Dr Smith's Classical Dictionary: an invaluable reference book compiled in Victorian times by William Smith, D.C.L., L.L.D.

Dry Blackthorn: one of the two brands of dry cider commonly available on draught in English pubs.

ferret, slip the: penetrate sexually (by analogy with the sportsman who inserts a ferret into a rabbit hole in order to expel the rabbits from their warren; the word "cunt" comes from the old English term for rabbit—although "cunny" is nowadays rendered in script as "coney" and pronounced, euphemistically, as if it did not rhyme with "honey," while the similarly euphemistic "bunny" has been consigned to the use of children).

Gap: a chain of clothing merchants whose products are aimed at young people.

Headrow, The: the main street of Leeds, site of the Town Hall, the Central Library, and numerous imposing lampposts.

hen party: the female equivalent of a stag party, in which "friends" of a bride-to-be get her roaring drunk and play vicious practical jokes; because female imitations of lad culture (qv) tend to be a little less vindictive, a hen party's worst excesses of violence and calculated humiliation tend to be visited upon innocent bystanders (e.g., male strippers) rather than upon the bride-to-be herself.

Jez: although "Jez" is used in the south of England as a contraction of Jeremy, Jeremys are very rare in Yorkshire; the likelihood is that the Jez in the story was actually christened Jesse but employs the harder pronunciation because Yorkshire slang tends to equate a "Jessie" with "a big girl's blouse" (i.e., an effeminate male).

lad culture: an aspect of the male backlash against feminism that became well established in Britain in the 1990s, encouraged and sustained by such popular magazines as *Loaded*; it renews and magnifies the pride taken by young males in their love of association football, their capacity for bitter ale and their deep-seated fear of all things feminine, while simultaneously (and perhaps paradoxically) converting them into helpless fashion victims.

lavvy: a contraction of "lavatory" widely employed in regions of England where the word "toilet" is considered to be too Frenchified for polite use.

letter, French: a slag term for a condom, used by people who consider themselves too posh to say "Johnny."

M1: the motorway connecting Leeds to London.

naff: somewhat lacking in good taste, and therefore seriously uncool.

New Labour: After nineteen years of Conservative government the Labour party finally won a British general election in 1998, having rebranded its ideology and policies as "New

Labour"—i.e., indistinguishable from those of the Conservative party.

Peel, John: a long-serving Liverpudlian radio disc jockey, held in such affectionate esteem by people who were young in the 1960s that he has now become a curious national institution.

piss, taking the: holding someone or something up to ridicule.

pull-a-pig contest: an alleged ritual of British lad culture (qv) in which a group of young men in a pub or nightclub place bets as to which of them can find, take home, and have sexual intercourse with the ugliest woman. Proof has to be provided in the form of Polaroid photographs, preferably displaying the unclad victims in supposedly hilarious, compromising positions, which may be submitted to an unbiased referee in order to determine who scoops the pool.

Redondan Cultural Foundation Newsletter, The: a periodical devoted to the affairs of the Kingdom of Redonda, a loose-knit literary society created by M. P. Shiel (who was taken to the eponymous uninhabited rock near Montserrat in his youth and crowned king thereof by his father). Royal Redondan Naval Reserve T-shirts are, however, an American product.

slag: a derogatory term for a sexually active woman.

striker: an attacking player in association football whose job is scoring goals.

Strongbow: the other brand of dry cider commonly available on draught in English pubs.

sweeper: a defensive player in association football who never strays far enough into the other team's half to get scoring chances.

Tesco: a supermarket chain.

United: in Leeds, the association football club Leeds United; as noted by the narrator, the term has different referents in Manchester, Sheffield, and Dundee (not to mention Newcastle and Carlisle). The Leeds United stadium is in Elland Road, on the opposite side of the road from the only greyhound racing stadium in England whose track is so narrow that there is only room for five dogs to race on it, instead of the usual six.

You learn something new every day: a popular English cliché, which probably holds true only for people who take the trouble to read glossaries.

S. P. Somtow

Vanilla Blood

IN A PROFESSION *filled with colorful authors,* S. P. SOMTOW *is one of the most colorful. Born in Bangkok and related to the royal family of Thailand, he has written many highly regarded fantasies and works of science fiction, notably* Vampire Junction, The Pavilion of Frozen Women, Starship and Haiku, Mallworld, *and* Light on the Sound. *He is also a musical prodigy who has conducted several of the world's orchestras, and is an avant-garde composer whose music has been performed in more than a dozen countries on four continents. Now if you've been keeping count, it's been a close race in* The Vampire Sextette *between sympathetic and diabolical vampires. "Vanilla Blood" closes the tally with some particularly nasty bloodsuckers!*

WELL, THEN. We might as well begin in the middle. Because the beginning has been done to death, hasn't it? The discovery of the bodies, the cross-country chase, even the allegations of police brutality . . . you've seen it on CNN. *60 Minutes. 20/20. Hard Copy.* Graphic detail. You saw it all.

You saw her face. Pale as Ophelia in the bathtub of blood. The half-formed smile. The eyes, wide, emerald green, the soggy blonde hair that wound about the corpse like a seaweed garnish; the skin, luminescent, of a piece with the porcelain she lay in; naked, of course, but they didn't show that on TV. If you were lucky, you caught the nudity when the camera lingered on the photos that first day on Court TV, marking the exhibits one by one, starting with the crime-scene photographs.

You saw it; we can dispense with it.

You saw the perp on the cover of *Newsweek*. How young he looked! Anyone's kid, really—a nice southern boy. Tried as an adult? You didn't really want to agree with the prosecutors— he seemed so good-looking, so vulnerable, so . . . in need of a friendly social worker. Stared right through the camera and into your eyes . . . and into your heart.

Even the Pope sent a letter. As if that would have done much good here, right in the heart of Catholic-hating Klan country.

And then there was the lawyer. Pro bono, of course. A man who had been on every dream team in every high-profile trial in the last ten years. A talking head on Court TV. Once rendered Pat Buchanan speechless on *Crossfire*. He, too, had made the cover of *Newsweek*. But that was the "Superlawyers" cover story last year.

The prosecutor. An ice queen. Considered more robot than human . . . at least until Flynt released the nude pics. You know this. You've spent whole watercooler breaks discussing her anatomy. Oh, yes, she was a natural redhead all right. Unless, of course, she had taken the trouble to dye . . . down there.

What a bitch! But an appealing one.

And the judge. He fumbled his way through the last big one, an eighteen-month soap opera of celebrity murder, money, and sex. Now he had learned his lesson, and he was breathing fire, not taking any shit.

You are familiar with all these figures, I'm sure—there aren't many people in America who aren't. The *Saturday Night Live* parody alone said more than this brief memoir ever could.

So, instead, we'll start in the middle . . . just seconds after Judge Trepte kicked the cameras out of the courtroom.

We'll even go so far as to begin in the middle of a sentence.

—gone yet? Good, good.

—Sir? Get that thing out of my courtroom. Thank you. All the way out. When I kick out the cameras, sir, I kick out the cameras; I don't mean to have them lurking about in the ante-room. I mean, out, out, *out*.

—But, Your Honor, we've paid generously for the broadcast rights to—all right, Your Honor. Yes, sir. Good-bye, sir. Thank you, sir.

. . .

—and now, Counselor, you will reveal to this court exactly why your next witness is arriving in so remarkable a fashion.

—He always travels this way, Your Honor.

—Objection! The defense is attempting to offer a *corpse* as a defense witness!

—You must admit, Counselor, that the prosecution does have a point.

—He's not exactly *dead*, Your Honor. He just travels this way.

—In a *coffin*.

—Yes, Your Honor.

—Well, I'll be damned. Strike that. I think you will all agree that I made the right call in getting rid of the press. We can all relax now and get to the bottom of this nonsense, without getting yet *another* lead story on the *CBS Evening News*. Miss Anderson, strike all that—all of it. This is not going to be a trial for the TV trial junkies. No. This is life and death . . . some would add even undeath. Don't expect me to run this courtroom like Judge Itoh. More like Judge Dredd. Strike that, too, Miss Anderson, strike, strike, strike, strike, strike. Now I'll stop pontificating and turn things over to you overpaid lawyers.

—The prosecution continues to object, Your Honor.

—Sustained.

—Your Honor, we cannot present this case without this witness's testimony.

—Then I will reconsider the objection when the witness deigns to get out of the coffin.

—He can't yet, Your Honor. But I believe he will be able to in about five minutes . . .

—Five minutes you may have. The court will recess for five minutes . . . no, let's say ten. Some of us still smoke.

. . .

—Well, Counselor?

—I don't understand it, Your Honor, but the witness doesn't appear to have stirred.

—Does the defense counsel propose to attempt to resuscitate the witness? We do have paramedics on call, do we not? Or will smelling salts do the trick?

—Your Honor, this has gone on far enough. Defense's sense of the theatrical is a little ill-timed, don't you think? I mean, they defend a few big-name actors, they think they're Perry Mason. Can I continue to state my objection?

—Your objection stands. Bring on your next witness, Counselor.

—We confess, Your Honor, we're sort of at a loss. In view of the apparent immobility of our star witness, we'd like to . . . ah . . . may I look at my notes? . . . Jeremy Kindred. Yes. He's on the list.

—Very well.

—State your name for the record.

—Jeremy William Kindred.

—How old are you, Jeremy?

—I'm . . . I don't know exactly. Fifteen, sixteen.

—Are you a vampire?

—Yes.

—Are you a member of the group variously known as the Brotherhood of Blood, the Cult, the Vampire Society?

—I was, sir.

—You were?

—I was for a while, sir, but it was just what you'd call peer pressure, and no sir, I didn't kill nobody, didn't drink nobody's blood.

—Just answer the question, young man.

—Uh, sure, Your Honor.

—Tell us about it . . . in your own words, if you'd like.

—Objection! This is all irrelevant. The witness wasn't even *at* the killing. He's just wasting the jury's time.

—I think it's important to my case, Your Honor, that we

clearly illustrate the circumstances under which these kids could come to believe that these crimes were not only acceptable, but desirable.

—Listen. The cameras are off, Counselors. There's no more need for posturing. The jury is going to zone out completely unless you entertain them with a good story. So, kid, let's have it.

—Uh . . .

—You may proceed, Jeremy.

—Well, sir, I really joined it for the sex. I mean, there was a rumor that the Brotherhood had these orgies in the old Hanson house.

—That's an abandoned house?

—Yes, sir, by the cemetery. I don't know why it ain't been tore down yet; it's kinda an eyesore. It's condemned, though. I always used to walk past it on my way to school. It's a big old place, creaky doors, peeling paint, scary statues of devils with leathery wings . . . and the big angel with the bronze sword . . . not shiny anymore, green mostly . . . not since the ringleaders of the Brotherhood was all put in jail. But that used to be the weirdest thing about that place. It was all crumbling and dirty except for that sword. That tall angel stood next to them wrought-iron gates and it held its sword high in the air and the sword was all polished . . . and you know, walking to school in winter, with the sun just rising, you could of swore that thing was on fire. The way it caught the sunlight. So the kids called it the Flaming Sword, like the preacher says about the Angel of Death. Anyways . . . there was this rumor that someone had wild parties there . . . you might call them raves, I guess . . . lotta E, lotta dope, lotta loose wenches, if you know what I mean. So when Cat Sperling kept looking at me from the other end of the hall, she was a senior and all, with tits like balloons, you could say I was interested. Everyone knew that Cat had something to do with them parties. And everyone wanted that bitch, shit, even the girls wanted her. But there's something weird about her that you need to know. It wasn't no big Hollywood special-effect kinda thing but . . . she carried the night around with her . . .

—Could you explain that a little more clearly, Jeremy? Take your time.

—Well, sir, it didn't matter if the sun was out, or if all the lights was on inside that school room. She always had like a shadow on her. Her skin was real pale, and it glimmered . . . well, like the moon was shining . . . but just on her, you understand, just on her. There was a silvery thing about her eyes, too . . . you know like when you're in the woods all alone at night and you catch the moonlight dancing amongst the leaves . . . you catch my drift, sir?

—You're saying she was attractive. She had a unique look. Some kind of makeup, perhaps.

—Yeah well, it was like on no infomercial about pearly essence face cream . . . a lotta girls use that shit . . . she was different. It was like she was the real thing, and the others were all just imitating her. Did I tell you about the black hair? It was long, all the way to her waist. And she wore black lipstick. It matched.

—A Goth, then.

—More than that. Like I said. Not a wanna-be. The real thing.

—Objection, Your Honor, I fail to see how this catalog of feminine charms has any relevance whatsoever to the defense's case!

—Stop posturing, Counselor. I've sent away the cameras; and the jury looks awake for the first time since this sorry spectacle began. I'm going to allow it. You may proceed, Mr. Kindred.

—Just tell the story in your own words, Jeremy.

—Well, I still think he's fishing, Your Honor.

—I've already overruled your objection.

—Jeremy?

—Yes sir. Cat Sperling, sir.

—Cat Sperling let you know, through some kind of sign language or eye contact, that she had something to discuss with you.

—Not exactly, sir.

—What did she let you know?

—She wanted to fuck me, sir.

—Watch your language, young man! Try to act in a manner consistent with the dignity and majesty of the law—what's left of it!

—I'm sorry, Your Honor; I don't know no other word for what she was trying to say.

—Very well, then. The court will take into account the deprived environment you clearly come from.

—I ain't no trailer trash, Your Honor!

—Quite so, young man, quite so. Why don't you finish telling your story to the court?

—Sure, Your Honor. Like I said, I got the Look from her. There ain't no mistaking the Look, sir. From all the way across the hall, and I knew she wanted me. Well, so there's a place you go to when you give someone the Look . . . at least that's how it works at Edward Kramer High. The place is up on a hill, you know, the hill just north of the cemetery. There's a road that winds up, and a hiking trail as well. At Kramer, we don't need to pass notes; it's a tradition; you get the Look, and if you give the Look back, then you go meet on the hill. If you hold up one finger, it means *tonight*; two fingers means we'll set a time later. Well, Cat held up one finger; everyone saw it, even if they didn't say nothing; Kramer ain't a kiss-and-tell kind of a school.

—It's an ancient tradition, then.

—I'd say so, sir.

—One that your parents would know about. That even a few members of this jury may well have experienced, if they happened to have gone to your high school.

—Did Cat Sperling meet you on the hill that night?

—Yes, sir.

—Did she then proceed to initiate you into the Brotherhood of Blood?

—Oh, no, sir. You can't get in just like that.

—Tell the court what happened, Jeremy.

—Well, that night, I went up to the hill. I borrowed my

mom's Malibu. I don't have a license, but you said I'd have immunity, right?

—This is a multiple-murder case, Jeremy. I don't think the court is too worried about your license.

—Okay, okay. Well, she was waiting there all right. She was every bit as enticing as the rumors said. It was windy and her hair was flying every which way . . . and catching the moonlight. She leaned against a tree with a joint in one hand . . . I can say that, can't I? . . . and her eyes were wild. I couldn't believe my luck. I mean, to tell you the truth, I'd never done it before. Unless you count, one time, in summer camp—

—That's all right, Jeremy. I don't think the court needs an exegesis of your sexual experiences.

—Okay. So she says to me, Jeremy Kindred, I've had my eye on you. You're a good-looking kid. And I says, Yeah, they say that. I'm tall for my age, almost six feet already. And she says, You got that unplucked look. Like a glistening round apple in a tree . . . a fresh smell, apple-scented shampoo maybe, a little-kid smell in a big-kid body . . . and I know how much you want me, seen how you stare at me—across the hallway or last week when we had that big assembly with the Yankee AIDS speaker. Here, take a drag of this, it'll relax you; I know your heart's pounding, boy. Really pull on it, hard, I mean hard. Come closer. You always wanted to touch them, didn't you? Here. Put your hand on them. Through the sweater for now, I ain't no whore . . . I know you like it, Jeremy Kindred. So well, I felt them titties, and they were fine. Firmer than I thought they'd be. Fairly straining against the wool they was. Got a rise out of me, lemme tell you. It was something to be alone on the hill with Cat Sperling. It sure turned my head. I didn't even think nothing of it when she asked for a drop of blood.

—So let me get this straight, Jeremy. This woman, this older woman—

—She won't but three years older than me, sir, if that!—

—Well, for the sake of argument, a slightly older and certainly much more sophisticated woman . . . lures you to a well-known trysting spot . . . gets you all hot and bothered . . . and suddenly asks to drink your blood?

—She didn't say drink, sir. You're jumping the gun on the story. She just said, Jeremy, you cute-as-a-button boy toy, let me have a drop of blood. The drinking didn't rightly occur to me, not at that moment . . . I don't know *what* was occurring to me, really, excepting I wanted to get inside her jeans something fierce. I knew she was a member of that Brotherhood thing, so blood had to figure in it somewhere . . . like swearing blood brotherhood with your best buddy in junior high or something. Well, she asked for a drop of blood, and by now we were in the backseat of the Malibu, I forgot to say that, didn't I? . . . and I was reaching into her jeans . . . it didn't feel down there like I thought it would . . . more leathery . . . and slick . . . like a beat-up old wallet. And she was all, I have a needle here, and I just need a little bit, just a thimbleful would do the trick right fine. And she reached into a back pocket and pulled out a hypodermic. The needle glinted in the moonlight that reflected off the rearview mirror and you know what, it made me mighty hard, more than I'd ever felt before in my life, 'cause I guess there was something dark about it, something forbidden . . . and this was how she did it . . . she yanked my pants down to my knees and kinda crouched down and pushed me up into her, and at the same time she jabbed that needle into my chest, like she was fixing to impale my heart. Well, I can't tell you how that made me feel, I mean, I just about burst right then and there, after being inside of her only a minute . . . and then I thought, well, I'm screwed for sure, because Cat Sperling ain't gonna want a green kid who can't last but a minute inside the famousest pussy in town.

—Your Honor, I simply have to object. I just don't see how this catalog of adolescent fumbling can possibly relate to the defense's case.

—If you'd bear with me for a second, Your Honor, I believe the witness is about to reach a crucial point of evidence in the defense's case . . . the blood.

—All right, Counselor. But if you don't reach some kind of relevance within the next two minutes—

—Jeremy, tell the court about what happened next.

—Well, sir, she didn't seem to pay no mind to the fact that I come inside her. She was only interested in the blood. When she saw that stream of red gushing into that syringe, she started thrashing and heaving and carrying on something fierce. She was all moaning, too . . . and shrieking . . . like a passel of cats in a back alley. I never seen anything like it, sir, and I've watched a lot of pornos. And then she's all shuddering to a climax right there in the backseat of my Malibu. And the blood's dribbling from her lips . . . but it's not a scary thing . . . it's warming her, lighting up her face . . . her cheeks were pale before, but now they're all blushing just a bit. And then she says to me, I want you to join. Join what? I asks her, but I already know what she means. I said, I heard there's a lotta parties, and in them parties you all get down, if you know what I mean. Parties right in the cemetery's what I heard. She smiled. You're coming to the very next one, she says, and it's on Friday the Thirteenth . . . next weekend . . . but it'll probably last until Sunday morning . . . when some of us, the ones that aren't in too deep, who can still stand the vibes, why, we go to church. I'm thinking that it can't be *that* bad if they go to church afterwards. So I say, Sure, I'll come. And she says, Be sure and bring your best friend Jody.

—Who did she mean by that?

—Jody Palmer, my best friend.

—The defendant?

—Yes sir, he sure is.

—I trust the prosecution is now satisfied as to the relevance of this witness?

—We continue to object, Your Honor. All this is fascinating in a prurient sort of way . . . I can see the reporter from CBS in the back there, desperately looking for an opening to demand the cameras back . . . but the fact remains that Jody Palmer killed several people, including his mother . . . and that he's being tried for murder.

—Your Honor, we must have some latitude here. The prosecution's perfectly aware that we're trying to establish that the defendant was under such crippling social and emotional pressure that he believed he no longer had a choice. You must allow the witness to—

—Your Honor! The coffin lid is shaking!

—Well, hold it down, Bailiff!

—I can't! There's something inside . . . struggling to get out!

—Jesus Christ, I forgot daylight savings time! Sunset's an hour later!

—Cut the profanity, Counselor.

—I'm sorry, Your Honor, but—

—I'm fining you a thousand dollars for contempt. Get your checkbook out this minute, Counselor. Bailiff! Control that coffin!

—Blast! The lid's off!

—Well, put it back on.

—It's fighting back! Someone's inside—and he—she—it's trying to sit up!

—Well, restrain him, Bailiff.

—It's a woman, Your Honor . . . a young woman.

—Cat!

—The witness will refrain from speaking unless it is in response to a question from counsel, or from myself.

—Oh. Yes, Your Honor. Yes, sir. I didn't mean to—

—Counsel for the defense . . . you've been referring to this witness in the masculine gender from the beginning. And now that your witness has deigned to emerge from her . . . ah . . . conveyance, she appears to be very, very feminine indeed. Exceptionally so, and flaunting it besides. Do you always instruct your witnesses to appear in court in flimsy negligees? Is this a courtroom or a Frederick's of Hollywood catalogue? For God's sake, madam, cover yourself! Bailiff . . . a cloak for the witness. I won't have the jury distracted by her endowments. In fact, I won't have the jury distracted at all; Counsel, I want an explanation.

—Your Honor, could we have a brief sidebar? This isn't the witness we had in mind for this portion of the testimony. There appears to have been a . . . misunderstanding.

—Oh, Jeremy . . . you sure are a sight! You look real small

and scared and powerless up there in that witness box. But it's okay, baby. Cat's here now. Cat will hold your hand. It's gonna be all right. You didn't do nothing wrong . . . and it's not you that's on trial.

—But Cat . . . you're *dead!* I saw you die!

—Death ain't nothing, baby. Just another kind of doorway. And there's more than one way of going through that doorway . . . you can let them shove you through, and you can let them flush the key down the toilet bowl of eternity . . . or you can wrest that key out of their hand and take it with you . . . so they can't slam the door in your face . . . so you can live forever on the edge of life and death . . . I did it, baby, just like I said I would . . . I did it, baby. Oh, yes, I crossed over, and I crossed back. Just like the Duke said. And you can do it, too. Don't be afraid, Jeremy. Oh, and Mr. Counsel . . . the Duke says he's sorry, but he can't be in court tonight. Something's come up. He sent me instead. I can give all the evidence you need.

—The Duke, as you call him, Miss . . . Sperling, is it? . . . is under subpoena.

—Subpoenas don't work too good on dead people, Mr. Judge. If the Duke wants to come to your court, he'll come; but your laws don't really apply to him. The undead have their own laws. There's nothing in the constitution about them.

—On the contrary, Ms. Sperling. Just because creatures you're calling the *undead* are not specifically mentioned in law doesn't make them outside the law at all. Anyone who is evidently capable of rational discourse and capable of appearing here and making remarks, relevant or otherwise, is a *prima facie* candidate for personhood, and I can damn well hold them in contempt if I so choose!

—Your Honor, the witness is . . . well . . . she's sort of swirling, melting into some kind of mist . . . and now there's a black cat running around the courtroom . . . it doesn't seem very friendly, sir . . . in fact, it's got poor Mrs. Coates trying to climb up one of the pillars . . . it could be rabid, Your Honor.

—Shoot the critter! I won't have any more disruptions!

—Sir, the cat appears to have leapt out of the window.

—That's four stories, Bailiff! Surely even a *cat* can't leap four stories and survive . . . now what? It's flying into the night? You see great leathern wings against the face of the full moon, Bailiff? Is this *Batman* or is it a court of law? Put that camera away, Mr. Prinze, or I'm kicking CNN out completely. And I'm hereby instructing the jury to ignore all of this—the woman climbing out of the coffin, the soap-opera dialogue between Ms. Sperling and the witness, the bizarre metamorphosis from female to feline, *and* Mrs. Coates's screams. None of this ever happened, do you hear? *None of it!*

—Your Honor . . .

—What is it now, Counselor? My patience is wearing pretty thin.

—In view of the fact that we have let the wrong . . . ah, cat out of the bag, and in view of the fact that the witness currently on the stand hasn't yet completed his testimony . . .

—Quite, quite, Counselor. I think there's been quite enough claptrap for one day. Court will reconvene tomorrow at nine o'-clock sharp, corpses and all.

—The corpse . . . and I will try to make sure we have the right one on hand tomorrow, Your Honor . . . will not actually be able to *say* anything until sundown . . . might an allowance be made? Please don't consider it contempt; consider it rather to be a medical condition that prevents the witness from testifying during daylight hours.

—All right. I'm going to give you a lot of leeway, Counselor. But any cats, bats, or talking corpses are going to have to abide by my rules. Court will reconvene at three P.M., then—we will allow the current witness to finish his touching story—by which time sundown will have arrived and we will be able to continue with your key witness—assuming him, or her, to have completed his, or her beauty sleep at that time.

—So, Jeremy . . . having had your blood sipped by the sexiest girl at Kramer High in what can only be described as a somewhat erotic experience . . . did you then accept Ms. Sperling's invitation to an event which you believed would be some kind of wild, gothic orgy?

—Yes, sir.

—And did you bring the defendant with you on that occasion?

—Uh, yes, sir.

—And did you and the defendant drink blood at that event?

—Yes, sir. Vanilla.

—Vanilla?

—When the new ones drink blood for the first time . . . they mix it with vanilla syrup. Kinda kills the taste. Gets you used to it. It's like, uh, you wouldn't give your kid brother a straight shot of JD the first time, not without mixing it with a Coke or something. He'll get just as drunk, but it won't burn his throat as bad.

—What did you tell the defendant to get him to come to this event?

—Oh, that was easy. Jody's a big vampire fan. He watches vampire movies all the time, and he plays role-playing games, live-action ones, too. Last year, we hitchhiked down to some sci-fi convention in Chattanooga, and he got into a live-action vampire thing that lasted the whole weekend, 24/7. He didn't even try to pick up no bitches or get fucked up, he was so caught up in the game. See, when it came to Cat Sperling's big event, orgy, whatever you wanted to call it, I was just looking to get laid, but Jody wanted something deeper. When I told him that she'd asked me to bring him, asked for him by name even, he got all glassy-eyed and weird, and he was all, "Finally. This is it. The call. The embrace of ultimate darkness." Which sounds like the script of a video game, but he said it all like it was for real. Jody has these deep eyes, that cornflower blue color, you know, that the bitches like so much; he could have had bitches, except he wouldn't play any of the games they wanted him to play. So when he starts talking about *ultimate darkness,* and he puts on this weird, toneless kind of voice, like he's, I don't know, *possessed* or something, it gets creepy. That's why the kid had no friends. He scared people. Even so, I wouldn't exactly call him guilty of murder.

—Objection! The witness is speculating wildly about the defendant's guilt . . . even without counsel calling for such speculation. He's not here to speak to these issues.

—Yes, yes. The jury will disregard that, of course; the defendant's guilt is for the jury to decide, not this benighted young man. Please confine your testimony to the facts, Mr. Kindred . . . if any.

—All right, Jeremy. You do understand what the judge is saying, right? Just tell us what happened. No opinions, just facts.

—Yes sir.

—You passed Cat Sperling's invitation on to the defendant.

—Yes.

—How did you convince the defendant to attend?

—I told him it was the wildest live-action role-playing game of all time.

—You didn't mention the . . . erotic element?

—Oh, yes, sir. I told him there would be an orgy.

—And how did he react to that?

—He said, you can have the sex, Jeremy, long as I can have the violence.

—So is it fair to say that the defendant had a tendency towards violence?

—He was just kidding, sir! I never knew Jody to harm a flea, except in some fantasy or game, and then, of course, he'd go crazy . . . ripping off heads or wrapping himself in entrails . . . you know, movie-special-effects kind of shit. But in real life, no sir, Jody was gentle. I've seen him walk sideways so he wouldn't step on a bug. Most guys kinda enjoy stepping on bugs . . . taking a life, you know, even if it's just a bug's life. Jody wasn't like that. Loner, though. At lunch, he'd always be by himself, because even though I'm his best friend, you didn't want to be seen hanging around with a loser; he understood that; we only hung together after school, or at the mall. But even sitting by himself, munching on them Power Bars which was all he ever had packed for his lunch, he had an audience . . . there was always bitches eyeing him from a distance, wanting him. I guess it was the eyes. That's why he was on the cover of *Newsweek,* wasn't it? The eyes. I assumed that's why Cat wanted me to bring him. And I know he's been getting a lot of mail from bitches all around the country, since that magazine cover; he told me that one time when they let me visit him in jail. I thought he'd be more, you know, fucked up by jail, what with all them big dudes named Bubba, but he says ain't none of them touched him; they're all scared of him. It's been put out that he has powers, you know, going through keyholes, transforming into bats, and all that vampire-movie shit; but what I wanna know is, if that's true, why hasn't he escaped from jail? Well okay, I guess I'm getting off the subject again. You wanna know about the party in the cemetery, the Friday-the-Thirteenth thing . . . and how my friend Jody come to be accused of wiping out his family and a passel of his friends.

—Yes, Jeremy. Take your time. I know some of this is painful. But the jury needs to get the whole picture.

—Where was I?

—Perhaps you could go back to the vanilla blood.

—Yeah. It was like a cocktail almost. They served it in tall cone-shaped glasses, flutes they called them; champagne comes the same way, I heard tell. When me and Jody got there, it was close to midnight. That's because Jody took some convincing, even though he loved vampires; these weren't his kind of people. Leastways, we assumed that it would be mostly the school Goth crowd, the Nine Inch Nails types, the Anne Rice readers; actually it was kinda surprising who *was* there. It wasn't even confined to kids from Kramer High. I mean, Miss Higginbotham, the social studies teacher, was there . . . and she was bare-ass *nekkid*, and lying on top of a big old gravestone with her hippo-sized haunches in the air . . . and moaning. And this . . . well, this *black* dude was all on her shit, and he won't wearing nothing but a pair of black leather Pampers, and a nose ring the size of a golf ball, which must have tickled old Higginbotham's clit something fierce . . . well, she was moaning every time his head bobbed up and down, and her titties were flapping around like a couple of beached flounders. Shit, she was a sight, all moaning and wet in the moonlight like that. And there were other people scamming against grave markers; some guy was even trying to pork the stone angel that guards the cemetery gate. And there was this girl I'd never seen before, passing around the glasses, I mean flutes, filled with vanilla blood, and that was the only food they had at the whole party, if you can call it food. Well, just about everyone seemed occupied with someone else, and no one paid much mind to me and Jody, and the only one who said anything to us was the girl with the tray of blood; she stopped to ask us if we were new, and when we said yes, she told us drink up, it's real important for the new ones to drink up, can't really be part of the action until you've taken the first step; so we did.

—What sensation did you associate with drinking this, ah, "vanilla blood?"

—Hey, I don't rightly know if I should tell you what it was really like—this being a court of law and all.

—You're under oath, Jeremy. And also, you have immunity.

—So you can't use *nothing* I say against me? Nothing at all?

—Well—no.

—Objection! The witness only has use immunity.

—I'll sustain that, but I want to hear the witness's answer.

—Jeremy, the judge isn't going to do anything to you for what you say. He just wants to hear your answer.

—Well, sir, did you ever try E?

—Are you saying that the effects of this "vanilla blood" were somewhat akin to the drug E—Ecstasy—a drug popular among the "rave" segment of the student population?

—Well, if I answered that, I'd have to say that I'd *used* E before, and the judge just sustained that mean-looking bitch's objection. So I'll just say it gave me a boner the size of a baseball bat, and I wanted to screw the first thing I saw.

—Which was?

—Objection! Irrelevant.

—Actually, Your Honor, this answer speaks directly to the defendant's motivation.

—All right, I'll allow the question, but you'd better proceed very quickly to something important. Or the gentleman from CNN is liable to wet his pants.

—Jeremy, and what was the first thing you saw that you wanted to, as you so delicately put it, screw?

—Well, this is kinda embarrassing, sir. I mean, I wouldn't want you to think I'm gay or nothing, but I was so horny I wanted to do Jody . . . well, okay, there was something about him, the eyes, or whatever, anyway, on Brother Thompson's Christian summer camp last year, we all learned about circle jerks from the brother himself, so it wasn't like . . .

—Order in the court!

—And I mean, people were going crazy in that graveyard. I swear, I saw Mr. Smith, the football coach, getting boned up the butt by Mr. Oliver, who's like a police sergeant down at—

—Order in the goddamn court!

—Your Honor, we're not here to discuss the sexual antics of half the town. Could the witness confine himself to—

—Brother Thompson was even there, and he was handcuffed to a gravestone, and these motorcycle bitches were prodding him with cigarettes, and he was all moaning.

—That's enough, Mr. Kindred. Counselor, instruct your witness to get to the point.

—So, Jeremy, you, ah, made a pass at your best friend.

—Well, not exactly. It was more like this: I swallowed a couple of mouthfuls of that blood-cocktail thing, and everything went all misty . . . well, okay, and I felt like my veins were on fire . . . like this burning sensation, this tingling, everywhere, especially, you know, down there . . . and the next thing I knew, I was on Jody's leg, like a dog or something, rubbing myself up and down on it. But he wasn't getting horny off that blood at all. It wasn't affecting him the same way. Even though there was couples, threesomes, getting down every which way, in the light of the moon, with a dark, pounding music pouring out of a ghetto blaster somewhere . . . like one of them imperial orgy scenes in *Caligula*, you know? . . . Jody wouldn't have none of it. He shook me off of him like you'd shake off, well, a dog. "Don't," he said. "You're like all them others. To me the blood feels different. I think maybe I ain't the same kind as you, maybe I don't belong with the likes of you. What you're all doing seems so empty to me. Blood sings a different music to me. When I look into the dark, I look right past all of you and all your sleazy thrills, your wanna-be games, I see you all just flirting with the darkness . . . not willing to embrace it . . . to become a part of it . . . no, you're not like me after all, and it makes me sad because you've been a good friend to me, Jeremy, all these years when no one would talk to me because I'm like the school outcast, the mutant in the hallway . . . today I'm starting to learn who I really am."

—So the defendant had, as it were, an epiphanic moment from the drinking of human blood?

—I don't rightly know what that means, sir.

—Doesn't matter. That evening changed him, didn't it?

—Maybe so. What he said to me, though, was he found his true self.

—And his true self was what? A vampire?

—Won't that simple, sir. But anyways, I didn't have time to listen to him ranting on at that point, because, as I said, I was thinking with my dick. And soon my dick found something to play with. There was this mousy girl, no one anyone would look at twice in the daylight . . . her name was Constance Thorpe . . . and the only time I ever spent more than five seconds in her company was when me and her was paired off cutting up rats in biology lab one time. You know, she always used to make me nervous. She had nerd glasses, and she had a way of pulling out them rat intestines that made it look like she was enjoying it too much. And she dressed like a refugee from the sixties, parents must've been hippies or something and she forgot to rebel. Well, I saw her leaning against a tombstone, and she wasn't the same bitch at all, lemme tell you. She'd lost the glasses and she even had a spot of makeup on. But I didn't really give a shit, because of whatever it was in that blood; all I cared about was that she made a beeline for me and kinda nose-dived toward my crotch. Before you knew it she'd unzipped me and she was all up on me like a noisy old vacuum cleaner. I mean, I wouldn't have been seen dead with her normally, but you should have seen her suck, I mean, that girl could suck. She was wild, too, licking up a storm on my balls and even thrusting down past them, I think she'd have stuck it up my butt if my pants had come all the way down, but the zipper was all tangled in her hair. Must've hurt, it yanking on that hair like that, sir, but she sucked with a will, like her life depended on it. So I sorta leaned back against a gravestone, closed my eyes, and slipped into like a kind of trance, just letting myself go with the flow of it . . . then I sort of came to with a shock because I could feel this pinprick, this sharp pain that wouldn't go away. I looked down and she had pulled out a syringe and she'd stuck me right in the shaft, and you know how much blood gets down there when you got a boner. I guess I kinda panicked, even though I knew that these people have a thing about blood, and I drew back, and well, I knocked the syringe out and I jizzed at the same time, and there was blood and cum everywhere . . . well, Constance was going crazy now, lapping up everything, sperm, blood, sweat, I could have pissed on her face and she'd've drunk it. Holy shit! I didn't like it. The high of the vanilla blood was coming down now. I was all dizzy. This wasn't how I thought it would feel. I felt all dirty inside. That's when I decided to go looking for Jody. I sorta pushed Constance out of the way. She was on all fours, the fucking nympho bitch, and already sniffing for a fresh piece of meat to chew on. I kept calling Jody's name, asked a couple people where he was, and they kept shrugging or being too involved with their own shit.

—And where did you in fact discover the defendant to be?

—Well, I'm getting to that, sir!

—Good. I see that the prosecution has become too, ah, involved in its prurient fascination with the material to object any further . . .

—There's no need for the defense to snipe, Your Honor,

when it is clearly burying itself with every word this so-called witness utters.

—Be that as it may . . . Mr. Kindred?

—Okay. Well, there's this big old structure bang in the middle of the cemetery, see, and it's the oldest monument there. I think it dates to long before the war.

—You mean the Civil War.

—Yes, sir.

—I think most of the jury are familiar with the monument you're referring to. It's the Forbin–St. Cloud Memorial, right? Built by a prominent French family, in the days when our little city was booming. Which times, since the banning of hemp cultivation, are long past. A bizarrely incongruous Gothic monstrosity, surrounded by a wrought-iron fence with strange-looking gargoyles on top, rumored to have underground passageways, under whose sheltering eaves the homeless of this town often rest, as the local police force rarely bothers to kick them out, rarely even patrols this area because of the mysterious death of Police Sergeant McKinley, found garroted and disemboweled and spread-eagled over the—

—Why is the defense now regaling us with a history lesson, Your Honor? Objection!

—I'll stop, Your Honor. I just thought the local color would be helpful. The Forbin–St. Cloud monument has . . . *vibes*. I want the jury to understand that. Since all of them heard the ghost stories when they were kids, and few were brave enough to go there. I know the prosecution is anxious to get back to the dirty bits. So how about it, Mr. Kindred? Let's have 'em. The dirty bits.

—Like I said, sir, I thought I saw the back of Jody's head, and he was squeezing through the iron bars into the Fo-for- . . . well, we don't call it that, sir.

—What *do* you call it?

—We call it the Hellhouse.

—Why?

—Well, sir, on account of . . . it's big enough to be a house, what with all the underground passages it's supposed to

have . . . and it's got this entranceway . . . well, a *fake* entranceway . . . that looks like the mouth of hell . . . a big old demon's
jaw in stone with a stone door that can't be opened. Well . . . I
didn't *think* it could be opened. But then . . . I saw Jody sort of
standing there . . . at the stone mouth . . . you could see the
sculpted flames of hell there . . . and he was just standing there.
Just staring. Like he'd seen something . . . supernatural. Well, I
kind of snuck up behind him. I guess I startled him because
when he felt me breathing down his neck he screamed up a
storm. I mean he had like a panic attack, and I hadn't *never* seen
him lose his cool before. I got him calmed down. I kept saying,
It ain't so bad, Jody, nothing bad's happened yet, maybe we just
lost a bit of blood is all. Maybe we're a bit weak from that, you
know, dizzy, seeing things. When you lose blood you see things.
We learned that in school. But he was all, I saw what I saw. I
said, What did you see? and he said, Nothing. Fucking nothing,
and don't ask me again. I ain't crazy. I said, Nobody said you
was. Just tell me what you seen there.

—And did the defendant respond?

—Yeah.

—What did he say?

—He more than said, sir. Well, at first he just murmured,
They went through the doorway, they just up and walked right
on through there like it was air, I can feel them inside there, feel
the heat of their souls inside the dead, empty space . . . but
pretty soon he was a-banging on that stone with his fists, like he
should have been able to melt right through it. Well, what do
you know? The wall started to give.

—He shattered a mausoleum wall with his fists?

—Not hardly, sir. I mean the wall and him seemed to kind
of meld together, and he was sort of sinking into it.

—What did you do, Jeremy?

—I thought he was going to die. I mean, getting sucked into
a Jell-o kind of a wall, it was one of them *Poltergeist*-style special effects, like you see in movies. So I guess I grabbed on to
him, and that's how I ended up getting pulled inside, too. The
stone felt mushy. Oily, you know. It made my flesh crawl. But

the wall closed right up again as soon as we got through, and it was dark as shit in there, and won't no way to get back out. I almost shat my pants, I don't mind telling you, sir, it was that scary. The air was all moist and stale-smelling. I don't know how dead people are supposed to smell, but I could *feel* death there. Well, after a time, you could start to see a bit of light. Water was dripping. Where we were was a kind of corridor leading downward. And we heard voices. From down below. I was shaking, sir. And then Jody said the strangest thing. He said, Jer, we been buddies for a long time, but there's places you weren't meant to go . . . places I have to go alone. You weren't meant to pass through to this place, but you held on to me, and maybe that's good, because if anything ever happens to me, you can bear witness one day, you can speak the truth about me, shout it out, even if nobody ever believes you, or even understands what you say. I ain't long for this world, Jer, but I'm meant to go out like a comet, not like a lil' old candle. You know that, don't you? I've always been different . . . like everyone's born facing the same way, their butts to the past, their faces to the future, but not me, I go sideways, past and future are a sidestream to me, a path I can never tread.

—Quite a speech for a teenager, don't you think?

—Objection! Calls for speculation.

—Ah, I see that the Madame Prosecutor has awakened. Sustained.

—That's all right, Your Honor, I was only being rhetorical. Mr. Kindred . . . Jeremy . . . I'll say it a different way. Did your friend, the defendant, often make long speeches like that?

—Not often. But more than any other kid I knew. If he got going, he could talk up a storm. Almost like a preacher, except it would be all about violence and death and dark things.

—Are you aware that the defendant hasn't said a word since he was taken into custody?

—I've heard that, sir.

—So he's definitely changed.

—Yes, sir. He ain't human no more.

—Literally?

—Well, sir, I was getting to that.

—Proceed.

—Well, like I said, there was voices. And the corridor leading downward. And the light, you see, the light came from down below. A flickering, red light, kind of like the flames of hell, I guess. And even though Jody told me, No, you stay up here, this is for me alone . . . well, I guess I couldn't help following him down there. I was curious, sure. But it was also creepy as shit, and I didn't want to be alone.

—Did the defendant know you were following him?

—Sort of. But you see, he was like in his own world. He really didn't pay me no mind at all. I was like a puppy dog or something . . . no, a shadow more like, a nothing.

—To whom did the voices belong?

—Well okay, we kept going down deeper and deeper, because the corridor ended in steps, and the steps led us deeper and deeper underground. Maybe we were going into the hillside, I don't know; I lost my sense of direction. Because now there were steps going up, and passageways leading sideways. It was like that story we learned in Mrs. Seymour's class one time, the one with the maze and the bullheaded man and the hero with his ball of yarn. The walls glowed. It was a cold light, millions of dots of light, you know, like you get in caves sometimes, phosphorescence I think it's called. I followed. After what seemed like a long time, it widened into a cave. I think it was part natural, this cave, but there was also a bunch of marble columns and statues of weeping angels and other cool gothic shit. The light came from flaming torches on the walls. Some parts of the walls had paintings, Egyptian stuff, guys with dogs' heads, other parts had been painted over. It was all coated with soot, and when the torches flickered, it looked like them pictures was moving. And at the far end, there were niches in the wall, and in the niches were dead people. I mean some were long dead, like skeletons, but some were fresh . . . and some of them I recognized. I mean, they went to my school. I mean, they weren't supposed to be dead at all. I mean, I would have heard of it if they'd died, I was in some of the same classes. Well, I wasn't that sure. Like I said, I was dizzy. And the sex thing hadn't totally worn off. I hid behind a big statue. An angel. The Archangel Michael, I think, with a flaming sword. The sword was metal and sort of attached to his hand with a leather thong. And a bronze cross around his neck. His wings were wide enough that I could crouch down and peep through a little chink where his elbow lifted up against his robe. Apart from the sword and the cross he was all marble, and cold. And, well, I wasn't dressed for the cold, so I was shivering as I huddled there, trying not to breathe too much.

—What did the defendant do at that point?

—He stood there, in a semicircle of light, facing all of them dead folks, and I saw there was three coffins laying there, fine old coffins made of carved wood with all gold on them. The coffins are just laying there, and the middle one, the grandest one of them all, is closed, but the other two have their lids on the ground next to them, and they're empty, you see. And there's people here. They're hard to see at first, because they're all blended with the shadows, and it takes me a while to make them out. They ain't the same kind of people as the ones in the orgy up there in the cemetery grounds. They're, well, pale-looking. What was that word for the way the walls was all glowing? Phosphorescent. Yeah. That was in their faces, too. When you looked at one of them a long time you could see the cold light clinging to their faces. They all wore black. I don't mean all Dracula capes and stuff. I mean, some of them had capes, but there were clothes from olden times, and clothes you could see down at the Goth coffeehouse over in the next town. There was leather and fishnet stockings. There was black lipstick. Sunken eyes. Some had sweeping robes, you know, the kind that rustle when you walk. And, well, standing next to one of the empty coffins was Cat Sperling, and she was totally naked. And by the other coffin was . . . shit man, it's weird to think of it now, but it was Constance Thorpe, the little geek that done went down on me next to that gravestone up above. She was naked, too. She looked better than I thought she would. I couldn't believe it. The only two bitches I'd ever really messed around with, and they were standing around bare-ass naked in front of a bunch of ghouls in black. I gotta admit, it was making me, you know, all hot down there all over again. I watched my friend Jody. They didn't seem to notice him at first, them two girls, because they were busy staring into each other's eyes. I mean, I thought I was trapped inside of a lesbo porno. I mean, this was fucking wild. I never dreamed them two would have a thing for each other, I mean, the sexiest girl at Kramer High and some gap-toothed nerd with a thing for cutting up mice and frogs . . . secretly wanting to dyke it out? . . . I could see it in their eyes. Cat went without saying, but Constance looked different. A glow in her flesh. Gleaming. Maybe it was sweat. She had hard little nipples. They were inching toward each other. I was all, Holy shit, they're gonna get it on right here, in front of all these people . . . if they even *are* people. Cat's upper lip was quivering. The sweat was beading up on it. I could barely look at their pussies. I'd glimpsed pussy before, and in pornos you watch it all you want, but it's on a TV screen. This was different. I was afraid if I stared too long, I don't know, I was gonna have an accident.

—Your Honor, could the witness get to the point already?

—Sustained.

—I'm afraid he's right, Jeremy. The jury doesn't really need to know about your . . . accidents.

—Well, I didn't have no accident anyways, sir.

—Why?

—Just when I thought the two of them were going to really, you know, get down, the lid of the coffin in the middle started to creak open.

—A little like yesterday's little incident?

—Oh, no, sir. It was real slow, like. And then all the people there fell on the floor. I don't mean they tripped, I mean they fell to their knees, faces in the dust, even the two naked bitches. It was like, you know, I seen this movie about an ancient Chinese emperor, it was death to look him directly in the face. I could feel . . . fear in the room . . . and power. Real power. I was scared. I narrowly avoided one kind of accident, and now I was fixing to have another kind. Well, the lid was creaking open. Dust was flying. The lid swung up, and this old man was sitting up slowly. He was old, real old. Okay, he didn't *look* that old, but you could feel it in him. And he spoke. Slowly. Like he was having trouble remembering how to speak. Later they done told me that his kind don't have much use for talking amongst themselves; it's chiefly for the benefit of the ones that are still human. Oh, it won't English, neither. But one of the guys in black got up off his knees and crept up closer, and he translated everything in a flat, echoey voice. The first thing he says is, The Duke asks what new creatures come before him today.

—Meaning the two girls?

—Yes, sir, I guess, because the sex goddess and the geek stand up, and they're all coyly looking at the floor and half smiling, and their nipples are still hard. And they both say, Your Grace, we humbly beg for the honor of attending you. Well, His Grace mumbles something, and the translator says, How may you prove your worthiness? And they answer, We are yours entirely, body, soul, in life and death and undeath. We wish to become consorts of the darkness. We wish the everlasting night. We pine for the sunset. We abhor the light. We have listened in the wilderness and heard the music of the night.

—The sex goddess and the geek, as you call them, said all that? In those precise words?

—I reckon it was learned from a book or something, sir.

—So this appeared to be some kind of ritual?

—Yes, sir.

—Your Honor, I thought that this trial was about the defendant, not the erotic fantasies of some disturbed adolescent. I must continue to protest this undignified latitude in allowing endless filth to spew forth from the witness without any real connection to the defendant's guilt or innocence!

—Yes, yes, sustained, sustained, though I'm sure the lurid details will all be in your next book, Counselor!

—I resent that, Your Honor!

—Be quiet and let the kid tell the rest of his story. If the defense would care to continue . . . I'm as anxious to get to the relevance of this as anyone else here.

—Yes, Your Honor. Mr. Kindred . . . Jeremy . . . go on. Go easy on the sex. Unless it specifically concerns the defendant.

—All right, sir.

—Tell us about the defendant and his role in all this, then.

—Well, the translator guy, he says to the two girls, You know that before you can cross over, you must bid the flesh farewell . . . and you must find a willing lamb . . . a sacrifice. And Cat Sperling said, We have such a lamb, Your Grace. We've tracked him, we've lured him, we've cornered him, and we have him.

—And by "him," they meant the defendant?

—I guess so, sir, cause Jody done stepped forward.

—What was the defendant's demeanor?

—Huh?

—How did he look?

—Pale, sir, real pale. But determined, too. Whatever was about to happen, it looked like he'd thought it over and was gonna do it, no matter what. Grim, sir, real grim. It's amazing to me how young he looks at that moment. I know he's really older than me, but he comes off like a little kid. Scrawny. And so pale. Maybe that phosphorescence shit was rubbing off on him. He looked back only once. Looked me right in the eye. *Knew* I was there, knew I was watching. No one else saw, no one else knew. I thought about what he said to me earlier. *I ain't long for this world, Jer, but I'm meant to go out like a comet, not like a lil' old candle.* Jody was fixing to die. I realized that. All of a sudden. Something had happened between him and Cat Sperling. Something that had pushed him over the edge. Like the preacher says on *Hour of Power*, Into the abyss.

Well, the translator dude says to Jody, Do you come here of your own free will? And Jody's all, I do. Then the guy says, You will lose a lot of blood. Perhaps you will even die. But if you survive this ritual, you will be on the way to a different plane of existence. The one who brings you to us, the woman formerly called Cat, she was once such a lamb. To surrender yourself to the dark, to let the undead feast upon you, is to step blindfolded off the edge of the bottomless pit. You must trust. You must believe. Darkness will love you. Darkness will enfold you. Darkness will shield you. Do you accept such a destiny? If you do not, speak now, and in the morning you will wake up in your own bed, and remember nothing. But if you say aye, you will never again know where you will wake up in the morning: in your own bed, on a bed of thorns, in a coffin, in the wormy earth. Think carefully before you answer, Jody Palmer. It may be that you will never again see daylight. Some who have a special affinity for our kind . . . make the passage in a single night . . . and wake to eternal darkness. For most . . . well, for some there is the true death . . . but they would never had made the crossing; anyway . . . it's a talent you're born with. And for some, a slow, agonizing sickness that may or may not lead to death and the crossing into undeath. We cannot tell. There is no science of vampirology. Do you understand what we are telling you?

And Jody was all, Yes.

. . .

—And?

—I'm sorry, sir. I was just trying to remember the details. After this it gets kinda all confused.

—Take your time, Jeremy.

—Yes sir. Thank you, sir.

—You're telling us that these . . . creatures . . . made an offer to your friend, and he accepted it. An offer that, he believed, would bring about his death and transfiguration . . . his metamorphosis into a creature beyond life.

—I reckon so, sir. I mean, there was nothing for him in the real world anyways. He was always kind of a throwaway kid.

—Did he give any impression of having been coerced into this choice?

—Maybe he didn't feel he *had* no choice.

—What did the defendant do next?

—He stepped forward. And the translator guy said, First comes the consummation of all carnal pleasure. Then comes the drawing of the blood. The first is your farewell to the flesh, you candidates for initiation into the Brotherhood of Blood; the second is your salutation of the spirit.

—So the defendant believed he was being initiated into some kind of vampiric existence?

—No, you got it all wrong. Them two girls was the initiates. Jody was the lamb, the offering, the sacrifice.

—He was willing to die for this?

—I reckon so.

—What happened next?

—It gets confusing, sir. Because the first part of the ritual, that was the "farewell to the flesh" thing, slowly shifted into the second part . . . the blood ritual. It started with the two girls undressing Jody, slowly, sexily . . . for example, Cat would undo one of his shirt buttons with her teeth, then Connie would do the next one down, while Cat was sort of sliding her tongue in and out between the buttons, teasing his chest. And they were all rubbing their titties up and down him. Now I knew that Jody really had never had no sex before, well, no more than third base, anyways. But when they finally got the pants off him, he wasn't even hard. He just stood there, with a faraway look, fixing on some dark future he had always dreamed about. But the two girls were at him like there was no tomorrow. I guess, for them, in a way, there wasn't. They surrounded him. They were a blur of arms and legs and lips and tongues and gleaming pussies. I couldn't believe it, but mousy Constance was the wilder of the two bitches. She was squeezing Jody's scrawny ass, pumping against him, even thrusting her tongue in his butt hole. But Cat was more playful. She skimmed her tongue along his arms, his fingers, and when she reached his balls and started flicking at them, he finally started to get aroused. I think he was holding himself in, trying to resist, thinking to himself that giving in to sex was some kind of weakness, that he was there for the violence, not the sex . . . but no red-blooded guy could stay soft forever with them two working him over. And now they were taking turns, one holding him upright while the other slid up and down on him, spinning him around, making him dizzy, and he was moaning now, I couldn't make out all of it but it was all sick, private stuff, about his childhood, his parents, I don't know . . . and then it started to turn toward violence . . . first one girl then the other was raking at him with her nails, nails that seemed to get longer and sharper . . . nails that seemed to curl up, tighten, into claws . . . the girls were bucking and heaving as they pushed him down against the middle coffin, where the vampire master dude was still sitting, watching, his eyes slowly reddening . . . or was that just the flickering of the torches? . . . I don't know . . . and the crowd in black was hemming in closer . . . making it harder for me to see . . . and I knew they weren't noticing me any more, I even felt safe creeping out from behind the statue . . . keeping low to the ground . . . peering through the sea of legs and cloaks . . . glimpses now . . . the girls licking their lips . . . their eyes slitting . . . bending over him . . . slicing at his chest, his abdomen with their animal claws . . . and biting now . . . I could see fangs. They all had fangs. All them black-clad people with them glowing white faces. Their fangs glistened in the dark like a thousand stars. And there were other sharp things. I saw spikes . . . razor blades . . . pocket knives . . . hypodermics . . . all ready to harvest my best friend's lifeblood. The girls were still all over him . . . pleasure transforming into pain . . . but the others were moving in now . . . I could see a razor slice just beneath his nipple . . . I could see a delicate mouth close in on his ankle . . . and Jody was all convulsing now, I couldn't tell if it was from like an orgasm or whether they was *killing* the fuck out of him. Jesus, I was scared. I wanted it to stop. Me against a hundred bloodsuckers, what was I thinking? But that was my best friend out there. But did you ever see a pig that's been hit on the head in the slaughterhouse? That's how it looked. I mean, he was shaking like a fucking pile driver. I couldn't stand it. I mean, Jody, you know? Friends since the sixth grade. Camp outs, swimming holes, dirty websites, all the shit young guys grow up together doing. Well, what I done was dumb.

—What did you do, Mr. Kindred?

—Well, I ripped the cross off the Archangel Michael's neck, and I pulled off the sword, and like a wild man I charged.

—You attacked a crowd of . . . sadistic vampire cultists?

—Cultists? Hell no, sir, these people was actual vampires.
'Cause when the shadow of the cross fell upon them, they
started screaming. And scattering. And I was screaming, too, a
pretty damn impressive scream for a kid, a scream like a ban-
shee, and swinging that big old heavy sword like it was nothing
more'n a letter opener. Shit, I *scared* the fuckers. I think. There
was this big flapping noise. Dust everywhere. Swirling. Mist.
Everything was whirling, and there was this roar, like a tornado
or something. I don't think I actually hit anything with the
sword. Everything was dissolving before I could smash bronze
against flesh. I saw Jody on the ground there in front of the middle coffin. He was naked, and I swear to God he was half
drained already. There was so much blood, just sluicing from a
hundred cuts on him, pouring out onto the rocky floor. I knelt
down and tried to lift him up, but he was heavy, there won't no
give to him at all, it was like he was already dead. I was still all
crazed and I shook him, I was all, Wake up, Jody, this is your
buddy telling you, come out of it, you ain't dead yet. And then
the weirdest thing of all happened. You know all that swirling
mist I was talking about? Well, it seemed to gather up the
coffins and the cave walls and even the swordless St. Michael
over there, and even the dirt beneath us, and it was all billowing about us and darkening, and the torches were blowing out
one by one, and my friend was stirring a little, and I was all,
Jody, don't die, don't die, don't die, when all at once the world
seemed to melt around us . . . like a dissolve in a movie . . . and
we were somewhere else. I smelled a fresh wind. Flowers. Old
trees and rotting leaves. We were in the hills. The cemetery was
way below us . . . and the moon was shining through the treetops. What happened? When I arrived at the cemetery, there'd
been cars everywhere, pickups, Mustangs, a Mercedes, a police
car . . . now I couldn't see a one in that parking lot . . . and the
graveyard was deserted. Jody was still lying across my lap . . .
still bleeding to death . . . or was he? In the bright moonlight I
saw . . . the wounds closing up . . . the scratches fading . . . the
blood sort of evaporating, melding into the night mist . . . I

didn't understand. I knew it won't no dream. I knew it had to be real . . . but . . . Jody was moaning now. I was all, Wake up, wake up . . . and, slowly, he did.

—I see. *And I awoke and found me here, on the cold hill's side.*

—Yeah. I guess so.

—You saved your friend's life.

—Maybe, but he sure didn't thank me for it.

—No?

—Shit, no, sir. When he come to, it was just about twilight, and I'd been watching him, and I'd covered him with my own jacket, and I was trying my ass off to make him come back into the world . . . and when he finally opened his eyes, well, he didn't look like he was fixing to thank me at all. He looked at me with slitted eyes, and I saw *hate*. Pure, naked hate. I sure was shocked. I said, Jody, it's me, your best friend, Jer. They were gonna *kill* you in there. I don't know what happened, but I got you out . . . somehow. And he whispers to me, gasping for breath between every word, like he's struggling to keep from slipping back into darkness, Jer, I wanted it. That was my chance. I'm nobody in this world. I was about to *be* something. Let go of me, Jeremy, and don't come near me again. And he shook off my jacket . . . stood up . . . just as the first rays of sunlight were breaking over the gravestones below yonder . . . he stood up, naked as the day he was born, stood up and walked away from me. He was so frail and thin he was almost like a little kid. But here's the weird thing . . . the scars was all healed. There won't a scratch on that boy. The sun painted him a golden sort of color, and he didn't hardly seem human. And he walked away. Away from the coming light . . . into the thickest part of the wood . . . like he was afraid of the sun.

—Did you speak to him after that?

—Not really. I think he tried to go back to one of their cemetery parties . . . they usually had them on the full moon . . . but I know he never was able to get back inside that monument. That stone carving of the jaws of hell . . . well, stone was all it was to him. He had lost the key. I took it from him. I was stupid, I guess. I really didn't understand him after all. He fell in with other kids. Started a new "secret society" of some kind. A wanna-be vampire society. I heard about it mostly from—

—Your Honor, this is all hearsay now.

—Sustained.

—Your Honor, we have already heard evidence about young Jody Palmer's secret society . . . from all sorts of expert witnesses as well as from the ex-members themselves. I'm not seeking to add anything to the record on that matter from this witness. In fact, I'm going to excuse him now. Perhaps my opponents would care to cross?

—Yes, we would. Just a couple of questions, Jeremy Kindred. You're still under oath.

—Yes, ma'am.

—Isn't it true that no one has related any of these outlandish incidents . . . except you? I'm not referring merely to the supernatural events you claim to have seen inside one of the town's most famous landmarks . . . but to these very imaginative orgies you describe as having occurred regularly at the cemetery. If these things were true, don't you think others would have reported them to the authorities?

—Hell no, ma'am. Half the authorities were *in* them orgies.

—So it's a kind of . . . ah, conspiracy? Half the town involved in dark goings-on, and covering up the mess from the other half?

—You tell me, ma'am. After all, you were there, too.

—Well!

—Your Honor, the witness has just claimed that the state's prosecutor was present at those proceedings, in the light of which—

—Oh, nonsense, Counselor. The boy's a raving lunatic.

—Your Honor, comments like that would tend to throw some doubt on your own impartiality—

—Shut up, Counselor! I'm running a courtroom, not a voodoo séance. If the prosecution would care to continue the cross—

—Ah . . . no further questions.

—The witness may stand down.

—I would like to remind the defense that this evening's extraordinary timing was designed to let us hear from whoever is supposed to be inside that coffin of yours, and that we are now ten minutes past sundown. And no one has been banging on the lid from the inside. Is that particular bit of nonsense over with?

—I don't think so, sir. At this time I would like to ask the bailiff to remove the coffin lid and invite the next witness to the stand.

—All right. Bailiff?

—There's nothing inside of here, sir, except a headless cat. And a large quantity of garlic.

—That, Counsel, is in very poor taste.

—I don't know *how* that could have happened, Your Honor! Our resident vampirologist assured us that—

—Ew, Your Honor! It's stiff.

—Dispose of it, Bailiff. So what is the meaning of this, Counsel? Vampire hunters been calling, I suppose?

—I have no idea what's happened at all, Your Honor. We'll have the witness for you tomorrow, I promise.

—Don't make promises you can't keep, Counselor; I'm told that the dead are notoriously inept at keeping their appointments.

—Your Honor is pleased to joke at my expense.

—My Honor has had enough for the day, and we'll reconvene tomorrow morning at . . . let's say ten o'clock.

—Dr. Shimada, you're a vampirologist.

—Just an avocation, actually. My day job is psychiatric resident at the juvenile division of the state hospital for the criminally insane. My study of vampires, real and imagined, grew out of the ramblings of a patient I have in my private practice; I can't elucidate further without breaching confidentiality, of course.

—And you've studied the defendant at some length.

—Oh, yes. Fascinating boy. Very disturbed.

—The defendant is not, however, in your professional opinion, a vampire.

—No.

—Nor any other supernatural creature.

—Well, I would take issue with the choice of "supernatural," sir, since, as a scientist, I would prefer a rational explanation for any phenomenon, however supernatural-*seeming*. But no, Mr. Palmer is by no means undead. He is quite, quite human. He's just like you and me.

—Except that he hasn't talked since . . . the events that have brought us all here for this trial.

—That is *almost* true. I was starting to make some progress with that. I think he needs a few more months before he'll actually . . . be able to say anything to shed light upon this case.

—You were making progress?

—He grunts now, sometimes. I even detected a whimper once. And one time, on my way out, in the doorway, I heard a distinct, if sotto voce, utterance of the phrase, "Fuck off."

—I see. Will he ever talk?

—Everything he wants to say is caged up inside him. It only needs . . . a key. I've been considering the possibility of circumventing the lengthy period of therapy and just jumping to Pentothal.

—Sodium Pentothal? The old "truth serum," that cliché of fifties B-grade detective thrillers?

—The very same.

—How many sessions did you have with the defendant?

—I've seen him twice a week since the arrest.

—In your opinion, is the defendant insane?

—I think that would be obvious even to a layman.

—Was he insane at the time of the crime?

—Clearly he was unable to distinguish right from wrong at the time of the multiple murders.

—What is the nature of the defendant's mental illness?

—In Freudian terms, his superego, the inner voice we often think of as our "conscience," weak to start off with from inadequate childhood reinforcement, has disappeared entirely. It has been replaced by what he perceives as supernatural "beings," creatures who control him. He has experienced a transference of the normal youthful libido . . . the sex urge . . . in the direction of violence and bloodshed. The weakening of the superego causes him to be unable to control his beast within, his id. That, of course, is the basic reason for all crime, but in his case the weakening of the ego is clearly at a pathological level.

—I see, Dr. Shimada. I'd like to move that Dr. Shimada's entire report . . . some two thousand three hundred ten pages of it . . . be admitted to the record as Exhibit, ah . . .

—Defense Exhibit QQ.

—Yes. Defense Exhibit QQ.

—I hope you're not expecting our benighted jurors to make head or tail of it, Counselor. Even the last few minutes have been a little, ah, dry.

—Dr. Shimada's learned testimony merely adds to that of seven other psychiatrists, Your Honor, who have all agreed that the defendant is hopelessly, irretrievably insane.

—Quite so.

—Dr. Shimada, if you would state again, in simple layman's terms, the defendant's state of mind before, during, and after the crimes were committed?

—In layman's terms, Jody Palmer was stark, staring bonkers, Counselor.

—No further questions.

—Cross?

—Well, yes, I do have a couple of quick questions. Dr. Shimada, in this two-thousand-page document which, I admit, I haven't read, although my researchers have combed through it pretty thoroughly . . . do you not basically say that the defendant had no conscience?

—I suppose you could put it that way.

—Well, well, well. No conscience. And for that, we're gonna let him off after he mutilated his parents, disemboweled his sister, devoured his two-year-old brother's liver, and led a gang of hooligans on a rampage that culminated in several more people becoming . . . unwilling blood donors . . . not to mention . . . necrophilia.

—Your Honor, the prosecution's grandstanding.

—Sustained. Just ask the questions.

—Right. Well, I really have just one more question. You say the defendant has retreated behind a wall of silence.

—Yes. It's called hysterical mutism. It's one of the ultimate defense mechanisms of the paranoid schizophrenic.

—So you compiled a two-thousand-page report about this patient . . . without exchanging a single bit of dialogue with him?

—As I spoke to him, I monitored his vital signs, his brain waves, the surface electrical activity of his skin.

—But he didn't actually *tell* you any of this.

—Scientists can read a great deal from—

—He didn't actually *tell* you. Answer the question, please.

—Ah . . . no.

—No further questions.

—Natalie McConnell, you've been given immunity because you appear not to have participated in the actual killing. But you saw everything, and your insight into the defendant's state of mind is vital to the court's understanding of his motives.

—Yes, sir.

—Are you currently enrolled in Kramer High?

—No, sir. I dropped out. I had to go to work in my dad's doughnut store.

—So you never knew the defendant until a few months before the incident.

—Yes, sir. I met him at Cat Sperling's funeral.

—You knew Cat Sperling, then.

—Oh, sure, sir. Everyone did. She was the town slut.

—How did you come to be aware of that?

—My daddy always said that if I behaved anything like her, he'd whup my butt till it was bloody.

—What kind of behavior constituted "behaving like Cat Sperling"?

—Um . . . too much lipstick . . . wearing leather . . . standing a certain way . . . talking in a sexy voice . . .

—Your father ever carry out his threat?

—Shit, yeah. He wore me out all the time. When he wasn't making me go down on him.

. . .

—Order in the court! Order! Order! Counselor, tell the witness to stay on the topic.

—Your Honor, the fact that the witness was one of the disenfranchised, the violated members of society . . . is not entirely irrelevant to this defense . . . although I did not intend to have the matter raised quite this abruptly.

—That's enough. The jury will ignore the witness's life story, and concentrate only on those facts she raises that bear on this case. Meanwhile, I'd like the bailiff to make a note of the girl's remarks and pass them on to the district attorney; we are state employees here, and there are mandatory reporting laws.

—Well, Judge, if you're gonna turn in my dad, you might as well turn in the pastor of Hillside Baptist Church as well. And the vice principal of Kramer High—he got me in the closet one day. Oh, and—

—Miss McConnell, enough of that. When your testimony is through, you are to report to Detective . . . ah . . . who's on duty out there? . . . Detective Arnold. He'll take it from there. Meanwhile, if the court would care to turn its attention back to the case . . . Counsel? Counsel?

—Oh. Yes, Your Honor. So, despite Cat Sperling's reputation, you went to her funeral?

—Yeah. Her dad had ordered ten dozen doughnuts, you see, for afterwards, and I stopped by to get directions to the house. And that's when I saw Jody . . . the defendant. He was standing in the distance . . . in the shade of an oak tree. He was all in black. Trench coat and all. He looked lonely. Not like he was really invited. He was staring at all the relatives, at the coffin, at everything. With a kind of longing in his eyes. The guy seemed so sad. I wanted to talk to him. So I did.

—What did you converse about?

—Well, at first, I was all, like, questions, how did she die and such. And he said, *Anemia.* Which wasn't what I heard, I'd heard it was from something to do with sex, AIDS or such. It didn't matter nohow, 'cause she was gone no matter how you looked at it. I got him to give me directions to the Sperling place, and then he got to staring at me in a way I never been stared at before. Like he could see right into my mind. And he said to me, Are you afraid of the dark? And I said, Yeah. And he said, Very afraid? And I said, Yeah. And he said, Why? And I said, Because things come to me in the night. And he said, I can take that fear away forever. I can take you on a journey with me. Across the river of death. To the farthest shore. To the kingdom of ultimate darkness. I look into your eyes and I see you're like me, you don't got nothing to lose. I said, You sure are right about that. He said, I'm gathering a group of people to take with me on this journey. It's a quest, you see. Like searching for the Holy Grail. The cup of blood. I just know you want to come with me, Natalie. I can see it in your eyes. One time, I met these creatures from a place beyond our world. They called out to me. But I stayed behind. I had work left to do in the world. I wanted to go, but I thought of all the dispossessed of the world, all the young ones crying out for release, and I knew I had to bring a few with me in order to be worthy of my place among the dark ones.

—Did the defendant mention Jeremy Kindred at all? The fact that his friend physically prevented him from being sucked into the vampire world?

—No.

—So you had no idea there was any side to the story other than what you were being told.

—That's right, sir.

—Did you believe him?

—Not really, sir. I thought he'd lost it. But there was something real hypnotic about his voice and such. He was sexy, too. In a scary kind of way.

—Sexy and scary?

—He was pale and thin. His cheeks were all sunken and his

eyes, too. He looked like he hadn't eaten in days and he'd stayed out of the sun . . . well, like he was dead, really. Dead but beautiful. I guess what was exciting about him was . . . there was a wrongness. About the way he moved. The way he smiled. Like they weren't *his* lips, *his* limbs. Do you know what I mean? Like something was animating his body and such. Possession or something. I touched his shoulder. Flinched from it. It was cold as ice. But then again I felt I wanted to warm him up all over. I wanted to give him what I'd denied all those other men who took what they wanted from me. He was different. I wanted to make love to him. And later, we went back to the doughnut van, and, in the back, I did make love to him. I think of it as that, though he didn't really do much. I did all the moving. I'd never used Dad's van for that before, and it was sticky on account of all the bits of custard filling and the little patches of spilled powdered sugar and all. He sat back against a pile of delivery boxes and I didn't care that they were getting all crushed. I just ate him up, impaled myself on him, rode him up and down, wrapped my titties around his face, but all the while he was muttering about other things . . . about banging and banging on the gates of hell till his fists were raw and bloodied from the rough stone . . . I didn't know what he meant until that night, when I met him again at the Forbin–St. Cloud monument and saw him kneeling at the carved mouth of hell and beating his fists against the granite . . . but I didn't care, you see, because I'd found someone as lost as me, maybe even more lost, someone I could give to freely, someone I could love.

—So you became a member of his . . . secret society.

—If you could call it that. It was just him and three of us girls. He called us the Brides of Dracula. He drank our blood. He mixed it with vanilla syrup and ice in a blender. Said he needed the ice because the heat of the blood would send him straight to the other world, and he wasn't ready yet, he still had things to do in the human world. The other two girls were Ramona and Chastity. They're dead now. He found Ramona lurking outside a homeless shelter over there in the city. Chastity was a runaway. I know what we done was wrong, but Jody,

well, he had a vision and such. When he talked, we felt we belonged to something big. He gave us a structure, too, our
nightly hunts. He taught us to pounce on alley cats and bite
their necks and slurp down the gushing blood. That was disgusting, but it was kinda thrilling, too. And now and then as a
really special treat he'd fuck us. But it was always with us doing
all the work, and him staring off into space, thinking I guess
about his great vision. Which he finally explained to us. The day
before . . . you know.

—He told you . . . what? That you were going to go on a
killing spree?

—Not exactly. I remember it perfectly because we were having another meeting in Dad's van. We always used it for meet-
ings now, because I could always get the van between deliveries,
and now, behind the smell of apple-cinnamon and chocolate,
there was also a permanent smell of sex. Because the three of us
. . . the girls I mean, not Jody . . . we'd do stuff in there while we
were waiting for him. Thing is, you know how it is when us girls
hang out together all the time . . . our periods kind of fall into
sync. And so all three of us were on the rag at the same time.
And we were all laughing about it, how it had gotten closer and
closer in the last two months and now, this time, third time
lucky and such, bang, same day, same second practically. And
we were all idly fingerbanging each other while we talked about
our fucked-up lives. So finally he shows up. And he's all, I smell
blood. God, I smell blood! It makes me feel all . . . oh, I want it,
I want it. And since we're all already with our panties down,
and all moist from playing with each other, he's all over us,
pulling out our tampons, lapping at us like a cat cleaning its ass.
God, it was hot! I never felt that way before. The way he flecked
my clitoris, the way he tickled my lips, teasing out every last
flake of coagulating blood . . .

—Your Honor, spare us this pornography! Objection, objection!

—Your Honor, this evidence speaks directly to the nature of
the defendant's mental illness . . . his delusional obsession with
the, ah, sanguinary aspects of the human body.

—Young lady, get it over with, and proceed to the question at hand.

—Yes, Your Honor. Um . . . what were you going to ask me, sir?

—Well, Natalie. You've just explained that Jody became unusually animated as a result of the smell of blood.

—That's true, sir. As I say, usually he would just lay there while we rubbed up and down on him, but that day he was excited. He even came. I mean, he just *spurted*.

—I don't think we need to know all that, but did the defendant then say anything about his grand vision?

—Oh, yes.

—What did he say?

—Well, as we all lay there in the back of the van, there was this good, warm feeling, you know, us against the world and such, a little tiny piece of heaven. But then Jody begins to talk about the dark path we have to trod. I had my foot in the door, he said, and I was pushing my way in, and they sent me back out into the world. They didn't think I was good enough. But I'm gonna show them. I'm the king of the vampires. No dead dude in a coffin is gonna be badder than me.

—Did this statement contradict previous statements of his to you and your group of followers?

—Yes, sir. He always told us he was sent up here from the other world, that he had given up the world beyond so he could find disciples and teach all of them the dark path before he went back. Now he sounded bitter and angry, and we didn't know what to do.

—What did he say next?

—We're going to do something really big, he said. An orgasm of blood and pain. We're gonna kill, maim, disembowel, decapitate, swim in the lubricous life force that spews from the veins of the dying. The way he said it, you gotta believe, it sounded . . . poetic . . . beautiful . . . I could feel the blood rushing joyfully from my pussy to meet his eager tongue . . . I could think about nothing but all that blood, swirling over me, carrying me toward the final climax in waves of crimson passion, oh

God, Jody made me feel that good, all of us, he made us want to kill and to die the way we wanted his arms around us, his cock inside us and such.

—And how do you feel about Jody now?

—I love him, sir.

—Do you think he hears you, hiding as he does behind his wall of self-imposed silence?

—I don't know. Yeah. Maybe not. Maybe he doesn't hear any of us no more, maybe he's listening to a different music, the rushing of the river of death.

—I want to spare the jury yet another description of the crimes themselves . . . the slashing, the torture . . . all the things you witnessed but did not participate in . . . because you . . . had a twinge of conscience.

—I chickened out. I shoulda done them things. Like all the other girls did.

—Then you would be in trouble, Natalie.

—I don't care! Do you understand? I love him. I want to go with him! Into the ultimate kingdom. Into the dark country. Jody, listen to me, you motherfucker . . . I didn't mean to betray you . . . I'm here because I want them to know the truth . . . what you mean to me . . .

—Your Honor, the witness isn't supposed to be talking to the defendant.

—Sustained. Kindly confine your comments to the questions asked of you, Miss—

—Your Honor! The coffin! It's busting open! The lid is sliding again!

—Got a stake handy, Bailiff? You can use my gavel as a mallet, you superstitious nincompoop. You people are . . . screw it, let whoever it is come out. If the ladies and gentlemen of the jury would refrain from panicking—and just what the hell do you think you're doing in my courtroom, young lady, in the nude? Have you no sense of propriety at all? Bailiff, fetch the witness a damn cloak.

—Jody.

—Young lady, you're not on the stand yet. Go and sit down right this minute or I'll cite you for contempt.

—Be silent!

—How dare you!

—In this human world, you may be a judge of men, Mr. Trepte, but there are darker courtrooms, and there are punishments more dire than death. I stand before you, a naked woman, whose flesh is colder than the grave. Touch me if you dare.

—Madam, there is no higher authority present in this chamber than this jury and this judge. If you have anything to say, you will have to wait your turn.

—So what do you plan to do, asshole, cite me for contempt?

—Bailiff, cuff her!

—Your Honor, she's just ripped off the bailiff's head!

—Sobering isn't it, Mr. Kangaroo Court, to see your enforcing officer's torso twitching on the carpet. I'm sorry that I won't be paying the dry-cleaning bill. Where I come from, we don't have money . . . or credit cards, for that matter.

—Uh—uh—

—Speechless, at last, Your Honor! Give me a minute while I take a sip from this poor man's gushing jugular. Excuse me while I wipe my lips clean with his matted hair. Where shall I throw it? You have a basket? Thanks. Now . . . where was I? Oh yes. The defendant. The silent one. You who heard voices in the night, who were labeled a paranoid schizophrenic by Dr. Shimada over there . . . you who have been true to your deep dark self, all this time, you who have kept the faith . . . I've come for you. I ain't Cat Sperling, the town slut, no more . . . I've worked on my accent some . . . you learn a lot when you hang with the undead . . . plenty of sixty-four-dollar words in *their* vocabulary when they've been around a couple of centuries. Look at me, silent boy. I like that you kept silent after it was over. You betrayed no one. Oh! Bullets! My, my. They go right through me. I feel nothing. No feeling, you know, when you cross over the river. No mortal feelings, anyways. Look at me, silent boy. I'm still beautiful, ain't I? Beautiful as the day you saw me. My body is as firm as when you first touched it, but now it's cold as marble. It's a dead body, Jody, a corpse. But oh, a corpse that everyone in this room wants, man *and* woman, a corpse that exudes a sensuality that the living can't match, a corpse that breathes *eternity, eternity* . . . Oh, Jody, you don't know how long you were watched, how long you were groomed for that moment of sacrifice that your friend ruined for you. Oh, he meant well. But he's just an ignorant human being. And human beings are just cattle. They're here to serve us. Their lives are over in an instant. I watched over you . . . saw you grow up alienated . . . knew you were marked to become one of us. In this world a throwaway, one of the disenfranchised . . . in the world beyond . . . a prince. When you had your fantasies of death . . . when you dreamed of death and woke up with a stiffie in the night . . . one of us was watching . . . perhaps in the shape of a mist, coiling about the keyhole of your bedroom door . . . or a black rat, sniffing its way along the floorboards . . . smelling the crimson of your dreams. Oh, Jody, it was all meant for you . . . my seduction of your dumb, sentimental friend . . . the party at the cemetery . . . partly real, partly a fabric of hypnotizing illusions. Do you understand that? Oh, your doctor noted it all down as a dementia—delusions of grandeur—megalomania—paranoia—when it was all nothing but the truth. You heard the music of the night when others heard only wind, rain, the rustling of leaves, frightened children murmuring in their sleep. Oh, we were disappointed when you didn't die the slow death that night! You have always been special to the dark ones. All your life you've heard that whispered in your ear, you've wondered if you were going mad. Those whispers were all true. You have been anointed from birth, Jody. I wasn't kidding when I called you a prince. That's exactly what you are. The Duke couldn't welcome you into the kingdom himself. His coffin has been taken faraway, for safekeeping. It's getting dangerous for us here, with all these movies and role-playing games. Lies, but flirting with the truth. He's sent me to fetch you, Jody. I told you we were all sad when you didn't come to us. Some of us wanted to fetch you by force. But the Duke said, in his wisdom, Leave him be. The darkness is strong in him. If he cannot find the true kingdom right away, he will strive to build his own kingdom . . . he will mirror our world in his own world . . . and he will make himself worthy . . . and when he is ready . . . we will bring him in. That's what I'm here for. To finish what we started. Look at me now. Look at me, translucent as alabaster, pale as moonlight; come to me. That's right. You don't need that ugly orange prison suit any more. Those cuffs are useless now. Come to me. I twist them off with a flick of my wrist. The undead have great strength. They draw their strength from the womb of Mother Earth herself. Oh, Jody, come, come. Unzip that uniform and stand before me naked. Touch me. Look at the horrified faces of the judge and jury. They are so unimportant now. Slide your finger against the bailiff's blood, congealing on my breasts. Lick them. Lick the blood from the areola. Slow now, slow. I kiss you now. My teeth meet soft flesh. I taste blood. Give me your blood. Warm my stone heart with your last life force. Oh, Jody, Jody, you are beautiful. Give me all of you. I bite your chest . . . your abdomen . . . my fangs tease at the sensitive tip of your penis . . . blood engorges it . . . blood stiffens it . . . blood that will soon run gushing down my throat . . . oh, Jody, Jody, this is the end for you, the end and the beginning . . . drink me now . . . as I drink you . . . the cold of death is absolute . . . the warmth of life is but a shadow . . . and now . . . come . . . come into my coffin . . . I don't want to sleep alone any more . . . come into the coffin . . . into the womb . . . into the tomb . . . oh, Jody, this is love . . . this is death.

The transcript ends here. At least, the decipherable portion of the transcript. What follows on the tape is chaos. Screaming. Here and there a single word: blood, shit, fuck, no, no, no.

There was also the fire. The courthouse razed to the ground, the judge, the superlawyers, many others hospitalized for third-degree burns. There was also the complete disappearance of the defendant. Not a charred husk of him . . . not a bone . . . not a tooth.

There was also the silence. Not a word in the press. Not a picture in the paper. Not a clip in the news.

But you know all that. You follow the media.

Perhaps you even know about the transcript, which has been pronounced a hoax by almost every expert who has been given the privilege of examining it.

Does it matter? As a certain Roman procurator once said to a certain rabbi, in a courtroom not unlike this courtroom, two thousand years ago . . . *What is truth?*

It really doesn't matter to most of you. So stop reading now. Close the book. There's nothing to be gained from idle speculation about the nature of light and darkness . . . about the relationship between love and death . . . between desire and self-destruction. Get on with your lives. Go on. Do it.

Unless, of course, you can hear the music of the night . . .

Chelsea Quinn Yarbro

In the Face of Death

CHELSEA QUINN YARBRO, *of Berkeley, California, is an award-winning fantasist perhaps best known for* The Saint-Germain Chronicles *and other vampire tales, one of which, "Advocates," was co-winner of the prestigious World Horror Award for Best Novelette. "In the Face of Death," tangentially linked to the Saint-Germain series, describes a plausible "period-piece" affair between a fascinating vampire and William Tecumseh Sherman (1820–1891), a West Coast banker who became one of the Civil War's most important Union generals, second only in importance to U. S. Grant. Sherman's military genius was surpassed by his hatred of war; his alleged penchant for bloodiness was a reputation reportedly engineered by his enemies in the South and North. According to Ms. Yarbro, Sherman's family was indeed absent from the scene during the period in which her story takes place.*

I know of no courage greater . . . than the courage to love in the face of death.
—WILLIAM TECUMSEH SHERMAN TO QUEEN VICTORIA

FROM THE JOURNAL of Madelaine de Montalia
San Francisco, 18 May, 1855
At last! And only four days later than anticipated when we left the mountains. Had I been willing to travel on the river from Sacramento, we would have arrived on the date anticipated. . . . My native earth should be in one of the warehouses, waiting for me, which is just as well, as I have got down to less than a single chest of it.

My escorts brought me to a very proper boardinghouse on Sacramento Street, and have gone on themselves to find suitable lodgings. A Mrs. Imogene Mullinton, a very respectable widow from Vermont, owns this place and takes only reputable single women. She has given me a suite of three rooms at the top of the house, her best, and for it I am to pay $75 a month, or any fraction of a month, a very high price for such accommodations, but I have discovered that everything in San Francisco is expensive. The suite will do until I can arrange to rent a house for three or four months . . .

Tomorrow I will have to pay off my escorts, which will require a trip to the bank to establish my credit here, and to begin making my acquaintance with the city. Doubtless the excellent Mrs. Mullinton can direct me to Lucas and Turner; the documents from their Saint Louis offices should be sufficient bona fides to satisfy them.

At the corner of Jackson and Montgomery, the new Lucas and Turner building was one of the most impressive in the burgeoning city; located near the shore of the bay and the many long wharves that bristled far out into the water, the bank was well situated to sense the thriving financial pulse of San Francisco.

Madelaine, wearing the one good morning dress she had left from her long travels, stepped out of the hackney cab and made her way through the jostling crowds on the wooden sidewalk to the bank itself. As she stepped inside, she felt both relief and regret at once again being back in the world of commerce, progress, and good society. Holding her valise firmly, she avoided the tellers' cages and instead approached the nearest of the desks, saying, "Pardon me, but will you be kind enough to direct me to the senior officer of the bank?"

The man at the desk looked up sharply. "Have you an appointment, ma'am?" he asked, noticing her French accent with faint disapproval, and showing a lack of interest that Madelaine disliked, though she concealed it well enough. He was hardly more than twenty-two or -three and sported a dashing mustache at variance with his sober garments.

"No, I am just arrived in San Francisco," she said, and opened her valise, taking out a sheaf of documents, her manner determined; she did not want to deal with so officious an underling as this fellow. "I am Madelaine de Montalia. As you can see from this—" she offered him one of the folded sheets of paper "—I have a considerable sum on deposit with your Saint Louis bank and I require the attention of your senior officer at his earliest convenience."

The secretary took the letter and read it, his manner turning from indulgent to impressed as he reviewed the figures; he frowned as he read through them a second time, as if he was not convinced of what he saw. Folding the letter with care, he rose and belatedly gave Madelaine a show of respect he had lacked earlier. "Good gracious, Madame de Montalia. It is an unexpected pleasure to welcome you to Lucas and Turner."

"Thank you," said Madelaine with a fine aristocratic nod she had perfected in her childhood. "Now, if you will please show me to the senior officer? You may use those documents to introduce me, if that is necessary."

"Of course, of course," he said, so mellifluously that Madelaine had an urge to box his ears for such obsequiousness. He opened the little gate that separated the desks from the rest of the floor, and stood aside for her as she went through, her head up, the deep-green taffeta of her morning dress rustling as she moved. "If you will allow me to go ahead and . . ." He made a gesture indicating a smoothing of the way.

She sighed. "Is that necessary?"

He made an apologetic grimace. "Well, you see, there are very few wealthy young women alone in San Francisco. And you were not expected." Again he gestured to express his concern.

"No doubt," she said, and halted in front of a large door of polished oak. While the secretary rapped, Madelaine examined her brooch watch, thinking she would be fortunate to be out of the bank much before noon.

"Come in," came the crisp order from a sharp, husky voice.

The secretary made a slight bow to Madelaine, then stepped

into the office, discreetly closing the door behind him, only to emerge a few minutes later, all smiles and half bows, to open the door wide for her in order to usher her into the oak-paneled office of the senior officer of the bank.

The man who rose behind the orderly desk surprised Madelaine a little; he was younger than she expected—no more than his mid-thirties—sharp-featured, wiry and tall, with bright-red hair and steel-colored eyes, and a pinched look about his mouth as if he were in constant discomfort. His dark suit was neat as a uniform, and he greeted her with fastidious correctness. "William T. Sherman, senior officer of Lucas and Taylor in San Francisco, at your service, Madame de Montalia."

She took his hand at once. "A pleasure, Mr. Sherman," she said, liking his decisive manner. "I hope you will be willing to help me establish an account here."

His face did not change, but a glint appeared in his eyes. "Certainly." He signaled to the secretary. "Jenkins, leave us to it. And don't close the door."

Madelaine saw that the secretary was flustered. "But I thought—" he said.

"I will handle the opening of this account. Given the size of this woman's resources, such an account would need my authorization in any case." He came around the end of the desk not only to bring a chair for Madelaine, but to hurry Jenkins out of his office. He carried the Queen Anne chair to a place directly across the desk from his, and held it for Madelaine. "Madame?"

As she sat down, Madelaine smiled up at Sherman. "Thank you," she said and noticed a quick frown flicker across his face.

Taking his place behind the desk once more, Sherman spread out two of the letters in her packet of documents on the wide expanse of leather-edged blotter. "I see you deposited ninety-five thousand pounds sterling in the Saint Louis office of this bank in 1848. The most recent accounting, from a year ago, shows your balance only slightly reduced." He regarded her with curiosity. "That is a considerable fortune, Madame. And odd, that it should be in pounds sterling, not francs."

"I inherited most of it," she said, not quite truthfully, for in the last century she had been able to increase her wealth far beyond what her father had amassed. "And I have lived in London for more than ten years before I came here. Much of my money is in England." She made no mention of funds she had in France, Italy, and Switzerland.

"And you have not squandered it, it would seem. Very prudent. Unusual, you will permit me to say, in a young woman." He looked at her with increasing interest. "What do you want me to do for you? How much were you planning to transfer to this bank? In dollars?"

"I would think that twenty-five thousand would be sufficient," she said. "In dollars."

He coughed once. "Yes; I should think so. More than sufficient. Unless you are determined to cut a dash in society, you will find the sum ample. That's five times my annual salary." He confided this with a chuckle and a scowl. "Very well, Madame," he went on affably. "I will put the transaction in order. In the meantime, you will be free to draw upon funds up to . . . shall we say, five thousand dollars?"

Madelaine nodded. "That would be quite satisfactory, since you are able to contrive to live on it for a year, though prices here are much higher than I anticipated. Still, I should be able to practice good economy."

"You certainly have until now, given the state of your account." He cocked his head, a speculative light in his eyes, his long fingers moving restlessly as if searching for a pencil or a cigar. "Unless these funds have only recently been passed to your control? In that case, I would recommend you seek an able advisor, to guide you in the matters of investment management—"

"Mr. Sherman—" she interrupted, only to be cut off.

"Forgive me. None of my business. But I can't help but wonder how it comes about that you want twenty-five thousand now and have spent less than half of that in the last seven years?" He braced his elbows on the desk and leaned forward, his chin propped on his joined hands.

"My studies did not require it," she answered, determined not to be affronted by his directness.

"Ah. You were at school," he said, his expression lightening. He slapped his hands on the blotter and sat back, his question answered to his satisfaction.

"Something of the sort," she responded, in a manner she thought was almost worthy of Saint-Germain.

San Francisco, 23 May, 1855

Mrs. Mullinton has given me the address of an excellent dressmaker, and the first of my new clothes should be delivered tomorrow. There are six other ensembles on order, to be delivered in three weeks. Once I have settled in, I will need to order more . . . I suppose it is worth getting back into corsets for the pleasure of wearing silk again.

There is a private concert tomorrow afternoon that Mrs. Mullinton wishes to attend and has asked me to accompany her to. Now that she knows I have money and social position, she is determined to make the most of both of them, convinced I will add to her consequence in the town. If I am to remain here for three or four months, I will need to enlarge my acquaintances or risk speculation and gossip, which would do me no good at all. . . . Perhaps I will find someone who is to my liking, whom I please, who is willing to be very, very discreet. In a place like this, lapses are not easily forgotten by anyone . . .

My chests are at the Jas. Banner Warehouse near where Columbus and Montgomery Streets converge. I must make arrangements to retrieve them soon, not only because I am low on my native earth, but because the costs for storing the chests are outrageous. I had rather keep them in the safe at Lucas and Turner for such sums . . .

The house on Jackson Street was a fine, ambitious pile, made of local redwood timber and newly painted a deep-green color, unlike many of its paler neighbors, with the trim of yellow to contrast the white-lace curtains in most of the windows. It faced the street squarely with an Italianate portico of Corinthian columns; it was set back from the roadway and approached by a half-moon drive.

When Mrs. Mullinton alighted from the rented carriage, she fussed with her bonnet before stepping aside for her guest to join her.

Madelaine de Montalia had donned her new dress, an afternoon frock suitable for early suppers and garden parties, and as such, unexceptionable for this concert. It was a soft shade of lavender, with bared shoulders framed by a double row of ruched silk. The bodice was fitted and came to a point in the front over a skirt of three tiers of ruched silk spread over moderate crinolines. For jewelry, she wore a necklace of pearls and amethysts; her coffee-colored hair was gathered in a knot with two long locks allowed to escape and fall on her shoulders. An embroidered shawl was draped over her arms, and in one hand she held a beaded reticule. As she descended from the carriage, Madelaine silently cursed her enveloping skirts.

A Mexican servant, whose angular features revealed a significant admixture of Indian blood, ushered them into the house and explained in heavily accented English that the host and hostess were in the ballroom to receive their guests, while bowing in the direction they should go.

"We are not the first, are we?" Mrs. Mullinton asked, afraid that she had committed an intolerable gaffe.

"Oh, no. There are others here already," the servant assured the two women with a respectful lowering of his eyes.

"Thank goodness," Mrs. Mullinton said in an undervoice to Madelaine as they went along the corridor to the rear of the house. "It would not do to have it said we came early."

"Whyever not?" asked Madelaine, who had become more punctual as she grew older.

"My dear Madame," said Mrs. Mullinton in shock, "for women to arrive while only the host and hostess are present smacks of impropriety, particularly since you are new in town." Her long, plain face took on an expression of consternation as she considered this outrage.

"Then it would be better to arrive late?" asked Madelaine, trying to determine what Mrs. Mullinton sought to achieve.

"Heavens, no, for then it would seem that we did not appreciate the invitation," said Mrs. Mullinton. "I am very pleased that we have made our arrival so well." She raised her voice as she stepped into the ballroom antechamber. "You may find our entertainment sadly dull, Madame, after the excitement of London."

"Possibly," said Madelaine. "But as I have not seen London for eight years, I think what you offer here will suit me very well." She smiled at the couple approaching them—he of medium height and bristling grey hair; she a very pretty woman with a deep bosom and fair hair, in a fashionable dull-red afternoon dress that did not entirely become her; she was at least a decade her husband's junior.

"Mrs. Mullinton," said their hostess. "How nice of you to join us." She took Mrs. Mullinton's hand and kissed the air near her right cheek. "This must be your new guest." She turned to Madelaine. "I am Fanny Kent."

"And I am Madelaine de Montalia," she said, curtsying slightly to her hostess before taking her hand, though they made no other move toward each other.

"My husband, the Captain," added Fanny, indicating her partner. "My dear, you know Mrs. Mullinton. And this is Madelaine de Montalia."

Horace Kent bowed over Madelaine's hand. "Enchanted, Madame," he declared, and then shook Mrs. Mullinton's hand in a nominally polite way.

The four other couples in the room were presented, and by that time another pair of guests had arrived, and Madelaine gave herself over to the task of learning the names of the people in the room, hoping she would not confuse any of them as their numbers steadily increased.

"I have already had the pleasure," said the latest arrival, some twenty minutes later. Sherman bowed slightly to Madelaine.

"Yes," said Madelaine, taking refuge in a familiar face. "I met Mr. Sherman on my second day in the city."

"At the bank, I suppose," said the man accompanying him, another foreigner, with a Russian accent. He beamed at Madelaine and continued in French. "It is an honor to meet such a distinguished lady traveling so far from home. We are two strangers on these shores, are we not?"

Sherman looked from one to the other. "Madame, let me present Baron deStoeckl. Baron, Madame de Montalia."

"Delighted, Baron," said Madelaine, and went on, "I had thought that everyone in California except for the Indians were here as strangers, and far from home."

"Touché, Madame." As the Baron kissed her hand, he said, still in French, "I hope you will excuse my friend's curt manner. There is no changing him."

"And remember," said Sherman in rough-accented French, "he understands what you say." With that, he gave Madelaine a polite nod and passed on to greet General Hitchcock, who had just entered the ballroom.

"He misses the army, or so it seems to my eyes," said the Baron to Madelaine. "If you will excuse me?"

She gestured her consent, and a moment later had her attention claimed by her hostess, who wished her to meet Joseph Folsom. "He is one of the most influential men in the city," Fanny confided. "You will be glad to know him."

Madelaine allowed herself to be led away; she saw Mrs. Mullinton deep in conversation with an elderly lady in lavish half-mourning, and thought it best not to interrupt her.

It was almost an hour later, after the string quartet had beguiled them with Mozart and a medley of transcribed themes from *Norma*, that Madelaine once again found herself in Sherman's company. He had just come from the bustle around the punch bowl bearing a single cup when he saw her standing by the window, looking out into the fading day. He strolled to her side, and remarked, "The fog comes in that way throughout the summer."

She turned to him, a bit startled, and said, "So Mrs. Mullinton has warned me, and advised that I carry a wrap no matter how warm the day." She went on, "What do you think of these musicians?"

"More to the point, Madame, what do *you* think of them? Undoubtedly you have more experience of these things than I do." He sipped from his cup and then said, before she could answer his first question. "I would fetch you something, but that would cause idle tongues to wag. With my wife away, I cannot risk giving any cause for gossip that would distress her."

"Certainly not," said Madelaine, regarding Sherman with some surprise. "On occasions such as this—"

"You will forgive me, Madame, for saying that you do not know these sniping cats who have nothing better to do with their conversation than to blacken the reputations of those around them." He bowed slightly and was about to turn away when he looked down at her. "You may find it difficult to move about in society, single as you are. If you were not so beautiful a young woman, Madame, and so vivacious, there would be little to fear, but—" And with that, he was gone.

As Madelaine and Mrs. Mullinton were taking their leave of the Kents at the end of the concert, Fanny Kent drew Madelaine aside, with signs of apprehension about her. She made herself come to the point at once. "I could not but notice that you and Mr. Sherman spoke earlier."

Madelaine knew well enough not to laugh. "Yes, some minor matters about when I could sign certain papers at the bank. Mr. Sherman wished to know when I would be available to tend to them. I gather they will be ready earlier than I had been told."

Fanny looked reassured, her rosy cheeks flaming with embarrassment. "Oh, Madame. I am so sorry. I have mistaken the . . . But as you have just come here, and have not yet learned . . . I was afraid you were wanting to fix your interest . . . oh, good gracious."

"Dear Mrs. Kent," Madelaine said pleasantly enough but with grim purpose, "I am aware that Mr. Sherman is a married man."

"Yes, he is," said Fanny Kent flatly. "With three hopeful children."

"I have no intention of making his life awkward for him.

What a goose I should be to do such a foolish thing. Great Heaven, Mrs. Kent, he is my banker. I rely upon him to look after my financial welfare while I am in San Francisco." She smiled easily. "And because he is, I will have to speak with him upon occasion, and call at his office to take care of transactions that married women leave to their husbands to perform, but which I must attend to for myself. I hope that people understand the reasons are those of business; I have no motives beyond that."

"Of course, of course," said Fanny hastily.

"It would be most inconvenient to have to contend with malicious speculation over such minor but necessary encounters." This time her smile had purpose to it.

Now Fanny let out a long sigh, one hand to her opulent bosom. "It is very sad that Mrs. Sherman has had to be away from him just now," she said. "The run on the bank left him exhausted, and his asthma, you know, has been particularly bad. To care for those two children as well—" She put her hand to her cheek. "Not that you have any reason to be concerned. I'm sure the worst is behind him. He managed the crisis of the run quite successfully, and now Lucas and Turner is likely to stand as long as the city. It would be a terrible thing if scandal should fix to his name after he has won through so great a trial."

Madelaine blinked as she listened, and realized that Sherman had been right to warn her about gossip.

San Francisco, 29 May, 1855

I must look for a house. I need someplace where I can lay down my native earth and restore myself through its strength, and I do not want to pay Mrs. Mullinton another $75 for my apartments, pleasant though they are. A few of the other women here are starting to question how I live, especially my refusal to dine with them, and I must make an effort to stop their speculations as soon as possible. If I had an establishment of my own, and my own staff, I could deal with these problems summarily. No doubt Lucas and Turner can assist in finding what I want. . . .

. . . .

"This is an unexpected surprise," said Sherman, coming out of his office to greet Madelaine shortly before noon two days later. He motioned Jenkins aside and indicated that he wanted her to follow him. "I have the papers ready for you to sign. They'll go off on the next ship, and the funds will arrive as quickly as possible after that. In these days we can handle these transactions in less than two months. But let us discuss your matters less publicly. If you will be kind enough—?"

"Of course. And I thank you for giving me a little time; I am sure you are very busy." As she made her way back to his office, Madelaine realized that many of the customers and about half the staff in the bank were staring at her, either directly or covertly. She knew it was not just because she had worn her newest walking dress—a fetching mode in grape-colored fine wool; she drew her short jacket more closely around her as she took the chair Sherman offered, aware that once again, he had left the door half open.

He settled himself behind his desk and held out a pen to her as he reached for the papers needing her signature. "Now then, Madame, what more are we to have the pleasure of doing for you?"

Madelaine squared her shoulders. "I want to rent a house. At least through August, possibly for longer."

Sherman stared at her. "Rent a house?" he repeated as if she had spoken in a language he did not adequately understand.

She went on without remarking on his surprise. "Yes. Something not too lavish, but as comfortable and suitable as possible. And I will need to hire a staff for it." She swiftly reviewed the permission form and signed first one, then the second, the pen spattering as the ink dried on the nib. "Probably no more than three or four will serve me very well."

"You want to rent a house," Sherman said again, as if he had at last divined her meaning. "But why? Is there something not to your liking at Mrs. Mullinton's?"

"Only the price and the lack of privacy," said Madelaine as politely as she could. "That is not to say anything against Mrs. Mullinton. She has been all that is courteous and attentive, and

Mrs. Mullinton's establishment is a fine one, but not for what I am engaged in doing."

"And what might that be?" asked Sherman, disapproval scoring his sharp features.

"I am writing a book," said Madelaine candidly.

Sherman's glower vanished only to be replaced by an indulgent smirk; Madelaine decided she liked the glower better, for it indicated genuine concern, and this showed nothing of the sort.

"A book?"

"On my studies here in America," she said with a coolness she did not feel.

"Have you any notion of what must go into writing a book? It is far different than making entries in a diary; it requires discipline and concerted effort." He continued to watch her with a trace of amusement.

Stung, Madelaine said. "Yes. I have already written three volumes on my travels in Egypt."

"When you were an infant," said Sherman. "You told me you have spent your time here at school, and before that—"

"Actually, I said I had been studying," Madelaine corrected him. "You were the one who said I had been at school."

Sherman straightened in his chair as he took the two papers back from her. "You were not in the convent!" he declared with conviction. "You have not the manner of it."

Madelaine had managed to regain control over her impulsive tongue; she said, "That is nothing to the point. All that matters is that I find an appropriate house to rent. If you are not willing to help me in this endeavor, you need only tell me and I will go elsewhere."

This indirect challenge put Sherman on his mettle. "Certainly I will do what I can. As your financial representative, I must question anything that does not appear to be in your best interests." He gave her a severe stare. "If you will let me know your requirements and the price you had in mind to pay, I will have Jenkins begin his inquiries."

"Thank you," said Madelaine, her temper beginning to cool. "I will need a small- or medium-sized house in a good location, one with room for a proper study. I will need a bed-chamber and a dressing room, a withdrawing room and a parlor, a dining room, a pantry, and a reasonably modern kitchen, with quarters for a staff of three." She had established these requirements for herself over eighty years ago. She added the last in an off-handed way. "Also, I must be able to reach the foundation with ease."

"The foundation!" Sherman repeated in astonishment. "Why should the foundation concern you?"

Madelaine thought of the trunks of her native earth and felt the pull of it like exhausted muscles yearning for rest. "I have learned that it is wise to know what the footing of a house may be," she answered.

"Most certainly," Sherman agreed, pleasantly surprised that Madelaine should have so practical a turn of mind. "Very well. I will stipulate that in my instructions to Jenkins: easy access to the foundations." He regarded her with the manner of one encountering a familiar object in an unfamiliar setting. "How soon would you like to occupy the house?"

"As soon as possible," said Madelaine. "I want to get my work under way quickly, and I cannot do that until I have a place where I may examine my notes and open all my records—I assure you, they are extensive—for review; at the moment most of them are still in trunks and are of little use to me there." She smiled at him, noticing for the first time that he had dark circles under his eyes. "If you will excuse me for mentioning it, you do not appear to have slept well, Mr. Sherman. Are you unwell?"

He shrugged, looking slightly embarrassed. "My son was fussy last night; he is very young and misses his mother. I wanted to comfort him, and so I . . ." He made a brusque gesture of dismissal, then relented. "And for the last few days my asthma has been bothering me. It is a childish complaint, one that need not concern you, Madame."

Madelaine regarded him with sympathy. "I know what it is to suffer these conditions, for I, myself, cannot easily tolerate direct sunlight." She hesitated, thinking that she did not want to create gossip about the two of them. Then she offered, "I have some preparations against such continuing illnesses. If you would let me provide you with a vial of—"

"I have nitre paper," Sherman said, cutting her off abruptly. He stared at the blotter on the desk, and the papers she had signed. "But I thank you for your consideration."

"If you change your mind, you have only to let me know," said Madelaine, noticing that Sherman's face was slightly flushed. "Think of it as a gesture of gratitude for finding my house."

He nodded stiffly. "If you will call back on Monday, I will let you know what Jenkins has discovered. What was the price you had in mind again?"

"Anything reasonable. You know better than I what that would be, and you know what my circumstances are," Madelaine said as if she had lost interest in the matter. "And you know what is a reasonable amount for a landlord to ask, even with prices so very high."

Sherman nodded, his expression distant. "And the matter of staff? You said two or three?"

"If you will recommend someone to help me in hiring them, I would appreciate it." Why was she feeling so awkward? Madelaine wondered. What had happened in the last few minutes that left her with the sensation that she had done something unseemly? Was it something in her, or was it in Sherman?

"There are employment services in the city," said Sherman, looking directly at her. "I will find out which is most reputable."

Madelaine was startled at the intensity of his gaze. "I don't know what to say to you, Mr. Sherman, but thank you."

He rose stiffly. "On Monday then, Madame de Montalia."

She took his hand; it might as well have been made of wood. "On Monday, Mr. Sherman."

San Francisco, 6 June, 1855

It is still in his eyes. When Mr. Sherman and I met at the soiree given by General Hitchcock, I saw him watching me; never have I experienced so searching an expression, as if he wanted to fathom me to the depths. It is not like Saint-Germain, who looks at me with knowing: Sherman is questing. This considered inspection had nothing to do with the soiree: the fare was musical, for the General has some talent on the flute, and he, with the accompaniment of Mrs. Kent at the piano, regaled his guests with a variety of airs by Mozart and Handel, all very light and pleasant. Yet for all his watching me, Sherman hardly spoke to me during the evening. If he seeks to avoid gossip in this way, he will not succeed, for his Russian friend, deStoeckl asked me why Sherman was making such a cake of himself, an old-fashioned question I cannot answer . . .

I have been given descriptions of three houses Mr. Sherman thinks would be suitable for my needs. One is on Shotwell Street; there is a second house on Franklin, somewhat larger than the first—it is quite modern and comes with many furnishings included. The third is on Bush Street, where the hill becomes steeper; it is not as well situated as the other two. I will go inspect them in the next few days, to make up my mind . . .

The rooms in the house on Franklin Street echoed eerily as Madelaine made her way from the front parlor to the withdrawing room.

"I am sorry that the landlord has not carpeted the place," said Sherman, walking slightly behind her. "I have discussed the matter with him, and he is willing to make an adjustment in the rent charged because of the lack. You will be expected to provide the carpets, as well as the draperies and the bed. The rest is as you see," he added, indicating the furniture all swathed in Holland covers.

"Actually, I don't see," said Madalaine. "But I know the furnishings are here." She continued through the withdrawing room to the hall leading through the dining room to the kitchen and pantry beyond. "And the servants' quarters? Where are they? Upstairs?"

"They are in the rear of the house," said Sherman, the roughness in his voice not entirely due to a recent attack of asthma. "A detached cottage with three apartments."

Madelaine paused in the door to the kitchen, thinking that

having the servants' quarters out of the house could be a real advantage. "Are they adequate? Do they have sufficient heat? If the summers are as chilly as you say they are, Mr. Sherman, it will be necessary to provide heating for them, even in July."

"There are stoves in each of the apartments," Sherman said stiffly. "That will be sufficient to their needs."

"And they will dine in the kitchen?" she said, looking into that room.

"Naturally," said Sherman, and veiled a cough.

"What of the location? Is it . . . acceptable?" she asked.

"Well enough," answered Sherman, and added, as if against his will, "I have only recently moved from Green Street to a fashionable house on Rincon Hill. To please my wife."

"Who is visiting her family," Madelaine finished for him.

"Yes." He waited until the silence was too laden with unspoken things; he then chose the most trivial of them to break it. "There are so few areas where reputable women may live safely alone in this city, though this comes as close to being that as any neighborhood might do. The location is not the most fashionable, but it is not inappropriate for a single woman keeping her own house, conserving her money, and assuring her good character in society."

"All of which is important." Madelaine turned to him. "I will need to find a good draper. I will need heavy curtains and draperies for the windows in the front parlor and the withdrawing room, as well as for the front bedrooms."

"Which face west," he said, looking impressed by her resolution. "You have not yet seen the third house, Madame de Montalia."

"Why should I waste your time and my own when this suits my needs so well?" Madelaine asked, coming toward him.

Again he masked a cough, a sign of discomfort in him. "You haven't seen the bedrooms upstairs. They might not suit your purposes, or you could decide that the withdrawing room will not serve you well as your study," he pointed out. "I do not want you to contract for this house and then complain to me later that it is not what you wanted."

Madelaine smiled at him, annoyed that he would not admit she knew her own mind, and decided to enjoy herself at his expense. "Dear me, Mr. Sherman, are you always so hesitant yourself?" She could see that he was uneasy with this challenge, and she pressed her advantage, feeling his uncertainty about her as if there were a third person in the house with them, a silent judge who evaluated all that passed between them. "From what General Hitchcock told me the other afternoon, I thought you were of a decisive nature. Captain Buell says the same thing about you."

Stung, Sherman regarded her through narrowed eyes. "What do you mean, Madame?"

"I mean that you doubt my capacity to choose that which suits me," she answered, coming closer still to him. "This house will do well. The cellar is large enough and secure enough for my purposes, the rooms are pleasant, the location is satisfactory, and it requires very little attention from me, once I select the carpets and draperies. You tell me the rent is not too high for the house. Since it has so much to recommend it, I am willing to take it on a lease through . . . shall we say September?"

"You will have your book written in that time?" He flung this back at her, his face nearly expressionless.

"The greater part of it, certainly," she answered, unflustered; she enjoyed the awkwardness he felt in response to her emerging confidence.

He shrugged, making it plain that he washed his hands of the whole affair. "Be it on your head then, Madame." His eyes belied the indifference of his demeanor. "I will arrange for the lease to be drawn up this afternoon; you may sign it at my office this evening, if that is convenient."

"Excellent," she said. "And perhaps you can recommend a firm to move my things to this house at the beginning of next week? We might as well be about this as soon as possible."

He offered her a small salute. "Certainly, Madame."

"When I have established myself here, you must advise me how best to entertain, so that I will not offend any of the important hostesses in San Francisco." She meant what she said, and was relieved that for once Sherman seemed convinced.

"If my wife were here . . ." he began, then let his words trail off as he stared at her.

"If your wife were here, we should not be having this conversation, Mr. Sherman," said Madelaine, being deliberately provocative, and wondering what it was about him that so intrigued her, aside from his apparent fascination with her.

"No," he said, and looked away toward the vacant window and its view of the street beyond.

San Francisco, 10 June, 1855

I am now in my house on Franklin Street, near the intersection of Grove Street, and very pleasant it is, too. The draper is making up curtains, draperies, and valences for me; they will be installed by the day after tomorrow, or so he has assured me, which will do much to make the place more comfortable during the day. With my chests of native earth in the basement, and my mattress and shoes relined, I am already quite at home. In a week or so, all should be in order. I think I shall go on very well here.

This afternoon I interviewed over thirty applicants for my three staff positions, and have chosen a housekeeper-cum-maid who has but recently arrived from Sweden, a woman of middle years named Olga Bjornholm. I have also found a man-of-all-work named Christian van der Groot who came here to find gold but realized that he could do better helping to build houses and guard them than panning in the mountain rivers, and so here he is. I have yet to hire a cook for the household, but I have found a coachman to drive for me as needed.

I am reluctant to ask Mr. Sherman for more assistance, for I sense that his attraction is deepening, which causes him distress. It is apparent when he speaks to me that he does it with confusion springing from his attraction. If only my attraction were not deepening as well. It has been so long since I have let myself be loved knowingly; for the last decade I have taken my pleasure—such as it has been—in the dreams of men who have been interesting to me, and interested in me. And that has sufficed; it is gratification but not nourishment. For that, there must be intimacy without fantasy. And I cannot help but long for that intimacy, for knowledge and acceptance—although why I believe I should find either from William T. Sherman, I cannot tell, except for what is in his eyes.

Madelaine arrived at the French Theatre on Montgomery Street and found herself in a crush of carriages trying to get into position at the front of the theatre, where the sidewalk was broader and two wide steps were in place for those leaving their carriages. Ushers were at the edge of this boardwalk helping the arriving audience to alight.

"I don't think I can get much closer, Madame, not in another ten minutes, and you would then be late," said Enrique, her coachman, as he looked over the line of vehicles waiting to discharge their passengers. "It is less than a block from here."

"It is satisfactory, Enrique," said Madelaine with decision, handing him a small tip as she prepared to get out. "I will walk the rest of the way; if you will watch me, to be sure I am not—"

"I will watch, Madame," he said, drawing the coach up to the boardwalk. "Do you need me to let the steps down?"

"No," she replied. "I can manage well enough. The street is well lit, and I doubt anyone will importune me with so much activity about." With that, she opened the door panel, set her lap rug aside, and stepped down from the carriage, swinging the door behind her to close it. She was about to turn when she felt her cloak snag on the door latch; as she struggled to free it, she stumbled back against the coach.

"Allow me, Madame," said a voice from behind her; William Sherman reached out and freed her cloak, then held out his hand to assist her to the wide, wooden sidewalk. "Good evening, and permit me to say that I am surprised to see you here."

"At the French Theatre? Where else should I be?" Madelaine recovered her poise at once. "Thank you for your concern, Mr. Sherman. Why should you be surprised?"

He answered indirectly as he glanced at his pocket watch. "The curtain will rise in five minutes. You will have to join your company at once."

"Then I will have to hurry," said Madelaine, starting along

the boardwalk in the direction of the French Theatre. "But there is no one I am joining, Mr. Sherman. And no one is joining me. I am a Frenchwoman here for the pleasure of hearing her own language spoken, not to indulge in the entertainment of society."

"Surely you do not go to the theatre unescorted?" He gazed at her in dismay. "No, no; Madame, you must not."

"But why?" she asked reasonably. "I have attended the theatre alone in London." As soon as she said it, she realized she had slipped; it was rare for her to make such an error.

"Never tell me you went alone to the theatre as a child," he countered. "Not even French parents are so indulgent."

"Not as a child, no," she allowed, irritated that her tongue should have got her into such a pass with Sherman, of all people. He was too acute for her to forget herself around him.

He stopped walking, and looked down at her, cocking his head; the lamplight made his red hair glow like hot coals. "As a gentleman, I should never ask a lady this question, but I fear I must."

She returned his look. "What question is that? I have told you the truth, Mr. Sherman."

"Of that I have no doubt." He answered so directly that she was startled. "I can perceive the truth of you as if it grew on stalks. No, the question I ought not ask is: How old are you?" Before she could answer, he added, "Because I have received an accounting of your money in the Saint Louis office of Lucas and Turner, and with a portrait and a description to verify your identity. It would seem that you have not altered in any particular in the last decade. You appeared to be about twenty when you first went there, and you appear to be about twenty now."

Very carefully she said, "If I told you when I was born, you would not believe me."

He studied her eyes and was satisfied, "That, too, was the truth." He again looked at his pocket watch. "We are going to miss the curtain."

"Does this mean you are escorting me?" asked Madelaine, unable to resist smiling at him.

"Perforce," answered Sherman, his eyes creasing at the corners.

"But what of the gossip you have warned me about? And your wife is still with her parents." Madelaine noticed that the theatregoers had all but disappeared from the street. She glanced at Sherman. "Are you really set on seeing Racine?"

His face did not change, but his voice softened. "No."

"Nor am I," said Madelaine, who had seen *Phaedre* more than twenty times in the last sixty years. "Surely there is somewhere we can go that will not cause tongues to wag?"

Most of those going to the theatre were in their place. The few who remained on the street hurried to reach their seats before the curtain went up; they paid no attention to Madelaine and Sherman.

He coughed once. "There are rooms at the casinos, private rooms. Men dine there, in private. Sometimes these rooms are used for assignations."

"Would that bother you?" asked Madelaine. "Going to such a place?"

"It should bother you," said Sherman sternly. Then he made up his mind. He took her by the elbow and started to lead her in the direction away from the French Theatre. "My carriage is in a livery around the corner on Pine Street," he said.

"I wish you would not hold on to my arm in that manner," she said to him. "It's uncomfortable."

He released her at once, chagrined. "I meant nothing unsuitable, Madame." He put more than two feet between them. "You must understand that I only sought to guard—"

"Oh! for all the saints in the calendar!" Madelaine burst out, then lowered her voice. "I meant nothing but what I said: I dislike having my arm clutched. But I am glad of your company, Mr. Sherman, and your protection. I know these streets can be dangerous."

He paused at the corner of Pine Street. "I will take you home."

"My coachman will do that, thank you," said Madelaine amiably, "after we have our private discussion."

This time there was an eagerness in his eyes as he looked down at her. "What did you mean by discussion, since you are clarifying your meaning, Madame?"

"That, in large part, is up to you," said Madelaine, regarding him steadily. "I will not seduce you, or demand what you are unwilling to give; I want no man who is not enthusiastic to have me."

He laughed abruptly. "What man would that be? One who is dead, or prefers the bodies of men?"

Madelaine answered him seriously. "I do not mean only my body, Mr. Sherman. If that is all I sought, it is there for the taking, all around us, at acceptable prices. I mean a man who is willing to see into my soul. And to let me see into his."

Taken aback, Sherman straightened up and stared down the dark street. "Well, your candor is admirable." He paused thoughtfully. "Let me make myself plain to you, Madame, and if what I say is repugnant to you, then I will not impose upon you any longer, and I will forget that any of this was said. No matter what you may stir in me, I cannot, and I will not, compromise my obligations to my family. I am married, and that will not be changed by any desire I may feel for you."

"I don't recall asking you to change, or to hurt your family," said Madelaine as she put her hand through his arm. "I only remember suggesting that we spend the evening together."

"And that I may have you if that is what I wish," he said, as if to give her one more chance to change her mind.

Madelaine's smile was quick. "I am not challenging you, Mr. Sherman. I am seeking to spend time with you."

"Whatever that means," said Sherman.

"Whatever that means," Madelaine concurred.

San Francisco, 16 June, 1855
  . . . Tonight will be better.

The sheets were fine linen, as soft as antique satin, and there were six pillows and a damask comforter flung in glorious disarray about the bed. In the wan spill of moonlight from the window, Sherman was standing, wearing only a loosely belted dressing robe, and smoking a thin cigar as he gazed out into the darkness. "The other evening and now this. What must you think of me?"

"Nothing to your discredit," said Madelaine quietly, hardly moving as she spoke. "I think you do not trust what you want." She pulled the sheet up to cover her breasts.

"That's kind," he said tightly. "Many another woman would be offended."

Madelaine turned on her side to look at him, regarding him with a serious expression. "If that's not it, what is bothering you?"

He met her eyes. "You are."

"Why do I bother you? Would you rather not be here?" she asked, more puzzled than apprehensive.

"No. There is no place I would rather be," he answered evenly.

"Then why—?" she began, only to be cut off.

"Because it *is* what I want," he said bluntly, and stubbed out his cigar in the saucer she had set out for that purpose. "A man in my position, with a wife and a good marriage, has other women for convenience and amusement. It isn't that way with you. You are not a convenience or an entertainment. You are not convenient at all. You are what I want. All of you. And I should not. I must not." He started toward the bed, tugging at his sash and flinging it aside as he reached her. He stared down at her as his robe fell open. "Do you know what it means to want you so much, to go beyond reason with wanting you? I want to possess you, and I fear you will possess me. I am afraid that once I touch you, I will be lost."

"Is that so terrifying a prospect?" she asked, moving to make a place beside her in the bed.

"Yes." In a shrug he dropped his dressing robe to the floor, letting it lie in a velvet puddle.

"Then come and stretch out beside me. We can talk as friends, all through the night." She piled up the pillows. "I don't require you to take me."

"How do you mean?" he asked sharply.

"If you do not want to touch me at all, you need not." She regarded him kindly. "If you would like to, then you may."

He scowled. "How can you say that you want me, that you have me here in your house, in your bed, and not care if I—"

She sighed. "I've told you before, William."

"Don't call me William," he interrupted, seeking a distraction from the confusion that warred within him.

"I won't call you Mr. Sherman, not here," she said, slapping one of the pillows with the back of her hand; though it was dark, she could see his face clearly and knew he was deeply troubled. She strove to lighten the burdens of desire that so plagued him, and decided to stay on safe ground. "What does the *T* in your name stand for?"

"My friends and . . . and family call me Cump," he said, swallowing hard.

"Cump?" She was baffled.

"My given name is Tecumseh," he said at last. "The Ewings added William when they took me in after my father's death. So that I could be baptized into Maria Ewing's Catholic religion." He sat on the edge of the bed and absently reached out to stroke her hair.

Madelaine knew he had just given her a very special gift. "You're named for the chief of the Shawnee."

"Yes," he said with urgency as he reached out and wrapped his long-fingered hands around her upper arms. "How do you know about Tecumseh?"

"I know he had a twin brother, Tenskwatawa, and they were both called The Prophet." It was not a direct answer, but it was all she was prepared to give now. "Come to me, Tecumseh. You don't have to do anything if you don't want to."

He glowered at her, then looked down at himself, sighed, and swung his legs up and under the covers. He stared up at the ceiling in the darkness. "What should we talk about?" he asked, his manner forbidding.

"Anything you wish or nothing at all. Either will please me if that is what you want." As much as she desired to lie next to him, to feel his flesh against hers for the length of her body, she, too, lay on her back and stared at the ceiling, noticing a faint crack in the ornamental plasterwork. She wanted to bridge the rift between them, and sought for something she could give him, as he had offered his name to her. "Let us share secrets, as friends do," she suggested impulsively. "If you like, I will tell you how old I am."

"That is a wonderful secret for a lady to share with a friend, and quite an admission for any woman to make." He laughed once, then looked grave. "Very well. On my honor I promise I will never repeat it," he told her somberly.

"You had best not," said Madelaine, and plunged ahead, telling herself that surprise was an advantage with this man. "For I was born on the twenty-second day of November, 1724, at Montalia, my family estate, in the south of France."

For several seconds Sherman was silent. Then he chuckled. "Seventeen-twenty-four, not 1824. That would make you more than a century old, Madame."

"I am," she said, beginning to worry.

He turned toward her, trying hard to keep the incredulity out of his voice. "All right. I deserved that. For the sake of argument, we will say you are ancient, a veritable crone. You are one hundred thirty-one years old, or will be in November." His chuckling continued, rich and easy, the hard lines in his face relaxing so that he, himself, now appeared younger than he was. "And how did you attain this great age without looking older than a girl just out?"

"Because I died on the fourth of August, 1744. I *was* just out," she replied, trying to keep her voice from trembling, though she could not disguise the chill that seized her, making her quiver.

"The fourth of August, 1744," he repeated, as if hearing the words again would change them. His chuckle turned to coughing, and he took a minute to bring his breathing under control. He lay back on the pillows, willing himself not to cough. "You don't expect me to believe this, do you?"

"Why not?" she answered, fighting the desolation that swept over her. She was afraid her teeth would chatter. "Tecumseh, you know when I am lying. I am not lying now, am I? This is the truth."

"The truth?" he scoffed. "Well, Madame, you sure look mighty pretty for a corpse." He rolled onto his side, propped himself on his elbow, and stared at her. "How can you claim to exchange confidences and then tell such bald-faced . . ." The words straggled; when he spoke again, he was awed. "You *are* telling the truth, aren't you?"

"Yes," she said as if from a great distance.

"But how . . . ?" He touched her face with one long finger; he did his best to comprehend the enormity of what she said. "Dear God, Madelaine, how?"

She gave him Saint-Germain's answer. "I drink the Elixir of Life. And I do not die. I cannot die."

This was not nearly sufficient to convince Sherman. "Then tell me something of your youth." His steel-colored eyes grew sharp. "Who was ruling France then?"

"When I came to Paris, Louis XV was king," she answered calmly, though she continued to shiver as much from the strength of her memories as from apprehension about Sherman. "That was in the fall of 1743. I went to my aunt so that she could introduce me into society."

"What sort of fellow was he, Louis XV?" demanded Sherman, making her answer a test. "I warn you, I know something about the man, and will not be fobbed off with vague answers."

"Venal, luxury-loving, indolent, handsome, overindulged, manipulative. In a word, spoiled." She stared at him, surprised when he took her hands in his. "I escaped the Terror, which is just as well."

Sherman managed a kind of laugh. "A lovely corpse without a head—that would be difficult," agreed Sherman in ill-concealed excitement. "Limiting, I should think."

"A corpse is all I would have been. Those who taste the Elixir of Life are not proof against all death. Madame la Guillotine is as deadly to me as to you. So is fire." She looked directly into his eyes. "In the time I have lived, can you imagine the number of times I have said good-bye?" And how many more times I will, she added silently to herself. She thought of Trowbridge then, of his devotion which had cost him his life to save hers; and Falke, going willingly into the furnace of the Egyptian desert in order to be free of her and the life she gave.

"No, Madelaine. Don't despair," he said, with the urgency of one who knew despair well. His arms went around her, and he drew her close to him as if to protect her from the weight of grief. "It is unbearable," he murmured, pressing his lips to her hair.

She rested her head on his chest, listening to his heart beat, hearing the pulse quicken. "I am told one learns, in time." Her breath was deep and uneven.

He reached out to turn her face up to his, searching out secrets. "What are you, then? I'd better warn you, I don't hold any truck with the supernatural. And don't preach religion at me, whatever you do. I get enough of that from Maria Ewing." He made an impatient gesture at the mention of his mother-in-law.

"No religion," she promised. "Other than that most religion is against those of us who come to this life." She stretched out to kiss him, feeling yearning and resistance in his mouth. "We die, but slip the hold death has on us, and we live—"

"On the Elixir of Life," he said, one hand sliding down her flank. "And how is this mysterious Elixir obtained?"

"It is taken from those who are willing to give it," she answered quietly. "Where there is understanding, and passion, there is also great . . . joy."

"Joy," he echoed, as if the word were terrible even as he pulled her inexorably nearer, kissing her with what he had intended as roughness but what became a tenderness of such intensity that he felt all his senses fill with her. He tried to push her away, but his body would not answer the stern command of his will; and as she guided his hands over the treasure of her flesh, he surrendered to her with all the strength of his desire.

"Slowly," she whispered as she flicked her tongue over his nipples, seeing his shock and delight. "It is better if you savor it."

"God and the devils! I am ready to explode!" He kicked

back the sheet to show her, proud and embarrassed at once. "Hurry, Madelaine. I am at the brink."

"Not yet," said Madelaine, bending to kiss him again as she straddled him. "Do not deny yourself the full measure of your passion, for you also deny me. This is not a race where glory goes to the swiftest." Then, with exquisite languor, she guided him deep within her.

His breath hissed through his clenched teeth. "I can't—"

"You can," she promised, remaining very still until he opened his eyes. Then she began to move with him, feeling his guard fall away as his ardor became adoration; at this instant her lips brushed his throat.

They lay together until the first predawn call of birds warned them of coming day.

"I don't want to leave," Sherman said, kissing the corner of her mouth. "You have enthralled me, Madelaine."

"And I am bound to you, Tecumseh," she said.

With sudden emotion, he pulled her close against him, his long fingers tangled in her hair. "What have you done to me?"

"Touched you," she answered, "And you me."

As he rose, gooseflesh on his pale skin, he brushed the arch of her lip with his fingers. "We will have to be very careful, very discreet. They know, the women here, that a man has appetites, but they will not look upon you with the same understanding."

"Yes," she agreed. "I know," and turned her head to kiss the palm of his hand.

He gathered up his clothes with care and dressed quickly, listening for sounds in the street. "I don't want anyone to know I've come here," he told her, his manner stern. "For both our sakes."

She got out of bed and pulled on a heavy silken peignoir. "I am not about to cry it to the world."

He paused in the door, regarding her steadily. "No, you are not," he conceded with a curious mixture of relief and exasperation. "It isn't in you to do that." Then he smiled, and the harshness left his face. He held his arms open, and she ran into them.

. . .

San Francisco, 1 July, 1855

Yesterday I met Tecumseh's two children, though he tells me he has a third child, Minnie, living with her grandparents, an arrangement that does not entirely please him. The children currently living with him were at a puppet show presented near the old Mission San Francisco de Assisi. I came with the Kents. . . .

He is clearly fond of both children, but takes the keenest delight in his son, Willy, who is still a baby; the boy has hair almost as red as his father's, and is quick and amiable. It is no wonder his father dotes on him . . .

Most of my notes are prepared and ready and I am about to set to work in earnest. . . .

Sherman read the first three pages in growing disbelief. "Indians," he said to her at last. *"Indians!* What in infernal damnation do you mean with this?"

Madelaine watched him as he began to pace her front parlor, ignoring the raised, cautioning finger Baron deStoeckl offered him. "It is the subject of my studies." She was in a deep-green afternoon dress, and her hair was neatly arranged, as suited any woman prepared to receive guests; the filmy light from her curtained windows gave the whole room a soft, pale glow.

Sherman would not be stilled. "Indians! What is the matter with you? How can you be such a romantic fool, to go among savages?" He was dusty from riding and made no excuse for it as he prowled his way about the room, refusing to look directly at her, for fear he might give himself away. "What do you know about Indians?"

"Enough not to call them savages. I have been studying them," said Madelaine, determined not to argue uselessly.

"Studying! A nice word for adventuring! But what do you *know* about them?" He put down the pages in triumph.

"Not nearly enough," she answered steadily. "That is why I study them, to end my ignorance."

"But you do not know what they are like; you prove that by what you're saying now," Sherman persisted. "You are one of the dreamers, thinking you have come upon discarded wisdom or neglected perceptions. You haven't a notion what kind of superstitious, bloody barbarians they are."

"Some might say the same of me," Madelaine interjected in an undervoice, then spoke up. "I have already spent time among the Osage, the Kiowa, the Pawnee, the Arapaho, the Cheyenne, the Ute, the Shoshone, and the Miwok, without anything untoward happening to me. I am working from my journals and other records I have made. For my book."

Sherman stared at her, aghast. "Is *that* what you are doing in America? Living with *Indians*?"

"For the most part, yes," said Madelaine, her face betraying no emotion.

"Don't you know how dangerous that is?" Sherman insisted, this time looking directly at her. "You think that they are noble, but they are not. I have fought Indian skirmishers, while I was mapping in the South for the army. I know what they can be. I do not need a pitched battle to show me the cruelty they embody."

"They did me no harm, and I do not think they would ever do me any," said Madelaine. "Once they realized what I wanted to know, and were convinced of my sincerity, they were most cooperative. They permitted me to study them. As I expected they would do, since they are reasonable peoples." It was not quite the truth. "Most of them," she appended, aware of Sherman's keen gaze.

"You were luckier than you had any right to be," said Sherman brusquely, breaking away from the spell of her violet eyes.

"How can you say that?" Madelaine asked, unable to keep from responding to his challenge, though she realized he was deliberately provoking her. "What danger is one European woman to them?"

"I was referring to the danger one European woman was in from them, little as she is willing to acknowledge it," said Sherman dryly. "I have some experience of Indians, remember. I have seen Seminole, Madame, and I know to my cost what implacable enemies they can be. They killed troopers who were doing them no harm whatsoever. They would ambush a few men and pick them off with arrows and blowguns. Indians are dangerous. And if the European woman is not willing to heed me, then be it on her head."

Baron deStoeckl cleared his throat. "Perhaps each of you has a point? In your own ways," he suggested in French. "I do not mean to increase dissension, but it seems to me that there is good reason to concede as much to each other."

Sherman rounded on him, his brows drawn down, his mouth a thin line. "I do not want any misfortune to befall her."

"And I do not want any misfortune to befall my Indian friends, since they have endured so much already, although they do not complain of it," said Madelaine, sensing that Sherman might understand this better then he admitted. "You know that many of them have been forced to change their way of life since the Europeans arrived here."

"As Europeans were forced to change their way of life when they came to the American wilderness." Sherman sighed once, his breathing strained. "It was not like visiting another European country, coming to this one. It still isn't, though we have cities and a few of the amenities of life. Not as we do in the East, of course, but this is not the frontier, as it was when I was here eight years ago. Then there were only a dozen streets in the whole of San Francisco." He sat down abruptly, his face draining of color as the severity of his asthma attack increased.

Madelaine recognized the symptoms; she asked Baron deStoeckl to tend to Sherman for a moment so that she could fetch something that would ease his labored breathing.

"Certainly," said Baron deStoeckl.

"No need," wheezed Sherman.

"Because it offends your pride to be helped?" Madelaine suggested, then excused herself and hurried toward the back of the house, calling to Olga to assist her. "I have a number of large stoneware jars in the cellar. Will you please bring me the one with the green seal. At once."

By the time Olga returned, Madelaine had made a hot brandy toddy, and as she peeled off the seal with a knife, she explained, "This is a very old remedy. I obtained it while traveling in Egypt." She poured some of the contents into the toddy. "If you will seal the jar again and put it back where you found it?" As Olga obeyed, Madelaine took the toddy and hurried back to the parlor where she could hear Sherman trying not to cough as he labored to breathe.

Baron deStoeckl was patting Sherman on the back and frowning when Madelaine moved him aside and held out the cup and saucer to her stricken guest.

"What's this?" Sherman demanded with difficulty.

"A toddy. It will make you better directly," she promised. "Drink it before it is too cool to help ease your trouble."

Sherman glowered at her, but took the proffered cup and winced as he sipped. "It's hot." When the cup's contents were half gone, he was noticeably improved, his breathing more regular and less labored. "Thank you, Madame," he said as soon as he was sitting straight once again.

"Finish the toddy, Mr. Sherman. You are better but not yet restored." Madelaine watched him sternly as he drank the rest and set the cup and saucer aside on the rosewood end table beside his chair. "Very good."

"I am pleased you think so, Madame," said Sherman with a wry smile. "What a stern taskmistress you are."

"I am concerned with your well-being, Mr. Sherman. Who else would handle my affairs as well as you have done?" This was intended to return their conversation to more formal tones, but it did not succeed.

"What other banker would care enough to ignore the impropriety of your studies?" Sherman countered with a gesture of capitulation that made the sharp-eyed Baron deStoeckl raise his brows in surprise.

"I doubt you will do that, Mr. Sherman. I suspect you will adopt a flanking strategy and try to wear down my resolve through a series of skirmishes, like the Seminole." Madelaine did her best to make this a teasing suggestion, one that could not be taken seriously by either man.

Sherman grinned. "Yes, a series of skirmishes along your flanks would be most . . . rewarding."

The Baron lifted his hands to show he was helpless against

these blatant flirtations. He leaned down and made one last attempt. "My good friend William, I think you are taking advantage of our hostess."

"I would certainly like to," said Sherman incorrigibly. Now that he was feeling markedly better, he was seized with high spirits. "A covert campaign is required."

"God and the archangels!" Baron deStoeckl burst out. "What of your reputation? What of hers?"

Sherman regarded his friend with a canny look. "What danger are we in? You will not repeat what we say here, will you? I know Madame de Montalia will not, and neither will I, so where is the problem? You will keep our secret." He got up and strode to Madelaine's side, purpose in every line of his body. "Don't preach to me about good sense and prudence. Not now. Not here." With that, he caught her up in his arms and bent to kiss her.

Few things flustered Madelaine; this unexpected demonstration unnerved her thoroughly. She felt her face redden, and when she could speak, she said, "What a burden you are imposing on your friend. Think, Tecumseh." She glanced at the Baron, about to apologize for the impropriety of it all when Sherman took her by the shoulders and nearly shook her.

"Damn it, woman, I want someone to know." Sherman looked down into her eyes, and his sternness vanished. He went on quietly. "I want at least one man I can trust to see what I feel for you, so that I will be able to talk with him about what you mean to me when . . . this is over."

"When your wife returns," said Madelaine.

"When you leave," said Sherman.

Baron deStoeckl bowed to them. "You may rely on my discretion," he promised them in French.

San Francisco, 21 July 1855

After an absence of sixteen days, Tecumseh has returned to my bed. This time he had no hesitation, no awkward beginnings. His embraces were long and deep and he undertook to follow my lead, to find out how long he could build his passion before spending. He was merry as a boy with a prize, and he romped with me for more than an hour before fatigue finally overcame him. When I woke him an hour before dawn, he was as refreshed as if he had passed a full night in slumber, and was in good spirits when he left. He promised to come again in three nights, and said he would find good reasons for us to be in one another's company without attracting undue attention or gossip, which pleased me very much, for it is enervating to live with such close scrutiny as attends on single women in this city. I pointed out to him that this would require careful planning, to which he replied that he is very good at strategy and swore he would relish the opportunity, thinking it worthy of his talents . . .

The warmth of the day was quickly fading before the chilling fingers of fog came, caressing the hills from the west. As they turned down the steep hill, the wind nipping at their backs, Sherman signaled Madelaine to swing her horse off the main road to the wooded copse, indicating through gestures that they could then dismount and put on their coats.

"The Spanish call those two hills the Maiden's Breasts," he said to her as he lifted her out of the sidesaddle under the trees. He indicated the slope they had just descended. "I like yours better." He took the reins from her hand and secured them to one of the low-growing oak branches, next to where his grey was tied.

"Less hectic to ride, I imagine," said Madelaine in spite of herself.

"I wouldn't say that," Sherman whispered as he bent down to wrap her in his arms, his lips seeking hers. He took his time about it, feeling her warm to him; it promised well for the night ahead. When he moved back, he said impishly, "Isn't there any other land you would like to inspect, with the prospect of making an offer to purchase? I would have to escort you to advise you and negotiate for you, wouldn't I? I could not allow you to venture abroad without suitable protection. I would be remiss in my duties if I did—everyone would agree to that." He bent again, and moving the thick knot of hair at the nape of her neck aside, kissed her just under her ear. "Where you kiss me, Madelaine. When you pledge me your bond." His lips were light, almost playful.

It took her a while to gather her thoughts, and when she did, she struggled to voice them. "That is a good notion, on its own; never mind the chance for privacy it offers us. If you know of any property I might like, tell me of it, and I will arrange to see it for myself," she said quite seriously. "I am in earnest, Tecumseh. I want to purchase some land here."

"So far speculation has been very profitable, at least in this area." He nodded, doing his best to fall into his role as banker. "All the West is going to be valuable, someday. When Congress finally comes to its senses and builds a railroad linking the East Coast with the West, then land here will appreciate dramatically, but that will not happen until there is a railroad. Not even a good wagon road would help as the railroad would. But a wagon road would be better than nothing," he said, letting his rancor show. "Politicians! They cannot think beyond the next election. There is no sense in their reluctance to authorize the railroad other than their usual damned lack of foresight. The telegraph link with the Mississippi only begs the question, but it is typical of Congress to settle for half measures when full ones are wanted. As long as they keep California isolated, it will have little to attract investors beyond the gold fields, and that is not investment but exploitation, and it will continue as long as there is no land connection but trails across the continent. Only when goods and people may cross quickly and comfortably will the Pacific come into its own, and assume its place in the scheme of things, bringing the Occident and Orient together as no gang of Chinese laborers and cooks can do now. Until that time, it will be the last point of escape for the dreamers and scoundrels who seek their own private paradise, and attempt to create it for themselves here. It is shortsighted political chicanery to refuse to unite East and West by rail, I am convinced of it. The trouble is that California is an enigma; not even those who live here understand it." He folded his arms, his shirtsleeves suddenly too little protection for the encroaching fog. "I will get my coat."

"Bring mine, will you?" She strolled deeper into the small

grove of trees, listening to the sounds around her, the rustlings and flutters that reminded her that there were other occupants of the copse, many of which began their day when the sun went down—just as she would do if she did not line the soles of her shoes with her native earth. It was cool enough to be unpleasant, and she was relieved when Sherman came and held up her nip-waisted coat for her as she slid her arms into the leg-o'-mutton sleeves. He rested his hands on her shoulders as he stood behind her, then slid them down to cover her breasts.

"How can I give this up?" he murmured, drawing her back against him, holding her tightly as his hands moved down the front of her body; he did this with ease, being more than a head taller then Madelaine. He stopped his rapt exploration abruptly. "I must be mad."

"For planning to give me up or for wanting me in the first place?" She avoided any hint of accusation in her mild rebuke, but she could not shake off the sadness that swept through her at the realization that she would have to leave San Francisco and Sherman before long.

"Both," said Sherman with utmost conviction, turning her to face him, staring down into her violet eyes as if he wanted to meet her in combat. "I am not a man who loves easily, and I am . . . possessed by you. What is it about you? You are more of a mystery than this place." His countenance was stern, his brows drawn downward. "Had I thought I would be so . . . so wholly in your thrall, I would never have begun with you."

"*Bien perdu, bien connu,*" said Madelaine, hoping to conceal the sting she felt from his harsh words.

"But you are *not* well lost; that is the trouble. I do not need to lose you to know you, Madelaine." He surrounded her with his arms, his mouth rough on hers. He strained to press them more tightly together, then broke away from her. "But I will not compromise my marriage."

"So you have said from the first," Madelaine reminded him, as much to assure him that she still understood his requirements of her as to lessen his defensiveness. "And I have never protested your devotion to your family. I will not do so now."

"I meant it. I mean it still." He reached out and took her face in his long-fingered hands. "I treasure you as I have never treasured another woman, and may I be thrice-damned for it."

"Tecumseh," she said gently. "I have no wish to bring you pain."

He released her and moved away, leaves crackling underfoot. His voice was low and his words came quickly. "But you will, and that is the problem. There's nothing that can be done about it now: you are too deeply fixed in my soul for that. Oh, it is no fault of yours; you have been honorable from the first, if that is a word I may use for our adultery. Never have you asked, or hinted, that you want me to leave my wife: it is just as well, no matter what sorcery you work on me. Yet when you go, as go you must, you will leave a wound in me that no enemy could put there. When you are gone . . ." He stared down at the ground as if to read something there in the dying light. "I have never known anyone who has so completely won me as you have."

Madelaine did not go after him. "Then we must make the most of the short time we have, so that our joy will be greater than your hurt, and you will remember our time together with happiness." She did not add that she longed for his ecstasy to sustain her in the long, empty months ahead.

"How can we?" He met her eyes in the dimness. "Why take the risk? We have been discreet so far, but I must resist my impulse to set caution aside."

"Why? Who is to know what passes between us? When we are private, there is no reason for caution," said Madelaine, feeling some of his contained anguish as her own.

"No reason? Can you not think of one?" He shook his head, unwilling to look directly at her any longer. "It may be there is the greatest reason of all, for when we are alone together, I have no strength to resist you."

"You are managing to resist me well enough now," she said, more sharply than she had intended.

"Do you think so?" he asked, his voice very quiet and deep, the lines in his face severe.

The silence between them lengthened, opening as if it were

a chasm deep as the pits of hell. A scuttling in the underbrush as a fox hurried to find his supper provided a momentary distraction, then Madelaine took a step toward him, her hands turned palms up. "Tecumseh, do you recall what I told you of the bond the blood makes between us?"

His features grew less formidable, and he reached out to caress her face as if compelled to do it. "Yes, Madelaine. How can I forget?"

"Then believe that when we are parted, we will not be separated," she said as she touched his fingers.

He put his hands into hers but would not close the gap between them. "What else would you call it?"

For once she had an answer. "Tell me, when you cannot see the sun or stars, do you still know which direction is north?"

"North?" he repeated, baffled, and then said, "Yes, of course."

"And how do you know it?" she asked him.

He frowned, hitching up one shoulder. "I . . . sense it."

She nodded. "Then understand that I will always sense you, no matter where you are, or where you go. It is the way of those of us who have become vampires."

He winced at this last. "Vampires."

"Yes," she confirmed.

He regained his skepticism with effort. "For heaven's sake, isn't there another word for it? What a ludicrous notion. Vampires. Legends for the credulous and childish. Surely there is another explanation to account for what has happened." He lacked conviction, but he glowered at her, anyway. "How can you expect me to believe such a fable?"

"I don't," she said wearily. "But it is still the truth. Oh, I have read that Polidori tale, and the little horrors Hoffmann writes, and I cannot blame you for how you think of us. If I were not what I am, I would be inclined to feel as you do, and scoff at the very idea of vampires." She came a step nearer to him. "But I am what you may become, and you need to know the dangers you may face."

His laughter crackled, brittle as autumn leaves. "Very well, you have warned me. If we continue as lovers, I could become a vampire when I die if my spine or my nervous system or my body is not destroyed. I will have to avoid direct sunlight and running water and mirrors. That covers all the hazards, I think. Yes, and I will need my native Ohio earth to sustain me. And blood. Should it come to pass, I will take the precautions you advise, on the odd chance they may be necessary." Then, with a deep sound that was half sigh, half groan, he pulled her into his arms again and bent to open her mouth with his own.

San Francisco, 30 August, 1855
 In the last ten days I have seen Tecumseh once, and that was in his carriage with his children, taking them on an outing to the Chinese market where Willy had purchased a paper kite in the shape of a dragon's head that he was attempting to fly off the back of the carriage, which annoyed the horses. Tecumseh was meticulously polite, doing nothing anyone could construe as pay-ing untoward attention to me, but his eyes were haunted. Why he should be so distant now, I do not know, but it saddens me . . .

Rain was turning the streets from dust to mud as the afternoon wound down toward night. Along the streets, lamps were being lit early to stave off the coming darkness as the first storm of au-tumn whipped over the hills.

Madelaine sat at her desk, busying herself with writing, when she heard the knocker on the front door. She looked up, annoyed at the interruption, recalling that Olga had taken the evening off. Clicking her tongue impatiently, Madelaine blotted the half-finished page and reached to pull a vast woolen shawl around her shoulders before hurrying to the front of the house to answer the urgent summons.

"Madelaine," said William Tecumseh Sherman as the door swung open. He was wet and bedraggled, his hair quenched of fire and rain-slicked to his skull. He glanced over his shoulder at the street. "May I come in? Will you let me?"

"Tecumseh," said Madelaine, holding the door wider. "Wel-come."

His head bowed, he hesitated, and asked in a whisper, "You are willing to speak to me? After my inexcusable behavior?"

Perplexed, Madelaine stepped aside to admit him. "Certainly. Come in. You have done nothing that would keep me from knowing you. What do you want?" It was the only question that came clearly to mind, and it was out before she could soften or modify it in any way.

He pressed the door closed quickly. "I don't think anyone saw me," he said cautiously.

"Possibly not," said Madelaine, her bafflement increasing as she looked at him. "You are soaked to the skin."

"It doesn't matter," he said, squaring his shoulders and daring to look directly into her violet eyes. "I have been a fool and a coward, and I wouldn't blame you if you tossed me out on my ass."

Had she truly been as young as she looked, Madelaine might have taken advantage of the offer; as it was, she shook her head. "No, I won't do that. But I have a few questions I hope you will answer." She indicated the way to the parlor.

"Thank you, Madame," he said with unwonted humility. He turned and locked the door himself, leaning against it as if he had been pursued by the hounds of hell. "Let me say what I must, Madelaine; if you stop me, my courage may fail me, and then I will be thrice-damned." He looked directly at her, keeping his voice quite low. "I have chastised myself every day for not coming to you, and with every passing day it grew more difficult to act at all. I have all but convinced myself that you do not wish to see me because of my cravenness. So I must come to you now, or mire hopelessly in my own inaction. Poor Hamlet had to bear the same trouble, in his way; I don't think I ever grasped the full scope of his predicament until now." He passed his hand over his eyes. "I'm maundering. Forgive me; I don't want to do that." He straightened up and moved a few steps to stand directly in front of her. "I'm no stranger to suffering. I have not yet fought a war, but I have seen men fall of fatal wounds, in Seminole ambushes, and I have held my comrades while they bled to death so that they would not be wholly alone."

"What has that to do with you and me?" Madelaine asked, growing confused.

"Let me continue," he said forcefully. "There are things I should have said to you days ago."

She realized now how determined he was. "If you think it is necessary, go on."

Sherman took a stance as if to fend off attack. "You would think that one who is . . . or, rather, has been a soldier would not have such weakness." He held up his hands to stop any protests she might make. Now he looked away, unwilling to let Madelaine see the shine of tears in his eyes.

"Tecumseh . . ." Madelaine said gently, searching for a phrase to end his self-condemnation.

He fixed her with his gaze, determined to admit his faults. "You have been so self-possessed, that I—"

"I may appear that way to you, but I am far from feeling so, you may believe," she said, hoping to turn him away from further abasement. "You have no reason to cast me in such an angelic role."

"You conduct yourself like a good officer, Madelaine." This was the highest praise he could give her.

"If that is true and useful, then it pleases me you think so." She tried to smile and nearly succeeded. "Well, I will consider myself fortunate that I have some poise, and will tell you I am grateful to you for holding it in high regard. Let me get you a cup of coffee, or something to eat."

"No," he insisted. "I am not finished, and I am not hungry." He put his hands together so that he would not be tempted to reach out for her. "It is inexcusable of me not to offer you any succor I can provide. My only excuse is that I am filled with anxiety about my children, and so have kept close to them for these past several days, for with their mother away, they are— You cannot blame me more than I blame myself."

"Doubtless," she said dryly.

"I am sorry I deserted you." He faltered, struggling to finish. "I am . . . tremendously proud of you."

It would have been easy to give him a facile answer, Madelaine realized; it would also shut him away from her as no barred door could do. She considered her response carefully. "I know how hard it is to say these things to me."

"As it should be," he agreed in self-disgust.

"The more so because you have taken all the responsibility upon yourself, as if you were the only person who might protect me," said Madelaine, her understanding of him making this a precarious revelation.

"But I am . . . your lover," he protested. "You yourself say there is a bond between us."

"And so there is," she said, "which is why I do not hold you in the contempt you dread and hope I might. My sensibilities are not so delicate that I must have constant reassurance for my—"

His supplication gave way to aggravation. "For heaven's sake, Madame, get angry with me. Denounce me for my desertion. Rail at me for not coming to you before now. Tell me what a poltroon you think I am."

"But I don't wish to do any of those things," she said reasonably as she attempted to move nearer to him without upsetting him. "I think you are what you say you are—a father who is worried about his family."

He nodded, the first dawning of hope in his steel-colored eyes. "There is some truth in that."

"The more so because you have castigated yourself for things I have not held against you. The accusations you make against yourself are of your own creation, not mine. I do not hold you to the account you hold yourself. And just as well, given the catalogue of offenses you have conjured for yourself." She went and stood next to him, not quite touching him. "You have assumed I would not recognize your desire to protect your family, and would expect you to devote yourself to me."

"As I should have done," he interjected harshly.

"You may think so; I do not." She put her hand on his shoulder, noticing again how wet he was, then looked up into his face. "Tecumseh, listen to me: I will not deny that I would like to have you here with me, for I would."

"It would be poor recompense to tarnish your reputation."

He put his hand over hers where it rested on his shoulder. "I am taking a chance coming here now. Your housekeeper might—"

"My housekeeper will not be back until late tonight. I have told her she need not look in on me; she may go directly to her apartment and retire. My man-of-all-work is dining with his cousin's family." She smiled at him.

He did not return the smile. "You mean they left you alone?" he demanded. "What kind of servants do you have, Madame, that they leave you by yourself?"

"I have servants who do as I instruct them." Now Madelaine grew impatient. "What nonsense you talk, Tecumseh," she said with asperity. "You would think I am a hothouse flower, incapable of fending for myself, when you should realize I have managed on my own for decades."

"Visiting Indians," he said, determined to make his point.

"Among others," she responded, refusing to be dragged into yet another dispute with him.

"Oh, yes; those travels in Egypt," he grumbled. "Hard going, no doubt."

"They were," she said. "Some of the time. The expedition was a small one, and we were four hundred miles up the Nile." She recalled the endless heat and sand; she remembered the Nile at flood, and the profusion of insects and vermin that came with the water; she saw the faces of Falke and Trowbridge and the Coptic monk Erai Gurzin, and the death of Professor Baudilet.

"What is it?" Sherman asked, reading something of her memories in her face. "What's the matter?"

"Nothing," she said. "It's all in the past, all behind me." She shook off the hold of the memories and made herself pay closer attention to him. "Your hand is like ice," she said. "You're wet to the skin. You may not want any food, but you need to get warm and clean once again."

"It's not important," he claimed.

"It is if you are taken ill because of it," she said briskly, and slipped her hand from under his, but only to seize it and lead him through the gloom of her house to the curtained alcove off the kitchen where her bathtub was kept. "I will start heating water right now," she declared as she went to the stove, opened the tinderbox, and stirred the embers to life. She pulled two split logs of wood from the box near the stove and put them, one on top of the other, on the glowing coals. "This will be hot shortly, the kitchen will be warm, and your bath will be ready in a half hour." She paused to hold out her hand to him again. "Do this for me, Tecumseh."

Sherman regarded her tenderly. "A bath. I wish I could stay for it," he said in a rueful voice, his fingers lacing through hers.

"Do you tell me you will not?" she asked.

"I fear I must," he said by way of apology.

She closed the stove grate and put her hands on her hips. "And why can't you? And no farragoes, please, about my reputation. No one saw you come, and only I know you are here."

He looked somber. "My children are—"

"Your nurse is more than competent to care for them," said Madelaine, who had met the woman several times and had been impressed with her reliability. "And don't tell me you have never got home later than expected."

"But—" he began, only to be cut short.

"You need to get warm and dry before venturing out into that weather; I will supply you with an oilskin against it. You would tell me the same if I had paid you a visit, and well you know it, you need not bother to say otherwise." She stared at him, waiting for his answer.

"What would be the point?" Sherman said. "You wouldn't believe me if I did. And neither would I."

"Good; at least you admit that much: we make progress," said Madelaine as she lifted the side of the curtain and took the first of four large pots from the shelf next to the bathtub. She carried this to the pump at the sink and began to work the handle to fill the pot.

"You're never going to be able to lift that," said Sherman, reaching out to heft it for her. "Let me."

It was tempting to let him take the pot, but Madelaine kept her hold on the two handles and hoisted the eight-gallon pot from the sink to the stove without effort. "Unnecessary; I can do it, thank you. I told you those of my blood acquire extra strength; this pot is a minor thing," she said, unwilling to permit him to claim otherwise, even if there were no reason for it other than good manners.

"But it isn't fitting," Sherman protested as Madelaine reached for the second pot. "No, Madelaine. No, I can't allow it. You should not have to do such menial work, not while I am here to help you."

"Why not?" Madelaine asked, setting the pot in the deep sink and starting to work the pump handle once again. "What is the vice in menial work that you think I should disdain it? Why should anyone feel shame, doing necessary work? Don't tell me you never filled a pot, or carried one, before now?"

"Of course I've done both," he blustered. "That's different."

"Because you did it?" Madelaine guessed, and shook her head. "Where did you learn such intolerance?"

He glared. "It is what everyone expects of well-bred men and women."

"Isn't that a bit . . . extreme?" Madelaine asked. "To require well-bred men and women to become dependent puppets requiring the labor of servants to make their way in the world?"

He did not answer her question, and stood, with an expression of distant blankness, staring at the two windows at the rear of the kitchen. The anemic light filtering into the room banished most of the colors, turning the figures of both Sherman and Madelaine a ghostly, washed-out shade of sepia with pale beige faces. As if to be rid of this perception, Sherman shook himself and found the nearest kitchen lamp and a box of lucifers to go with it. As the flame rose, the kitchen seemed to warm with the return of color. "There. That should make your task easier."

Madelaine did not point out that the increasing dusk made little difference to her; she saw in darkness almost as well as she saw in moderate light. Instead, she nodded her thanks and carried the second pot to the stove while Sherman took the third from the shelf and set it in the sink under the pump, and started to ply the handle with vigor. "The wood is catching; that will make everything more comfortable," she remarked as she glanced at the tinderbox of the stove.

Sherman continued to fill the third pot of water, then carried it to the stove, setting it in place with care. "Since you are determined to do this, I suppose I ought to lend my assistance."

"If you like," said Madelaine, handing him the fourth pot and saying, "Just fill it with water." She then tugged the curtain aside so that the bath alcove was completely open, revealing the large enameled-copper tub and a wall of shelves where the various requirements for bathing were placed. "I have set out bath salts, if you want them. And I have a razor and shaving supplies, if you need them."

"You are always prepared," he said, intending it as a complaint, but making it into a compliment. "Yes, I will rid myself of this stubble," he said, and went on slyly, "or I might have to explain where all the scratches on your body came from. Since you insist on doing this, I shall do it properly. Perhaps I should grow a beard again."

Madelaine could not stop herself from smiling, knowing now that he would remain with her for several hours, if not all night. The weight of his absence lifted from her and she said playfully, "In fact, given the circumstances, shaving would be a prudent thing to do."

"Prudent," he repeated ironically. "What a word to use for anything pertaining to you and me, Madelaine."

"All the more reason it is necessary," she said, satisfying herself that the tub would be ready when the water was hot. She set out two large sponges and a rough washing cloth on the rack next to the tub, and then pulled out a brass towel rack. "I'll get a robe for you from the linen closet."

He extended his arms to block her progress and pulled her to him, bending to kiss her as his embrace enfolded her.

She shifted against his arm, then gave herself over to his caresses as if she had never before experienced them. Finally when she could speak at all, she said softly to him, "Tecumseh, I have no wish to compel you to do anything that displeases you."

"I know that," he said indulgently as he stroked her breasts through her clothes.

"You're distracting me," she objected without any determination to stop him.

"Good," he approved. "I intend to." His kiss was light and long, full of suggestions that left both of them breathless. "Why don't you let me help you out of that rig you've got on?"

"Tecumseh," she said again, making a last-ditch effort to keep from giving in to him completely. "You will not be angry, will you? For my turning you from your purpose?"

"Why should I be angry?" He kissed the corner of her mouth. "And what purpose do you mean? I only wanted to apologize for failing you."

"You mean you had not resolved to break off with me?" she asked.

He stared at her, a hint of defiance in his answer. "After what I have done, I am shocked that *you* are not angry with *me*." He reached up and pulled the long pins from the neat bun at the back of her neck. "That's better," he said as he loosened her hair with his fingers.

"I could not be angry with you, not when I have tasted your blood," she said.

"That again," he muttered; he became patiently courteous, all but bowing to her. "And why is that, Madame Vampire?"

"Because I know you, and I know what you are." She looked up at him, and read vexation in his eyes. "I know that you despise weakness, especially in yourself, and you often regard your feelings for me as weakness."

He looked at her in amazement. "How the devil—?"

"It is your nature," Madelaine said swiftly. "It is intrinsic to your soul. You have decided that if you love me, you are weakened. I don't know how to make you see that loving is strength, not weakness—that it takes courage to love because love's risk is so great."

Sherman shook his head, scowling down at her. "If I were not married, what you tell me might be true, for there truly are risks in loving. But as I have a wife, and you, my dear, are not she, I must look upon this as an indulgence."

"But you don't," she said softly, "look upon this as an indulgence."

The light in his eyes warmed and gentled, and he drew her tightly against him. "No, I don't."

This time their kiss was deep, passionate, and long; it was the strangest thing. Madelaine thought in a remote part of her mind, but it was as if Sherman wanted to absorb her into himself, to pull her into him with all the intensity of appetence. Then she let all thought go and gave herself over to the desire he ignited in her.

When they broke apart, Sherman had to steady himself against the table, laughing a little with shy embarrassment. "Sorry. That was clumsy of me. I was . . . You made me dizzy."

"You weren't paying attention," said Madelaine as she ran her hands under the lapels of his jacket and peeled it off him.

He did not protest this, but set to unfastening his waistcoat and the shirt beneath it, working so precipitously that he got the shirt tangled in his suspenders and had to let Madelaine disengage them for him, which she did merrily. "It isn't funny," he grumbled.

"If you say not," she told him with a smile that pierced his heart.

He caressed her hair as she continued to unfasten his clothing, and said dreamily. "If I were truly a brave man, I would take you and my children, and we would sail away to the Sandwich Islands together, and live there, the world well lost. But I'm not that brave."

She interrupted her task and said somberly, "You would come to hate me within a year or two, for making you forsake your honor."

"But you *don't* ask that," he said, holding her face in his hands and scrutinizing her features.

"In time you would persuade yourself I had," she said with grim certainty. "And I am not brave enough to sustain your loathing."

"How could I do that?" He asked her, marveling at the forthrightness she displayed in the face of his examination.

"You would," she said, and moved back to let him step out of his trousers. "I will fill the tub for you; the water is nearly warm enough." She could see the first wisps of steam rising from the large pots. "Then you will bathe and we will have time together." She reached for the pot holders and lifted the first of the vessels from the stove. As she emptied it into the bathtub, a warm cloud rose, made tangy by bath salts.

Sherman was down to his underwear and shoes; he started to protest her labors, but stopped and offered, "Shall I help you out of your clothes, as well?"

Madelaine emptied the second pot. "No. I will do that once you are in the bath," she assured him.

"Where I can watch," he ventured.

"Of course." By the time she had poured the contents of the third pot into the tub, Sherman was naked and shivering. "Hurry. Get in," she said, gathering up his clothes and setting them out on the butcher's block to dry.

"It feels so good it hurts," Sherman sighed as he sank into the water, taking the sponge and soap from the stand beside the tub.

"Then enjoy it," said Madelaine, reaching to release the fastenings of her bodice as she went toward the bathtub.

San Francisco, 8 September, 1855

I am almost finished with my chapter on the Utes, which pleases me tremendously. I tell myself I have captured the spirit of their legends and other teachings clearly enough so that the most opinionated of university-bound scholars cannot misinterpret what I have said. But I know such lucidity is impossible, so I must be content to accept my satisfaction as sufficient to the task.

Tecumseh has been with me for five nights out of the last ten, and he alternates between anguish at his laxness and joy for our passion. When he is not berating himself, he tells me he has never been so moved before, that I have revealed pleasures and gratification that he thought did not exist except between the

covers of novels. But this rapture is always accompanied by the
warning that he will not shame his wife any more than he has
done already, and that he will never leave his children. He re-
fuses to be convinced that I do not wish him to run off with me,
and nothing I have said to the contrary has made any lasting im-
pression on him.

Tomorrow I go to an afternoon party given by Mr. Folsom
to celebrate the tenth anniversary of the marriage of Captain
and Mrs. Kent—or so reads the invitation that was delivered to
me last week. Baron deStoeckl has offered to be my escort, and
I suppose I will accept . . .

Fanny Kent was radiant in a flounced gown of peach-colored
tarlatan over petticoats *à la Duchesse;* her eardrops were
baroque pearls surmounted by rubies, and she wore an extravagant and hideous necklace of diamonds and rubies, the gift her
husband had given her for this occasion. She took advantage of
every opportunity to show off these splendid presents, coquet-
ting prettily for all those who were willing to compliment her.

Beside her, Captain Kent was in a claw-tail coat of dark-
blue superfine over a waistcoat of embroidered white satin. He
was beaming with pride as he lifted his champagne glass to his
wife and thanked her for "the ten happiest years of my life." He
was delighted by the applause that followed.

"I won't bother to bring you wine," the Russian Baron
whispered to Madelaine after they had greeted their host. "But
excuse me if I get some for myself."

"Please do," said Madelaine, returning the wave Fanny
Kent gave her. "You do not have to wait upon me, Baron."

"You are gracious, as always," said deStoeckl, and went off
to have some of the champagne.

Madelaine had no desire to go sit with the widows and
dowagers in the kiosk, nor did she want to join the younger
wives, all of whom seemed to spend their time talking about the
unreliability of servants, the precocity of their children, and the
ambitions they had for their husbands. She would have nothing
to contribute to their conversation, so instead, she went to

where a new bed of flowers had been planted; she occupied her time identifying the plants, her thoughts faintly distracted by the realization that she would have to make more of the compounds Saint-Germain had taught her to concoct nearly a century ago; she did not hear Fanny Kent's light, tripping step behind her.

"Oh, Madame de Montalia," she enthused, prettily half turning so that the tiers of her skirt fluttered becomingly around her. "I was so happy to see you arrive with Baron deStoeckl."

"Why is that?" Madelaine asked, adding. "My felicitations on your anniversary. May all those to come be as happy."

"Thank you," said Fanny, a smug hint of a smile showing her delight in this occasion. "I am a fortunate woman; my husband is devoted to me."

"Yes, you are fortunate," said Madelaine. "The more so that you are fond of him."

Fanny clasped her hand to her throat, touching her new necklace. "Dear me, yes. I have seen marriages—well, we all have—where the partners do not suit, and one is forever trapped trying to win the other, with flattery and gifts and other signs of affection that gain nothing but aggravation. The greater the effort, the greater the failure in those sad cases. Fortunately, I am not of their number."

"Which must please all your friends," said Madelaine, thinking that festive small talk had not changed appreciably in the one hundred thirty years she had been alive. "I see the Captain has given you a wonderful remembrance."

"So he has," she preened. "How good of you to notice." She looked around, then moved a step nearer to Madelaine. "I mentioned Baron deStoeckl just now, in the hope that there might be . . . an interesting announcement from him?"

Madelaine realized at once what Fanny sought to know; she chuckled. "Do not let his affianced bride hear you say that, or she will never lend me his escort again."

Fanny's face wilted. "Oh. An affianced bride, you say?"

"So he has informed me," said Madelaine, her good humor unaltered. "Dear Mrs. Kent, you must know that even with your best efforts, few of us can become as happy as you are with your Captain. Although I appreciate your wish to see me thus." She regarded Fanny, trying not to lose patience with her.

"Yes," said Fanny naively. "It is true that happiness like ours is rare. But I think it is necessary for a woman to have a husband in this world. Life is quite impossible without one." Impulsively she put her hand on Madelaine's arm. "And I *hate* to see you so alone."

"I deal well enough with my single condition," said Madelaine, knowing that Fanny intended the best for her, but offended by the intrusion in spite of her intuition.

"But the *future*; think of the future, Madame." Her pretty face was now puckered with distress. "What will become of you? I cannot bear to think of it, not when I know you to be a prize any man would be glad to win."

"Please, Mrs. Kent," Madelaine said, her manner less conciliating than before, "do not think that you must make arrangements for me. I have no wish to be any man's prize. I am capable of caring for myself; I value your interest as I ought, but I must ask you not to pursue the matter."

Fanny dabbed a tear from her eye with her lace handkerchief. "If you insist, I will refrain, but why I should, I cannot grasp. Surely you must know that we all wish you well. Nothing would please us more than to see you well situated." She lowered her eyes to the flower beds. "This will be so splendid next spring. Don't you look forward to seeing it?"

"Yes," Madelaine answered, "and I regret that I will no longer be in San Francisco when they bloom."

Fanny's expression changed to shock. "What are you saying, Madame?"

"Only that my purpose for being in your country will take me away from here before much more time goes by; I will be leaving soon, ahead of winter setting in, for I do not like hazardous travel," said Madelaine, trying to make these statements calmly so that Fanny would not be too inquisitive about her plans.

"Gracious," said Fanny, nonplussed to the point of brief silence. "What purpose is that, Madame de Montalia?"

"I am making a study of America; the United States are part of my subjects." It was not a lie, Madelaine reminded herself, though it was also not quite the truth.

"But why would you want to do that?" Fanny marveled. "Why should a well-born woman like you undertake so arduous a task?"

"Curiosity," said Madelaine. "Women are supposed to be more curious than men, aren't we?"

"Well, I suppose so," said Fanny dubiously, then turned as she heard her name called. She waved in response, then looked guiltily at Madelaine. "Oh, dear. You must excuse me, Madame. My husband needs me."

"By all means," said Madelaine, and went back to her perusal of the flower beds. But she could not bring herself to concentrate on what she saw now, for Fanny Kent's well-meaning interference niggled at the back of her thoughts, and she remembered how Saint-Germain had cautioned her against making herself too noticeable in society. At the time, she had thought the advice too protective, but now she could perceive the reason for his warning, and she tried to think how best to undo the damage she had done.

A short while later, Baron deStoeckl found her once more. He carried a glass of champagne, and he smiled broadly, his whole manner amiable, his eyes shrewd. As usual, he addressed her in French. "How are you faring, Madame?"

"Well enough," she said, taking care not to appear too interested in him. "Fanny Kent was hoping she could make a match of us."

Baron deStoeckl chuckled. "And did you tell her of my promised bride at home?"

"Yes," said Madelaine. "I think she was more disappointed than shocked."

He strolled along beside her, content to say little as they went. Finally, as he reached the foot of the garden, he remarked, "I hope you will not allow yourself to worry about what she said to you."

"It is not my intention," said Madelaine, trying to sound

unconcerned, and went on impulsively, "but it galls me to think I have been foolish enough to expose myself to her . . ."

"Scrutiny?" suggested deStoeckl when Madelaine did not go on.

"Something of the sort," she admitted. "Though that may be too strong a word."

They started back to where most of the guests were gathered. DeStoeckl gestured to indicate the expansive garden. "You know, at the rate this city is growing, holdings of this size will soon vanish. Ask William what it was like when he was in California the first time. It was nothing like the place you see now. Once the Rush was on, San Francisco mushroomed. And it is mushrooming still." He grinned impishly. "William learned a great deal then, and it has stood him in good stead now. He claims that at the time, he had other things on his mind. Ask him why they called Monterey Bay 'Sherman's Punch Bowl,' six years ago."

"You may be right about the city," she said with verve, not wanting to be pulled into talking about Sherman. "Though it would be a pity to lose this garden."

"The price of land is rising steadily," deStoeckl reminded her. "And buildings are going up everywhere. I venture to guess that one day the city will stretch from the Bay to the Pacific itself." He saw the mayor signal to him. "I will return later," he said as he went to answer the summons.

It was too early to leave the party, but Madelaine wanted some relief from it. She went into the house and looked about for the library; the chance to read would diminish her growing anxiety.

There was no library, only two small shelves of books in the withdrawing room. With a sigh, she resigned herself to the limited fare, and taking a copy of *Bleak House* from the top shelf, sat down to read, deciding she would discover at last what it was Sherman so admired in Dickens.

"I wondered what had become of you," said a voice from the door; a young importer stood there, smiling fatuously at Madelaine. "No fair, you running off the way you did."

"It is too bright in the garden; I fear I do poorly in such bright sun," she said, noticing the fellow looked a bit flushed. "So do you, it would seem."

"The sun doesn't bother me," he boasted and held up his glass in a toast to her. "But not looking at you does. You're better than the sun any day of the week."

This flattery was more alarming than complimenting; Madelaine began to wonder if the high color in the young man's face did not result from too much champagne rather than too much sun; there was a certain glaze to his eyes that suggested it. A quiver of consternation went through her as she recalled other unwelcome encounters: Alain Baudilet in Omats' garden, Gerard le Mat on the road to her estate in Provence, Ralph Whitestone in her box after *The Duchess of Malfi*. "Thank you for the pretty words," she said automatically, continuing with great deliberation. "I think, perhaps, it is time to rejoin the others."

The young man gave her a lupine grin. "Not so fast. I thought we could have a little . . . talk on our own."

"Did you?" Madelaine closed the novel and put it back into its place on the shelf. "I fear you were mistaken." She rose and started toward the door, not so quickly that she would seem to confront the young man. With all the composure she could muster, she said, "Will you let me by?"

He extended his arm to block the door. "I don't think so. Not yet."

"Mr. . . ." She could not bring his name to mind; it was something simple, uncomplicated, but not as obvious as Smith. She maintained her outward equanimity. "There is no reason to do this."

"There's plenty of reason," said the intruder, enjoying his position of advantage. "And a Frenchwoman should not need to be told what it is."

Madelaine frowned. She could always scream, but that would defeat the whole purpose of her withdrawal from the garden—to remove herself from observation and the occasion for gossip. "I don't think you want to do this," she began reasonably. "Please stand aside." She thought she sounded like a schoolmistress with a recalcitrant pupil.

"Not on your life," the young man said, swaying toward her. "Not while I have this chance." He drank the last of the champagne in his glass, tossed it away without paying any notice to its shattering, then reached out for her.

Madelaine sought to get around him and was about to reach for something she could use as a weapon when Sherman abruptly forced his way into the withdrawing room, grabbing the young man by the front of his shirt to back him up against the wall, leaning hard on him, pinning him to the wainscoting. "You didn't hear the lady, sir. She asked you to step aside."

The young man blanched and sweat broke out on his forehead. "I . . . I . . ."

"And you will do it, won't you?" Sherman demanded through clenched teeth.

"I . . ." Though bulkier than Sherman, the young man was terrified, and he squirmed in an attempt to escape; Sherman leaned harder. "Oh, God."

The relief and gratitude that had filled Madelaine a moment before vanished in a wash of exasperation. "Mr. Sherman," she said crisply, "I think he has taken your meaning."

Sherman kept his relentless grip on the young man. "You will apologize to the lady, sir," he ordered.

"I . . . Sorry. I . . . didn't mean . . ." He stopped as Sherman released his hold and moved back. "I . . . just a mistake. Never meant anything . . . untoward. Upon my word, Madame." He was shaking and kept glancing quickly at Sherman, then at the windows, anything to avoid looking directly at Madelaine for fear of the red-haired banker's wrath.

"And because it was a mistake, you will say nothing to anyone, will you?" Sherman pursued, giving the fellow no chance to capitalize on his gaffe through boasting or smugness.

"No. No. I won't. Ever." With that, he bolted from the room. His hasty, uneven footsteps were loud.

The withdrawing room was still, neither Madelaine nor

Sherman being willing to speak first. She relented before he did. "Mr. Sherman. I didn't know you were here."

"I arrived not long after you did," he said, keeping his distance.

She had nothing to say to that. "How did you happen to follow that young man in here?"

"Winters? I heard him boast that he would get a better taste of France than mere champagne. When I saw him come into the house, I followed; I had an idea he might attempt something of this sort." He locked eyes with her. "I'm sorry I was right. I would not have you subjected to . . . such things for . . . anything."

"Thanks to your intervention, I wasn't," she said bluntly, and could read shock in his face. "His intentions were—"

"If he had touched you, I would have killed him," said Sherman with quiet certainty.

She achieved a rallying tone. "Now that *would* have been a grand gesture. And neither of our reputations would survive it, so it is just as well you arrived when you did." She managed to keep her hands from shaking as she slipped out the door. "Speaking of reputations, it might be wise if we did not leave this room at the same time. I will go back to the garden now; follow when you think best."

He nodded, and before she could turn away, he blew her a kiss.

San Francisco, 7 October, 1855

How still it is this evening. After a week of wind and fog, it has turned bright and hot. I was surprised at this sudden change, coming when it does in the year, though I now understand it is not unusual to this region. I was told that this is one of the reasons vintners have been flocking to the inland valleys north of here, where they can plant vines with a reasonable prospect of a long, warm growing season . . .

It is arranged that we will depart no later than 10 October, no matter what the weather. It is tempting to delay, but I must not, for my own sake as well as Tecumseh's . . .

· · ·

"I know it is what must be done, and I hate it," Sherman whispered, his hand tangled in her hair, his leg between hers, his body replete, tired, and yet unwilling to sleep; it was after midnight, and the city beyond the house on Franklin Street was quiet.

Madelaine shifted her position so that she could lift herself up enough to look into his face. "I will miss you. Tecumseh."

"I will miss you, too, and be damned for it," he said softly, the usual tension gone out of his features, making him look younger than he was. The hand in her hair moved down to brush her face lightly, and he stared into her eyes, wanting to pierce more than the night. "I should never have let myself become . . ." He drew her down to kiss her searchingly.

She gave herself over to his mouth, opening herself to his growing renewed need, lying back as he made his way down her body as if by passion alone he could take the whole of her into himself. As he moved between her thighs, he gave a harsh sigh, then lowered his head. Madelaine caught her fingers in his fine red hair. "What's the matter?" she asked, sensing the return of his ambivalence.

He raised his eyes enough to meet hers. "It has nothing to do with you," he told her, touching the soft, hidden folds of flesh and relishing the shiver that went through her.

"If it impairs our loving, it has something to do with me," she said as gently as she could.

"Later," he muttered.

"Now," she insisted, concern more than determination coloring her inflection.

"Very well," he said, and brought his elbows under his chest so that he could more easily look at her without moving from his place. "Since I cannot truly grasp the enormity of your leaving, I was thinking that this is one—one of many—delights I will lose with you. If I could contain myself, I would do this for hours, to have the pleasure of your transports." He laughed once, chagrined. "But I am not patient enough for that, and so I have to make the most of our desires and be content with memories."

Madelaine reached down and stroked his shoulder. "You are a generous lover, Tecumseh, more than you know, and you have learned . . ."

"To be less precipitous?" he ventured. "To increase our gratification by postponing its fulfillment?"

She touched his neck, feeling the strong pulse there. "It grieves me that you cannot be as generous in your marriage as we are together."

To his acute discomfort, he blushed. "Not all women have the capacity to enjoy these things." He rested one hand on her thigh, caressing her with delicious languor. "And many who claim to are suspect, since it is their profession to please men." He moved to adjust himself more comfortably between her legs, saying, "If I had been less infatuated, less off guard, I would have kept away from you, arranged things with one of the whorehouses for discreet . . ."

"Servicing," Madelaine supplied for him. "If that was your only alternative to me, then I am gratified your infatuation was—"

He stopped her. "It isn't infatuation," he said in a flat tone. "And you know it."

She looked at him, deep into his steel-colored eyes. "I know."

This time when he sighed, he slipped away from her, ending up at the foot of the bed, naked and cross-legged, with a mess of sheets in his lap. "I should not have permitted this to happen. My life ought to be better ordered than that. But what proof am I against you—you, with a face filled with light, and all the sweet delirium of the world in your body. No wonder I could not reason myself out of my fascination. It is mad of me to love you."

They were both silent for a short while, then Madelaine shivered and sat up, facing him down the length of the bed. "I cannot help but love you, madness or not."

"Because it is your nature," he said, repeating what she had told him so often. "Because you have tasted my blood."

"Yes," she said, trying not to fear his response.

"Yes," he echoed, wanting it to be an accusation and hearing himself make the single word a vow.

"And you accept it." She felt a surge of rapture go through her as no physical act would bring. That he finally recognized the bond between them! She would have laughed with utter joy had she not understood that would offend him.

"How can I not?" he asked in mock capitulation.

Certain his resistance was crumbling, she went to him in a single, sinuous motion, sweeping the sheets and comforter aside; she would not let him turn away from her. "Then tonight must stand for all the nights to come that we will not share, Tecumseh; why waste it in anticipating our separation when we may yet be together for a few hours more?"

It was more than he could bear, having her so close. With a sound that was not quite a groan, he reached out and pulled her tightly to him, his carnality igniting afresh as he embraced her. At last he took her firmly by the shoulders and held her back from him. "How can you endure parting?" There was pain in his voice and his body was taut.

"I can because I must," she answered, not resisting him. "Those of my blood do more parting than anything else. Or at least it seems that way to me."

"And when you have gone, there will be others, won't there?" He meant this to hurt; his long fingers tightened on her shoulders.

"Yes. There will." She looked directly at him, unflinching in the face of his accusation. "As you will have your wife, and those women you seek out for . . . didn't you call it necessity and amusement?"

He released his hold on her and looked away. "You are right, Madelaine; I have no basis for complaint. I, after all, made the conditions of our liaison: how ill-mannered of me to protest them now."

She took his hand. "Stop berating yourself," she said in discomfiture. "If you must know, I find your jealousy unrealistic but . . . flattering."

"I am not jealous." In spite of his forbidding demeanor, he

could not stop a quick burst of rueful laughter. "Fine pair we are," he told her at last. "It would serve us both right if we lost the whole night in bickering."

"If that would make parting easier, then—" she offered, only to be cut off by his lips opening hers.

He seemed determined to press the limits of their passion, for he went at her body as if it were territory to be won. He lavished attention on her face and mouth, on the curve of her neck and the swell of her breasts, using every nuance of excitation he knew to evoke a desire in her as intense as his own, all the while reveling in her tantalizing ministrations and ecstatic responses to the onslaught of his relentless fervor; it was an act of flagrant, erotic idolatry. "Now. Let me have. All of you," he whispered to her as he drew her onto his lap, guiding her legs around him, shuddering in anticipation as she sheathed him deep inside her. His kiss was as long and profound as his flesh was frenzied; while she nuzzled his throat, he clasped her as if to brand her body with his image until their spasms passed.

They were quiet together for some undefined time afterward, neither wanting to make the first move that would break them apart. Then he shifted, changing how he held her. "My foot's falling asleep," he apologized.

"Does it hurt?" Madelaine asked, moving off his lap entirely. In the predawn umber gloom her bedroom looked more like a sketch in charcoal than a real place; no birds yet announced the coming of the October sun, but Madelaine saw it heralded by more than the muting of darkness.

"No, it tingles," he said, wrapping his arm around her shoulder. As he pulled her close, he said, as he flipped his foot to restore circulation, "What a prosaic thing to happen."

"It might have been a leg cramp," said Madelaine as levelly as she could; she was still filled with the glory of their consummation.

"*That* would be a different matter, wouldn't it?" He chuckled once.

She turned her head and kissed the lobe of his ear. "Oh, entirely."

He ran his hand down her neck to her breast, cupping it and brushing her nipple with his thumb. "I hope you won't have bruises."

"No," she said. "I won't."

"Another of the things those of your blood don't do?" he asked deliberately lightly. "As you do not eat or weep?"

"Yes," she said quietly, and kissed the angle of his jaw where it met his neck.

"Is it difficult, not to eat or weep?" he asked, still holding on to her.

"Occasionally," she admitted, aware that she would have welcomed the release that weeping would bring her upon parting. She was about to move away from him when he tightened his arm, pulling her back close to him.

"Oh, God, Madelaine: I cannot give you up. I must, but I cannot." This was wrung from him, a cry of such utter despair that she was rendered still by its intensity.

"I know," she said, moved by his anguish; she sought to find some consolation to offer him but could think of nothing.

His eyes were frenzied as he pulled her around to face him. "I will not let this end. If I took you with me, if we left right now, we might be anywhere in the world in a month."

"If that is what you want, Tecumseh, then I will do it," she said, amazed at how deeply she meant what she said.

"It is, it is," he insisted. "It would be the joy of my life to have you at my side. Think of all the places we might go, and all the time we would have." He tried to smile, but succeeded only in stretching his lips over his teeth.

"That might not be the advantage you assume it would be," said Madelaine, a sadness coming over her that surprised her more than it surprised him. "You would grow old and I would not. You might not mind this year, or next year, but in time it would vex you. To say nothing as to what your children would think."

He stared at her. "My children?"

"Well, you would not leave them behind, would you?" she asked reasonably, and knowing what his answer would be.

"No," he admitted after a moment. "I could not do that."

Madelaine kept on. "They would see what you would see: they would grow older and I would not."

He did his best to deny what she told him. "If I could have you all to myself, then I would be happy, no matter what became of us. Or what my children might suspect."

"And how long would you be content?" Madelaine bent to kiss the fingers of his hand on her shoulder. "Even with your children along?"

"I would be thankful to the end of my days," he said with profound conviction.

"Do you think so?" Her voice was soft and poignant. "You tell me this is how you feel, but it is not. You would not like to face age as the living do, while I would hardly change at all."

"I wish you wouldn't say it that way," he protested.

"How would you like me to say it?" she challenged. "You would grow old, and I would appear not to. Vampires age very, very slowly. I have hardly changed in the last century. How would you—"

"I would accept it," he insisted, his fingers digging into her flesh, driven by the force of his emotions. "I might not like it, but I would be willing to accept it."

"Would you? What of the lovers I would have?" She made her question blunt deliberately.

"You wouldn't need them. You would have me," he told her firmly.

"For a time, perhaps," she responded, continuing with great care, "but I would need to find others, or you would soon be exhausted and come to my life." This was not quite the truth, but it was near enough that she knew she had to make him aware of what was likely to happen.

"Then we would carry on in vampire fashion," he said, his emphatic tone shoring up any doubts that might trouble him.

"But vampires cannot be lovers of vampires," she said, and felt him go still.

"And why not, pray?" His tone was harsh, sarcastic, as if he expected some self-serving answer.

"Because vampires must have life. It is the one thing we do

not have to give, and the one thing we need above all others," she said quietly. "Once you come to my life, you and I will not be able to—"

"It's not true!" he exclaimed, pushing her away.

"But it is," she said.

"So I must share you or lose you," he said thoughtfully.

"Yes," she said.

"And I take it there is no alternative to this?" He reached out for her hand. "Can we not devise some means to allow us to remain together without having to become estranged?"

"We can never be estranged," Madelaine said.

"Because you have tasted my blood," he said, a wistful note creeping into his statement.

"Yes, Tecumseh; because of that."

He had a sharp retort in mind, a single, pithy remark that would show his skepticism was flourishing; the words never came. Instead, he turned, took her face in his hands and scrutinized her features, memorizing them, before he kissed her with the sudden, harsh misery of parting. As he rose abruptly from the bed, he said, "Stay there. Please, Madelaine. Don't come to the door. I won't have the courage to go if you do."

"All right," she said, watching him dress, her violet eyes filled with anguish. Only when he was ready to leave did she say to him, "You are part of me, Tecumseh. You will always be part of me."

He paused in the door but would not look around. "And you of me." He waited for her to say good-bye; when she did not, he strode out of the room and down the stairs.

San Francisco, 8 October, 1855

Tomorrow I will be gone from this place. It is a harder parting than I would have thought possible, for I am torn between my certainty that I must and my reluctance to leave Tecumseh. I find his hold upon me quite astonishing, for I have been resigned from the first—or so I thought—to going before his wife returns. I had not thought I would find leaving so arduous, or the wrench of separation as painful as it is proving to be . . .

The two buckboard wagons are ready, one carrying my books and papers and personal things, one carrying four crates of my native earth. I have bought two horses to ride, and mules to pull the wagons, and I have paid off those I have hired. There only remains the closing of my account at Lucas and Turner; I have decided to do it as I am departing tomorrow, my last stop in this city before we turn to the south-southeast. It may be that Tecumseh will not handle the matter himself, but will deputize one of his assistants to tend to the matter . . .

"We're sorry to see you go, Madame," said Jenkins as he held open the low gate, admitting Madelaine to the realm of desks and files.

"I am sorry to leave," said Madelaine with as much sincerity as good manners. "I have truly enjoyed my stay here."

"Yes," said Jenkins, going on a bit too smoothly. "Mr. Sherman has your account information ready, if you'll just step into his office?"

Madelaine was a bit startled to hear this. "Very well," she said, and turned to walk toward the door at the end of the aisle between the desks. She had to steel herself against seeing Sherman this last time, and she waited a long moment before she knocked on the door.

"Enter," came the crisp order.

She obeyed, making herself smile as she went up to his desk. "I've come to say good-bye, Mr. Sherman. And to pick up my account records and traveling money."

Sherman had risen, but he did not take her proffered hand; instead he rummaged through a stack of papers on his desk. "I have your account information here, Madame de Montalia, and the funds you requested," he said in a voice that did not seem to belong to him.

"Thank you," she responded.

"I wish I could persuade you to carry less gold and cash with you." Concern roughened his tone. "You are not on the boulevards of Paris, Madame, and any signs of wealth are likely to attract attention you cannot want." His face was set in hard lines, but his eyes were full of anguish.

"I know something of the dangers of travel, Mr. Sherman, although I am grateful for your warning. I will heed your admonitions to the extent that circumstances allow." How formal and stiff she sounded in her own ears; she wanted so much to weep, and could not. It would not be seemly, she told herself, even if it were possible, and added aloud, "I will take all the precautions I can."

"Yes," he said. "Be sure you keep a loaded pistol to hand at all times. If you need one, you will need it instantly."

"I'll do that," she said, delaying taking her file of material into her hands, for that would be more final than closing the door.

"You will be wise to learn as much as you can about those you hire to guide you. Many of the men in that profession are scoundrels and not to be trusted." He spoke crisply, yet all the while his eyes revealed suffering he could not admit.

"I will be careful, Mr. Sherman," she promised him.

Sherman coughed twice, short, hard coughs that might signal an asthma attack. "Don't trouble yourself, Madame," he said brusquely, waving her away, although she had not moved. "It will pass. And I have a vial of your medicine, if it does not."

Madelaine had to stop herself from going around his desk to his side, to comfort him. "Well," she said rallyingly, "do not let pride keep you from using it."

"I won't," he said, and stared down at his desk in silence for several seconds, then asked, "Do you think you will ever come back to San Francisco, Madame?"

"Ever is a long time, Mr. Sherman," she pointed out. "I do not plan to now, but in time, who can tell?"

"Who, indeed," he said. "And we knew when you came that you would leave, didn't we?"

She nodded. "Soon or late, I would go."

"Off to study America," he said, trying to be jaunty; his voice cracked.

"Yes." She bit her lip to keep from saying more. With an effort, she remarked, "I suppose your children must be glad that their mother is coming home."

"Oh, yes," he said, grateful to have something safe to say. "Both of them are delighted."

"I'll think of them kindly," said Madelaine.

"You're very good." He fumbled with a square envelope, then held it out to her. "Here. I want you to have this."

"What is it?" Madelaine took the envelope cautiously, as if she expected something untoward from it.

"A sketch I did. Of you." He looked her directly in the eye, a world of longing in his gaze.

"Oh!" Madelaine said softly. "May I open it?"

"Not here, if you please," he said, his standoffishness returning. "I couldn't keep it with me, much as I wanted to. It . . . it is very revealing—oh, not of you, of me. If Ellen ever saw it, she—" He cleared his throat. "It is enough that one of us should have a broken heart. I will not chance giving such pain to her."

Madelaine nodded, unable to speak; she slipped the envelope into her leather portfolio which she had brought to contain her account records.

"This is too difficult," Sherman whispered as he took the file and thrust it toward her. "If you do not leave now, I don't think I will be able to let you go. And let you go I must."

"Yes," said Madelaine as she took the file and put it into the portfolio.

"And your cash and gold," he went on with ruthless practicality, handing her a heavy canvas sack with Lucas and Turner stenciled on its side. "Be careful where you stow this."

"I will," she said, and turned to leave.

"Madel—am," he said, halting her. "I wish, with all my heart, you . . . your stay here wasn't over."

"You're very kind, Mr. Sherman," said Madelaine, struggling to retain her composure.

"As it is," he went on as if unable to stop. "I will think of you each . . . often."

"And I of you," said Madelaine, wishing she could kiss him one last time and knowing she must not.

"If only you and I . . ." He let his words falter and stop.

Madelaine backed away, reaching behind her for the door. "Our . . . our friendship is not at an end simply because we part," she told him, forcing herself to speak steadily. She pulled the door open, readying herself to leave the bank.

His reply struck her with the full weight of his constrained emotions, as if he wanted to impart to her all that he could not say: "I know, Madelaine; I know."

Presidio de Santa Barbara, 14 November, 1855

We have found an inn near the Presidio itself, and I am assured we will be safe here. . . . This part of California is much more Spanish than the north, more like Mexico; I suspect it is because there are fewer men willing to prospect in the deserts than in the mountains. Perhaps the hold of the Spanish landlords is stronger here than in the North, as there are fewer newcomers to challenge their rule and their Land Grants. Thanks to gold, San Francisco has become quite an eclectic place, what with miners arriving from every part of Europe and America. But here, I am told, it is not so dramatically changed. For the most part, the Camino Real, which our guide calls the Mission Road, is well enough maintained that we made good progress along it, and lost only one day to rain. Our average progress has been a respectable ten to twelve miles a day, although we did slow in our climb through the mountains around San Luis Obispo. Generally, however, we have traveled swiftly, and at this pace, we should reach San Diego by Christmas, from whence we will turn east.

I have sent two letters back to Tecumseh, though I have had no replies and expect none; I have not yet found a way to thank him sufficiently for the sketch he made of me and gave me the morning I left. He is right: it is too easily read for him to keep it by him, where it might be discovered and understood. In execution it is simple enough: he has drawn me seated on a fallen log, my hat in my hand, in all considerations a most innocuous pose—but there is something about it that smolders, so that I half expect the paper to burst into flame. He included a short note which said he would have to carry my likeness burning in his heart; that is very gallant of him, as well as being very nearly accurate, if this sketch is any indication of his sentiments. I am surprised to discover how strong the bond between us is, though why I should feel so, I cannot think.

I wonder if Saint-Germain is right, and I am developing a weakness for Americans?

Tanith Lee

The Isle Is Full of Noises

TANITH LEE, *the internationally renowned, award-winning fanta-sist, makes her home on the southern seacoast of England. Her many superb novels and short-story collections include* The Birth-grave, Companions on the Road, Dark Dance, Drinking Sapphire Wine, East of Midnight, Red as Blood, *and many other books and tales. Her fantasies appear regularly in my anthologies, the most re-cent being a specially commissioned new story, "The Pandora Heart," in* Don't Open This Book! *(Doubleday Direct, 1998). "The Isle Is Full of Noises," whose title derives from Shakespeare's* The Tempest, *features a vampire the likes of which—trust me!—you have never before encountered.*

. . . and if you gaze into the abyss, the abyss gazes also into you.
—NIETZSCHE

1

IT IS AN ISLAND here, now.

At the clearest moments of the day—usually late in the morning, occasionally after noon, and at night when the lights come on—a distant coastline is sometimes discernible. This coast is the higher area of the city, that part which still remains intact above water.

The city was flooded a decade ago. The Sound possessed it. The facts had been predicted some while, and various things were done in readiness, mostly comprising a mass desertion.

They say the lower levels of those buildings which now

form the island will begin to give way in five years. But they were saying that, too, five years back.

Also there are the sunsets. (Something stirred up in the atmosphere apparently, by the influx of water, some generation of heat or cold or vapour.) They start, or appear to do so, the sunsets, about three o'clock in the afternoon, and continue until the sun actually goes under the horizon, which in summer can be as late as seven forty-five.

For hours the roof terraces, towerettes, and glass lofts of the island catch a deepening blood-and-copper light, turning to new bronze, raw amber, cubes of hot pink ice.

Yse lives on West Ridge, in a glass loft. She has, like most of the island residents, only one level, but there's plenty of space. (Below, if anyone remembers, lies a great warehouse, with fish, even sometimes barracuda, gliding between the girders.)

Beyond her glass west wall, a freak tree has rooted in the terrace. Now nine years old, it towers up over the loft, and the surrounding towers and lofts, while its serpentine branches dip down into the water. Trees are unusual here. This tree, which Yse calls Snake (for the branches), seems unfazed by the salt content of the water. It may be a sort of willow, a willow crossed with a snake.

Sometimes Yse watches fish glimmering through the tree's long hair, that floats just under the surface. This appeals to her, as the whole notion of the island does. Then one morning she comes out and finds, caught in the coils of her snake-willow, a piano.

Best to describe Yse, at this point, which is not easy.

She might well have said herself (being a writer by trade but also by desire) that she doesn't want you to be disappointed, that you should hold on to the idea that what you get at first, here, may not be what is to be offered later.

Then again, there is a disparity between what Yse seems to be, or is, and what Yse *also seems* to be, or *is*.

Her name, however, as she has often had to explain, is

pronounced to rhyme with "please"—more correctly, *pleeze*: Eeze. Is it French? Or some sport from Latin-Spanish? God knows.

Yse is in her middle years, not tall, rather heavy, dumpy. Her fair, greying hair is too fine, and so she cuts it very short. Yse is also slender, taller, and her long hair (still fair, still grey-ing) hangs in thick silken hanks down her back. One constant, grey eyes.

She keeps only a single mirror, in the bathroom above the wash basin. Looking in it is always a surprise for Yse: Who on earth is that? But she never lingers, soon she is away from it and back to herself. And in this way, too, she deals with Per Laszd, the lover she has never had.

Yse had brought the coffeepot and some peaches onto the ter-race. It is a fine morning, and she is considering walking along the bridgeway to the boat stop, and going over to the cafés on East Heights. There are always things on at the cafés, psychic fairs, art shows, theatre. And she needs some more lamp oil.

Having placed the coffee and fruit, Yse looks up and sees the piano.

"*Oh,*" says Yse, aloud.

She is very, very startled, and there are good reasons for this, beyond the obvious oddity itself.

She goes to the edge of the terrace and leans over, where the tree leans over, and looks at the snake arms which hold the piano fast, tilted only slightly, and fringed by rippling leaves.

The piano is old, huge, a type of pianoforte, its two lids fast shut, concealing both the keys and its inner parts.

Water swirls round it idly. It is intensely black, scarcely marked by its swim.

And has it been swimming? Probably it was jettisoned from some apartment on the mainland (the upper city). Then, stretch-ing out its three strong legs, it set off savagely for the island, de-termined not to go down.

Yse has reasons, too, for thinking in this way.

She reaches out, but cannot quite touch the piano.

There are tides about the island, variable, sometimes rough. If she leaves the piano where it is, the evening tide may be a rough one, and lift it away, and she will lose it.

She *knows* it must have swum here.

Yse goes to the table and sits, drinking coffee, looking at the piano. As she does this a breeze comes in off the Sound, and stirs her phantom long heavy soft hair, so it brushes her face and neck and the sides of her arms. And the piano makes a faint twanging, she thinks perhaps it does, up through its shut lids that are like closed eyes and lips together.

"What makes a vampire seductive?" Yse asks Lucius, at the Café Blonde. "I mean, irresistible?"

"His beauty," says Lucius. He laughs, showing his teeth. "I knew a vampire once. No, make that twice. I met him twice."

"Yes?" asks Yse cautiously. Lucius has met them all, ghosts, demons, angels. She partly believes it to be so, yet knows he mixes lies with the truths; a kind of test, or trap, for the listener. "Well, what happened?"

"We walk, talk, drink, make love. He bites me. Here, see?" Lucius moves aside his long locks (luxurious, but greying, as are her own). On his coal-dark neck, no longer young, but strong as a column, an old scar.

"You told me once before," says Yse, "a shark did that."

"To reassure you. But it was a vampire."

"What did you do?"

"I say to him, Watch out, monsieur."

"And then?"

"He watched out. Next night, I met him again. He had yellow eyes, like a cat."

"He was undead?"

"The undeadest thing I ever laid."

He laughs. Yse laughs, thoughtfully. "A piano's caught in my terrace tree."

"*Oh* yeah," says Lucius, the perhaps arch liar.

"You don't believe me."

"What is your thing about vampires?"

"I'm writing about a vampire."

"Let me read your book."

"Someday. But Lucius—it isn't their charisma. Not their beauty that makes them irresistible—"

"No?"

"Think what they must be like . . . skin in rags, dead but walking. Stinking of the grave—"

"They use their hudja-magica to take all that away."

"It's how they make *us* feel."

"Yeah, Yse. You got it."

"What they can do to *us*."

"Dance all night," says Lucius, reminiscent. He watches a handsome youth across the café, juggling mirrors that flash unnervingly, his skin the colour of an island twilight.

"Lucius, will you help me shift the piano into my loft?"

"Sure thing."

"Not tomorrow, or next month. I mean, could we do it today, before sunset starts?"

"I love you, Yse. Because of you, I shall go to heaven."

"Thanks."

"Shit piano," he says. "I could have slept in my boat. I could have paddled over to Venezule. I could have watched the thought of Venus rise through the grey brain of the sky. Piano huh, piano. Who shall I bring to help me? That boy, he looks strong, look at those mirrors go."

The beast had swum to shore, to the beach, through the pale, transparent urges of the waves, when the star Venus was in the brain-grey sky. But not here.

There.

In the dark before star rise and dawn, more than two centuries ago. First the rifts, the lilts of the dark sea, and in them these mysterious thrusts and pushes, the limbs like those of some huge swimmer, part man and part lion and part crab—but also, a manta ray.

Then, the lid breaks for a second through the fans of water, under the dawn star's piercing steel. Wet as black mirror, the closed lid of the piano, as it strives, on three powerful beast legs, for the beach.

This Island is an island of sands, then of trees, the sombre sullen palms that sweep the shore. Inland, heights, vegetation, plantations, some of coffee and sugar and rubber, and one of imported kayar. An invented island, a composite.

Does it crawl onto the sand, the legs still moving, crouching low like a beast? Does it rest on the sand, under the sway of the palm trees, as a sun rises?

The Island has a name, like the house which is up there, unseen, on the inner heights. Bleumaneer.

(*Notes:* Gregers Vonderjan brought his wife to Bleumaneer in the last days of his wealth . . .)

The piano crouched stilly at the edge of the beach, the sea retreating from it, and the dark of night falling away . . .

It's sunset.

Lucius, in the bloody light, with two men from the Café Blonde (neither the juggler), juggle the black piano from the possessive tentacles of the snake-willow.

With a rattle, a shattering of sounds (like slung cutlery), it fetches up on the terrace. The men stand perplexed, looking at it. Yse watches from her glass wall.

"Broke the cock thing."

"No way to move it. Shoulda tooka crane."

They prowl about the piano, while the red light blooms across its shade.

Lucius tries delicately to raise the lid from the keys. The lid does not move. The other two, they wrench at the other lid, the piano's top (pate, shell). This, too, is fastened stuck. (Yse had made half a move, as if to stop them. Then her arm fell lax.)

"Damn ol' thing. What she wan' this ol' thing for?"

They back away. One makes a kicking movement. Lucius shakes his head; his long locks jangle across the flaming sky.

"*Do* you want this, girl?" Lucius asks Yse by her glass.

"Yes." Shortly. "I said I did."

" 'S all broke up. Won't play you none," sings the light-eyed man, Carr, who wants to kick the piano, even now his loose leg pawing in its jeans.

Trails of water slip away from the piano, over the terrace, like chains.

Yse opens her wide glass doors. The men carry the piano in and set it on her bare wooden floor.

Yse brings them, now docile as their maid, white rum, while Lucius shares out the bills.

"Hurt my back," whines Carr the kicker.

"Piano," says Lucius, drinking, "pian-o—O pain!"

He says to her at the doors (as the men scramble back into their boat), "That vampire I danced with. Where he bit me. Still feel him there, biting me, some nights. Like a piece of broken bottle in my neck. I followed him, did I say to you? I followed him and saw him climb in under his grave just before the sun came up. A marble marker up on top. It shifted easy as breath, settles back like a sigh. But he was beautiful, that boy with yellow eyes. Made me feel like a king, with him. Young as a lion, with him. *Old* as him, too. A thousand years in a skin of smoothest suede."

Yse nods.

She watches Lucius away into the sunset, of which three hours are still left.

Yse scatters two bags of porous litter-chips, which are used all over the Island, to absorb the spillages and seepages of the Sound, to mop up the wet that slowly showers from the piano. She does not touch it. Except with her right hand, for a second, flat on the top of it.

The wood feels ancient and hollow, and she thinks it hasn't, perhaps, a metal frame.

As the redness folds over deeper and deeper, Yse lights the oil lamp on her worktable, and sits there, looking forty feet across the loft, at the piano on the sunset. Under her right hand now, the pages she has already written, in her fast untidy scrawl.

Pian-o. O pain.

Shush, says the Sound tide, flooding the city, pulsing

through the walls, struts, and girders below.

Yse thinks distinctly, suddenly—it is always this way—about Per Laszd. But then another man's memory taps at her mind.

Yse picks up her pen, almost absently. She writes:

"Like those hallucinations which sometimes come at the edge of sleep, so that you wake, thinking two or three words have been spoken close to your ear, or that a tall figure stands in the corner . . . like this, the image now and then appears before him.

"Then he sees her, the woman, sitting on the rock, her white dress and her ivory-coloured hair, hard-gleaming in a poststorm sunlight. Impossible to tell her age. A desiccated young girl, or unlined old woman. And the transparent sea lapping in across the sand . . .

"But he has said, the Island is quite deserted now."

2. Antoinelle's Courtship

Gregers Vonderjan brought his wife to Bleumaneer in the last days of his wealth.

In this way, she knew nothing about them, the grave losses to come, but then they had been married only a few months. She knew little enough about him, either.

Antoinelle was raised among staunch and secretive people. Until she was fourteen, she had thought herself ugly, and after that, beautiful. A sunset revelation had put her right, the westering glow pouring in sideways to paint the face in her mirror, on its slim, long throat. She found, too, she had shoulders, and cheekbones. Hands, whose tendons flexed in fans. With the knowledge of beauty, Antoinelle began to hope for something. Armed with her beauty she began to fall madly in love—with young officers in the army, with figures encountered in dreams.

One evening at a parochial ball, the two situations became confused.

The glamorous young man led Antoinelle out into a summer garden. It was a garden of Europe, with tall dense trees of twisted trunks, foliage massed on a lilac northern sky.

Antoinelle gave herself. That is, not only was she prepared to give of herself sexually, but to give herself *up* to this male person, of whom she knew no more than that he was beautiful.

Some scruple—solely for himself, the possible consequences—made him check at last.

"No—no—" she cried softly, as he forcibly released her and stood back, angrily panting.

The beautiful young man concluded (officially to himself) that Antoinelle was "loose," and therefore valueless. She was not rich enough to marry, and besides, he despised her family.

Presently he told his brother officers all about this girl, and her "looseness."

"She would have done anything," he said.

"She's a whore," said another, and smiled.

Fastidiously, Antoinelle's lover remarked, "No, worse than a whore. A whore does it honestly, for money. It's her work. This one simply does it."

Antoinelle's reputation was soon in tatters, which blew about that little town of trees and societal pillars, like the torn flag of a destroyed regiment.

She was sent in disgrace to her aunt's house in the country.

No one spoke to Antoinelle in that house. Literally, no one. The aunt would not, and she had instructed her servants, who were afraid of her. Even the maid who attended Antoinelle would not speak, in the privacy of the evening chamber, preparing the girl for the silent evening supper below, or the lumpy three-mattressed bed.

The aunt's rather unpleasant lapdog, when Antoinelle had attempted, unwatched, to feed it a marzipan fruit, had only turned its ratlike head away. (At everyone else, save the aunt, it growled.)

Antoinelle, when alone, sobbed. At first in shame—her family had already seen to that, very ably, in the town. Next in frustrated rage. At last out of sheer despair.

She was like a lunatic in a cruel, cool asylum. They fed her, made her observe all the proper rituals. She had shelter and a place to sleep, and people to relieve some of her physical wants. There were even books in the library, and a garden to walk in on sunny days. But language—*sound*—they took away from her. And language is one of the six senses. It was as bad perhaps as blindfolding her. Additionally, they did not even speak to each other, beyond the absolute minimum, when she was by— coarse-aproned girls on the stair stifled their giggles, and passed with mask faces. And in much the same way, too, Antoinelle was not permitted to play the aunt's piano.

Three months of this, hard, polished months, like stone mirrors which reflected nothing.

Antoinelle grew thinner, more pale. Her young eyes had hollows under them. She was like a nun.

The name of the aunt who did all this was Clemence— which means, of course, clemency—mild, merciful. (And the name of the young man in the town who had almost fucked Antoinelle, forced himself not to for his own sake, and then fucked instead her reputation, which was to say, her *life* . . . his name was Justus.)

On a morning early in the fourth month, a new thing happened.

Antoinelle opened her eyes, and saw the aunt sailing into her room. And the aunt, glittering with rings like knives, *spoke* to Antoinelle.

"Very well, there's been enough of all this. Yes, yes. You may get up quickly and come down to breakfast, Patice will see to your dress and hair. Make sure you look your best."

Antoinelle lay there, on her back in the horrible bed, staring like the dead newly awakened.

"Come along," said Aunt Clemence, holding the awful little dog untidily scrunched, "make haste now. What a child!" As if Antoinelle were the strange creature, the curiosity.

While, as the aunt swept out, the dog craned back and chattered its dirty teeth at Antoinelle.

And then, the third wonder, Patice was chattering, breaking like a happy stream at thaw, and shaking out a dress.

Antoinelle got up, and let Patice see to her, all the para-phernalia of the toilette, finishing with a light pollen of powder, even a fingertip of rouge for the matt pale lips, making them moist and rosy.

"Why?" asked Antoinelle at last, in a whisper.

"There is a visitor," chattered Patice, brimming with joy.

Antoinelle took two steps, then caught her breath and dropped as if dead on the carpet.

But Patice was also brisk; she brought Antoinelle round, crushing a vicious clove of lemon oil under her nostrils, slapping the young face lightly. Exactly as one would expect in this effi-ciently cruel lunatic asylum.

Presently Antoinelle drifted down the stairs, light-headed, rose-lipped and shadow-eyed. She had never looked more lovely or known it less.

The breakfast was a ghastly provincial show-off thing. There were dishes and dishes, hot and cold, of kidneys, eggs, of cheeses and hams, hot breads in napkins, brioches, and choco-late. (It was a wonder Antoinelle was not sick at once.) All this set on crisp linen with flashing silver, and the fine china nor-mally kept in a cupboard.

The servants flurried round in their awful, stupid (second-hand) joy. The aunt sat in her chair and Antoinelle in hers, and the man in his, across the round table.

Antoinelle had been afraid it was going to be Justus. She did not know why he would be there—to castigate her again, to apologise—either way, such a boiling of fear—or something—had gone through Antoinelle that she had fainted.

But it was not Justus. This was someone she did not know.

He had stood up as she came into the room. The morning was clear and well lit, and Antoinelle had seen, with a dreary sagging of relief, that he was old. Quite old. She went on think-ing this as he took her hand in his large one and shook it as if carelessly playing with something, very delicately. But his hand was manicured, the nails clean and white-edged. There was one ring, with a dull colourless stone in it.

Antoinelle still thought he was quite old, perhaps not so old as she *had* thought.

When they were seated, and the servants had doled out to them some food and drink, and gone away, Antoinelle came to herself rather more.

His hair was not grey but a mass of silvery blond. A lot of hair, very thick, shining, which fell, as was the fashion then, just to his shoulders. He was thickset, not slender, but seemed immensely strong. One saw this in ordinary, apparently unrelated things—for example, the niceness with which he helped himself now from the coffeepot. Indeed, the dangerous playfulness of his handshake with a woman; he could easily crush the hands of his fellow men.

Perhaps he was not an old man, really. In his forties (which would be the contemporary age of fifty-five or -six). He was losing his figure, as many human beings do at that age, becoming either too big or too thin. But if his middle had spread, he was yet a presence, sprawled there in his immaculately white ruffled shirt, the broad-cut coat, his feet in boots of Spanish leather propped under the table. And to his face, not much really had happened. The forehead was both wide and high, scarcely lined, the nose aquiline as a bird's beak, scarcely thickened, the chin undoubled and jutting, the mouth narrow and well shaped. His eyes, set in the slightest rouching of skin, were large, a cold, clear blue. He might actually be only just forty (that is, fifty). A fraction less.

Antoinelle was not to know, in his youth, the heads of women had turned for Gregers Vonderjan like tulips before a gale. Or that, frankly, now and then they still did so.

The talk, what was that about all this while? Obsequious pleasantries from the aunt, odd anecdotes he gave, to do with ships, land, slaves, and money. Antoinelle had been so long without hearing the speech of others, she had become nearly word-deaf, so that most of what he said had no meaning for her, and what the aunt said even less.

Finally the aunt remembered an urgent errand, and left them.

They sat, with the sun blazing through the windows. Then Vonderjan looked right at her, at Antoinelle, and suddenly her face, her whole body, was suffused by a savage burning blush.

"Did she tell you why I called here?" he asked, almost indifferently.

Antoinelle, her eyes lowered, murmured childishly, thoughtlessly, "No—she—she hasn't been speaking to me—"

"Hasn't she? Why not? Oh," he said, "that little business in the town."

Antoinelle, to her shock, began to cry. This should have horrified her—she had lost control—the worst sin, as her family had convinced her, they thought.

He knew, this man. He knew. She was ashamed, and yet unable to stop crying, or to get up and leave the room.

She heard his chair pushed back, and then he was standing over her. To her slightness, he seemed vast and overpowering. He was clean, and smelled of French soap, of tobacco, and some other nuance of masculinity, which Antoinelle at once intuitively liked. She had scented it before.

"Well, you won't mind leaving her, then," he said, and he lifted her up out of her chair, and there she was in his grip, her head drooping back, staring almost mindlessly into his large, handsome face. It was easy to let go. She did so. She had in fact learnt nothing, been taught nothing by the whips and stings of her wicked relations. "I called here to ask you," he said, "to be my wife."

"But . . ." faintly, "I don't know you."

"There's nothing to know. Here I am. Exactly what you see. Will that do?"

"But . . ." more faintly still, "why would you want me?"

"You're just what I want. And I thought you would be."

"But," nearly inaudible, "I was—disgraced."

"We'll see about that. And the old she-cunt won't talk to you, you say?"

Antoinelle, innocently, not even knowing this important word (which any way he referred to in a foreign argot), only shivered. "No. Not till today."

"Now she does because I've bid for you. You'd better come with me. Did the other one, the soldier-boy, have you? It doesn't matter, but tell me now."

Antoinelle threw herself on the stranger's chest—she had not been told, or heard his name. "No—no—" she cried, just as she had when Justus pushed her off.

"I must go slowly with you then," said this man. But nevertheless, he moved her about and, leaning over, kissed her.

Vonderjan was an expert lover. Besides, he had a peculiar quality, which had stood him, and stands those like him, in very good stead. With what he wanted in the sexual way, providing they were not unwilling to begin with, he could spontaneously communicate some telepathic echo of his needs, making them theirs. This Antoinelle felt at once, as his warm lips moved on hers, his hot tongue pierced her mouth, and the fingers of the hand which did not hold her tight, fire-feathered her breasts.

In seconds her ready flames burst up. Business-like, Vonderjan at once sat down, and holding her on his lap, placed his hand, making nothing of her dress, to crush her centre in an inexorable rhythmic grasp, until she came in gasping spasms against him, wept, and wilted there in his arms, his property.

When the inclement aunt returned with a servant, having left, she felt, sufficient time for Vonderjan to ask, and Antoinelle sensibly to acquiesce, she found her niece tearstained and dead white in a chair, and Vonderjan drinking his coffee, and smoking a cigar, letting the ash fall as it wished onto the table linen.

"Well then," said the aunt, uncertainly.

Vonderjan cast her one look, as if amused by something about her.

"Am I to presume—may I—is everything—"

Vonderjan took another puff and a gout of charred stuff hit the cloth, before he mashed out the burning butt of the cigar on a china plate.

"Antoinelle," exclaimed the aunt, "what have you to say?"

Vonderjan spoke, not to the aunt, but to his betrothed. "Get up, Anna. You're going with me now." Then, looking at the servant (a look the woman said after was like that of a basilisk),

"Out, you, and put some things together, all the lady will need for the drive. I'll supply the rest. Be quick."

Scarlet, the aunt shouted, "Now sir, this isn't how to go on."

Vonderjan drew Antoinelle up, by his hand on her elbow. *He* had control of her now, and she need bother with nothing. She turned her drooping head, like a tired flower, looking only at his boots.

The aunt was ranting. Vonderjan, with Antoinelle in one arm, went up to her. Though not a small woman, nor slight like her niece, he dwarfed her, made of her a pygmy.

"Sir—there is her father to be approached—you must have a care—"

Then she stopped speaking. She stopped because, like Antoinelle, she had been given no choice. Gregers Vonderjan had clapped his hand over her mouth, and rather more than that. He held her by the bones and flesh of her face, unable to pull away, beating at him with her hands, making noises but unable to do more, and soon breathing with difficulty.

While he kept her like this, he did not bother to look at her, his broad body only disturbed vaguely by her flailing, weak blows. He had turned again to Antoinelle, and asked her if there was anything she wished particularly to bring away from the house.

Antoinelle did not have the courage to glance at her struggling and apoplectic aunt. She shook her head against his shoulder, and after a little shake of his own (at the aunt's face) he let the woman go. He and the girl walked out of the room and out of the house, to his carriage, leaving the aunt to progress from her partial asphyxia to hysterics.

He had got them married in three days by pulling such strings as money generally will. The ceremony did not take place in the town, but all the town heard of it. Afterwards Vonderjan went back there, without his wife, to throw a lavish dinner party, limited to the male gender, which no person invited dared not attend, including the bride's father, who was trying to smile off, as does the death's-head, the state it has been put into.

At this dinner, too, was Justus. He sat with a number of his friends, all of them astonished to be there. But like the rest, they had not been able, or prepared, to evade the occasion.

Vonderjan treated them all alike, with courtesy. The food was of a high standard—a cook had been brought from the city—and there were extravagant wines, with all of which Gregers Vonderjan was evidently familiar. The men got drunk, that is, all the men but for Vonderjan, who was an established drinker, and consumed several bottles of wine, also brandy and schnapps, without much effect.

At last Vonderjan said he would be going. To the bowing and fawning of his wife's relatives he paid no attention. It was Justus he took aside, near the door, with two of his friends. The young men were all in full uniform, smart as polish, only their bright hair tousled, and faces flushed by liquor.

"You mustn't think my wife holds any rancour against you," Vonderjan announced, not loudly, but in a penetrating tone. Justus was too drunk to catch himself up, and only idiotically nodded. "She said, I should wish you a speedy end to your trouble."

"What trouble's that?" asked Justus, still idiotically.

"He has no troubles," added the first of his brother officers, "since you took that girl off his hands."

The other officer (the most sober, which was not saying much—or perhaps the most drunk, drunk enough to have gained the virtue of distance) said, "Shut your trap, you fool. Herr Vonderjan doesn't want to hear that silly kind of talk."

Vonderjan was grave. "It's nothing to me. But I'm sorry for your Justus, naturally. I shouldn't, as no man would, like to be in his shoes."

"What shoes are they?" Justus belatedly frowned.

"I can recommend to you," said Vonderjan, "an excellent doctor in the city. They say he is discreet."

"*What?*"

"What is he saying—"

"The disease, I believe they say, is often curable, in its earliest stages."

Justus drew himself up. He was almost the height of Vonderjan, but like a reed beside him. All that room, and waiters on the stair besides, were listening. "I am not—I have no—*disease*—"

Vonderjan shrugged. "That's your argument, I understand. You should leave it off, perhaps, and seek medical advice, certainly before you consider again any courtship. Not all women are as softhearted as my Anna."

"What—what?"

"Not plain enough? From what you showed her she knew you had it, and refused you. Of course, you had another story."

As Vonderjan walked through the door, the two brother officers were, one silent, and one bellowing. Vonderjan half turned, negligently. "If you don't think so, examine his prick for yourselves."

Vonderjan did not tell Antoinelle any of this, but a week later, in the city, she did read in a paper that Justus had mysteriously been disgraced, and had then fled the town after a duel.

Perhaps she thought it curious.

But if so, only for a moment. She had been absorbed almost entirely by the stranger, her strong husband.

On the first night, still calling her Anna, up against a great velvet bed, he had undone her clothes and next her body, taking her apart down to the clockwork of her desires. Her cry of pain at his entry turned almost at once into a wavering shriek of ecstasy. She was what he had wanted all along, and he what she had needed. By morning the bed was stained with her virginal blood, and by the blood from bites she had given him, not knowing she did so.

Even when, a few weeks after, Vonderjan's luck began to turn like a sail, he bore her with him on his broad wings. He said nothing of his luck. He was too occupied wringing from her again and again the music of her lusts, forcing her arching body to contortions, paroxysms, screams, torturing her to willing death in blind-red afternoons, in candlelit darkness, so that by daybreak she could scarcely move, would lie there in a stupor in the bed, unable to rise, awaiting him like an invalid or a corpse, and hungry always for more.

3

Lucius paddles his boat to the jetty, lets it idle there, looking up.

Another property of the flood vapour, the stars by night are vast, great liquid splashes of silver, ormolu.

The light in Yse's loft burns contrastingly low.

That sweet smell he noticed yesterday still comes wafting down, like thin veiling, on the breeze. Like night-blooming jasmine, perhaps a little sharper, almost like oleanders.

She must have put in some plant. But up on her terrace, only the snake tree is visible, hooping over into the water.

Lucius smokes half a roach slowly.

Far away the shoreline glimmers, where some of the stars have fallen off the sky.

"What you doing, Yse, Yse-do-as-she-please?"

Once he'd thought he saw her moving, a moth shadow crossing through the stunned light, but maybe she is asleep, or writing.

It would be simple enough to tie up and climb the short wet stair to the terrace, to knock on her glass doors. (How are you, Yse? Are you fine?) He had done that last night. The blinds were all down, the light low, as now. But through the side of the transparent loft he had beheld the other shadow standing there on her floor. The piano from the sea. No one answered.

That flower she's planted, it is sweet as candy. He'd never known her do a thing like that. Her plants always died, killed, she said, by the electrical vibrations of her psyche when she worked.

Somewhere out on the Sound a boat hoots mournfully.

Lucius unships his paddles, and wends his craft away along the alleys of water, towards the cafés and the bigger lights.

Whenever she writes about Per Laszd, which, over twenty-seven years, she has done a lot, the same feeling assails her: slight guilt. Only slight, of course, for he will never know. He is a man who never reads anything that has nothing to do with what he does. That was made clear in the beginning. She met him only twice, but has seen him, quite often, then and since, in newspapers, in news footage, and on network TV. She has been able therefore to watch him change, from an acidly, really too-beautiful young man, through his thirties and forties (when some of the silk of his beauty frayed, to reveal something leaner and more interesting, stronger and more attractive), to a latening middle age, where he has gained weight, but lost none of his masculine grace, nor his mane of hair which—only perhaps due to artifice—has no grey in it.

She was in love with him, obviously, at the beginning. But it has changed, and become something else. He was never interested in her, even when she was young, slim, and appealing. She was not, she supposed, his "type."

In addition, she rather admired what he did, and how he did it, with an actor's panache and tricks.

People who caught her fancy she had always tended to put into her work. Inevitably Per Laszd was one of these. Sometimes he appeared as a remote figure, on the edge of the action of other lives. Sometimes he took the centre of the stage, acting out invented existences, with his perceived actor's skills.

She had, she found though, a tendency to punish him in these roles. He must endure hardships and misfortunes, and often, in her work, he was dead by the end, and rarely of old age.

Her guilt, naturally, had something to do with this—was she truly punishing him, not godlike, as with other characters, but from a petty personal annoyance that he had never noticed her, let alone had sex with her, or a single real conversation. (When she had met him, it had both times been in a crowd. He spoke generally, politely including her, no more than that. She was aware he had been arrogant enough, if he had wanted to, to have demandingly singled her out.)

But really she felt guilty at the liberties she took of necessity, with him, on paper. How else could she write about him? It was

absurd to do otherwise. But describing his conjectured nakedness, both physical and intellectual, even spiritual (even supposedly "in character"), her own temerity occasionally dismayed
Yse. How dare she? But then, how dare ever to write anything,
even about a being wholly invented.

A mental shrug. *Alors* . . . well, well. And yet . . .

Making him Gregers Vonderjan, she felt, was perhaps her
worst infringement. Now she depicted him (honestly) burly
with weight and on-drawing age, although always hastening to
add the caveat of his handsomeness, his power. Per himself, as
she had seen, was capable of being majestic, yet also mercurial.
She tried to be fair, to be at her most fair, when examining him
most microscopically, or when condemning him to the worst
fates. (But, now and then, did the pen slip?)

Had he ever sensed those several dreadful falls, those calum-
nies, those *deaths*? Of course not. Well, well. There, there. And
yet . . .

How wonderful that vine smells tonight, Yse thinks, sitting up
in the lamp dusk. Some neighbour must have planted it. What
a penetrating scent, so clean and fresh, yet sweet.

It was noticeable last night, too. Yse wonders what the
flowers are that let out this aroma. And in the end, she stands
up, leaving the pen to lie there, across Vonderjan and Antoinelle.

Near her glass doors, Yse thinks the vine must be directly
facing her, over the narrow waterway under the terrace, for here
its perfume is strongest.

But when she raises the blinds and opens the doors, the
scent at once grows less. Somehow it has collected instead in the
room. She gazes out at the other lofts, at a tower of shaped glass
looking like ice in a tray. Are the hidden gardens there?

The stars are impressive tonight. And she can see the hem of
the star-spangled upper city.

A faint sound comes.

Yse knows it's not outside, but in her loft, just like the scent.
She turns. Looks at the black piano.

Since yesterday (when it was brought in), she hasn't paid it that much attention. (Has she?) She had initially stared at it, tried three or four times to raise its lids—without success. She had thought of rubbing it down, once the litter-chips absorbed the leaking water. But then she had not done this. Had not touched it very much.

Coming to the doors, she has circled wide of the piano.

Did a note sound, just now, under the forward lid? How odd, the two forelegs braced there, and the final leg at its end, more as if it balanced on a tail of some sort.

Probably the keys and hammers and strings inside are settling after the wet, to the warmth of her room.

She leaves one door open, which is not perhaps sensible. Rats have been known to climb the stair and gaze in at her under the night blinds, with their calm, clever eyes. Sometimes the criminal population of the island can be heard along the waterways, or out on the Sound, shouts and smashing bottles, cans thrown at brickwork or impervious, multiglazed windows.

But the night's still as the stars.

Yse goes by the piano, and through the perfume, and back to her desk, where Per Laszd lies helplessly awaiting her on the page.

4. Bleumaneer

Jeanjacques came to the Island in the stormy season. He was a mix of black and white, and found both peoples perplexing, as he found himself.

The slave trade was by then defused, as much, perhaps, as it would ever be. He knew there were no slaves left on the Island; that is, only freed slaves remained. (His black half lived with frenzied anger, as his white half clove to sloth. Between the two halves, he was a split soul.)

There had been sparks on the rigging of the ship, and all night a velour sky fraught with pink lightning. When they reached the bay next morning, it looked nearly colourless, the sombre palms were nearly grey, and the sky cindery, and the sea only transparent, the beaches white.

The haughty black master spoke in French.

"They call that place *Blue View*."

"Why's that?"

"Oh, it was for some vogue of wearing blue, before heads began to roll in Paris."

Jeanjacques said, "What's he like?"

"Vonderjan? A falling man."

"How do you mean?"

"Have you seen a man fall? The instants before he hits the ground, before he's hurt—the moment when he thinks he is still flying."

"He's lost his money, they were saying at Sugarbar."

"They say so."

"And his wife's a girl, almost a child."

"Two years he's been with her on his Island."

"What's she like?"

"White."

"What else?"

"To me, nothing. I can't tell them apart."

There had been a small port, but now little was there, except a rotted hulk, some huts, and the ruins of a customs house, thatched with palm, in which birds lived.

For a day he climbed with the escorting party up into the interior of the Island. Inside the forest it was grey-green-black, and the trees gave off sweat, pearling the banana leaves and plantains. Then they walked through the wild fields of cane, and the coffee trees. Dark figures still worked there, tending the kayar. But they did this for themselves. What had been owned had become the garden of those who remained, to do with as they wanted.

The black master had elaborated, telling Jeanjacques how Vonderjan had at first sent for niceties for his house, for china and Venetian glass, cases of books and wine. Even a piano had been ordered for his child-wife, although this, it seemed, had never arrived.

The Island was large and overgrown, but there was nothing, they said, very dangerous on it.

Bleumaneer, *Blue View*, the house for which the Island had come to be called, appeared on the next morning, down a dusty track hedged by rhododendrons of prehistoric girth.

It was white-walled, with several open courts, balconies. Orange trees grew along a columned gallery, and there was a Spanish fountain (dry) on the paved space before the steps. But it was a medley of all kinds of style.

"Make an itinerary and let me see it. We'll talk it over, what can be sold."

Jeanjacques thought that Vonderjan reminded him most of a lion, but a lion crossed with a golden bull. Then again, there was a wolflike element, cunning and lithe, which slipped through the grasslands of their talk.

Vonderjan did not treat Jeanjacques as what he was, a valuer's clerk. Nor was there any resentment or chagrin. Vonderjan seemed indifferent to the fix he was in. Did he even care that such and such would be sorted out and taken from him—that glowing canvas in the salon, for example, or the rose-mahogany cabinets, and all for a third of their value, or less, paid in banknotes that probably would not last out another year. Here was a man, surely, playing at life, at living. Convinced of it and of his fate, certainly, but only as the actor is, within his part.

Jeanjacques drank cloudy orjat, tasting its bitter orange-flowers. Vonderjan drank nothing, was sufficient, even in this, to himself.

"Well. What do you think?"

"I'll work on, and work tonight, present you with a summary in the morning."

"Why waste the night?" said Vonderjan.

"I must be ready to leave in another week, sir, when the ship returns."

"Another few months," said Vonderjan consideringly, "and maybe no ship will come here. Suppose you missed your boat?"

He seemed to be watching Jeanjacques through a telescope,

closely, yet far, far away. He might have been drunk, but there was no smell of alcohol to him. Some drug of the Island, perhaps?

Jeanjacques said, "I'd have to swim for it."

A man came up from the yard below. He was a white servant, shabby but respectable. He spoke to Vonderjan in some European gabble.

"My horse is sick," said Vonderjan to Jeanjacques. "I think I shall have to shoot it. I've lost most of them here. Some insect, which bites."

"I'm sorry."

"Yes." Then, lightheartedly, "But none of us escape, do we?"

Later, in the slow heat of the afternoon, Jeanjacques heard the shot crack out, and shuddered. It was more than the plight of the unfortunate horse. Something seemed to have hunted Vonderjan to his Island and now picked off from him all the scales of his world, his money, his horses, his possessions.

The clerk worked at his tally until the sun began to wester about four in the evening. Then he went up to wash and dress, because Vonderjan had said he should dine in the salon with his family. Jeanjacques had no idea what he would find. He was curious, a little, about the young wife—she must by now be seventeen or eighteen. Had there been any children? It was always likely, but then again, likely, too, they had not survived.

At five, the sky was like brass, the palms that lined the edges of all vistas like blackened brass columns, bent out of shape, with brazen leaves that rattled against each other when any breath blew up from the bay. From the roof of the house it was possible also to make out a cove, and the sea. But it looked much more than a day's journey off. Unless you jumped and the wind blew you.

Another storm mumbled over the Island as Jeanjacques entered the salon. The long windows stood wide, and the dying light flickered fitfully like the disturbed candles.

No one took much notice of the clerk, and Vonderjan behaved as if Jeanjacques had been there a year, some acquaintance with no particular purpose in the house, neither welcome nor un.

The "family," Jeanjacques saw, consisted of Vonderjan, his wife, a housekeeper, and a young black woman, apparently Vrouw Vonderjan's companion.

She was slender and fine, the black woman, and sat there as if a slave trade had never existed, either to crucify or enrage her. Her dress was of excellent muslin, ladyishly low cut for the evening, and she had ruby eardrops. (She spoke at least three languages that Jeanjacques heard, including the patois of the Island, or house, which she exchanged now and then with the old housekeeper.)

But Vonderjan's wife was another matter altogether.

The moment he looked at her, Jeanjacque's blood seemed to shift slightly, all along his bones. And at the base of his skull, where his hair was neatly tied back by a ribbon, the roots stretched themselves, prickling.

She was not at all pretty, but violently beautiful, in a way far too large for the long room, or for any room, whether spacious or enormous. So pale she was, she made her black attendant seem like a shadow cast by a flame. Satiny coils and trickles of hair fell all round her in a deluge of gilded rain. Thunder was the colour of her eyes, a dark that was not dark, some shade that could not be described visually but only in other ways. All of her was a little like that. To touch her limpid skin would be like tasting ice cream. To catch her fragrance like small bells heard inside the ears in fever.

When her dress brushed by him as she first crossed the room, Jeanjacques inadvertently recoiled inside his skin. He was feeling, although he did not know it, exactly as Justus had felt in the northern garden. Though Justus had not known it, either. But what terrified these two men was the very thing which drew other men, especially such men as Gregers Vonderjan. So much was plain.

The dinner was over, and the women got up to withdraw. As she passed by his chair, Vonderjan, who had scarecely spoken to her throughout the meal (or to anyone), lightly took hold of his wife's hand. And she looked down at once into his eyes.

Such a look it was. Oh God, Jeanjacques experienced now all his muscles go to liquid, and sinking, and his belly sinking down into his bowels, which themselves turned over heavily as a serpent. But his penis rose very quickly, and pushed hard as a rod against his thigh.

For it was a look of such explicit sex, trembling so colossally it had grown still, and out of such an agony of suspense, that he was well aware these two lived in a constant of the condition, and would need only to press together the length of their bodies to ignite like matches in a galvanic convulsion.

He had seen once or twice similar looks, perhaps. Among couples kept strictly, on their marriage night. But no, not even then.

They said nothing to each other. Needed nothing to say. It had been said.

The girl and her black companion passed from the room, and after them the housekeeper, carrying a branch of the candles, whose flames flattened as she went through the doors on to the terrace. (*Notes:* This will happen again later.)

Out there, the night was now very black. Everything beyond the house had vanished in it, but for the vague differential between the sky and the tops of the forest below. There were no stars to be seen, and thunder still moved restlessly. The life went from Jeanjacques's genitals as if it might never come back.

"Brandy," said Vonderjan, passing the decanter. "What do you think of her?"

"Of whom, sir?"

"My Anna." (Playful; who else?)

Jeanjacques visualized, in a sudden unexpected flash, certain objects used as amulets, and crossing himself in church.

"An exquisite lady, sir."

"Yes," said Vonderjan. He had drunk a lot during dinner, but in an easy way. It was evidently habit, not need. Now he said again, "Yes."

Jeanjacques wondered what would be next. But of course

nothing was to be next. Vonderjan finished his cigar, and drank down his glass. He rose, and nodded to Jeanjacques. *"Bon nuit."*

How could he even have forced himself to linger so long? Vonderjan demonstrably must be a human of vast self-control.

Jeanjacques imagined the blond man going up the stairs of the house to the wide upper storey. An open window, drifted with a gauze curtain, hot, airless night. Jeanjacques imagined Antoinelle, called Anna, lying on her back in the bed, its nets pushed careless away, for what bit Vonderjan's horses to death naturally could not essay his wife.

"No, I shan't have a good night," Jeanjacques said to Vonderjan in his head. He went to his room, and sharpened his pen for work.

In the darkness, he heard her. He was sure that he had. It was almost four in the morning by his pocket watch, and the sun would rise in less than an hour.

Waveringly she screamed, like an animal caught in a trap. Three times, the second time the loudest.

The whole of the inside of the house shook and throbbed and scorched from it.

Jeanjacques found he must get up, and standing by the window, handle himself roughly until, in less than thirteen seconds, his semen exploded onto the tiled floor.

Feeling then slightly nauseous, and dreary, he slunk to bed and slept gravely, like a stone.

Antoinelle sat at her toilette mirror, part of a fine set of silvergilt her husband had given her. She was watching herself as Nanetta combed and brushed her hair.

It was late afternoon, the heat of the day lying down but not subsiding.

Antoinelle was in her chemise; soon she would dress for the evening dinner.

Nanetta stopped brushing. Her hands lay on the air like a black slender butterfly separated in two. She seemed to be listening.

"More," said Antoinelle.

"Yes."

The brush began again.

Antoinelle often did not rise until noon, frequently later. She would eat a little fruit, drink coffee, get up and wander about in flimsy undergarments. Now and then she would read a novel, or Nanetta would read one to her. Or they would play cards, sitting at the table on the balcony, among the pots of flowers.

Nanetta had never seen Antoinelle do very much, and had never seen her agitated or even irritable.

She lived for night.

He, on the other hand, still got up mostly at sunrise, and no later than the hour after. His man, Stronn, would shave him. Vonderjan would breakfast downstairs in the courtyard, eating meat and bread, drinking black tea. Afterwards he might go over the accounts with the secretary. Sometimes the whole of the big house heard him shouting (except for his wife, who was generally still asleep). He regularly rode (two horses survived) round parts of the Island, and was gone until late afternoon, talking to the men and women in the fields, sitting to drink with them, rum and palm liquor, in the shade of plantains. He might return about the time Antoinelle was washing herself, powdering her arms and face, and putting on a dress for dinner.

A bird trilled in a cage, hopped a few steps, and flew up to its perch to trill again.

The scent of dust and sweating trees came from the long windows, stagnant yet energizing in the thickening yellow light.

Nanetta half turned her head. Again she had heard something far away. She did not know what it was.

"Shall I wear the emerald necklace tonight?" asked Antoinelle sleepily. "What do you think?"

Nanetta was used to this. To finding an answer.

"With the white dress? Yes, that would be effective."

"Put up my hair. Use the tortoiseshell combs."

Nanetta obeyed deftly.

The satiny bright hair was no pleasure to touch, too electric, stickily clinging to the fingers—full of each night's approaching storm. There would be no rain, not yet.

Antoinelle watched as the black woman transformed her. Antoinelle liked this, having only to be, letting someone else put her together in this way. She had forgotten by now, but never liked, independence. She wanted only enjoyment, to be made and remade, although in a manner that pleased her, and which, after all, demonstrated her power over others.

When she thought about Vonderjan, her husband, her loins clenched involuntarily, and a frisson ran through her, a shiver of heat. So she rationed her thoughts of him. During their meals together, she would hardly look at him, hardly speak, concentrating on the food, on the light of the candles reflecting in things, hypnotizing herself and prolonging, unendurably, her famine, until at last she was able to return to the bed, cool by then, with clean sheets on it, and wait, giving herself up to darkness and to fire.

How could she live in any other way?

Whatever had happened to her? Had the insensate cruelty of her relations pulped her down into a sponge that was ultimately receptive only to this? Or was this her true condition, which had always been trying to assert itself, and which, once connected to a suitable partner, did so, evolving also all the time, spreading itself higher and lower and in all directions, like some amoeba?

She must have heard stories of him, his previous wife, and of a black mistress or two he had had here. But Antoinelle was not remotely jealous. She had no interest in what he did when not with her, when not about to be, or actually in her bed with her. As if all other facets, both of his existence and her own, had now absolutely no meaning at all.

About the hour Antoinelle sat by the mirror, and Vonderjan, who had not gone out that day, was bathing, smoking one of the cigars as the steam curled round him, Jeanjacques stood among a wilderness of cane fields beyond the house.

That cane was a type of grass tended always to amaze him,

these huge stripes of straddling stalks, rising five feet or more above his head. He felt himself to be a child lost in a luridly unnatural wood, and besides, when a black figure passed across the view, moving from one subaqueous tunnel to another, they now supernaturally only glanced at him, catlike, from the sides of their eyes.

Jeanjacques had gone out walking, having deposited his itinerary and notes with Vonderjan in a morning room. The clerk took narrow tracks across the Island, stood on high places from which (as from the roof) coves and inlets of the sea might be glimpsed.

The people of the Island had been faultlessly friendly and courteous, until he began to try to question them. Then they changed. He assumed at first they only hated his white skin, as had others he had met, who had refused to believe in his mixed blood. In that case, he could not blame them much for the hatred. Then he understood he had not assumed this at all. They were disturbed by something, afraid of something, and he knew it.

Were they afraid of her—of the white girl in the house? Was it that? And why were they afraid? Why was he himself afraid—because afraid of her he was. Oh yes, he was terrified.

At midday he came to a group of hut houses, patchily colour-washed and with palm-leaf roofs, and people were sitting about there in the shade, drinking, and one man was splitting rosy gourds with a machete, so Jeanjacques thought of a guillotine a moment, the red juice spraying out and the *thunk* of the blade going through. (He had heard they had split imported melons in Marseilles, to test the machine. But he was a boy when he heard this tale, and perhaps it was not true.)

Jeanjacques stood there, looking on. Then a black woman got up, fat and not young, but comely, and brought him half a gourd, for him to try the dripping flesh.

He took it, thanking her.

"How is it going, Mother?" he asked her, partly in French, but also with two words of the patois, which he had begun to recognize. To no particular effect.

"It goes how it go, monsieur."

"You still take a share of your crop to the big house?" She gave him the sidelong look. "But you're free people, now."

One of the men called to her sharply. He was a tall black leopard, young and gorgeous as a carving from chocolate. The woman went away at once, and Jeanjacques heard again that phrase he had heard twice before that day. It was muttered somewhere at his back. He turned quickly, and there they sat, blacker in shade, eating from the flesh of the gourds, and drinking from a bottle passed around. Not looking at him, not at all.

"What did you say?"

A man glanced up. "It's nothing, monsieur."

"Something came from the sea, you said?"

"No, monsieur. Only a storm coming."

"It's the stormy season. Wasn't there something else?"

They shook their heads. They looked helpful, and sorry they could not assist, and their eyes were painted glass.

Something has come from the sea.

They had said it, too, at the other place, farther down, when a child had brought him rum in a tin mug.

What could come from the sea? Only weather, or men. Or the woman. She had come from there.

They were afraid, and even if he had doubted his ears or his judgement, the way they would not say it straight out, that was enough to tell him he had not imagined this.

Just then a breeze passed through the forest below, and then across the broad leaves above, shaking them. And the light changed a second, then back, like the blinking of the eye of God.

They stirred, the people. It was as if they saw the wind, and the shape it had was fearful to them, yet known. Respected.

As he was walking back by another of the tracks, he found a dead chicken laid on a banana leaf at the margin of a field. A propitiary offering? Nothing else had touched it, even a line of ants detoured out onto the track, to give it room.

Jeanjacques walked into the cane fields and went on there for a while. And now and then other human things moved through, looking sidelong at him.

Then, when he paused among the tall stalks, he heard them whispering, whispering, the stalks of cane, or else the voices of the people. Had they followed him? Were they aggressive? They had every right to be, of course, even with his kind. Even so, he did not want to be beaten, or to die. He had invested such an amount of his life and wits in avoiding such things.

But no one approached. The whispers came and went.

Now he was here, and he had made out, from the edge of this field, Vonderjan's house with its fringe of palms and rhododendrons (Blue View) above him on the hill, only about a half hour away.

In a full hour, the sun would dip. He would go to his room and there would be water for washing, and his other clothes laid out for the dinner.

The whispering began again, suddenly, very close, so Jeanjacques spun about, horrified.

But no one was there, nothing was there.

Only the breeze, that the black people could see, moved round among the stalks of the cane, that was itself like an Egyptian temple, its columns meant to be a forest of green papyrus.

"It's black," the voices whispered. "Black."

"Like a black man," Jeanjacques said hoarsely.

"Black like black."

Again, God blinked his eyelid of sky. A figure seemed to be standing between the shafts of green cane. It said, "Not black like men. So black we filled with terror of it. Black like black of night is black."

"Black like black."

"Something from the sea."

Jeanjacques felt himself dropping, and then he was on his knees, and his forehead was pressed to the powdery plant-drained soil.

He had not hurt himself. When he looked up, no one was in the field that he could see.

He got to his feet slowly. He trembled, and then the trembling, like the whispers, went away.

. . .

The storm rumbled over the Island. It sounded tonight like dogs barking, then baying in the distance. Every so often, for no apparent reason, the flames of the candles flattened, as if a hand had been laid on them.

There was a main dish of pork, stewed with spices. Someone had mentioned there were pigs on the Island, although the clerk had seen none, perhaps no longer wild, or introduced and never wild.

The black girl, who was called Nanetta, had put up her hair elaborately, and so had the white one, Vonderjan's wife. Round her slim pillar of throat were five large green stars in a necklace like a golden cake-decoration.

Vonderjan had told Jeanjacques that no jewelry was to be valued. But here at least was something that might have seen him straight for a while. Until his ship came in. But perhaps it never would again. Gregers Vonderjan had been lucky always, until the past couple of years.

A gust of wind, which seemed to do nothing else outside, abruptly blew wide the doors to the terrace.

Vonderjan himself got up, went by his servants, and shut both doors. That was, started to shut them. Instead he was standing there now, gazing out across the Island.

In the sky, the dogs bayed.

His heavy bulky frame seemed vast enough to withstand any night. His magnificent mane of hair, without any evident grey, gleamed like gold in the candlelight. Vonderjan was so strong, so nonchalant.

But he stood there a long while, as if something had attracted his attention.

It was Nanetta who asked, "Monsieur—what is the matter?"

Vonderjan half turned and looked at her, almost mockingly, his brows raised.

"Matter? Nothing."

She has it too, Jeanjacques thought. He said, "The blacks were saying, something has come from the sea."

Then he glanced at Nanetta. For a moment he saw two rings of white stand clear around the pupil and iris of her eyes. But she looked down, and nothing else gave her away.

Vonderjan shut the doors. He swaggered back to the table. (He did not look at his wife, nor she at him. They kept themselves intact, Jeanjacques thought, during proximity, only by such a method. The clerk wondered, if he were to find Antoinelle alone, and stand over her, murmuring Vonderjan's name, over and over, whether she would fall back, unable to resist, and come, without further provocation and in front of him. And at the thought, the hard rod tapped again impatiently on his thigh.)

"From the sea, you say. What?"

"I don't know, sir. But they were whispering it. Perhaps Mademoiselle knows?" He indicated Nanetta graciously, as if giving her a wanted opening.

She was silent.

"I don't think," said Vonderjan, "that she does."

"No, monsieur," she said. She seemed cool. Her eyes were kept down.

Oddly—Jeanjacques thought—it was Antoinelle who suddenly sprang up, pushing back her chair, so it scraped on the tiles.

"It's so hot," she said.

And then she stood there, as if incapable of doing anything else, of refining any desire or solution from her own words.

Vonderjan did not look at her, but he went slowly back and undid the doors. "Walk with me on the terrace, Anna."

And he extended his arm.

The white woman glided across the salon as if on runners. She seemed weightless—*blown*. And the white snake of her little narrow hand crawled round his arm and out on to the sleeve, to rest there. Husband and wife stepped out into the rumbling night.

Jeanjacques sat back and stared across the table at Nanetta. "They're most devoted," he said. "One doesn't often see it, after the first months. Especially where the ages are so different. What is he, thirty, thirty-two years her senior?"

Nanetta raised her eyes and now gazed at him impenetrably, with the tiniest, most fleeting smile.

He would get nothing out of her. She was a lady's maid, and he a jumped-up clerk, but both of them had remained slaves. They were calcined, ruined, defensive, and armoured.

Along the terrace he could see that Vonderjan and the woman were pressed close by the house, where a lush flowering vine only partly might hide them. Her skirts were already pushed askew, her head thrown sideways, mouth open, and eyes shut. He was taking her against the wall, thrusting and heaving into her.

Jeanjacques looked quickly away, and began to whistle, afraid of hearing her cries of climax.

But now the black girl exclaimed, "Don't whistle, don't do that, monsieur!"

"Why? Why not?"

She only shook her head, but again her eyes—the black centres were silver-ringed. So Jeanjacques got up and walked out of the salon into Vonderjan's library across the passage, where now the mundane papers, concerning things to be sold, lay on a table.

But it has come, it has come through the sea, before star rise and dawn, through the rifts and fans of the transparent water, sliding and swimming like a crab.

It has crawled onto the sand, crouching low, like a beast, and perhaps mistaken for some animal.

A moon (is it a different moon each night? Who would know?) sinking, and Venus in the east.

Crawling into the tangle of the trees, with the palms and parrot trees reflecting in the dulled mirror of its lid, its carapace. Dragging the hind limb like a tail, pulling itself by the front legs, like a wounded boar.

Through the forest, with only the crystal of Venus to shatter through the heavy leaves of sweating bronze.

Bleumaneer, La Vue Bleu, Blue Fashion, Blue View, seeing through a blue eye to a black shape, which moves from shadow to shadow, place to place. But always nearer.

Something is in the forest.

Nothing dangerous. How can it hurt you?

5

Yse is buying food in the open-air market at Bley. Lucius had seen her, and now stands watching her, not going over.

She has filled her first bag with vegetables and fruit, and in the second she puts a fish and some cheese, olive oil and bread.

Lucius crosses through the crowd, by the place where the black girl called Rosalba is cooking red snapper on her skillet, and the old poet paints his words in coloured sand.

As Yse walks into a liquor store, Lucius follows.

"You're looking good, Yse."

She turns, gazing at him—not startled, more as if she doesn't remember him. Then she does. "Thank you. I feel good today."

"And strong. But not *this* strong. Give me the vegetables to carry, Yse."

"Okay. That's kind."

"What have you done to your hair?"

Yse thinks about this one. "Oh. Someone put in some extra hair for me. You know how they do, they hot-wax the strands on to your own."

"It looks fine."

She buys a box of wine bottles.

"You're having a party?" Lucius says.

"No, Lucius. I don't throw parties. You know that."

"I know that."

"Just getting in my stores. I'm working. Then I needn't go out again for a while, just stay put and write."

"You've lost some weight," Lucius says, "looks like about twenty-five pounds."

Now she laughs. "*No.* I wish. But you know I do some-times, when I work. Adrenaline."

He totes the wine and the vegetables, and they stroll over to the bar on the quay, to which fresh fish are being brought in from the Sound. (The bar is at the top of what was, once, the Aquatic Museum. There are still old cases of bullet-and-robber-proof glass, with fossils in them, little ancient dragons of the deeps, only three feet long, and coelacanths with needle teeth.)

Lucius orders coffee and rum, but Yse only wants a mineral water. Is she dieting? He has never known her to do this. She has said dieting became useless after her forty-third year.

Her hair hangs long, to her waist, blonde, with whiter blonde and silver in it. He can't see any of the wax-ends of the extensions, or any grey either. Slimmer, her face, hands, and shoulders have fined right down. Her skin is excellent, luminous and pale. Her eyes are crystalline, and outlined by soft black pencil he has never seen her use before.

She says sharply, "For a man who likes men, you surely know how to look a woman over, Lucius."

"None better."

"Well, don't."

"I'm admiring you, Yse."

"Well, still don't. You're embarrassing me. I'm not used to it any more. If I ever was."

There is, he saw an hour ago—all across the market—a small white surgical dressing on the left side of her neck. Now she absently touches it, and pulls her finger away like her own mother would do. They say you can always tell a woman's age from her hands. Yse's hands look today like those of a woman of thirty-five.

"Something bite you, Yse?"

"An insect. It itches."

"I came by in the boat," he says, drinking his coffee, leaving the rum to stand in the glass. "I heard you playing that piano."

"You must have heard someone else somewhere. I can't play. I used to improvise, years ago. But then I had to sell my piano back then. This one . . . I haven't been able to get the damn lid up. I'm frightened to force it in case everything breaks."

"Do you want me to try?"

"Thanks—but maybe not. You know, I don't think the keys can be intact. How can they be? And there might be rats in it."

"Does it smell of rats?"

"Oddly, it smells of flowers. Jasmine, or something. Mostly at night, really. A wonderful smell. Perhaps something's growing inside it."

"In the dark."

"Night-blooming Passia," Yse says, as if quoting.

"And you write about that piano," says Lucius.

"Did I tell you? Good guess then. But it's not about a piano. Not really. About an Island."

"Where is this island?"

"Here." Yse sets her finger on a large notebook that she has already put on the table. (Often she will carry her work about with her, like a talisman. This isn't new.)

But Lucius examines the blank cover of the book as if scanning a map. "Where else?" he says.

Now Yse taps her forehead. (*In my mind.*) But somehow he has the impression she has also tapped her left ear, directly above the bite—as if the island was in there, too. *Heard* inside her ear. Or else, heard, felt—inside the *bite*.

"Let me read it," he says, *not* opening the notebook.

"You can't."

"Why not?"

"My awful handwriting. No one can, until I type it through the machine and there's a disc."

"You write so bad to hide it," he says.

"Probably."

"What's your story really about?"

"I told you. An Island. And a vampire."

"And it bit you in the neck."

Again, she laughs. "*You're* the one a vampire bit, Lucius. Or has it gone back to being a shark that bit you?"

"All kinds have bit me. I bite them, too."

She's finished her water. The exciting odour of cooking spiced fish drifts into the bar, and Lucius is hungry. But Yse is getting up.

"I'll carry your bag to the boat stop."

"Thanks, Lucius."

"I can bring them to your loft."

"No, that's fine."

"What did you say about a vampire," he asks her as they wait above the sparkling water for the water bus, "not what they are, what they *do* to you—what they make you feel?"

"I've known you over five years, Lucius—"

"Six and a half years."

"Six and a half then. I've never known you to be very interested in my books."

The breeze blows off the Sound, flattening Yse's shirt to her body. Her waist is about five inches smaller, her breasts formed, and her whole shape has changed from that of a small barrel to a curvy egg timer. Woman-shape. Young woman-shape.

He thinks, uneasily, will she begin to menstruate again, the hormones flowing back like the flood of the Sound tides through the towers and lofts of the island? Can he scent, through her cleanly showered, soap and shampoo smell, the hint of fresh blood?

"Not interested, Yse. Just being nosy."

"All right. The book is about, among others, a girl, who is called Antoinelle. She's empty, or been made empty, because what she wants is refused her—so she's like a soft, flaccid, open bag, and she wants and wants. And the soft wanting emptiness pulls him—the man—inside. She drains him of volition, and of his good luck. But he doesn't care. He also wants this. Went out looking for it. He explains that in the next section, I think . . ."

"So she's your vampire."

"No. But she makes a vampire possible. She's like a blueprint—like compost, for the plant to grow in. And the heat there, and the decline, that lovely word *desuetude*. And empty spaces that need to be continually *filled*. Nature abhors a vacuum. Darkness abhors it, too, and rushes in. Why else do you think it gets dark when the sun goes down?"

"Night," he says flatly.

"Of course not," she smiles, "nothing so ordinary. It's the black of outer space rushing to fill the empty gap the daylight filled. Why else do they call it *space?*"

She's clever. Playing with her words, with quotations and vocal things like that.

Lucius can see the tired old rusty boat chugging across the water.

(Yse starts to talk about the planet Vulcan, which was discovered once, twice, a hundred or a hundred and fifty years ago, and both times found to be a hoax.)

The bus boat is at the quay. Lucius helps Yse get her food and wine into the boat. He watches as it goes off around this drowned isle we have here, but she forgets to wave.

In fact, Yse has been distracted by another thought. She had found a seashell lying on her terrace yesterday. This will sometimes happen, if an especially high tide has flowed in.

She's thinking about the seashell, and the idea has come to her that, if she put it to her left ear, instead of hearing the sound of the sea (which is the rhythm of her own blood, moving), she might hear a piano playing.

Which is how she might put this into the story.

By the time the bus boat reaches West Ridge, sunset is approaching. When she has hauled the bags and wine to the doors of her loft, she stands a moment, looking. The snake-willow seems carved from vitreous. The alley of water is molten. But that's by now commonplace.

Even out here, before she opens her doors, she can catch the faint overture of perfume from the plant which may—must—be growing in the piano.

She dreamed last night she followed Per Laszd for miles, trudging till her feet ached, through endless lanes of shopping mall, on the mainland. He would not stop, or turn, and periodically he disappeared. For some hours, too, she saw him in conversation with a slender, dark-haired woman. When he vanished yet again, Yse approached her. "Is he your lover?" "No," chuckled the incredulous woman. "Mine? No." In the end Yse had gone on again, seen him ahead of her, and at last given up, turned her back, walked away briskly, not wanting him to know she had pursued him such a distance. Then only did she feel his hands thrill lightly on her shoulders—

At the shiver of memory, Yse shakes herself.

She's pleased to have lost weight, but not so surprised. She hasn't been eating much, and change is always feasible. The extensions cost a lot of money. Washing her hair is now a nuisance, and probably she will have them taken out before too long.

However, seeing her face in the mirror above the wash basin, she paused this morning, recognizing herself, if only for a moment.

A red gauze cloud drifts from the mainland.

Yse undoes her glass doors, and in the shadow, there that other shadow stands on its three legs. It might be anything but what it is, as might we all.

6. Her Piano

On the terrace below the gallery of orange trees, above the dry fountain, Gregers Vonderjan stood checking his gun.

Jeanjacques halted. He felt for a moment irrationally afraid—as opposed to the other fears he had felt here.

But the gun, plainly, was not for him.

It was just after six in the morning. Dawn had happened not long ago, the light was transparent as a windowpane.

"Another," said Vonderjan enigmatically. (Jeanjacques had noticed before, the powerful and self-absorbed were often obscure, thinking everyone must already know their business, which of course shook the world.)

". . . Your horses."

"My horses. Only two now, and one on its last legs. Come with me if you like, if you're not squeamish."

I am, extremely, Jeanjacques thought, but he went with Vonderjan nevertheless, slavishly.

Vonderjan strode down steps, around corners, through a grove of trees. They reached the stables. It was vacant, no one about but for a single man, some groom.

Inside the stall, two horses were together, one lying down. The other, strangely uninvolved, stood aloof. This upright one was white as some strange pearly fish animal, its eyes almost blue, Jeanjacques thought, but perhaps that was a trick of the pure light. The other horse, the prone one, half lifted its head, heavily.

Vonderjan went to this horse. The groom did not speak. Vonderjan kneeled down.

"Ah, poor soldier—" then he spoke in another tongue, his birth-language, probably. As he murmured, he stroked the streaked mane away from the horse's eyes, tenderly, like a father, caressed it till the weary eyes shut, then shot it, quickly through the skull. The legs kicked once, strengthlessly, a reflex. It had been almost gone already.

Jeanjacques went out and leaned on the mounting block. He expected he would vomit, but did not.

Vonderjan presently also came out, wiping his hands, like Pilate.

"Damn this thing, death," he said. The anger was wholesome, *whole*. For a moment a real man, a human being, stood solidly by Jeanjacques, and Jeanjacques wanted to turn and fling his arms about this creature, to keep it with him. But then it vanished, as before.

The strong handsome face was bland—or was it *blind*?

"None of us escape death."

That cliché once more, masking the *horror*—but what *was* the horror? And was the use of the cliché, only acceptance of the harsh world, precisely what Vonderjan must have set himself to learn?

"Come to the house. Have a brandy," said Vonderjan.

They went back, not the way they had come, but using another flight of stairs. Behind them the groom was clearing the beautiful dead horse like debris or garbage. Jeanjacques refused to look over his shoulder.

Vonderjan's study had no light until great storm shutters were undone. It must face, like the terrace, towards the sea.

The brandy was hot.

"All my life," said Vonderjan, sitting down on his own writing table, suddenly unsolid, his eyes wide and unseeing, "I've had to deal with fucking death. You get sick of it. Sick to death of it."

"Yes."

"I know you saw some things in France."

"I did."

"How do we live with it, eh? Oh, you're a young man. But when you get past forty, Christ, you feel it, breathing on the back of your neck. Every death you've seen. And I've seen plenty. My mother, and my wife. I mean, my first wife, Uteka. A beautiful woman, when I met her. Big, if you know what I mean. White skin and raven hair, red-gold eyes. A Viking woman."

Jeanjacques was mesmerized, despite everything. He had never heard Vonderjan expatiate like this, not even in imagination.

They drank more brandy.

Vonderjan said, "She died in my arms."

"I'm sorry—"

"Yes. I wish I could have shot her, like the horses, to stop her suffering. But it was in Copenhagen, one summer. Her people everywhere. One thing, she hated sex."

Jeanjacques was shocked despite himself.

"I found other women for that," said Vonderjan, as if, indifferently, to explain.

The bottle was nearly empty. Vonderjan opened a cupboard and took out another bottle, and a slab of dry, apparently stale bread on a plate. He ripped off pieces of the bread and ate them.

It was like a curious Communion, bread and wine, flesh, blood. (He offered none of the bread to Jeanjacques.)

"I wanted," Vonderjan said, perhaps two hours later, as

they sat in the hard stuffed chairs, the light no longer window-pane pure, "a woman who'd take that, from me. Who'd want me pushed and poured into her, like the sea, like they say a mermaid wants that. A woman who'd take. I heard of one. I went straight to her. It was true."

"Don't all women—" Jeanjacques faltered, drunk and heart racing, "take—?"

"No. They give. Give, give, give. They give too bloody much."

Vonderjan was not drunk, and they had consumed two bottles of brandy, and Vonderjan most of it.

"But she's—she's taken—she's had your *luck*—" Jeanjacques blurted.

"Luck. I never wanted my luck."

"But you—"

"Wake up. I had it, but who else did? Not Uteka, my wife. Not my wretched mother. I hate cruelty," Vonderjan said quietly, "And we note, this world's very cruel. We should punish the world if we could. We should punish God if we could. Put Him on a cross? Yes. Be damned to this fucking God."

The clerk found he was on the ship, coming to the Island, but he knew he did not want to be on the Island. Yet, of course, it was now too late to turn back. Something followed through the water. It was black and shining. A shark, maybe.

When Jeanjacques came to, the day was nearly gone and evening was coming. His head banged and his heart galloped. The dead horse had possessed it. He wandered out of the study (now empty but for himself) and heard the terrible sound of a woman, sick-moaning in her death throes: Uteka's ghost. But then a sharp cry came; it was the other one, Vonderjan's second wife, dying in his arms.

As she put up her hair, Nanetta was thinking of whispers. She heard them in the room, echoes of all the other whispers in the house below.

Black—it's black—not black like a man is black . . . black as black is black . . .

Beyond the fringe of palms, the edge of the forest trees stirred, as if something quite large were prowling about there. Nothing else moved.

She drove a gold hairpin through her coiffure.

He was with her, along the corridor. It had sometimes happened he would walk up here, in the afternoons. Not for a year, however.

A bird began to shriek its strange stupid warning at the forest's edge, the notes of which sounded like *"J'ai des lits! J'ai des lits!"*

Nanetta had dreamed this afternoon, falling asleep in that chair near the window, that she was walking in the forest, barefoot, as she had done when a child. Through the trees behind her something crept, shadowing her. It was noiseless, and the forest also became utterly still with tension and fear. She had not dared look back, but sometimes, from the rim of her eye, she glimpsed a dark, pencil-straight shape, that might only have been the ebony trunk of a young tree.

Then, pushing through the leaves and ropes of a wild fig, she saw it, in front of her not at her back, and woke, flinging herself forward with a choking gasp, so that she almost fell out of the chair.

It was black, smooth. Perhaps, in the form of a man. Or was it a beast? Were there eyes? Or a mouth?

In the house, a voice whispered, "Something is in the forest."

A shutter banged without wind.

And outside, the bird screamed, *I have beds! I have beds!*

The salon: it was sunset and thin wine light was on the rich man's china, and the Venice glass, what was left of it.

Vonderjan considered the table, idly, smoking, for the meal had been served and consumed early. He had slept off his brandy in twenty minutes on Anna's bed, then woken and had her a third time, before they separated.

She had lain there on the sheet, her pale arms firm and damask with the soft nap of youth.

"I can't get up. I can't stand up."

"Don't get up. Stay where you are," he said. "They can bring you something on a tray."

"Bread," she said, "I want soft warm bread, and some soup. And a glass of wine."

"Stay there," he agreed again. "I'll soon be back."

"Come back quickly," she said. And she held out the slender, strong white arms, all the rest of her flung there and limp as a broken snake.

So he went back and slid his hand gently into her, teasing her, and she writhed on the point of his fingers, the way a doll would, should you put your hand up its skirt.

"Is that so nice? Are you sure you like it?"

"Don't stop."

Vonderjan had thought he meant only to tantalize, perhaps to fulfill, but in the end he unbuttoned himself, the buttons he had only just done up, and put himself into her again, finishing both of them with swift hard thrusts.

So, she had not been in to dine. And he sat here, ready for her again, quite ready. But he was used to that. He had, after all, stored all that, during his years with Uteka, who, so womanly in other ways, had loved to be held and petted like a child, and nothing more. Vonderjan had partly unavoidably felt that the disease, which invaded her body, had somehow been given entrance to it because of this omitting vacancy, which she had not been able to allow him to fill—as night rushed to engulf the sky once vacated by a sun.

This evening the clerk looked very sallow, and had not eaten much. (Vonderjan had forgotten the effect brandy could have.) The black woman was definitely frightened. There was a type of magic going on, some ancient fear-ritual that unknown forces had stirred up among the people on the Island. It did not interest Vonderjan very much, nothing much did, now.

He spoke to the clerk, congratulating him on the efficiency of his lists and his evaluation, and the arrangements that had been postulated, when next the ship came to the Island.

Jeanjacques rallied. He said, "The one thing I couldn't locate, sir, was a piano."

"Piano?" Puzzled, Vonderjan looked at him.

"I had understood you to say your wife—that she had a piano—"

"Oh, I ordered one for her years ago. It never arrived. It was stolen, I suppose, or lost overboard, and they never admitted to it. Yes, I recall it now, a pianoforte. But the heat here would soon have ruined it, anyway."

The candles abruptly flickered, for no reason. The light was going, night rushing in.

Suddenly something, a huge impenetrable shadow, ran by the window.

The woman, Nanetta, screamed. The housekeeper sat with her eyes almost starting out of her head. Jeanjacques cursed. *"What was that?"*

As it had run by, fleet, leaping, a mouth gaped a hundred teeth—like the mouth of a shark breaking from the ocean. Or had they mistaken that?

Did it have eyes, the great black animal which had run by the window?

Surely it had eyes—

Vonderjan had stood up, and now he pulled a stick from a vase against the wall—as another man might pick up an umbrella, or a poker—and he was opening wide the doors, so the women shrank together and away.

The light of day was gone. The sky was blushing to black. Nothing was there.

Vonderjan called peremptorily into the darkness. To Jeanjacques the call sounded meaningless, gibberish, something like *Hooh! Hoouah!* Vonderjan was not afraid, possibly not even disconcerted or intrigued.

Nothing moved. Then, below, lights broke out on the open space, a servant shouted shrilly in the patois.

Vonderjan shouted down, saying it was nothing. "Go back inside." He turned and looked at the two women and the man in the salon. "Some animal." He banged the doors shut.

"It—looked like a lion," Jeanjacques stammered. But no. It

had been like a shark, a fish, which bounded on two or three legs, and stooping low.

The servants must have seen it, too. Alarmed and alerted, they were still disturbed, and generally calling out now. Another woman screamed, and then there was the crash of glass.

"Fools," said Vonderjan, without any expression or contempt. He nodded at the housekeeper. "Go and tell them I say it's all right."

The woman dithered, then scurried away—by the house door, avoiding the terrace. Nanetta, too, had stood up, and her eyes had their silver rings. They, more even than the thing which ran across the window, terrified Jeanjacques.

"What was it? Was it a wild pig?" asked the clerk, aware he sounded like a scared child.

"A pig. What pig? No. Where could it go?"

"Has it climbed up the wall?" Jeanjacques rasped.

The black woman began to speak the patois in a singsong, and the hair crawled on Jeanjacques's scalp.

"Tell her to stop it, can't you?"

"Be quiet, Nanetta," said Vonderjan.

She was silent.

They stood there.

Outside the closed windows, in the closed dark, the disturbed noises below were dying off.

Had it had eyes? Where had it gone to?

Jeanjacques remembered a story of Paris, how the guillotine would leave its station by night, and patrol the streets, searching for yet more blood. And during a siege of antique Rome, a giant phantom wolf had stalked the seven hills, tearing out the throats of citizens. These things were not real, even though they had been witnessed and attested, even though evidence and bodies were left in their wake. And, although unreal, yet they existed. They grew, such things, out of the material of the rational world, as maggots appeared spontaneously in a corpse, or fungus formed on damp.

The black woman had been keeping quiet. Now she made a tiny sound.

They turned their heads.

Beyond the windows—dark blotted dark, night on night.

"*It's there.*"

A second time Vonderjan flung open the doors, and light flooded, by some trick of reflection in their glass, out across the place beyond.

It crouches by the wall, where yestereve the man carnally had his wife, where a creeper grows, partly rent away by their movements.

"In God's sight," Vonderjan says, startled finally, but not afraid.

He walks out, straight out, and they see the beast by the wall does not move, either to attack him or to flee.

Jeanjacques can smell roses, honeysuckle. The wine glass drops out of his hand.

Antoinelle dreams, now.

She is back in the house of her aunt, where no one would allow her to speak, or to play the piano. But she has slunk down in the dead of night, into the sitting-room, and rebelliously lifted the piano's lid.

A wonderful sweet smell comes up from the keys, and she strokes them a moment, soundlessly. They feel . . . like skin. The skin of a man, over muscle, young, hard, smooth. Is it Justus she feels? (She knows this is very childish. Even her sexuality, although perhaps she does not know this, has the wanton ravening quality of the child's single-minded demands.)

There is a shell the inclement aunt keeps on top of the piano, along with some small framed miniatures of ugly relatives.

Antoinelle lifts the shell, and puts it to her ear, listens to hear the sound of the sea. But instead, she hears a piano playing, softly and far off.

The music, Antoinelle thinks, is a piece by Rameau, for the harpsichord, transposed.

She looks at the keys. She has not touched them, or not enough to make them sound.

Rameau's music dies away.

Antoinelle finds she is playing four single notes on the keys, she does not know why, neither the notes, nor the word they spell, mean anything to her.

And then, even in the piano-dream, she is aware her husband, Gregers Vonderjan, is in the bed with her, lying behind her, although in her dream she is standing upright.

They would not let her speak or play the piano—they would not let her have what she must have, or make the sounds that she must make . . .

Now *she* is a piano.

He fingers her keys, gentle, next a little rough, next sensually, next with the crepitation of a feather. And, at each caress, she sounds, Antoinelle, who is a piano, a different note.

His hands are over her breasts. (In the dream, too, she realizes, she has come into the room naked.) His fingers are on her naked breasts, fondling and describing, itching the buds at their centres. Antoinelle is being played. She gives off, note by note and chord by chord, her music.

Still cupping, circling her breasts with his hungry hands, somehow his scalding tongue is on her spine. He is licking up and up the keys of her vertebrae, through her silk-thin skin.

Standing upright, he is pressed behind her. While lying in the bed, he has rolled her over, crushing her breasts into his hands beneath her, lying on her back, his weight keeping her pinned, breathless.

And now he is entering her body, his penis like a tower on fire.

She spreads, opens, melts, dissolves for him. No matter how large, and he is now enormous, she will make way, then grip fierce and terrible upon him, her toothless springy lower mouth biting and cramming itself full of him, as if never to let go.

They are swimming strongly together for the shore.

How piercing the pleasure at her core, all through her now, the hammers hitting with a golden quake on every nerve-string.

And then, like a beast (a cat? a lion?), he has caught her by the throat, one side of her neck.

As with the other entry, at her sex, her body gives way to

allow him room. And, as at the very first, her virgin's cry of pain changes almost at once into a wail of delight.

Antoinelle begins to come (to enter, to arrive).

Huge thick rollers of deliciousness, purple and crimson, dark and blazing, tumble rhythmically as dense waves upwards, from her spine's base to the windowed dome of her skull.

Glorious starvation couples with feasting, itching with rubbing, constricting, bursting, with implosion, the architecture of her pelvis rocks, punches, roaring, and spinning in eating movements and swallowing gulps—

If only this sensation might last and last.

It lasts. It lasts.

Antoinelle is burning bright. She is changing into stars. Her stars explode and shatter. There are greater stars she can make. She is going to make them. She does so. And greater. Still she is coming, entering, arriving.

She has screamed. She has screamed until she no longer has any breath. Now she screams silently. Her nails gouge the bedsheets. She feels the blood of her virginity falling drop by drop. She is the shell and her blood her sounding sea, and the sea is rising up and another mouth, the mouth of night, is taking it all, and she is made of silver for the night which devours her, and this will never end.

And then she screams again, a terrible divine scream, dredged independently up from the depths of her concerto of ecstasy. And vaguely, as she flies crucified on the wings of the storm, she knows the body upon her body (its teeth in her throat) is not the body of Vonderjan, and that the fire-filled hands upon her breasts, the flaming stem within her, are black, not as black is black, but black as outer space, which she is filling now with her millions of wheeling, howling stars.

7

The bird which cries *Shadily! Shadily!* flies over the island above the boiling afternoon lofts, and is gone, back to the upper city mainland, where there are more trees, more shade.

In the branches of the snake-willow, a wind chime tinkles, once.

Yse's terrace is full of people, sitting and standing, with bottles, glasses, cans, and laughing. Yse has thrown a party. Someone, drunk, is dog-paddling in the alley of water.

Lucius, in his violet shirt, looks at the people. Sometimes Yse appears. She's slim and ash-pale, with long, shining hair, about twenty-five. Closer, thirty-five, maybe.

"Good party, Yse. Why you throw a party?"

"I had to throw something. Throw a plate, or myself away. Or something."

Carr and the fat man, they got the two lids up off the piano by now. It won't play, everyone knew it wouldn't. Half the notes will not sound. Instead, a music centre, straddled between the piano's legs, rigged via Yse's generator, uncoils the blues.

And this in turn has made the refrigerator temperamental. Twice people have gone to neighbours to get ice. And in turn these neighbours have been invited to the party.

A new batch of lobsters bake on the griddle. Green grapes and yellow pineapples are pulled apart.

"I was bored," she says. "I couldn't get on with it, that vampire story."

"Let me read it."

"You won't decipher my handwriting."

"Some. Enough."

"You think so? All right. But don't make criticisms, don't tell me what to do, Lucius, all right?"

"Deal. How would *I* know?"

He sits in the shady corner, (*Shadily*! the bird cried mockingly [*J'ai des lits*!] from Yse's roof) and now he reads. He can read her handwriting, it's easier than she thinks.

Sunset spreads an awning.

Some of the guests go home, or go elsewhere, but still crowds sit along the wall, or on the steps, and in the loft people are dancing now to a rock band on the music centre.

"Hey, this piano don't play!" accusingly calls Big Eye, a late learner.

Lucius takes a polite puff of a joint someone passes, and passes it on. He sits thinking.

Sunset darkens, claret colour, and now the music centre plays Mozart.

Yse sits down by Lucius on the wall.

"Tell me, Yse, how does he get all his energy, this rich guy? He's forty, you say, but you say that was like fifty, then. And he's big, heavy. And he porks this Anna three, four times a night, and then goes on back for more."

"Oh that. Vonderjan and Antoinelle. It's to do with obsession. They're obsessive. When you have a kink for something, you can do more, go on and on. Straight sex is never like that. It's the perversity—so-called perversity. That revs it up."

"Strong guy, though."

"Yes."

"Too strong for you?"

"Too strong for me."

Lucius knew nothing about Yse's "obsession" with Per Laszd. But by now he knows there is something. There has never been a man in Yse's life that Lucius has had to explain to that he, Lucius, is her friend only. Come to that, not any women in her life, either. But he has come across her work, read a little of it—never much—seen this image before, this big blond man. And the sex, for always, unlike the life of Yse, her books are full of it.

Lucius says suddenly, "You liked him, but you never got to have him, this feller."

She nods. As the light softens, she's not a day over thirty, even from two feet away.

"No. But I'm used to that."

"What is it, then? You have a bone to pick with him for him getting old?"

"The real living man, you mean? He's not old. About fifty-five, I suppose. He looks pretty wonderful to me still."

"You see him?" Lucius is surprised.

"I see him on TV. And he looks great. But he was—well, fabulous when he was younger. I mean actually like a man out of a fable, a myth." She's forgotten, he thinks, that she never confided like this in Lucius. Still though, she keeps back the name.

Lucius doesn't ask for the name.

A name no longer matters, if it ever did.

"You never want to try another guy?"

"Who? Who's offering?" And she is angry, he sees it. Obviously, he is no use to her that way. But then, did she make a friendship with Lucius for just that reason?

"You look good, Yse."

"Thank you." Cold. Better let her be. For a moment.

A heavenly, unearthly scent is stealing over the evening air.

Lucius has never seen the plant someone must have put in to produce this scent. Nothing grows on the terrace but for the snake-willow, and tonight people, lobster, pineapple, empty bottles.

"This'll be a mess to get straight," he says.

"Are you volunteering?"

"Just condoling, Yse."

The sunset totally fades. Stars light up. It's so clear, you can see the Abacus Tower, like a Christmas tree, on the mainland.

"What colour are his eyes, Yse?"

". . . Eyes? Blue. It's in the story."

"No, girl, the other one."

"Which—? Oh, *that* one. The vampire. I don't know. Your vampire had yellow eyes, you said."

"I said, he made me feel like a king. But the sex was good, then it was over. Not as you describe it, extended play."

"I did ask you not to criticise my work."

"No way. It's sexy. But tell me his eyes' colour?"

"Black, maybe. Or even white. The vampire is like the piano."

"Yeah. I don't see that. Yse, why is it a piano?"

"It could have been anything. The characters are the hotbed, and the vampire grows out of that. It just happens to form as a piano—a sort of piano. Like dropping a glass of wine, like a cloud—the stain, the cloud, just happens to take on a shape, randomly, that seems to resemble some familiar thing."

"Or is it because you can play it?"

"Yes, that, too."

"And it's an animal."

"And a man. Or male. A male body."

"Black as black is black. Not skin-black."

"Blacker. As black as black can be."

He says quietly, "La Danse aux Vampires."

A glass breaks in the loft, and wine spills on the wooden floor—shapelessly? Yse doesn't bat an eyelash.

"You used to fuss about your things."

"They're only things."

"We're all only things, Yse. What about the horses?"

"You mean Vonderjan's horses. This is turning into a real interrogation. All right. The last one, the white one like a fish, escapes, and gallops about the Island."

"You don't seem stuck, Yse. You seem to know plenty enough to go on."

"Perhaps I'm tired of going on."

"Looked in the mirror?"

"What do you mean?"

"Look in the mirror, Yse."

"Oh that. It's not real. It won't last."

"I never saw a woman could do that before, get fifteen years younger in a month. Grow her hair fifty times as thick and twenty times longer. Lose forty pounds without trying, and nothing *loose*. How do you *feel*, Yse?"

"All right."

"But do you feel good?"

"I feel all right."

"It's how they make you feel, Yse. You said it. They're not beautiful, they don't smell like flowers or the sea. They come out of the grave, out of beds of earth, out of the cesspit shit at the bottom of your soul's id. It's how they make you feel, what they can do to change you. Hudja-magica. Not them. What they can do to *you*."

"You are crazy, Lucius. There've been some funny smokes on offer up here tonight."

He gets up.

"Yse, did I say, the one I followed, when he went into his grave under the headstone, he say to me, *You come in with me, Luce. Don't mind the dark. I make sure you never notice it.*"

"And you said no."

"I took to my hot heels and ran for my fucking life."

"Then you didn't love him, Lucius."

"I loved my fucking life."

She smiles, the white girl at his side. Hair and skin so ivory pale, white dress and shimmering eyes, and who in hell is she?

"Take care, Yse."

"Night, Lucius. Sweet dreams."

The spilled wine on the floor has spilled a random shape that looks like a screwed-up sock.

Her loft is empty. They have all gone.

She lights the lamp on her desk, puts out the others, sits, looking at the piano from the Sound, forty feet away, its hind lid and its forelid now raised, eyes and mouth.

Then she gets up and goes to the piano, and taps out on the keys four notes.

Each one sounds.

D, then E, then A. And then again D.

It would be *mort* in French, *dood* in Dutch, *tod* in German. Danish, Czech, she isn't sure . . . but it would not work.

I saw in the mirror.

PianO. O, pain.

But, it doesn't hurt.

8. Danse Macabre

A wind blew from the sea, and waxy petals fell from the vine, scattering the lid of the piano as it stood there, by the house wall.

None of them spoke.

Jeanjacques felt the dry, parched cinnamon breath of Nanetta scorching on his neck, as she waited behind him. And in front of him was Vonderjan, examining the thing on the terrace.

"How did it get up here?" Jeanjacques asked, stupidly. He knew he was being stupid. The piano was supernatural. It had run up here.

"Someone carried it. How else?" replied Vonderjan.

Did he believe this? Yes, it seemed so.

Just then a stifled cry occurred above, detached itself and floated over them. For a moment none of them reacted to it; they had heard it so many times and in so many forms.

But abruptly Vonderjan's blond head went up, his eyes wide. He turned and strode away, half running. Reaching a stair that went to the gallery above, he bounded up it.

It was the noise his wife made, of course. But she made it when he was with her (inside her). And he had been here—

Neither Nanetta nor Jeanjacques went after Gregers Vonderjan, and neither of them went any nearer the piano.

"Could someone have carried it up here?" Jeanjacques asked the black woman, in French.

"Of course." But as she said this, she vehemently shook her head.

They moved away from the piano.

The wind came again, and petals fell again across the blackness of its carapace.

Jeanjacques courteously allowed the woman to precede him into the salon, then shut both doors quietly.

"What is it?"

She looked up at him sleepily, deceitfully.

"You called out."

"Did I? I was asleep. A dream . . ."

"Now I'm here," he said.

"No," she said, moving a little way from him. "I'm so sleepy. Later."

Vonderjan stood back from the bed. He gave a short laugh,

at the absurdity of this. In the two years of their sexual marriage, she had never before said anything similar to him. (And he heard Uteka murmur sadly, "Please forgive me, Gregers. Please don't be angry.")

"Very well."

Then Antoinelle turned, and he saw the mark on her neck, glowing lushly scarlet as a flower or fruit, in the low lamplight.

"Something's bitten you." He was alarmed. He thought at once of the horses dying. "Let me see."

"Bitten me? Oh, yes. And I scratched at it in my sleep, yes, I remember."

"Is that why you called out, Anna?"

She was amused and secretive.

Picking up the lamp, he bent over her, staring at the place.

A little thread, like fire, still trickled from the wound, which was itself very small. There was the slightest bruising. It did not really look like a bite, more as if she had been stabbed on purpose by a hat pin.

Where he had let her put him off sexually, he would not let her do so now. He went out and came back, to mop up the little wound with alcohol.

"Now you've made it sting. It didn't before."

"You said it itched you."

"Yes, but it didn't worry me."

"I'll close the window."

"Why? It's hot, so hot—"

"To keep out these things which bite."

He noted her watching him. It was true she was mostly still asleep, yet despite this, and the air of deception and concealment which so oddly clung to her, for a moment he saw, in her eyes, that he was old.

When her husband had gone, Antoinelle lay on her front, her head turned, so the blood continued for a while to soak into her pillow.

She had dreamed the sort of dream she had sometimes dreamed before Vonderjan came into her life. Yet this had been much more intense. If she slept, would the dream return? But she slept quickly, and the dream did not happen.

Two hours later, when Vonderjan came back to her bed, he could not at first wake her. Then, although she seemed to welcome him, for the first time he was unable to satisfy her. She writhed and wriggled beneath him, then petulantly flung herself back. "Oh finish, then. I can't. I don't want to."

But he withdrew gently, and coaxed her. "What's wrong, Anna? Aren't you well tonight?"

"Wrong? I want what you usually give me."

"Then let me give it to you."

"No. I'm too tired."

He tried to feel her forehead. She seemed too warm. Again, he had the thought of the horses, and he was uneasy. But she pulled away from him. "Oh, let me sleep, I must sleep."

Before returning here, he had gone down and questioned his servants. He had asked them if they had brought the piano up on to the terrace, and where they had found it.

They were afraid, he could see that plainly. Afraid of unknown magic and the things they beheld in the leaves and on the wind, which he, Vonderjan, could not see and had never believed in. They were also afraid of a shadowy beast, which apparently they, too, had witnessed, and which he thought he had seen. And naturally, they were afraid of the piano, because it was out of its correct situation, because (and he already knew this perfectly well) they believed it had stolen by itself out of the forest, and run up on the terrace, and *was* the beast they had seen.

At midnight, he went back down, unable to sleep, with a lamp and a bottle, and pushed up both the lids of the piano with ease.

Petals showered away. And a wonderful perfume exploded from the inside of the instrument, and with it a dim cloud of dust, so he stepped off.

As the film cleared, Vonderjan began to see that something lay inside the piano. The greater hind lid had shut it in against the piano's viscera of dulcimer hammers and brass-wire strings.

When all the film had smoked away, Vonderjan once more

went close and held the lamp above the piano, leaning down to look, as he had with his wife's bitten throat.

An embalmed mummy was curled up tight in the piano.

That is, a twisted knotted thing, blackened as if by fire, lay folded round there in a preserved and tarry skin, tough as any bitumen, out of which, here and there, the dull white star of a partial bone poked through.

This was not large enough, he thought, to be the remains of a normal adult. Yet the bones, so far as he could tell, were not those of a child, nor of an animal.

Yet it was most like the burnt and twisted carcass of a beast.

He released and pushed down again upon the lid. He held the lid flat, as if it might lunge up and open again. Glancing at the keys, before he closed them away, too, he saw a drop of vivid red, like a pearl of blood from his wife's neck, but it was only a single red petal from the vine.

Soft and loud. In his sleep, the clerk kept hearing these words. They troubled him, so he shifted and turned, almost woke, sank back uneasily. *Soft and loud*—which was what *pianoforte* meant . . .

Jeanjacques's mother, who had been accustomed to thrash him, struck him round the head. A loud blow, but she was soft with grown men, yielding, pliant. And with him, too, when grown, she would come to be soft and subserviently polite. But he never forgot the strap, and when she lay dying, he had gone nowhere near her. (His white half, from his father, had also made sure he went nowhere near his sire.)

Nanetta lay under a black, heavily furred animal, a great cat, which kneaded her back and buttocks, purring. At first she was terrified, then she began to like it. Then she knew she would die.

Notes: The black keys are the black magic. The white keys are the white magic. (Both are evil.) Anything black, or white, must respond.

Even if half black, half white.

. . .

Notes: The living white horse has escaped. It gallops across the Island. It reaches the sea and finds the fans of the waves, snorting at them, and canters through the surf along the beaches, fish-white, and the sun begins to rise.

Gregers Vonderjan dreams he is looking down at his dead wife, (Uteka) in the rain, as he did in Copenhagen that year she died. But in the dream she is not in a coffin, she is uncovered, and the soil is being thrown onto her vulnerable face. And he is sorry, because for all his wealth and personal magnitude, and power, he could not stop this happening to her. When the Island sunrise wakes him at Bleumaneer, the sorrow does not abate. He wishes now she had lived, and was here with him. (Nanetta would have eased him elsewhere, as she had often done in the past. Nanetta had been kind, and warm-blooded enough.) (Why speak of her as if she, too, were dead?)

Although awake, he does not want to move. He cannot be bothered with it, the eternal and repetitive affair of getting up, shaving and dressing, breakfasting, looking at the accounts, the lists the clerk has made, his possessions, which will shortly be gone.

How has he arrived at this? He had seemed always on a threshold. There is no time left now. The threshold is that of the exit. It is all over, or soon will be.

Almost all of them had left. The black servants and the white, from the kitchen and the lower rooms. The white housekeeper, despite her years and her pernickety adherences to the house. Vonderjan's groom—he had let the last horse out, too, perhaps taken it with him.

Even the bird had been let out of its cage in Antoinelle's boudoire, and had flown off.

Stronn stayed, Vonderjan's man. His craggy indifferent face said, *So, have they left?*

And the young black woman, Nanetta, she was still there, sitting with Antoinelle on the balcony, playing cards among the Spanish flowers, her silver and ruby earrings glittering.

"Why?" said Jeanjacques. But he knew.

"They're superstitious," Vonderjan, dismissive. "This sort of business has happened before."

It was four in the afternoon. Mornings here were separate. They came in slices, divided off by sleep. Or else, one slept through them.

"Is that—is the piano still on the terrace? Did someone take it?" said Jeanjacques, giving away the fact he had been to look, and seen the piano was no longer there. Had he dreamed it?

"Some of them will have moved it," said Vonderjan. He paced across the library. The windows stood open. The windows here were open so often, anything might easily get in.

The Island sweated, and the sky was golden lead.

"Who would move it?" persisted Jeanjacques.

Vonderjan shrugged. He said, "It wasn't any longer worth anything. It had been in the sea. It must have washed up on the beach. Don't worry about it."

Jeanjacques thought, if he listened carefully, he could hear beaded piano notes, dripping in narrow streams through the house. He had heard them this morning, as he lay in bed, awake, somehow unable to get up. (There had seemed no point in getting up. Whatever would happen would happen, and he might as well lie and wait for it.) However, a lifetime of frantic early arisings, of hiding in country barns and thatch, and up chimneys, a lifetime of running away, slowly curdled his guts and pushed him off the mattress. But by then it was past noon.

"Do they come back?"

"What? What did you say?" asked Vonderjan.

"Your servants. You said, they'd made off before. Presumably they returned."

"Yes. Perhaps."

Birds called raucously (but wordlessly) in the forest, and then grew silent.

"There was something inside that piano," said Vonderjan, "a curiosity. I should have seen to it last night, when I found it."

"What—what was it?"

"A body. Oh, don't blanch. Here, drink this. Some freakish

thing. A monkey, I'd say. I don't know how it got there, but they'll have been frightened by it."

"But it smelled so sweet. Like roses—"

"Yes, it smelled of flowers. That's a funny thing. Sometimes the dead do smell like that. Just before the smell changes."

"I never heard of that."

"No. It surprised me years ago, when I encountered it myself."

Something fell through the sky—an hour. And now it was sunset.

Nanetta had put on an apron and cooked food in the kitchen. Antoinelle had not done anything to assist her, although, in her childhood, she had been taught how to make soups and bake bread, out of a sort of bourgeois pettiness.

In fact, Antoinelle had not even properly dressed herself. Tonight she came to the meal, which the black woman had meticulously set out, in a dressing robe, tied about her waist by a brightly coloured scarf. The neckline drooped, showing off her long neck and the tops of her round, young breasts, and the flimsy improper thing she wore beneath. Her hair was also undressed, loose, gleaming and rushing about her with a water-wet sheen.

Stronn, too, came in tonight, to join them, sitting far down the table, and with a gun across his lap.

"What's that for?" Vonderjan asked him.

"The blacks are saying there's some beast about on the Island. It fell off a boat and swam ashore."

"You believe them?"

"It's possible, *mijnheer,* isn't it. I knew of a dog that was thrown from a ship at Port-au-Roi, and reached Venice."

"Did you, indeed."

Vonderjan looked smart, as always. The pallid topaz shone in his ring, his shirt was laundered and starched.

The main dish they had consisted of fish, with a kind of ragout, with pieces of vegetable, and rice.

Nanetta had lit the candles, or some of them. Some repeatedly went out. Vonderjan remarked this was due to something in the atmosphere. The air had a thick, heavy saltiness, and for once there was no rumbling of thunder, and constellations showed, massed above the heights, once the light had gone, each star framed in a peculiar greenish circle.

After Vonderjan's exchange with the man, Stronn, none of them spoke.

Without the storm, there seemed no sound at all, except that now and then, Jeanjacques heard thin little rills of musical notes.

At last he said, "What is that I can hear?"

Vonderjan was smoking one of his cigars. "What?"

It came again. Was it only in the clerk's head? He did not think so, for the black girl could plainly hear it, too. And oddly, when Vonderjan did not say anything else, it was she who said to Jeanjacques, "They hang things on the trees—to honour gods—wind gods, the gods of darkness."

Jeanjacques said, "But it sounds like a piano."

No one answered. Another candle sighed and died.

And then Antoinelle—*laughed*.

It was a horrible, terrible laugh. Rilling and tinkling like the bells hung on the trees of the Island, or like the high notes of any piano. She did it for no apparent reason, and did not refer to it once she had finished. She should have done, she should have begged their pardon, as if she had belched raucously.

Vonderjan got up. He went to the doors and opened them on the terrace and the night.

Where the piano had rested itself against the wall, there was nothing, only shadow and the disarrangement of the vine, all its flower-cups broken and shed.

"Do you want some air, Anna?"

Antoinelle rose. She was demure now. She crossed to Vonderjan, and they moved out onto the terrace. But their walking together was unlike that compulsive, gliding inevitablility of the earlier time. And, once out in the darkness, they *only* walked, loitering up and down.

She is mad, Jeanjacques thought. This was what he had seen in her face. That she was insane, unhinged and dangerous, her loveliness like vitriol thrown into the eyes of anyone who looked at her.

Stronn poured himself a brandy. He did not seem unnerved, or particularly *en garde,* despite the gun he had lugged in.

But Nanetta stood up. Unhooking the ruby eardrops from her earlobes, she placed them beside her plate. As she went across the salon to the inner door, Jeanjacques noted her feet, which had been shod in city shoes, were now bare. They looked incongruous, those dark velvet paws with their nails of tawny coral, extending long and narrow from under her light gown; they looked lawless, in a way nothing of the rest of her did.

When she had gone out, Jeanjacques said to Stronn, "Why is she barefoot?"

"Savages."

Old rage slapped the inside of the clerk's mind, like his mother's hand. Though miles off, he must react. "Oh," he said sullenly, "barbaric, do you mean? You think them barbarians, though they've been freed."

Stronn said, "Unchained is what I mean. Wild like the forest. That's what it means, that word, savage—forest."

Stronn reached across the table and helped himself from Vonderjan's box of cigars.

On the terrace, the husband and wife walked up and down. The doors stayed wide open.

Trees rustled below, and were still.

Jeanjacques, too, got up and followed the black woman out, and beyond the room he found her, still in the passage. She was standing on her bare feet, listening, with the silver rings in her eyes.

"*What can you hear?*"

"You hear it, too."

"Why are your feet bare?"

"So I can go back. So I can run away."

Jeanjacques seized her wrist and they stood staring at each other in a mutual fear, of which each one made up some tiny element, but which otherwise surrounded them.

"What—" he said.

"Her pillow's red with blood," said Nanetta. "Did you see the hole in her neck?"

"No."

"No. It closes up like a flower—a flower that eats flies. But she bled. And from her other place. White bed was red bed with her blood."

He felt sick, but he kept hold of the wand of her wrist.

"There *is* something."

"You know it, too."

Across the end of the passageway, then, where there was no light, something heavy and rapid, and yet slow, passed by. It was all darkness, but a fleer of pallor slid across its teeth. And the head of it one moment turned, and, without eyes, as it had before, it gazed at them.

The black girl sagged against the wall, and Jeanjacques leaned against and into her. Both panted harshly. They might have been copulating, as Vonderjan had with his wife.

Then the passage was free. They felt the passage draw in a breath.

"Was in my room," the girl muttered, "was in my room that is too small anything so big get through the door. I wake, I see it there."

"But it left you alone."

"It not want me. Want *her*."

"The white bitch."

"Want her, have her. Eat her alive. Run to the forest," said Nanetta, in the patois, but now he understood her, "run to the forest." But neither of them moved.

"No, no, please, Gregers. Don't be angry."

The voice is not from the past. Not Uteka's. It comes from a future now become the present.

"You said you have your courses. When did that prevent you before? I've told you, I don't mind it."

"No. Not this time."

He lets her go. Lets go of her.

She did not seem anxious, asking him not to be angry. He is not angry. Rebuffed, Vonderjan is, to his own amazement, almost relieved.

"Draw the curtains round your bed, Anna. And shut your window."

"Yes, Gregers."

He looks, and sees her for the first time tonight, how she is dressed, or not dressed.

"Why did you come down like that?"

"I was hot . . . does it matter?"

"A whore in the brothel would put on something like that." The crudeness of his language startles him. (Justus?) He checks. "I'm sorry, Anna. You meant nothing. But don't dress like that in front of the others."

"Nanetta, do you mean?"

"I mean, of course, Stronn. And the Frenchman."

Her neck, drooping, is the neck of a lily drenched by rain. He cannot see the mark of the bite.

"I've displeased you."

Antoinelle can remember her subservient mother (the mother who later threw her out to her aunt's house) fawning in this way on her father. (Who also threw her out.)

But Vonderjan seems uninterested now. He stands looking instead down the corridor.

Then he takes a step. Then he halts and says, "Go along to your room, Anna. Shut the door."

"Yes, Gregers."

In all their time together, they have never spoken in this way, in such platitudes, ciphers. Those things used freely by others.

He thinks he has seen something at the turn of the corridor. But when he goes to that junction, nothing is there. And then he thinks, of course, what *could* be there?

By then her door is shut.

Alone, he walks to his own rooms, and goes in.

The Island is alive tonight. Full of stirrings and displacements.

He takes up a bottle of Hollands, and pours a triple measure.

Beyond the window, the green-ringed eyes of the stars stare down at Bleumaneer, as if afraid.

When she was a child, a little girl, Antoinelle had sometimes longed to go to bed, in order to be alone with her fantasies, which (then) were perhaps "ingenuous." Or perhaps not.

She had lain curled up, pretending to sleep, imagining that she had found a fairy creature in the garden of her parents' house.

The fairy was always in some difficulty, and she must rescue it—perhaps from drowning in the birdbath, where sparrows had attacked it. Bearing it indoors, she would care for it, washing it in a teacup, powdering it lightly with scented dust stolen from her mother's box, dressing it in bits of lace, tied at the waist with strands of brightly coloured embroidery silk. Since it was seen naked in the teacup, it revealed it was neither male nor female, lacking both breasts and penis (she did not grossly investigate it further), although otherwise it appeared a full-grown specimen of its kind. But then, at that time, Antoinelle had never seen either the genital apparatus of a man or the mammalia of an adult woman.

The fairy, kept in secret, was dependent totally upon Antoinelle. She would feed it on crumbs of cake and fruit. It drank from her chocolate in the morning. It would sleep on her pillow. She caressed it, with always a mounting sense of urgency, not knowing where the caresses could lead—and indeed they never led to anything. Its wings she did not touch. (She had been told, the wings of moths and butterflies were fragile.)

Beyond Antoinelle's life, all Europe had been at war with itself. Invasion, battle, death, these swept by the carefully closed doors of her parents' house, and by Antoinelle entirely. Through a combination of conspiracy and luck, she learned nothing of it, but no doubt those who protected her so assiduously reinforced the walls of Antoinelle's self-involvement. Such lids were shut down on her, what else was she to do but make music with her-self—*play* with herself . . .

Sometimes in her fantasies, Antoinelle and the fairy quar-relled. Afterwards they would be reconciled, and the fairy would hover, kissing Antoinelle on the lips. Sometimes the fairy got inside her nightdress, tickling her all over until she thought she would die. Sometimes she tickled the fairy in turn with a goose feather, reducing it to spasms identifiable (probably) only as hysteria.

It never flew away.

Yet, as her own body ripened and formed, Antoinelle began to lose interest in the fairy. Instead, she had strange waking dreams of a flesh-and-blood soldier she had once glimpsed under the window, who, in her picturings, had to save her—not from any of the wild armies then at large—but from an escaped bear . . . and later came the prototypes of Justus, who kissed her until she swooned.

Now Antoinelle had gone back to her clandestine youth. Alone in the room, its door shut, she blew out the lamp. She threw wide her window. Standing in the darkness, she pulled off her garments and tossed them down.

The heat of the night was like damp velvet. The tips of her breasts rose like tight buds that wished to open.

Her husband was old. She was young. She felt her young-ness, and remembered her childhood with an inappropriate nos-talgia.

Vonderjan had thought something might get in at the win-dow. She sensed this might be true.

Antoinelle imagined that something climbed slowly up the creeper.

She began to tremble, and went and lay down on her bed.

She lay on her back, her hands lying lightly over her breasts, her legs a little apart.

Perhaps after all Vonderjan might ignore her denials and come in. She would let him. Yes, after all she had stopped men-struating. She would not mind his being here. He liked so much to do things to her, to render her helpless, gasping and abandoned, his hands on her making her into his instrument, making her utter sounds, noises, making her come over and over. And she, too, liked this best. She liked to do nothing, simply to be made to respond, and so give way. In some other life she might have become the ideal fanatic, falling before the godhead in fits whose real, spurious nature only the most sceptical could ever suspect. Conversely, partnered with a more selfish and less accomplished lover, with an ignorant Justus, for example, she might have been forced to do more, learned more, liked less. But that now was hypothetical.

A breeze whispered at the window. (What does it say?)

That dream she had had. What had that been? Was it her husband? No, it had been a man with black skin. But she had seen no one so black. A blackness without any translucence, with no blood inside it.

Antoinelle drifted, in a sort of trance.

She had wandered into a huge room with a wooden floor. The only thing in it was a piano. The air was full of a rapturous smell, like blossom, something which bloomed yet burned.

She ran her fingers over the piano. The notes sounded clearly, but each was a voice. A genderless yet sexual voice, crying out as she touched it—now softly, excitedly, now harsh and demanding and desperate.

She was lying on the beach below the Island. The sea was coming in, wave by wave—glissandi—each one the ripples of the wire harp-strings under the piano lid, or keys rippling as fingers scattered touches across them.

Antoinelle had drained Gregers Vonderjan of all he might give her. She had sucked him dry of everything but his blood. It was his own fault, exalting in his power over her, wanting to make her a doll that would dance on his fingers' end, penis's end, *power's* end.

Her eyes opened, and, against the glass windows, she saw the piano standing, its lids lifted, its keys gleaming like appetite, black and white.

Should she get up and play music on it? The keys would feel like skin.

Then she knew that if she only lay still, the piano would come to *her*. She was *its* instrument, as she had been Vonderjan's.

The curtain blew. The piano shifted, and moved, but as it did so, its shape altered. Now it was not only a piano, but an animal.

(*Notes:* Pianimal.)

It was a beast. And then it melted and stood up, and the form it had taken now was that of a man.

Stronn walked around the courtyard, around its corners, past the dry Spanish fountain. Tonight the husks of flowers scratched in the bowl, and sounded like water. Or else nocturnal lizards darted about there.

There was only one light he could see in Gregers Vonderjan's big house, the few candles left undoused in the salon.

The orange trees on the gallery smelled bittersweet.

Stronn did not want to go to bed. He was wide awake. In the old days, he might have had a game of cards with some of the blacks, or even with Vonderjan. But those times had ceased to be.

He had thought he heard the white horse earlier, its shod hoofs going along the track between the rhododendrons. But now there was no sign of it. Doubtless one of the people on the Island would catch the horse and keep it. As for the other animal, the one said to have escaped from a passing ship, Stronn did not really think it existed, or if it did, it would be something of no great importance.

Now and then he heard the tinkling noise of hudja bells the people had hung on the banana trees. Then a fragment like piano music, but it was the bells again. Some nights the sea breathed as loudly up here as in the bay. Or a shout from one of the huts two miles off might seem just over a wall.

He could hear the vrouw, certainly. But he was used to hearing that. Her squeaks and yowls, fetching off as Vonderjan shafted her. But she was a slut. The way she had come in tonight proved it, in her bedclothes. And she had never given the meester a son, not even tried to give him a child, like the missus (Uteka) had that time, only she had lost it, but she was never very healthy.

A low, thin wind blew along the cane fields, and Stronn could smell the coffee trees and the hairy odour of kayar.

He went out of the yard, carrying his gun, thinking he was still looking for the white horse.

A statue of black obsidian might look like this, polished like this.

The faint luminescence of night, with its storm choked within it, is behind the figure. Starlight describes the outline of it, but only as it turns, moving towards her, do details of its forward surface catch any illumination.

Yet too, all the while, adapting to the camouflage of its environment, it grows subtly more human, that is, more recognizable.

For not entirely—remotely—human is it.

Does she comprehend?

From the head, a black pelt of hair waterfalls away around it, folding down its back like a cloak.

The wide flat pectorals are coined each side three times. It is six-nippled, like a panther.

Its legs move, columnar, heavily muscled and immensely vital, capable of great leaps and astonishing bounds, but walking, they give it the grace of a dancer.

At first there seems to be nothing at its groin, just as it seems to have no features set into its face . . . except that the light had slid, once, twice, on the long rows of perfect teeth.

But now it is at the bed's foot, and out of the dark it has evolved, or made itself whole.

A man's face.

The face of a handsome Justus, and of a Vonderjan in his stellar youth. A face of improbable mythic beauty, and opening in it, like two vents revealing the inner burning core of it, eyes of grey ice, which each blaze like the planet Venus.

She can see now, it has four upper arms. They, too, are strong and muscular, also beautiful, like the dancer's legs.

The penis is large and upright, without a sheath, the black lotus bulb on a thick black stem. No change of shade. (No light, no inner blood.) Only the mercury-flame inside it, which only the eyes show.

Several of the side teeth, up and down, are pointed sharply. The tongue is black. The inside of the mouth is black. And the four black shapely hands, with their twenty long, flexible fingers, have palms that are black as the death of light.

It bends towards Antoinelle. It has the smell of night and of the Island, and of the sea. And also the scent of hothouse flowers, that came out of the piano. And a carnivorous smell, like fresh meat.

It stands there, looking at her, as she lies on the bed.

And on the floor, emerging from the pelt that falls from its head, the long black tail strokes softly now this way, now that way.

Then the first pair of hands stretch over onto the bed, and after them the second pair, and fluidly it lifts itself and *pours* itself forward up the sheet, and up over the body of the girl, looking down at her as it does so, from its water-pale eyes. And its smooth body rasps on her legs, as it advances, and the big hard firm organ knocks on her thighs, hot as the body is cool.

He walked behind her, obedient and terrified. The Island frightened him, but it was more than that. Nanetta was now like his mother (when she was young and slim, dominant and brutal). Once she turned, glaring at him, with the eyes of a lynx. "*Hush.*" "But I—" he started to say, and she shook her head again, raging at him without words.

She trod so noiselessly on her bare feet, which were the indigo colour of the sky in its darkness. And he blundered, try as he would.

The forest held them in its tentacles. The top-heavy plantains loomed, their blades of black-bronze sometimes quivering. Tree limbs like enormous plaited snakes rolled upwards. Occasionally, mystically, he thought, he heard the sea.

She was taking him to her people, who grasped what menaced them, its value if not its actual being, and could keep them safe.

Barefoot and stripped of her jewels, she was attempting to go back into the knowingness of her innocence and her beginnings. But he had always been overaware and a fool.

They came into a glade of wild tamarinds—could it be called that? A *glade*? It was an aperture among the trees, but only because trees had been cut down. There was an altar, very low, with frangipani flowers, scented like confectionary, and something killed that had been picked clean. The hudja bells chimed from a nearby bough, the first he had seen. They sounded like the sistra of ancient Egypt, as the cane fields had recalled to him the notion of a temple.

Nanetta bowed to the altar and went on, and he found he had crossed himself, just as he had done when a boy in church.

It made him feel better, doing that, as if he had quickly thrown up and got rid of some poison in his heart.

Vau l'eau, Vonderjan thought. Which meant, going downstream, to wrack and ruin.

He could not sleep, and turned on his side to stare out through the window. The stars were so unnaturally clear. Bleumaneer was in the eye of the storm, the aperture at its centre. When this passed, weather would resume, the ever-threatening presence of tempest.

He thought of the white horse, galloping about the Island, down its long stairways of hills and rock and forest, to the shore.

Half asleep, despite his insomnia, there was now a split second when he saw the keys of a piano, descending like the levels of many black and white terraces.

Then he was fully awake again.

Vonderjan got up. He reached for the bottle of schnapps, and found it was empty.

Perhaps he should go to her bed. She might have changed her mind. No, he did not want her tonight. He did not want anything, except to be left in peace.

It seemed to him that after all he would be glad to be rid of every bit of it. His wealth, his manipulative powers. To live here alone, as the house fell gradually apart, without servants, or any authority or commitments. And without Anna.

Had he been glad when Uteka eventually died? Yes, she had suffered so. And he had never known her. She was like a book he had meant to read, had begun to read several times, only to put it aside, unable to remember those pages he had already laboriously gone through.

With Anna it was easy, but then, she was not a book at all. She was a demon he had himself invented (Vonderjan did not realize this, that even for a moment, he thought in this way), an oasis, after Uteka's sexual desert, and so, like any fantasy, she could be sloughed at once. He had masturbated over her long enough, this too-young girl, with her serpentine body (apple tree and tempting snake together), and her idealized pleas always for more.

Now he wanted to leave the banquet table. To get up and go away and sleep and grow old, without such distractions.

He thought he could hear her, though. Hear her fast starved feeding breathing, and for once, this did not arouse him. And in any case it might not be Anna, but only the gasping of the sea, hurling herself far away, on the rocks and beaches of the Island.

It—he—paints her lips with its long and slender tongue, which is black. Then it paints the inside of her mouth. The tongue is very narrow, sensitive, incites her gums, making her want to yawn, except that is not what she needs to do—but she stretches her body irresistibly.

The first set of hands settles on her breasts.

The second set of hands on her rib cage.

Something flicks, flicks, between her thighs . . . not the staff of the penis, but something more like a second tongue. . . .

Antoinelle's legs open, and her head falls back. She makes a sound, but it is a bestial grunting that almost offends her, yet there is no room in her body or mind for that.

"No—" she tries to say.

The *no* means yes, in the case of Antoinelle. It is addressed, not to her partner, but to normal life, anything that may intrude, and warns *Don't interrupt.*

The black tongue wends, waking nerves of taste and smell in the roof of her mouth. She scents lakoum, pepper, ambergris, and myrrh.

The lower tongue, which may be some extra weapon of the tail, licks at a point of flame it has discovered, fixing a triangle with the fire-points of her breasts.

He—it—slips into her, forces into her, bulging and huge as thunder.

And the tail grasps her, muscular as any of its limbs, and, thick as the phallus, also penetrates her.

The thing holds Antoinelle as she detonates about it, faints and cascades into darkness.

Not until she begins to revive does it do more.

The terror is, she comes to already primed, more than eager, her body spangled with frantic need, as if the first cataclysm were only . . . foreplay.

And now the creature moves, riding her and making her ride, and they gallop down the night, and Antoinelle grins and shrieks, clinging to its obsidian form, her hands slipping, gripping. And as the second detonation begins, its face leaves her face, her mouth, and grows itself faceless and *only* mouth. And the mouth half rings her throat, a crescent moon, and the many side teeth pierce her, both the veins of her neck.

A necklace of emeralds was nothing to this.

Antoinelle drops from one precipice to another. She screams, and her screams crash through the house called Blue View, like sheets of blue glass breaking.

It holds her. As her consciousness again goes out, it holds her very tight.

And somewhere in the limbo where she swirls, fire on oil, guttering but not quenched, Antoinelle is raucously laughing with triumph at finding this other one, not her parasite, but her twin. Able to devour her as she devours, able to eat her alive as she has eaten or tried to eat others alive. But where Antoinelle has bled them out, this only drinks. It wastes nothing, not even Antoinelle.

More—more— She can never have enough.

Then it tickles her with flame so she thrashes and yelps. Its fangs fastened in her, it bears her on, fastened in turn to it.

She is arched like a bridge, carrying the travelling shadow on her body. Pinned together, in eclipse, these dancers.

More—

It gives her more. And indescribably yet more.

If she were any longer human, she would be split and eviscerated, and her spine snapped along its centre three times.

Her hands have fast hold of it. Which—it or she—is the most tenacious? Where it travels, so will she.

But for all the *more*, there is no more *thought*. If ever there was thought.

When she was fourteen, she saw all this, in her prophetic mirror, saw what she was made for and must have.

Perhaps many thousands of us are only that, victim or predator, interchangeable.

Seen from above: Antoinelle is scarcely visible. Just the edges of her flailing feet, her contorted forehead and glistening strands of hair. And her clutching claws. (Shockingly, she makes the sounds of a pig, grunting, snorting.)

The rest of her is covered by darkness, by something most like a manta ray out of the sea, or some black amoeba.

Then she is growling and grunting so loudly, on and on, that the looking glass breaks on her toilette table as if unable to stand the sound, while out in the night forest birds shrill and fly away.

More—always more. *Don't stop—* Never stop.

There is no need to stop. It has killed her, she is dead, she is re-alive and death is lost on her, she is all she has ever wished to be—nothing.

"Dearest . . . are you awake?"

He lifts his head from his arm. He has slept.

"What is it?" *Who are you?* Has she ever called him *dear* before?

"Here I am," she says, whoever she is. But she is his Anna. He does not want her. Never wanted her.

He thinks she is wearing the emerald necklace, something burning about her throat. She is white as bone. And her dark eyes . . . have paled to Venus eyes, watching him.

"I'm sorry," he says. "Perhaps later."

"I know."

Vonderjan falls asleep again quickly, lying on his back. Then Antoinelle slides up on top of him. She is not heavy, but he is; it impedes his breathing, her little weight.

Finally she puts her face to his, her mouth over his.

She smothers him mostly with her face, closing off his nostrils with the pressure of her cheek, and one narrow hand, and her mouth sidelong to his, and her breasts on his heart.

He does not wake again. At last his body spasms sluggishly, like the last death throe of orgasm. Nothing else.

After his breathing has ended, still she lies there, Venus-eyed, and the dawn begins to come. Antoinelle casts a black, black shadow. Like all shadows, it is attached to her. Attached very closely.

Is this her shadow, or is she the white shadow of *it*?

9

Having sat for ten minutes, no longer writing, holding her pen upright, Yse sighs, and drops it, like something unpleasant, dank, or sticky.

The story's erotographic motif, at first stimulating, had become, as it must, repulsive. Disgusting her—also as it should.

And the murder of Vonderjan, presented deliberately almost as an afterthought, (stifled under the slight white pillar of his succubus wife).

Aloud, Yse says almost angrily, "Now surely I've used him up. All up. All over. Per Laszd, I can't do another thing with you or to you. But then, you've used me up, too, yes you did, you have, even though you've never been near me. Mutual annihilation. That Yse is over with."

Then Yse rises, leaving the manuscript, and goes to make tea. But her generator, since the party, (when the music machine had been hooked into it by that madman, Carr) is skittish. The stove won't work. She leaves it, and pours instead a warm soda from the now improperly working fridge.

It is nighttime, or morning, about three-fifty A.M.

Yse switches on her small TV, which works on a solar battery and obliges.

And there, on the first of the fifteen mainland (upper city) channels, is he—is Per Laszd. Not in his persona of dead trampled Gregers Vonderjan, but that of his own dangerous self.

She stands on the floor, dumbfounded, yet not, not really. Of course, who else would come before her at this hour.

He looks well, healthy and tanned. He's even shed some weight.

It seems to be a talk show, something normally Yse would avoid—they bore her. And the revelation of those she sometimes admires as overordinary or distasteful, disillusions and frustrates her.

But him she has always watched, on a screen, across a room when able, or in her own head. Him, she knows. He could not disillusion her, or put her off.

And tonight, there is something new. The talk has veered round to the other three guests—to whom she pays no attention—and so to music. And now the TV show's host is asking Per Laszd to use the piano, that grande piano over there.

Per Laszd gets up and walks over to this studio piano, looking, Yse thinks, faintly irritated, because obviously this has been sprung on him and is not what he is about, or at least not publicly, but he will do it from a good showman's common sense.

He plays well, some melody Yse knows, a popular song she can't place. He improvises, his large hands and strong fingers jumping sure and finely trained about the keyboard. Just the one short piece, concluded with a sarcastic flourish, after which he stands up again. The audience, delighted by any novelty, applauds madly, while the host and other guests are all calling *encore*! (more! more! Again—don't stop). But Laszd is not manipulable, not truly. Gracious yet immovable, he returns to his seat. And after that a pretty girl with an unimportant voice comes on to sing, and then the show is done.

Yse finds herself enraged. She switches off the set, and slams down the tepid soda. She paces this end of her loft. While by the doors, forty feet away, the piano, dredged from the Sound, still stands, balanced on its forefeet and its phallic tail, hung in shade and shadow. It has been here more than a month. It's nearly invisible.

So why this now? This TV stunt put on by Fate? Why show her this, now? As if to congratulate her, giving her a horrible mean little failed-runner's-up patronizing nonprize. Per Laszd can play the piano.

Damn Per Laszd.

She is sick of him. Perhaps in every sense. But of course, she still wants him. Always will.

And what now?

She will never sleep. It's too late or early to go out.

She circles back to her writing, looks at it, sits, touches the page. But why bother to write anymore?

Vonderjan was like the enchanter Prospero, in Shakespeare's *Tempest*, shut up there on his sorcerous Island, infested with sprites and elementals. Prospero, too, kept close a strange young woman, who in the magician's case had been his own daughter. But then arrived a shipwrecked prince out of the sea, to take the responsibility off Prospero's hands.

(Per's hands on the piano keys. Playing them. A wonderful amateur, all so facile, no trouble at all. He is married, and has been for twelve years. Yse has always known this.)

Far out on the Sound, a boat moos eerily.

Though she has frequently heard such a thing, Yse starts.

Be not afeard: the isle is full of noises,
Sounds and sweet airs, that give delight, and hurt not.

She can no longer smell the perfume, like night-blooming vines. When did that stop? (Don't stop.)

Melted into air, into thin air . . .

10. Passover

They had roped the hut house round, outside and in, with their amulets and charms. There were coloured feathers and dried grasses, cogs of wood rough-carved, bones and sprinkles of salt and rum, and of blood, as in the Communion. When they reached the door, she on her bare, navy blue feet, Jeanjacques felt all the forest press at their backs. And inside the hut, the silver-ringed eyes, staring in affright like the staring stars. But presently her people let her in, and let him in as well, without argument. And he thought of the houses of the Chosen in Egypt, their lintels marked by blood, to show the Angel of Death he must pass by.

He, as she did, sat down on the earth floor. (He noted the earth floor, and the contrasting wooden bed, with its elaborate posts. And the two shrines, one to the Virgin, and one to another female deity.)

Nothing was said beyond a scurry of whispered words in the patois. There were thirty other people crammed in the house, with a crèche of chickens and two goats. Fear smelled thick and hot, but there was something else, some vital possibility of courage and cohesion. They clung together soul to soul, their bodies only barely brushing, and Jeanjacques was glad to be in their midst, and when the fat woman came and gave him a gourd of liquor, he shed tears, and she patted his head, calming him a little, like a dog hiding under its mistress's chair.

In the end he must have slept. He saw someone looking at him, the pale icy eyes blue as murder.

Waking with a start, he found everyone and thing in the hut tense and compressed, listening, as something circled round outside. Then it snorted and blew against the wall of the hut house, and all the interior stars of eyes flashed with their terror. And

Jeanjacques felt his heart clamp onto the side of his body, as if afraid to fall.

Even so, he knew what it was, and when all at once it retreated and galloped away on its shod hoofs, he said quietly, "His horse."

But no one answered him, or took any notice of what he had said, and Jeanjacques discovered himself thinking, *After all, it might take that form, a white horse. Or she might be riding on the white horse.*

He began to ponder the way he must go in the morning, descending towards the bay. He should reach the sea well in advance of nightfall. The ship would come back, today or tomorrow. Soon. And there were the old buildings, on the beach, where he could make a shelter. He could even jump into the sea and swim out. There was a little reef, and rocks.

It had come from the sea, and would avoid going back to the sea, surely, at least for some while.

He knew it was not interested in him, knew that almost certainly it would not approach him with any purpose. But he could not bear to *see* it. That was the thing. And it seemed to him the people of the Island, and in the hut, even the chickens, the goats, and elsewhere the birds and fauna, felt as he did. They did not want to *see* it, even glimpse it. If the fabric of this world were torn open in one place on a black gaping hole of infinite darkness, you hid your eyes, you went far away.

After that, he started to notice bundles of possessions stacked up in corners. He realized not he alone would be going down the Island to the sea.

Dreaming again, he beheld animals swimming in waves away from shore, and birds flying away, as if from a zone of earthquake, or the presage of some volcanic eruption.

Nanetta nudged him.

"Will you take me to St Paul's Island?"

"Yes."

"I have a sister there."

He had been here on a clerk's errand. He thought, ridiculously, *Now I won't be paid*. And he was glad at this wince of anxious annoyance. Its normalcy and reason.

11

Per Laszd played Bach very well, with just the right detached, solemn cheerfulness.

It was what she would have expected him to play. Something like this. Less so the snatch of a popular tune he had offered the talk show audience so flippantly. (But a piano does what you want, makes the sounds you make it give—even true, she thinks, should you make a mistake—for then that is what it gives you. Your mistake.)

As Yse raised her eyes, she saw across the dim sphere of her loft, still wrapped in the last flimsy paper of night, a lamp stood glowing by the piano, both of whose lids were raised. Her stomach jolted and the pain of shock rushed through her body.

"*Lucius*—?"

He was the only other who held a key to her loft. She trusted Lucius, who anyway had never used the key, except once, when she was gone for a week, to enter and water her (dying) plants, and fill her (then operable) refrigerator with croissants, mangoes, and white wine.

And Lucius didn't play the piano. He had told her, once. His *amouretta*, as he called it, was the drum.

Besides, the piano player had not reacted when she called, not ceased his performance. Not until he brought the twinkling phrases to their finish.

Then the large hands stepped back off the keys, he pushed away the chair he must have carried there, and stood up.

The raised carapace of the piano's hind lid still obscured him, all but that flame of light which veered across the shining pallor of his hair.

Yse had got to her feet. She felt incredibly young, light as thin air. The thick silk of her hair brushed round her face, her shoulders, and she pulled in her flat stomach and raised her head on its long throat. She was frightened by the excitement in herself, and excited by the fear. She wasn't dreaming. She had always known, when she *dreamed* of him.

And there was no warning voice, because long ago she had left all such redundant noises behind.

Per Laszd walked around the piano. "Hallo, Yse," he said.

She said nothing. Perhaps could not speak. There seemed no point. She had said so much.

But "Here I am," he said.

There he was.

There was no doubt at all. The low lamp flung up against him. He wore the loose dark suit he had put on for the TV program, as if he had come straight here from the studio. He dwarfed everything in the loft.

"Why?" she said, after all.

She, too, was entitled to be flippant, surely.

"Why? Don't you know? You brought me here." He smiled. "Don't you love me anymore?"

He was wooing her.

She glanced around her, made herself see everything as she had left it, the washed plate and glass by the sink, the soda can on the table, her manuscript lying there, and the pen. Beyond an angle of a wall, a corridor to other rooms.

And below the floor, barracuda swimming through the girders of a flooded building.

But the thin air sparkled as if full of champagne.

"Well, Yse," he said again, "here I am."

"But you are not *you*."

"You don't say. Can you be certain? How am I different?"

"You're what I've made, and conjured up."

"I thought it was," he said, in his dry, amused voice she had never forgotten, "more personal than that."

"*He* is somewhere miles off. In another country."

"This is another country," he said, "to me."

She liked it, this breathless fencing with him. Liked his persuading her. *Don't stop.*

The piano had not been able to open—or be opened—until

he—or she—was ready. (Foreplay.) And out of the piano came her demon. What was he? *What?*

She didn't care. If it were not him, yet it was, him.

So she said, archly, "And your wife?"

"As you see, she had another engagement."

"With you, *there*. Wherever you are."

"Let me tell you," he said, "why I've called here."

There was no break in the transmission of this scene, she saw him walk away from the piano, start across the floor, and she did the same. Then they were near the window-doors. He was standing over her. He was vast, overpowering, beautiful. More beautiful, now she could see the strands of his hair, the pores of his skin, a hundred tiniest imperfections—and the whole exquisite manufacture of a human thing, so close. And she was rational enough to analyse all this, and his beauty, and his power over her; or pedantic enough. He smelled wonderful to her as well, more than his clean fitness and his masculinity, or any expensive cosmetic he had used (for her?). It was the scent discernible only by a lover, caused by her chemistry, not his. Unless she had made him want her, too.

But of course he wanted her. She could see it in his eyes, their blue view bent only on her.

If he might have seemed old to an Antoinelle of barely sixteen, to Yse this man was simply her peer. And yet, too, he was like his younger self, clad again in that searing charisma which had later lessened, or changed its course.

He took her hand, picked it up. Toyed with her hand as Vonderjan had done with the hand of the girl Yse had permitted to destroy him.

"I'm here for you," he said.

"But I don't know you."

"Backwards," he said. "You've made it your business. You've bid for me," he said, "and you've got me."

"No," she said, "no, no, I haven't."

"Let me show you."

She had known of that almost occult quality. With what he wanted in the sexual way, he could communicate some telepathic echo of his desires. As his mouth covered and clasped hers, this delirium was what she felt, combining with her own.

She had always known his kisses would be like this, the ground flying off from her feet, swept up and held only by him in the midst of a spinning void, where she became part of him and wanted nothing else, where she became what she had always wanted . . . nothing.

To be nothing, borne by this flooding sea, no thought, no anchor, and no chains.

So Antoinelle, as her vampire penetrated, drank, emptied, reformed her.

So Yse, in her vampire's arms.

It's how they make us feel.

"No," she murmurs, sinking deeper and deeper into his body, drowning as the island will, one day (five years, twenty). None of us escape, do we?

Dawn is often very short and ineffectual here, as if to recompense the dark for those long sunsets we have.

Lucius, bringing his boat in to West Ridge from a night's fishing and drinking out in the Sound, sees a light still burning up there, bright as the quick green dawn. All Yse's blinds are up, showing the glass loft, translucent, like a jewel. Over the terrace the snake-tree hangs its hair in the water and ribbons of apple green light tremble through its coils.

Yse is there, just inside the wall of glass above the terrace, standing with a tall heavyset man, whose hair is almost white.

He's kissing her, on and on, and then they draw apart, and still she holds on to him, her head tilted back like a serpent's, bonelessly, staring up into his face.

From down in the channel between the lofts and towerettes, Lucius can't make out the features of her lover. But then neither can he make out Yse's facial features, only the tilt of her neck and the lush satin hair hanging down her back.

Lucius sits in the boat, not paddling now, watching. His eyes are still and opaque.

"What you doing, girl?"

He knows perfectly well.

And then they turn back, the two of them, farther into the loft where the light still burns, although the light of dawn has gone, leaving only a salty stormy dusk.

They will hardly make themselves separate from each other. They are together again and again, as if growing into one another.

Lucius sees the piano, or that which had been a piano, has vanished from the loft. And after that he sees how the light of the guttering lamp hits suddenly up, like a striking cobra. And in the ray of the lamp, striking, the bulky figure of the man, with his black clothes and blond hair, becomes transparent as the glass sheets of the doors. It is possible to see directly, too, through him, clothes, hair, body, directly through to Yse, as she stands there, still holding on to what is now actually invisible, drawing it on, in, away, just before the lamp goes out and a shadow fills the room like night.

As he is paddling away along the channel, Lucius thinks he hears a remote crash, out of time, like glass smashing in many pieces, but yesterday, or tomorrow.

Things break.

Just about sunset, the police come to find Lucius. They understand he has a key to the loft of a woman called Yse (which they pronounce *Jizz*).

When they get to the loft, Lucius is aware they did not need the key, since the glass doors have both been blown outwards and down into the water-alley below. Huge shards and fragments decorate the terrace, and some are caught in the snake-willow like stars.

A bored detective stands about, drinking coffee someone has made him on Yse's reluctant stove. (The refrigerator has shut off, and is leaking a lake on the floor.)

Lucius appears dismayed but innocuous. He goes about looking for something, which the other searchers, having dismissed him, are too involved to mark.

There is no sign of Yse. The whole loft is vacant. There is

no sign either of any disturbance, beyond the damaged doors which, they say to Lucius and each other, were smashed outwards but not by an explosive.

"What are you looking for?" the detective asks Lucius, suddenly grasping what Lucius is at.

"Huh?"

"She have something of yours?"

Lucius sees the detective is waking up. "No. Her book. She was writing."

"Oh, yeah? What kind of thing was that?"

Lucius explains, and the detective loses interest again. He says they have seen nothing like that.

And Lucius doesn't find her manuscript, which he would have anticipated, anyway, seeing instantly on her worktable. He does find a note—they say it is a note, a letter of some sort, although addressed to no one. It's in her bed area, on the rug, which has been floated under the bed by escaped refrigerator fluid.

"Why go on writing?" asks the note, or letter, of the no one it has not addressed. "All your life waiting, and having to invent another life, or other lives, to make up for not having a life. Is that what God's problem is?"

Hearing this read at him, Lucius's dead eyes reveal for a second they are not dead, only covered by a protective film. They all miss this.

The detective flatly reads the note out, like a kid bad at reading, embarrassed and standing up in class. Where his feet are planted is the stain from the party, which, to Lucius's for-a-moment-not-dead eyes, has the shape of a swimming, three-legged fish.

"And she says, 'I want more.'

" 'I want the terror and the passion, the power and the glory—not this low-key crap played only with one *hand*. Let me point out to someone, Yse is an anagram of Yes. *I'll drown my book*.' "

"I guess," says the detective, "she didn't sell."

They let Lucius go with some kind of veiled threat he knows is only offered to make themselves feel safe.

He takes the water bus over to the Café Blonde, and as the sunset ends and night becomes, tells one or two what he saw, as he has not told the cops from the tideless upper city.

Lucius has met them all. Angels, demons.

"As the light went through him, he wasn't there. He's like glass."

Carr says, slyly (inappropriately—or with deadly perception?), "No vampire gonna reflect in a glass."

12. Carried Away

When the ship came, they took the people out, rowing them in groups, in the two boats. The man Stronn had also appeared, looking dazed, and the old housekeeper, and others. No questions were asked of them. The ship took the livestock, too.

Jeanjacques was glad they were so amenable, the black haughty master wanting conscientiously to assist his own, and so helping the rest.

All the time they had sheltered in the rickety customs buildings of the old port, a storm banged round the coast. This kept other things away, it must have done. They saw nothing but the feathers of palm boughs blown through the air and crashing trunks that toppled in the high surf, which was grey as smashed glass.

In the metallic after-storm morning, Jeanjacques walked down the beach, the last to leave, waiting for the last boat, confident.

Activity went on at the sea's edge, sailors rolling a barrel, Nanetta standing straight under a yellow sunshade, a fine lady, barefoot but proud. (She had shown him the jewels she had after all brought with her, squeezed in her sash, not the ruby earrings, but a golden hair pin, and the emerald necklace that had belonged to Vonderjan's vrouw.)

He never thought, now, to see anything, Jeanjacques, so clever, so accomplished at survival.

But he saw it.

Where the forest came down on to the beach, and caves opened under the limestone, and then rocks reared up, white rocks and black, with the curiously quiescent waves glimmering in and out around them.

There had been nothing. He would have sworn to that. As if the reality of the coarse storm had scoured all such stuff away.

And then, there she was, sitting on the rock.

She shone in a way that, perhaps one and a quarter centuries after, could have been described as radioactively.

Jeanjacques did not know that word. He decided that she gleamed. Her hard, pale skin and mass of pale hair, gleaming.

She looked old. Yet she looked too young. She was not human-looking, nor animal.

Her legs were spread wide in the skirt of her white dress. So loose was the gown at her bosom, that he could see much of her breasts. She was doing nothing at all, only sitting there, alone, and she grinned at him, all her white teeth, so even, and her black eyes like slits in the world.

But she cast a black shadow, and gradually the shadow was embracing her. And he saw her turning over into it like the moon into eclipse. If she had any blood left in her, if she had ever been Antoinelle—these things he ignored. But her grinning and her eyes and the shadow and her turning inside out within the shadow—from these things he ran away.

He ran to the line of breakers, where the barrels were being rolled into a boat. To Nanetta's sunflower sunshade.

And he seemed to burst through a sort of curtain, and his muscles gave way. He fell nearby, and she glanced at him, the black woman, and shrank away.

"It's all right—" he cried. He thought she must not see what he had seen, and that they might leave him here. "I missed my footing," he whined, "that's all."

And when the boat went out, they let him go with it.

The great sails shouldered up into the sky. The master looked Jeanjacques over, before moving his gaze after Nanetta. (Stronn had avoided them. The other whites, and the housekeeper, had hidden themselves somewhere below, like stow-aways.)

"How did you find him, that Dutchman?" the master asked idly.

"As you said. Vonderjan was falling."

"What was the other trouble here? They act like it was a plague, but that's not so." (Malignly, Jeanjacques noted the master, too, was excluded from the empathy of the Island people.) "No," the master went on bombastically, "if you sick, I'd never take you on, none of you."

Jeanjacques felt a little better. "The Island's gone bad," he muttered. He would look, though, only up into the sails. They were another sort of white to the white thing he had seen on the rock. As the master was another sort of black.

"Gone bad? They do. Land does go bad. Like men."

Are they setting sail? Every grain of sand on the beach behind is rising up. Every mote of light, buzzing—

Oh God—*Pater noster—libera me*—

The ship strode from the bay. She carved her path into the deep sea, and through his inner ear, Jeanjacques hears the small bells singing. Yet that is little enough, to carry away from such a place.

13

Seven months after, he heard the story, and some of the newspapers had it, too. A piano had been washed up off the Sound, on the beach at the Abacus Tower. And inside the lid, when they hacked it open, a woman's body was curled up, tiny, and hard as iron. She was Caucasian, middle-aged, rather heavy when alive, now not heavy at all, since there was no blood, and not a single whole bone left inside her.

Sharks, they said.

Sharks are clever. They can get inside a closed piano and out again. And they bite.

As for the piano, it was missing—vandals had destroyed it, burned it, taken it off.

Sometimes strangers ask Lucius where Yse went to. He has nothing to tell them. ("She disappears?" they ask him again. And Lucius once more says nothing.)

And in that way, resembling her last book, Yse disappeared, disappears, is disappearing. Which can happen, in any tense you like.

"Like those hallucinations which sometimes come at the edge of sleep, so that you wake, thinking two or three words have been spoken close to your ear, or that a tall figure stands in the corner . . . like this, the image now and then appears before him.

"Then Jeanjacques sees her, the woman, sitting on the rock, her white dress and ivory-coloured hair, hard-gleaming in a poststorm sunlight. Impossible to tell her age. A desiccated young girl, or unlined old woman. And the transparent sea lapping in across the sand . . .

"But he has said, the Island is quite deserted now."